# Dizzying Heights

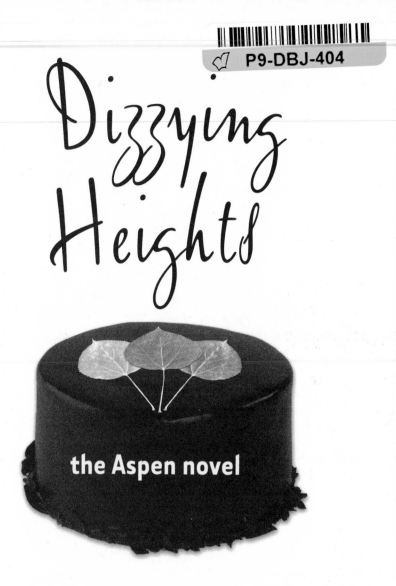

the Aspen novel

# BRUCE DUCKER

FULCRUM

GOLDEN, COLORADO

This is a work of fiction. Names, characters, places, or incidents either are the product of the author's imagination or are used fictitiously.

Library of Congress Cataloging-in-Publication Data
Ducker, Bruce.
  Dizzying heights : the Aspen novel / by Bruce Ducker.
     p. cm.
  ISBN-13: 978-1-55591-685-5
  ISBN-13: 978-1-55591-658-9 (pbk.)
  1. Computer programmers--Fiction 2. Aspen (Colo.)--Fiction. I. Title.
  PS3554.U267D59 2008
  813'.54--dc22

                              2007051817

Printed in the United States of America by Malloy Incorporated
0 9 8 7 6 5 4 3 2 1

Design: Jack Lenzo


Fulcrum Publishing
4690 Table Mountain Drive, Suite 100
Golden, Colorado 80403
800-992-2908 • 303-277-1623
www.fulcrumbooks.com

Also by Bruce Ducker

*Home Pool: Fly Fishing Stories* (Coming in September 2008)
*Mooney in Flight*
*Bloodlines*
*Lead Us Not into Penn Station*
*Marital Assets*
*Bankroll*
*Failure at the Mission Trust*
*Rule by Proxy*

For Sarah, Jack,
Logan, and Rowan

# Dramatis Personae

**Henry Wadsworth Longfellow Brush (Waddy)** – a callow young seeker
of truth and beauty

**Lisa Laroux** – Waddy's colleague, a software-designing femme fatale

**Frankie Rusticana** – owner of Pantagruel, Aspen's finest restaurant

**Mortimer Dooberry** – pop psychologist and TV personality

**Flavia Dooberry** – Mortimer's beautiful, Brazilian, and feral wife

**Justin Kaye** – clothing manufacturer; developer of the Isaac Walton Club

**Rochelle Kaye** – Justin's sensible wife

**Etta Eubanks** – Tulsa oil baroness and philosopher

**Sherry Topliff** – Etta's husband, an amateur sculptor

**Victor Grant** – noted financier and private equity manager

**Annalee** – the greeter at Pantagruel's

**Peyton Post** – heir to the toilet fortune and idler

**Chloe Post** – Peyton's wife; the brains of the family

**Carmen Siquieros** – chambermaid at the Hotel Jerome

**Philida Post** – crusader for all causes green or animate; Peyton's sister

**Marco Campaneris** – general contractor

**Irving "Silverheels" Brumberger** – lawyer and champion of Native
American tribes

**Tiffany Ashe** – superannuated soap opera actress

**Gene and Mary Finch** – old Aspen residents

**Gossage** – a prize-winning economist, without domicile

**Rodney Hollister** – the rock singer

**Matt Hempel** – undercover drug cop

**Morgan Atencio** – official of the Southern Utes

**Robert Yellowknife** – financial officer of the Northern Cheyenne

**Emanuel Johnstone** – registered representative and Shoshone

**A man with a white forelock** – Grant's security man

Imagine that these airy United States sit on a point of balance that is their center of population. A cosmic ball bearing. At the start of the republic, the fulcrum lodged somewhere north of Philadelphia, tucked snug against the coast, and the continent sloped off gently to the Pacific.

Slowly that fulcrum rolls westward, until one day, in late September toward the end of the last century, it finds perfect equilibrium. On that day the continent balances straight even, a day, you may remember, of warm breezes, when every love discovered is eternal and every duffer's putt runs plumb and true.

But the giant steel ball continues to edge westward, and the nation tilts now on an easterly slope. When that happens, Horace Greeley's ghost fluffs his pillow and shifts in his sleep, and the quicksilver that is Opportunity begins to run upstream, pooling in the shadow of the Rocky Mountains. ...

# I. The Summer

*The summer—no sweeter was ever*
*The sunshiny woods all athrill;*
*The greyling aleap in the river,*
*The bighorn asleep on the hill.*
*The strong life that never knows harness*
*The wilds where the caribou call;*
*The freshness, the freedom, the farness—*
*Oh God! how I'm stuck on it all.*

*—Robert Service, "The Spell of the Yukon"*

## One

Waddy Brush steered his car onto the cement curl to Rain-water Software and knew from the slight rush of G-force as he rounded the bend that he was atrack the perfect life. Beyond his windshield the Olympic Mountains shone under a recently washed sky, the pavement traced a measured and satisfying six-degree arc, and light from a rare April sun glinted off the window by his very workstation. Corridor F, Third Floor East. A yellow beam that spotlit his arrival, exactly as Jiminy Cricket highlighted the transubstantiation of Pinocchio from wood to flesh.

Waddy unpacked himself from the VW, pulled up the canvas top, and entered the sleek glass building owned by his employer. More than an employer. Rainwater Software was, he'd regularly been told, a family. The head of HR had a way of looking at you; the man could stare unflinchingly into your eyes and fix you with his sincerity.

Rainwater folk often spoke of family. At the summer picnic, when presenting the Christmas etching—employees were given a landscape rather than a check, last year it was a gnarled cypress on a hill—and again at the annual review. Every member of the family is treated the same, they told Waddy. Not in pay, of course, but in esteem. For two annual reviews, Waddy was Looked-on-Favorably, for the next three he was

Thought-of-Highly, and last year (Waddy felt the most expansive, though there was no official grading of these terms), he had been elevated from participle phrase to dependent clause. A Young Man We're Watching. With each year's good words, Waddy got a dollop of stock options, which, he was told, would make him rich if he continued to achieve harmony within the family. And of course if the options vested.

Harmony was easy. There were no discordant notes. Rainwater was a leading producer of retail software. Several of Waddy's projects had blossomed into video games, made it to the shelves, and he'd been promoted to the Virtual Reality Task Force. Rainwater was a great employer: full health, dental, and surgical, even pregnancy (which made Waddy, without an immediate application, nonetheless feel confident and adult). Vast athletic facilities, grander than those at Skakit Point High or Puget Community College. Waddy used them all, the fully equipped weight and cardio room, the indoor volleyball court, the jogging path that meandered through blooming tea roses and jonquil.

The environment was ideal, the opportunities unlimited, and the colleagues were, well, collegial. To a man and to a woman, intelligent, creative, accommodating. Indeed one (Waddy looked for her red Honda Civic as he exited the parking lot), one was perhaps too accommodating. Ah, Lisa Laroux.

The plink of closed-cycle streams filled the three-story atrium. But this day a dark presence skulked amid the white noise. A wall of summer-weight wool gathered around the reception desk where the pretty greeter was handing out ID badges. Two dozen young men and women who might be Latter Day Saints on their mission. If that's what they were, they outdressed the sinners. Waddy bounced up the helical stairwell that wound about the waterfall and thought no more of them. Turned to Third Floor East, Corridor F, strolled down the hallway to his team.

The magenta-walled cubicles of the Virtual Reality Task Force were personalized with photos of towheaded children in striped jerseys, ski and sail snapshots, and crayoned pictures. On Waddy's was tacked an eight-by-ten glossy of Satchmo and the Hot Five.

He booted up the computer and it responded with a familiar buzz. Business as usual. But when he looked up to click on his pearlescent screen, he saw the pygmy reflection of a visitor.

"Henry Wadsworth Longfellow Brush?"

Waddy swung his ergonomic stool around to face the man. A suit from the lobby. White, buttoned-down shirt, a tie in tiny blue paisley, business card at the ready. He was, he explained, from Rainwater's auditors.

"We're being dispatched today to inform the Rainwater employees of the transaction, to carry the message simultaneously and personally."

"Who's we?"

"Us. CPAs from the auditor."

"What message?"

The fellow looked relieved. "Rainwater," the fellow said, "considers its employees a family."

"Gee," said Waddy. "Thanks for taking time out to tell me."

"No, no. The message is the merger. Rainwater has received an offer from Pelican Fund to buy all of its assets. The Rainwater board met this weekend to approve. It's a merger."

"Really? Like a marriage?"

"Exactly. Pelican Fund will be buying you out at forty-one dollars a share."

"Buying me out? I don't own anything."

"I was speaking," the man glanced at his shoes, "collectively."

"Could you say it again? The price?"

The man, Waddy's age, spoke with ecclesiastic timbre. "Forty-one dollars a share, for a total of six hundred and fifty-two million, one hundred and eighty thousand dollars. Plus or minus."

"Is it good news?"

"It certainly is."

"What do I get for my stock options?"

The man sat down on the only guest chair, a wire straight-back with magenta seat pad, and placed a boxy attaché case on his lap. Cordovan belting leather, no small matter. Two snaps and it was open, revealing a lining of ivory silk.

"Your options? Options will depend on individual circumstances. As you know, top management wanted all the employees to share in Rainwater's good fortune." He found a computer printout and let it drape to the floor as he examined its listings. "Those who are vested can exercise and sell at closing."

Waddy waited.

"Or they can elect to take shares instead, the shares of CyberGullet. We encourage that. Hold on to Pelican shares and become part of their family."

"Thank you," said Waddy. It was comforting to know that another family was arriving. Corporations were far more solicitous of their children than people realized.

The man gave a tiny grunt, perhaps the result of mild dyspepsia. "Brush, Henry W. L. Here you are. Looks like you're out of luck. Your options would have vested next January. Only vested ex-employees can exercise."

"Which means?"

"No value."

"No money?"

"No money."

The young man nodded, an irregular bobbing of the head that a good welterweight might use. He asked Waddy to sign a form acknowledging he had been apprised of the merger and of the value of his stock options. In the blank for value, the man drew a perfect circle and halved it with a slash. He stowed the form and the printout, snapped up the case, and stood.

"I think that's all."

Waddy thought of something else. "You said *ex*-employees. Are you expecting some of us to quit?"

"No," the man said and took a backward step. "No. It applies to all of Rainwater Software. You see, Pelican Fund is buying the *assets* of Rainwater. It wants the patents and the product. All these wonderful games you've designed. *Eight Major Disasters*, *Buchenwald Adventure*, *Sinatra's Women*. But Pelican Fund will not be continuing to budget for the development business."

"And?" The man kept retreating. The two furrows on his brow deepened.

"And as a result, our client will be downsizing Rainwater to assets alone."

"I don't follow."

"They're downsizing Rainwater. How can I put this? They are outphasing all staffed functions, to alleviate incremental labor costs."

"They're firing me?"

The man had his back to the portable wall. "That's all I'm authorized to say."

One hand was groping for the plastic border around the opening. It was not possible, the young CPA knew, to become trapped in a modular workstation.

"Not just you. All of Rainwater. You will of course receive the proper notice. The law provides for ten days. And naturally you'll receive full pay for unused vacation and sick time."

"They're firing me?"

The man sidewinded across the corduroy wall and found the opening. Relief spread across his face like impetigo. He backed out.

"Yes. You could certainly ... ," he felt with his shoulder for the edge of the divider and slinked behind it, " ... say that."

He was gone.

~

Waddy pulled out the shutdown procedures. He knew them by heart, but company policy said to use the checklist. Encrypt new code in random access memory, download to storage, log off. There was no new code. He flicked off the machine. Facing him, Satchmo stood with horn in hand, happy at his work. Waddy made his way toward the communal zone. Scents of herbal teas floated smoky and fruited in the air. The kitchen was empty. He pulled a pint jar of mango-raspberry from the refrigerator and twisted off its top. Walked to the far stairwell and went down.

In the meditation garden, knots of people had gathered. Waddy finished the juice—there was no eating or drinking in the meditation garden—slipped off his shoes, donned a pair of paper slippers from the pile, and entered through the glass door.

The talk was angry, technical. "Selling against the box ... ," he heard someone say, and a response, " ... excessive multiple." He kept walking. A woman from the general counsel's office was crying and being comforted by the fellow who gave spot neck massages. "No place like it ... ," she was saying between sobs, and everyone agreed. Finally, Waddy spied his gang, the VR tekkies. Group Leader had his hand squarely on the Buddha's head, bracing against an animated attack from three program-mers. One of them was Lisa Laroux. Sharp-chinned as a Benin mask, undernourished and intense, Lisa was far from beauti-ful. But Waddy had had few women enter his life, and this one, by grace of a few civil words and a single frantic encounter (at her bay-view apartment, on a yellow futon beneath unframed Kandinsky prints), this one had early won him over.

"Two years of work pissed away?" a short Pakistani chap

was asking. "What happens to *You're Lee Harvey Oswald* and *Madonna's Boudoir*?"

Waddy shuffled across the stones to hear the answer.

"That's all been bought. New management will decide whether to proceed."

"And us? What are we supposed to do? Go out to pasture?"

Group Leader leaned back and closed his lids for a measured second. Waddy recognized the expression, intended to card his subordinates that he knew more than he was telling. It was, in fact, a false card.

"Oh, I'd guess Pelican Fund will come around. They'll want to pick off a few of us. After all, we're well known in the industry. The best VR staff, bar none."

The man was not satisfied. He said something unintelligible, said it again more loudly. Lisa asked Group Leader something Waddy couldn't hear, and GL ignored her. Instead, he toed the edge of a meditation rug so its corner flopped over, then carefully flattened the triangle under the sole of his grommeted hiking shoe.

"Well," Lisa announced, "I say it's the shits."

"A severance policy is in place," GL offered, palms out. "You'll get that."

"Two weeks?" asked Lisa. She moved in.

"The nonmanagement plan is, I believe, two weeks." GL backed up, but the Buddha blocked his retreat.

"For every year of service?"

"No. Just two weeks. Two weeks for every year of *service*, that's the management plan."

"Exactly. The shits."

A pimply fellow moved close, shouldering the front wheel of a racing bike. "What about the options? One month from vesting. What does that mean?"

"Well that's a bad break," said GL. "If they're vested, you can exercise."

"And if not?"

Again GL gave them the palms up, throw-it-here sign. "If not, they expire on the date of the merger. That's a bad break."

"Let me ask you something," said the fellow. His voice lowered, and the others leaned in to hear. "You, you're in the management program?"

"Yes," said GL and let slip an unfortunate smirk. "That's the way things go down."

"No it's not," said Lisa. "This is."

The punch was telegraphed. Waddy, indeed everyone, even GL, saw it start at her hip and travel the long ellipse up to GL's temple. But the early warning did not diminish its effect. GL went sprawling into the shallow water of the contemplation pool. Lisa marched out the glass door.

Waddy was not far behind.

"It's an outrage," Lisa muttered as he caught up with her. She headed toward the parking lot. "We're left to scramble."

Waddy wanted to share her outrage, but he was optimistic. He'd been paid a good wage and had some money saved up. "Perhaps it's an opportunity," he offered. "A new adventure." He opened the door to her red Honda Civic.

"Don't be a horse's ass. You want adventure, take a cruise around the world. For me it's the classifieds and pounding the pavement. Damn them all to hell." And with that she slammed the car door, fired the engine, and reversed out of his life.

He considered Lisa's words. Not a cruise—he tended toward mal de mer—and certainly not around the world. Exotic foods made him costive. But with Rainwater his first job out of college, he'd not been beyond Seattle, and had begun to think of his surroundings in pixels. At Rainwater they spoke of an analog life and a digitized life, with equal affection. Here was his chance to see the difference. He would find the American landscape for himself.

Henry Wadsworth Longfellow Brush had been at it—the quest for truth and beauty—only some twenty-six years. The youngest of three children, all named for American poets, raised by their mother in the picturesque town of Skakit Point, thirty miles west of Rainwater. Emily Dickenson Brush had become a teacher of Life Force and Basic Composition at an alternative school outside Medford, Oregon. Del—Delmora Schwartz Brush—had stayed in Skakit and started a lawn care business. Waddy had been a diligent student and an Eagle Scout.

It was neither these traits nor his Gary Cooper sincerity that produced a college scholarship, but rather a reliable jump shot from the top of the keyhole. He had come to attention from one game, the State one-A championship, where Waddy was high scorer for the Battling Crabs. Good things followed from the modest press. One scout, from a school for the deaf, promised, if Waddy would but apply, to overlook his hearing scores. He took a second offer, Puget Junior Community College. There, he found he was neither fast nor, at six-three, big, but simply an affable white guy with a single shot he could sink if left alone.

Two years of obscurity were followed by no further offers. Waddy finished a computer science degree by correspondence, at the top of his remote class. He lived at home, in off-hours learned how to animate a character to move naturally across a screen, and worked in his mother's catering business. Each weekend there were hundreds of halved egg whites yawning like baby robins for their deviled fillings, and from Advent through New Year, thousands. Squirting anchovy paste on sesame crackers, placing parsley around cut crusts, laying wax paper across trays of hors d'ouevres, Waddy dreamed of a larger world. His mother had made a go of her business, but serving snacks to an indifferent crowd was not his idea of destiny.

At Rainwater he rose quickly from checker, a tedious job

running algorithms, to programmer, and then assistant to the fabled editor Lisa Laroux. He worked under her, a locution he found distractingly erotic. Software editors were responsible for the product from origination to profit. GL had nixed Waddy's early ideas for software products—*In the Lab with Madame Curie*, *Thirty Merit Badges You Can Earn*, and *Founding Fathers*, a virtual trip to the Second Continental Congress—as off-market.

"Hang in there, Brock," Lisa told him. "Think box office. More Dionysus, less Apollo. You'll get the feel of it."

Eventually he had. His *Historic Executions* had been written up by *Software Tomorrow*, and *Sinatra's Women* earned him single-card credit as executive editor. He would have liked to show his mother, who had no grasp of what he did for a living, but the program bore a NC-18 rating, mostly for the trios.

The Pelican merger came at a perfect time. He was burned out. Maybe somewhere in the vast spaces he'd visited in *Summer Vacations for Windows Vista*, PG-13, there was a place to equal Skakit Point. In one weekend he closed his apartment. He packed a single valise with clothes and his CDs of Louis and Bessie Smith. He sold the rest of his possessions from the apartment-house lawn. In two hours they disappeared. The lava lamp, the rose-and-mauve Simmons hide-a-bed, a basketball signed by Bill Walton, "To Waddy Go Crabs, Bill," the works of Robert Louis Stevenson bound in simulated buckram, a VCR that didn't work and a sixteen-inch TV that did, one bottle of South Dakota Vouvray, three and a third place settings, and a poster of Kurt Vonnegut. All disappeared in hours.

And Monday morning, the mist blowing gray and green out of the Cascades and across the water, Waddy Brush folded his frame into the silver Volkswagen convertible, jiggled the gearshift as he'd been taught in Driver's Ed, put his arm out the window to signal that he was pulling out from the curb, eased the Bug into the street, and turned east toward the future.

Two

On the eve of Waddy's departure, across the country four masked amateurs entered a ground-floor window that had been left ajar by a sympathetic janitor. It was 10 P.M. eastern time. They were dressed identically—black chinos and turtlenecks, black watch caps purchased at the Harvard Co-op, one size fits all—costumed, as one of them pointed out, less for camouflage than for dramaturgy.

The lone woman was Philida Post, of the Post plumbing fortune, the very Philida Post featured in the *Time* story "Nuts in the Forest." Philida had dedicated her considerable net worth to the cause of living things not human. Her largesse had already benefited coco palms in Malasia, the South American marmoset, and the Tennessee snail darter.

The work at hand was an easy matter: an accomplice volunteering as a lab assistant to earn spare change had drawn them a floor plan. They flicked on their flashlights, found the basement, and opened all the cages in minutes. At first the mice crouched in the corner, but a sharp tap set them free and scrambling. The intruders taped to a blackboard a flyer announcing their mission: Leave Alone Lab Animals. Then all four stepped gingerly upstairs, stowed their burglar tools in green shoulder bags, removed a clutch of books, and walked out the front door, a knot of graduate students working late hours. They left the door ajar in the hope that the beneficiaries of their raid would seek wider freedom. But a chill was in the spring air, and the emancipated mice opted for the walls of the old building.

Mortimer Dooberry learned of that decision over breakfast the next morning.

"Eviction? What do you mean, eviction?"

"You're through, Dooberry. First the smell. Then the protests. Now I've got mice throughout my building. You're out. The deposit will go to pay an exterminator."

Dooberry contemplated the English marmalade on his English muffin. Did eviction matter? His experiment was ruined. The loss of the lease was, he could not resist a smile, the lesser of his worries. Even if he could recapture the mice, he couldn't start over, months into a controlled and well-funded experiment to test whether chlorophyll stimulated the libido. He had come across the relationship by accident, a tube of toothpaste that he credited for reviving, albeit briefly, his flagging interest in Flavia. Gone—his ardor, his mice. Loosed by those kooks from L.A.L.A.

With the manumission, his shot at masquerading as a serious psychologist was over. He had never liked real work, his success had come from celebrity. Celebrity was a weed—the more it grew, the more it grew. But a single legitimate experiment might have made his reputation. That's why he had chosen Cambridge in the first place, with its patina of scholarship, its access to hungry students prepared to work for low pay. It seemed the perfect place.

Dooberry would have reconsidered if he'd known: his student workers had been switching mice regularly, segregating the sexes to inhibit sexual contact, and rearranging control groups. They liked Dooberry and wanted him to succeed. After enforced celibacy, mice, they found, performed indefatigably. There was a side benefit. They brought their dates to view the goings-on, counting on the power of suggestion.

And of course, the grant would end. The grant money had been spent. It was too late to start over.

There was still a trickle of revenue from book sales—his famous Harmony series. *Harmonizing Your Multiple Personalities* had been a smash hit and could still be found, like browning lettuce in low-traffic supermarkets. And three sequels. *Harmonizing for Duets, Harmonizing the Old-Fashioned Way,* and *Harmonizing with Your Inner Child.* But each royalty check was smaller than the last. Celebrity was not a roller coaster, more a parachute ride. Once the winch of fame let you go, you couldn't reverse the fall. When his books went stale, the TV spots disappeared. No spots, no lectures, no advances. The long descent had begun.

Would they want the rest of the grant money back? Dooberry's stomach shriveled at the prospect of meals at the federal detention facility in Danbury, Connecticut. A fraud was one thing, a conviction for fraud quite another.

He would fess up—notify the National Science Foundation that the experiment had been sabotaged beyond recall. Too, the toothpaste manufacturer, which had matched the federal funds in exchange for commercial rights. The company's warehouses in Mitchell, South Dakota, were crammed with old chlorophyll product. He would have to tell them too.

These tasks were a joy compared to informing his wife. The Cambridge house would have to go, they could move into what they had intended to be a vacation home. Who knows when the next windfall would descend? The academic poseur's life is a dicey one.

Perhaps a new title? He called his agent that morning, proud of his idea.

"*Hungry Women Get Men From Hunger*? Not bad. What's it about?"

"About? I don't know. I don't have the book, I have the title."

The agent was quiet for a moment.

"Sweetie, look. Maybe you need a new McGuffin. You know? A new hustle."

We'll simply move into the mountain house. Flavia won't like it. Summers and winters there were fine, everyone in town, but the off-season was lonely. He licked an errant flake of marmalade from his thumb. Flavia will understand.

She didn't.

"You supposed to be some hotshot TV guy when I marry you, and now you want me to live all year on a mountain, snow and ice, no people?" She had just walked in from the morning's aerobics, fearsome in biking shorts of kelly green Lycra. The agent was quiet for a moment.

"There are people, dear, just not as many as here."

"How you got no money? Maybe I go back to Rio."

"It's not a question of money, dear. The intellectual center of the country is moving west. We want to be in that center, where a cutting-edge scientist ... "

He didn't finish his sentence. Her gym bag came at him head high. "Flavia, my darling, we will go west just as we'd planned and something will turn up. I promise."

"Ayyy, another promise. Your promises, Doo, your promises has no hair on it."

Dooberry wrote it off to some Brazilian idiom. She stormed upstairs toward the shower. He would sell the Cambridge house, the equity would get them through the year, and somehow he'd find new sponsors and a new hustle. If everything fell apart, if truly there were no more grants or guest shots, he had an offer to teach at a third-tier college. How hard could it be to turn Methodist? I've done a lot of things I'm not proud of, he thought, standing amid the oversized furniture, but I have never resorted to teaching.

The gym bag in his hand hefted of weight. What was she doing out on a Monday morning with eight pounds of gear?

Despite his love for Flavia, he had misgivings. His declining interest in sex, his declining balance sheet—could he continue to hold her? The landlord had described a burglary. An inside job. Were those tools in her bag; could she be a L.A.L.A.? Freud taught that suspicions must be attended. Premonitions, like mistakes, conceal truths. An indifferent student and an unsuccessful clinician, Dooberry had learned that much.

He walked to the stairwell and listened to make sure the shower was running. Then he unzipped the bag and emptied its contents on the hall table. Out spilled a dozen rollers, two mascara tubes, three metal eyeliner pencils, pots of blush, and a portable, self-charging hair dryer.

~

Waddy made Snoqualmie Pass under a lowering sky. At the summit, darkness parted to blue, as if curtaining off the eastern boundary of his history. Beyond lay the boreal valleys of central Washington, orchards and riverbeds, great and unscreened spaces of sky and farm. He pulled over, unlatched and carefully folded the convertible top—tucking the corners in, the manual said, will prevent rubbing and double the life of the canvas—and got back in. On the down side of the pass, the Bug was soon north of seventy. He threw his head back and let out a coyote howl.

Through the Columbia River Gorge, the spell of names of places. Wenatchee, Yakima, Horse Heaven Hills. Past meadows of spring wheat, hops, and barley, peered from under the soil, a bright new green, past regimental furrows of the Palouse hills, buds of asparagus. He spent the first night at a Motel Six outside Lewiston, Idaho. His dreams were electric and strange, the last an erotic scene involving the lost Lisa Laroux, a hot tub, and Chewbacca, the Wookiee from *Star Wars*.

By the afternoon of the second day, he had driven into

the shoulders of the Rockies, where the first syringa bloomed white among larkspur.

Waddy sang at the top of his voice.

"This land is made for you and meeee."

South and east, the hills flattened out and he rolled through dry lava tuff, toward Utah on the Emigration Trail. The symmetry of the landscape reminded Waddy of computer graphics—life was simpler in pixels.

Waiting behind the wheel for points on the horizon to near, Waddy reminisced. At Lisa Laroux, he dwelled not on that one odd night of passion, but on a dreamy indulgence of what might have gone right. The two had found themselves alone in Corridor F one gray November evening puzzling over a program error in *Battle of the Bulge*. She appeared at the opening of his cubby. His ideal woman. He'd had no time with her, and this sudden interlude, isolated by darkness and the misting rain, offered a romance he wouldn't have dared to fantasize.

"Any answers?" she asked.

"No, not yet."

"Me either. But I've narrowed it down. It's early in the sequence. I'm pretty sure it's in the definition of P-alpha."

"No, I've run that to ground."

Lisa's features tightened in disappointment. "Shit. Eight hours shot to hell. I'm through for the night. You staying?"

"No," said Waddy, at once seeing his opportunity, though he did not know for what. "I'll walk out with you." He had never shown his feelings to this woman, she could not be aware of his crush. He often imagined her softening to his words, her cartoon-heart-shaped mouth turning to his. Now might be a good time to hint, delicately of course. She was his superior and a lady, facts that inhibited his already shy nature when it came to matters of the heart and other organs.

They walked through the lobby. The fountains in the meditation garden dripped arhythmically. The open air would bring her close, under his umbrella, to keep from the rain. His brain was scanning possible scripts, cybersearching for Yes, when she turned to him.

"Tell me, Brush, what about sex?"

"What about it? I guess I'm in favor."

She looked at him sideways. "No, no. I mean what about it? *How* about it?"

"How?"

"Yes, how? You're a young, healthy male, I'm a healthy female. Occasionally I find it relaxing. Especially after the day I've had. If it's not P-alpha, I don't know where it is. Anyway, if you're so inclined, so am I. Unless you're married or something. Or gay. I don't mean to pry."

He forgot to offer his umbrella. Actually he forgot to open it.

Waddy found himself at top speed following her red Civic through the Seattle streets. She stopped twice, once at an Indian restaurant for a large bag and again at a laundry to fetch two neatly wrapped bundles.

The coupling was callisthenic and efficient. Waddy hoped surprise did not diminish his enthusiasm. A sense dogged him that he was a house painter called in at the last moment to touch up bare spots on the wall. Afterward, she spooned chicken vindaloo out of a white takeaway box onto a single plate.

"Help yourself, if you like," she said through a full mouth. "But I only ordered for one. Sorry."

Waddy excused himself. He was in fact famished, but the evening seemed to have ended. The incident was never again mentioned nor, not altogether to his disappointment, repeated.

❧

If the dry, bosky fields of southern Idaho cut grooves in Waddy's sensibilities, then the salt deserts of Utah scorched them closed. Why had Brigham Young called this the promised land? It seemed less a promise than a threat. Waddy drove through the day until the sun bounced out of bounds. A flickering neon sign enjoined him to Eat. Obediently, he parked and entered the scruffy café. There was no air-conditioning. On the radio a girl sang about losing her heart to a '79 TransAm. Silex coffee bubbled on two burners. Waddy took the rearmost booth, flopped down, and unfolded his map.

"Can I help you, son?" The waitress put a glass of ice water and a plastic menu in front of him.

"I'm thirsty," Waddy said.

She filled the already full glass so it splashed over. He sipped it down.

"Where am I?" he asked. She put her finger on a little town south of Malad City. A perfect, fire-red nail. Above that, decorating the first joint, an arthritic node the size of a BB. He looked up at her. She was the jowelled side of forty, and looked inexplicably familiar. The raptor beak, the darting black eyes, it came to him—she looked exactly like the Wicked Witch of the West. Except she wasn't green.

"I know, I know," she said pleasantly. "Margaret Hamilton. Only I'm not."

"It's quite a likeness."

"So far it's never gotten me a dime, let alone a roomful of flying monkeys."

The least expensive item on the menu was the vegetarian chili, and he ordered it. She served extra saltines on the plate. Waddy went at it, dousing its peppers with ketchup from a plastic tomato.

"Where you headed?"

"I don't know. I'm looking for someplace to settle."

"This is a nice town." She put a wedge of lemon meringue pie in front of him. He hadn't ordered it.

"Hey," he greeted the pie. "No offense, ma'am, but I'm hoping to find somewhere that's not so ... "

"Godforsaken?"

"I didn't mean that." Although he did.

"Remote? Plug ugly?"

"Yes. Remote. I grew up in a pretty place, and I thought I'd see if I could settle somewhere that was a little ... "

"I know what you mean, son. What do you do?"

"Well, it's complicated. But I can work food service. I know a lot about kitchens and cooking."

"Tell you what," said the witch, who clearly was not. "You take my job. Stay here until the dust storms are over and the 102-degree summers and the freeze-your-ass-off, colder-'n-witch's-tit winters and then, why, we'll switch back."

"Somewhere by the sea, maybe."

"Not much water around here. What we have chases whiskey."

"Or with mountains."

"Well, for mountains, there's Alta ... or, I tell you what," and she twisted Waddy's map around so she could read it.

"That's where I'd go," she told him. "I was down there on vacation ten years ago, and I can't tell you for pretty. Snowcaps year-round, warm sun come March, lots of green. And it's not fancy, you could live dirt cheap."

She had pointed to a little town on Colorado's Western Slope, a town that remains lovely today, where one can find not a single shirt embroidered with a polo pony. But readers of insubstantial fiction know all too well the part that Chance plays in our lives. As Waddy rotated the map back to see where she pointed, her finger canted ever so slightly. Her red nail now pointed miles to the south and east, to a town he was sure he had heard of.

"You think so?"

"Dirt cheap. Real folks. That's the place. You'd get on there, son."

She poured him an iced tea, for which she also neglected

to bill. Waddy, in gratitude, tipped far more than the cost of the tea and the pie. And so the currency of her generosity was not the economies she had intended, but the warmth both took away from the booth of chipped Formica.

The Bug fired up reliably. Waddy had lived alone for years and some time ago had begun to confide in his car.

"Aspen," he said to the carcass-splatted windshield, partly in camaraderie but also to assure himself that he had gotten it right. "Aspen, here we come."

## Three

As Waddy spoke the words, there were stirrings within the very heart of Aspen. Or rather, within its very stomach. For Pantagruel was the locus of gustatory Aspen, and at the celebrated restaurant, housed in the only Bauhaus building on Main Street, the first crowd of the season was assembling. Pantagruel's owner, Frankie Rusticana, counted his blessings in four-, six-, and eight-tops.

He had just seated two of the country's fifty wealthiest men—the current *Forbes* list was pinned to the corkboard in his office—and now walked back to assist his greeter. The greeting was one of Frankie's secrets of success. Each patron of this, the most expensive restaurant between Rodeo Drive and 21 West 52nd Street, could flourish without radicchio but not without recognition. Frankie affixed himself to the elbow of a new diner like a bone spur. "I'll keep an eye on your waiter," he would whisper. "Let me know if he's not up to standards."

Pantagruel waiters were often not up to standards. They were not waiters at all, but tanned and muscled bachelors of arts abiding until the ski season. Often the bank back home would insist they make a start on life, putting them in need not of a job, but of proof of a job.

The schmooze (for that was Frankie's word) was a second secret. The last was so pedestrian and evident, right under their noses, he smirked as a plate of the stuff passed him by. Greens. Greens, the cheapest way to make an impression. By the main course most diners had consumed several ounces of alcohol. Frankie served only the best greens—it allowed him to push entrées to their expiration. (One reviewer had written that the grouper had last seen an ocean in a past geologic era.) Mostly no one complained. They came to gawk and be gawked, remembered the schmooze, the salad, and the price. Each was dear. Arugula, oak dark and bitter, watercress flown in daily, frisée and sorrel from a Mennonite farm in Belize. Tenderloin might flirt with verdigris before appearing, but every Pantagruel leaf was fresh and crunchy.

His secrets worked. Tonight, as Frankie beamed, they had brought back Mortimer Dooberry, the distinguished TV psychologist and lecturer, hosting a table of six. Dooberry, Frankie knew, was not wealthy by Aspen standards. Last summer his account had been cleared only after the snow flew. But his spots on late-night talk shows qualified him for a table.

"Dr. Dooberry," Frankie enthused, "wonderful to have you back." Nearby diners turned their faces to catch the reflected sun. "A good winter?"

"Excellent, thank you, Frankie."

"And Mrs. Dooberry. *Como é você?*"

Flavia Dooberry opened her jet black eyes in tribute. Frankie's Portuguese was limited, but she loved to hear her language and appreciated his effort. She responded in kind, knowing he wouldn't understand. "*Muito bem agradeça-o, Frankie.*" Very well, thanks. He beamed at the mention of his name. She touched him on the arm and went on in tongue. "It was a wonderful winter. As you know, Mortimer can no longer get it up, but I fucked two cabbies, the doorman at the neighboring apartment, and a strapping fellow who visited one afternoon. I think to adjust the cable television."

Frankie took her last word to mean Dooberry's guest

appearances. He returned to English. "Yes, yes. Wonderful. They should give your husband that Leno show."

He took Flavia's upper arm and steered her toward the men's room. Gay and important chatter filled the air. "I've saved this table especially for you," he confided. "Most of the people who come here, blah, blah, blah. But you and your husband always have distinguished guests. A private table, real conversation. That is what I have chosen."

Eyes followed Flavia. She walked as if to a coronation, head level, chin pointed to God. Everyone noticed. It was a bearing developed on the runways in Rio, where Flavia had modeled lingerie.

Justin Kaye leaned across a plate of yearling lamb carpaccio to mutter to his wife. "A contradiction in terms, a full size eight." Justin knew his goods: every product of Kaye Designs, the fashion lines and home accessories, bore the imitable stamp of its sole stockholder. "What Dow Corning hath joined together," Justin ended, "let no man put asunder."

Frankie had been raised on the coast of New Jersey, where he knew the smell of fish too long beached. "I only have three servings of the sea bass left," he told Dooberry confidentially. "I'll hold them for you in case ... "

Dooberry had invited two likely people from the summer set. The cost was high, but marketing of this magnitude could not be calculated with precision. Each potential pigeon brought a companion. After the Cambridge fiasco, Dooberry was unwelcome at government, academic, and corporate troughs. That left only the rich. He arranged to be given the check.

People liked pop psychology. It had a gooey, comfortable quality. At other tables his competitors were selling each other on condos, philanthropy for several afflictions, the arts. He would supply the quid, they would supply the quo. Trouble was, he didn't yet have a quid. If only the idea would arrive, like Pantagruel's fit waiters, suddenly at one's side, ready to serve. What was the concept? "Nothing is accidental," wrote Freud. He'd keep himself open, keep the conversation in a certain neighborhood, and let Kismet fill in the spaces.

Dooberry seated Etta Eubanks to his right and to her right Peyton Post. He could thus engage both in one conversation. That was a calculated risk—the plumpest geese nearest the blade. These were sophisticated people. Nothing like candor to conceal one's guile. On his left hand he seated Peyton's trim and deft wife, Chloe. Overdressed in Nicole Miller black, but pretty enough to get away with it. And smart—rumor said she ran Peyton's money. To her left Sherry Topliff, Etta's saturnine husband, and across, his own Flavia.

Peyton Post slid the chair out for Chloe, eased it in under her. He moved quickly to render the same aid to Etta, but too late. She was down and chewing a Sicilian olive. Peyton seated himself leisurely, enjoying his moment of stature over the table. He waited two beats to display his easy grace, his camel's hair sport coat slightly tapered at the waist, his abiding tan.

He had been blessed from childhood with strength and balance. Movement came easily to him. His sister Philida had the brains, he the body, and he wouldn't trade for all the money in the world. For one thing, the Posts already had a discernible chunk of that very sum. Ever since Great-Great-Grandfather had invented the ball-cock assembly still found in the tanks of most modern toilets. An enduring gizmo, that. When sentiment overcame him, Peyton would find himself in a strange bathroom lifting the tank lid and gazing for a rapt moment at the wellspring of his comfort.

There was a second reason he did not envy his sister. Philida seemed so unhappy. Her energy had found countless outlets, all difficult. She had labored for whales, bamboo, Atlantic salmon, and a root with no known use being plowed under in Kenya. She'd gotten herself arrested, once outside Bergdorf's spraying paint on furs, once in Cambridge, where to publicize population control, she fixed to the statue of John Harvard an expensively forged, scale—or rather, an approximation of scale, since the measurements are nowhere recorded—bronze condom. When police connected her with a recent episode involving laboratory mice, Peyton leaned on his friends to find her a job in the West.

Philida's hijinks were an aberration in the family. The Posts were solid citizens. Not especially useful, but solid. Peyton himself had never lacked peaceable amusements. He liked sports. He golfed a three handicap, he'd shot upland bird over four continents, and he was particularly fond of a blend of Moroccan hash. Handsome, fit, browned most of the year by a sun he could afford to chase, he especially liked just walking about to be admired.

His ministries paid, Frankie Rusticana backed off. Etta Eubanks had too good a memory from years spent without to think the cause was other than her wealth. Ever since the first well, in what is now called the Eubanks Field, she had summered in Aspen. It happened that Etta fancied music, and there was music in Aspen. To the teasing of her Tulsa friends—What will the social set make of you?—Etta assured them that she didn't give a dusty fart.

Etta's husband was similarly indifferent, though the source of his remove was not philosophic but pharmacologic. One could not think of Sherry Topliff without thinking of bourbon. The two paired like Edison and electricity. Until Etta found him at a gallery opening and adopted him, Sherry had been a hanger-on. Art first-nighters, charity events, panels on postmodernism, Sherry was set out with the cashews. People recalled him as a promising sculptor, though it was unclear what his promise portended. Until Etta, he'd survived on hors d'oeuvres. He dressed all seasons in a tattered tweed coat over jeans, a denim shirt, his tie the only concession to fashion, passing in spring from Irish wool to Irish linen and back again in fall.

A waiter stepped up and announced his name. Dooberry waived him off.

"Dispense with the résumé, young man, and bring us food and drink." His guests ordered quickly, he was happy to see. This dinner would run him fifteen dollars a minute.

He had no sooner raised the wine list, upping his cost estimate, when the conversation sailed without him. This was a voluble group, and two rounds of cocktails were logged before Dooberry could gain his entrepreneurial feet. Talk bounced from who was in town to how long they'd been coming. Dooberry despaired of an opening.

Peyton described the travails of flying commercially, the rigors of airport security.

"Next time," Etta offered, "let me know. I'll have the old Flexible Flyer come get you."

"You'd think," Peyton said, "there'd be a way for honest citizens to bypass all that."

"Peyton," said Chloe, "that's a genuinely good idea. A database."

Everyone looked to her for more.

"In the nineties there was a boom of segmented consumer databases. The market got oversaturated. Now here's a need for one, voluntary at that, and nobody's filling it."

Etta drained the last of her Manhattan, chased the maraschino with her tongue, caught it. "Timing, honey. It's all in the timing."

Sherry asked what she meant.

"That field was hot, now it's cold. Someone will take a chance, put that together, make a jillion."

The steward presented a bottle of white wine. Dooberry fussily unfolded reading glasses, inspected the label. Then, with a sweep of the hand, he indicated that Etta's glass be filled. "I think you'll like this," Dooberry said to her in a stage whisper. Their waiter uncorked the bottle and handed it off.

The steward received it with the dismay of a forgetful surgeon and tipped the bottle forward to spill a few drops into the glass. There was silence. Etta sipped, smacked her lips, glanced up appreciatively.

"Look out," she said. "Look out gullet, Look out toes, Look out kidneys, Down she goes."

The bottle was emptied in one circuit. Dooberry answered the steward's look with a brisk nod. The conversation had taken a turn for the better—damn the costs. A second Vernaccia was opened and iced.

"A database," Dooberry wheedled. "So your ID is on file and once you prove who you are, you pass through."

"Not enough," said Chloe. "It has to be a superdatabase, the mother of all. Incorporate everything, consumer habits, credit, financials. You put yourself in, all voluntary. And it serves everything from airports to protection from identity theft to getting cash."

"Honey, you have an idea." Etta reached to the cuffs of her aqua leather cowgirl jacket and gave a firm tug.

Dooberry could hardly contain himself. He knew several colleagues who had made fortunes in just this business, helping catalogers flood the mails. It was a subject about which he could easily feign knowledge. The waiter set out appetizers.

"And it should do more," ventured Chloe. "It should have a personal hook. It should fill some need in your psyche, and do it in a way that locks you in. Otherwise it's just statistics, dead as," and she glanced around, "a salmon mousse."

Everyone stared at the plate in front of Flavia Dooberry. A glutinous pink paste in the shape of a fish was swimming through a fringe of cress.

"What do you have in mind, honey?"

"I don't know. But before the idea is a business, it needs something you can't copy. Something unique, proprietary."

They set into their plates.

"It's complicated, isn't it?" Dooberry said in his reflective voice. Geraldo had loved that voice, asked specially that he use it for the close.

The inevitable salads passed under the nose of Frankie Rusticana, followed closely by a third bottle of the white and the flawed sea bass. Frankie calculated, permitted himself an interior smile. Two drinks, eight ounces of wine per diner. No risk now—the fish will pass, undetected, out to sea.

Dooberry kept to the subject. He would need time to conjure its particular, and so retreated to the general. "We're really discussing a new tool. A combination of computer technology that includes an innovation to serve a contemporary need." Everyone's mouth was full, and Dooberry could never resist an unprotected listener.

"Tools change the way we think about things. The computer is to the mind the way Galileo's telescope is to the stars. This is the next frontier in scientific research. The people who back this will be," he gestured as if searching, "the Neil Armstrongs of their age."

It did not pass Etta Eubanks's notice that Dooberry used "back" rather than "do." Etta was an old hand at peddling oil leases, and in every human pairing she sniffed out buyer and seller. Best have it out early.

Chloe Post speared a mushroom and swirled it in the venison reduction. "I've never seen an invention yet that explored ourselves. Do you really think all this science helps the human animal?"

"Human animal," Flavia caught the phrase. Wine nourished the soft Portuguese accent. "Now you're talking. Scientists, man. Like my husban'. They not interested in the animal. They think drinking and fucking are places in China."

Entrées arrived and the conversation broke into groups. Peyton began to describe a bike trail. Sherry Topliff was leaning close to Flavia's cheek, forking into her mouth a taste of celery root roulade. Behind Dooberry stood a busboy, stationed like a page at the table of an English noble. The thought infused him with a regal well-being.

He turned to Chloe and inquired about the forthcoming music festival. "Perfect," he heard himself saying. "Opening with Mozart. How suitable. All music begins with Mozart."

Plates were cleared, the wine drunk, the liqueurs sipped, and Sherry's Black Jack Daniels sucked slick of its rocks. Dooberry was thanked by all. Etta insisted the three couples do it again. A provocative evening, she called it. The philosophical dimension of technology. The guests walked out into the June night. A late-rising moon shone behind Ajax Mountain and the air was insubstantial and chill.

Rusticana came over as Dooberry lingered. They shook hands enthusiastically.

"Frankie. Thanks for saving that sea bass for us. It was excellent."

*Four*

Waddy drove across the plateaus of the Colorado Grand Mesa. With every mile a gain in altitude brought a mild hypoxia, a quickening of pulse. As the air thinned Waddy breathed faster. Something was happening.

He liked it. It was the feeling of the state finals. All hands together, one heart, one team. The opening basket had been his, an easy pop from the foul line. Then five more jumpers. He could tell from the way the ball floated off his fingertips—he was on, he was the man. "Battling Crabs Eternal," played the band. Waddy sang along as the Bug labored up a hill.

> Battling Crabs eternal,
> Pincers held on high,
> Hearts fixed on the goal and
> Eyes fixed to the sky.
> Battling Crabs eternal,
> Battling Crabs supreme,
> We're fighting the fight and
> We're dreaming the dream.

The third quarter was a blur. After six in a row, he couldn't find the rim. Skakit fell behind as he lost the touch.

It returned in the fourth quarter. He closed the lead. The

last time-out. Bouncing cheerleaders patting him on the back as he came to the huddle. He wished he could have toweled off first. One in particular squeezed his arm: captain of the squad, the bosomy one with the heart-shaped lips. He was a sucker for heart-shaped lips.

> Waddy, Waddy, he's our man.
> If he can't do it, no one can.

He'd never had a night like this. Eleven for fifteen from the floor, dead on from the line. Thirty-three points. But with half a minute to go, it hadn't been enough. They were down by a single point.

"Okay," said Coach as they gathered round for the last time. "I want you to get it to Brush. He's on fire. Waddy, find space, any way you can. One shot is all we need. It's all come down to this, men. Remember your school. Remember your family. And remember this: those little cheerleaders don't suck the dicks of losers."

Back on the court. Waddy takes his position to the far left, sees the other guard walk casually to the keyhole to set up his pick. The ball is inbounded to his right, relayed to the corner. He makes his break. As he rounds the pick, the ball comes at him, his hands high. He doesn't hesitate. He is in the air, he launches.

It feels good. Soft, maybe too much arc, but on target. Better too much than too little he decides as he, his mother and his sisters, the cheerleading captain, the Skakit Point band, and most of the student body await the descent.

"Ahh," says the crowd, an ahh of ambiguity, of a hundred meanings all deconstructing into no meaning as the ball lands upon the back of the rim and bounces, softly falling, promising and seemingly straight. "Ahh," says the crowd as it bounces a second and lesser bounce off the front rim, not quite square and now falling softly, clearly describing a cone that fits within the circumference of the rim. And surely if the two bounces are within the circumference, then the ball is captured. It is only a matter of time, for Waddy has defined its geometry, Waddy the hero, Waddy—for even he in his virginity, bounding on the balls of his sneakers, has time for a fleeting, lubricious thought—Waddy the non-loser. Waddy has caused the inevitable, if only we can wait.

The ball descends and alights on the rim. The second bounce, millimeters awry, has sent the ball to sit the rim and now, in some perverse physic, to roll about the hoop. First on the inside, holding the arc and gaining speed around the curve like a carnival ride, and then, velocity exceeding drag (where is gravity when you most need it?), then finally and for all times, for all memory, taking the outside rim, careening off, falling away from the basket, no pass through that netted orifice, away and down to a wooden floor. A near miss.

Waddy levitated his hands from their grip on the wheel. That was a long time ago. He took a deep breath, let it out, and felt the anxiety burn through his system, fire in the cylinders of his lungs, and pass out with a sigh.

The countryside was spectacular. A maze of extended buttes carved by wind and water into an intricate pattern. To the south and east the hillsides were barren, but on the windward and northern sides, where snows gathered and held, forests of black-green ponderosa grew. And rivers—the Marvine and the White, the Dolores and the Eagle—all emptying into the mighty Colorado. Waddy's spirit responded to the romance of place, the only flavor of romance on his plate, though he knew if ever presented he would respond equally to the fleshy kind.

"Ye-ee-ee-ee-ss-ss," he shouted to the sky.

Waddy steered off the exit at a quaint little town and took the road that bordered the Roaring Fork River toward the couloirs in which Aspen nestled. The drive was a constant grade, in some fifty miles gaining three thousand feet. Waddy's spirits climbed as he ascended. The mountains grew craggy, their geology newer and the lines more severe, and the houses grew larger and more fantastical. Through it all, edging the road, ran a fierce and freestone river.

The setting did not disappoint him. The sky was a color you could use in a program of heaven. I ought to make a note of that, thought Waddy. Heaven as a video game. Until it came to him: he was no longer in the business.

The environs. Giant houses of every architectural excess, Greco moderne, Bauhaus, Provençal, Philip Johnson nihilist, ur-Tudor, PPG-bulk-sale. Michael Graves-end, Darien feudal, even something that looked like Colorado. The higher up on the cols one looked, the larger the houses grew, until in a band at the highest shelf, with its spectacular views of the ski runs and the wilderness beyond, Starwood, the crown in the jewel. There buildings poised on the fragile ledges like raptors peering down on the scurrying life below.

On Aspen's outskirts he passed an airport built against the base of a mountain. The craft on the aprons would have made any nation in the world a proud air force: Gulfstreams and Citations, and huddled over by the fuel pumps, infra dig, King Airs and Lears. Most bore no identifier except a tail number. One or two showed a discreet monogram, as might be embroidered on the linen of a peer of the realm.

And the town itself. Two- and three-story buildings lined the broad main street. Most had been freshly painted in gay colors, lavender and Prussian blue, real Victorians in buttercup yellow fringed in white cornices, white brackets, and friezes, brand-new Victorians with gingerbread, oculus windows, and roof crestings—the kind of work they don't do anymore, unless you pay for the apprenticeship first. Shops of pretty things, redbrick office buildings, restaurants, bookstores orderly and eager. At the main intersection stood the Hotel Jerome, three stories of renovated nineteenth-century luxury, faux gaslights, and carved wooden benches.

At the hotel's restaurant he ordered a coffee. When it came, he asked about staff. The young woman, wheat-blonde hair held back by a wide pink headband, shook her head sadly.

"We're booked up."

"I know a little something about food service," he said.

"You see that fellow." She pointed to a forty-ish man setting out silver. "He's a thesis away from a Stanford PhD. French lit. I have four languages. Knowing a little something won't help you around here."

Everywhere the same response. Nothing doing, all booked. Everyone was friendly and everyone sent him on. Toward the end of a long day, he stood outside a glass and chrome building and peered inside at Mediterranean tile. "How could you have missed this one?" a busboy had asked as he polished tulip Champagne glasses. "Probably Aspen's most expensive. Certainly its most pretentious. Just roll those dark eyes at them, bashful."

Waddy leaned against the brass push bar, moved the thick glass door, and found himself inside a small vestibule. He looked over the reservation book—tonight's page was filled, and its margin held a series of encrypted marks in red and yellow pen. Beyond, within the whites and grays of deep carpet and suede wall covering, stood forty tables resembling a symphony orchestra awaiting the baton.

"Sorry," said the pretty girl moving quickly toward him. "We're not open yet. Dinner from six."

"I'm looking for a job."

She appraised him carefully. Black Irish roots, those Calvin Klein looks the boss likes in his waitstaff. Callow, faintly carnivorous. Black hair roughly divided along what may have been intended as a part. Eyes ready for pleasant sights. A thin face so clearly young, optimistic, and confused that anywhere on earth, even without the tells of his dress—jeans, collared polo shirt, sockless tan ankles ending in Reeboks—he scanned American.

"We don't have anything." Annalee didn't yet have her lenses in and peered through her glasses at his disappointment.

"You want the official word?" She motioned toward double doors. "In the scarf."

Waddy passed through to the kitchen. A short Mediterranean fellow was wrestling a crate of strawberries, angrily jamming the claw of a hammer between wood planks and tossing curses at cowed men in toques. He wore an apron over his white linen shirt. Waddy watched him dunk the berries under the faucet and place them in a glass bowl. Water was accumulating in its bottom.

"Yes?" The man looked up, annoyed. He wore a floral cravat.

Waddy asked his question and got his answer. The same answer. He continued to stand there and stare.

"You want something else?"

"Well," Waddy began. "Those berries. They're *fraises des bois*. Wild strawberries."

"I know what they are, sonny. I just bought 'em."

"Well, they really shouldn't be stored like that. They're very delicate. A minimum of water and then layered in paper towels. They'll keep their flavor better."

The man stopped what he was doing and stared back. "Health department?"

"No," Waddy said. "I just know a little about berries."

"You've handled these?"

"No, sir. The most expensive berries we ever bought were Tributes. Even those I wouldn't drown like that."

Frankie Rusticana wiped his hands on his apron and handed the opened crate to a sous chef. He jerked his chin in the direction of his office and strode off. Waddy followed.

Frankie asked and Waddy, whose only human response since leaving the Utah diner had been rejection, answered.

Frankie sat meditatively flipping his lower lip with his thumb.

"Okay," the owner said at last. "One week, no pay. Things work out, day four you're a busboy. Day eight a paid one. Annalee will measure you for a uniform."

"The salary?"

"Nothing to talk about." Frankie mentioned a sum that might cover Pantagruel's warm duck salad. "Mostly tips."

He went back to the greeter and watched her make notes against the reservation list. She was pretty, in a homecoming contest way. Runner-up. Broad and forthright brow, hazel eyes not quite matched, the fatal heart-shaped lips. She was surprised the boss had taken him on.

"You must have something," she said as she wrote down the sizes he quoted her. At each number her eyes languidly measured the proportion, chest, waist, inner seam. Waddy was glad when it was over. Annalee was his age, late twenties, slender and tanned. She wore her thick, minky hair parted down the center. It billowed across her face, and she peered out from behind like a theater manager nervous about the house.

He drove back down valley. He'd passed a motel coming in—he'd get a simple room there, and in eight days he'd be on salary. Life's problems, his mother often told her children, are dirty dishes—they don't wash themselves.

Some needed Brillo. The motel manager quoted him a tourist's price. He thanked her and moved on. Prices went lower as he drove on, but at the rate of decline, he would not find an affordable bunk until Wyoming. Finally, almost an hour away, he took a modest room for the term of his probation. Nothing ventured, nothing gained, his mother had also counseled, although try as he might Waddy could not remember whether she had mentioned the converse.

Probation went well. Waddy attended with care, corrected placement of oyster forks. He performed the usual busboy duties. Fresh wine goblets were first on the list—when the white was cleared, the red was positioned, and when a new grape was chosen the suite was replaced. Glassware rolled Vesuvially out of the kitchen, and Frankie emphasized the importance of wine supply. "It is our plasma," he explained, dipping at the knees for emphasis. "The flow must be uninterrupted." When not attending, the busboy was to stand in readiness, imparting that the diners had a menial for their bidding. That's all there was to it. For his labors, he received a quarter of the tips. Half went to the waiter, the rest to the house.

When he asked Annalee how one lives on these amounts, she looked at him with innocence.

"Aren't you a DIB?"

"What is a DIB?"

"A distributable income beneficiary."

"Beneficiary of what?"

"Of a trust, silly. These people are all beneficiaries, mostly DIBs." It was an hour before opening on his fourth day. They sat folding linen napkins into swans. Around them the wait-staff busied itself.

"She's a mandatory income beneficiary, and he," she pointed to a tall lad with a ponytail, "he's lucky. He has the power to invade corpus. Without distributable income you're in tough shape around here. Frankie lays off most of the staff in October and they're on their own until ski season. You better be thinking about an off-season job."

Life was too glorious to worry. Days were bright with sun, there were expanses of countryside to hike, the nights were cool and starlit. Dinner began at four with setup and often lasted until one or two on the weekends. His waiter generated handsome tips, but not enough. He needed to stem the outflow of cash.

He mentioned his plight to Annalee.

"I'm looking for a roommate," she said after a silence. "One hundred a week in advance, no smokes, no guests. I'd rather have a girl, but I need the dough. For that you get half a bed in a trailer at the Alpenview Court, share a bath. No closets, keep your shit in your car."

"You had a roommate?"

"For two years."

"So what happened?"

"She went away."

"The view sounds nice."

"The view?"

"Alpenview. It sounds like you can see the mountains."

Annalee regarded him sadly. Contact lenses lent her eyes an aqueous sympathy.

"Right, my little rabbit. You can see the mountains, the river is Chardonnay, and every Sunday the Easter Bunny brings us a bowl of hash."

❧

Waddy rose early the next day to get in a jog and inspect his prospective digs before work. He had taken to jogging on the bike path through the canyon east of Glenwood Springs. He drove to the parking lot at the Shoshone Power Station. There the Colorado River backed up into a deep pool that let out through whooshing rapids. This June the water gushed coral, running as it did off sandstone hills. He ran two miles out and two miles back. On the return leg Waddy kept apace the river as it tumbled downhill. He could run forever. Follow it through its canyons, over its dams, he could race it to the Pacific.

By the time he returned—checked his watch, twenty-three minutes, ten seconds later—a monogram of moisture darkened the front of his T-shirt. He took a towel, doused it in the stream, and sponged himself off. The water was ice cold—yesterday's snowmelt. He downed a bottle of Gatorade and set out on the floor of the trunk fresh underwear, a crisp white shirt, and black-wash pants. A quick look around, and in one motion he stripped off his jock and running shorts. Just as they hit his ankles, a bright orange raft turned the corner of the canyon and drifted down toward him.

Behind that raft came three more, a high school senior class trip. The first, filled with teenaged girls, was steering straight for his shoreline. His panic was disrupted by wolf whistles and hoots. Six cell phone conversations—some raft-to-raft, some ship-to-shore—were interrupted as their cameras were held on high. He spun around and faced the maw of the trunk. "Great buns," someone called. "Hey, mountain man, watch the birdie." He managed to get his feet into the leg holes of his boxers. Eager to hoist them full mast, he stumbled and went headfirst into the open trunk. It was a solution of sorts. Waddy lay there, face down, hearing the hoots and ignoring the hot chrome bumper that divided his body at a strategic latitude, until the last raft was out of earshot. Then he rose and finished dressing.

As he came around to the driver's side, a woman—at least he guessed it was a woman—in military blouse and khaki shorts was kicking down the stand of her red Lambretta scooter. Braid ran from one epaulet under her arm, Scout-style. Wraparound sunglasses masked her eyes. All he could make out were two puny images of himself, tinted rose.

"Aren't you a little old for that, mister?"

"Old for what?"

"Mooning those kids."

"That's not what happened. I can explain."

She pulled her lips in tighter. They all but disappeared. "I've a good mind to make you explain to the Garfield County Court."

"Are you a cop?"

Waddy had never seen a cop in knee-length hose, British army tan knee socks turned down with a symmetrical cuff, wearing a badge that migrated as your view shifted from an image of the earth to a happy face.

"I'm an eco-cop. We're safeguarding your quality of life. FFE, Friends of the Friendless Earth. I'm empowered to give out summonses."

She was six feet-plus and cast a shadow Waddy could hide in. No lipstick, blouse puffy but without definition. "Well I'm glad you're on the job, officer."

"Mooning those teenagers. You ought to be ashamed."

Waddy turned to his trunk for evidence of his jogging story, but at the sight of his jock, soaked shirt and shorts, he decided to stand on a broad denial.

"Listen, officer. You have it wrong, believe me."

She took his license and registration, noted his name.

"I'm passing you this time, Brush. But I don't want to see that bony ass glistening in the Colorado sun again. You got it?"

"Yes, sir," he said. "I got it. You won't." He slammed the trunk lid and made to enter the car. From inside, he corrected himself.

"Ma'am."

"Hey! You fixing to leave that trash behind?"

"No, sir. Ma'am." He got out, walked around to fetch the Gatorade jar, climbed under the car to scour for the lid, and tossed both into the backseat. "No," he squinted to read the brass name bar over her two-tone, holographic badge. "No, Officer Post."

"Well it's a good thing. For that I *will* bust you. Now high-tail it out of here."

Waddy fired up the VW and floored its accelerator. He hoped to give the impression of burning rubber, hightailing, but the car's repertoire had at its top speed a leisurely pace.

❧

The trailer park lay in the leafy bottom of the river valley, only fifteen miles from Aspen. Tin barracks like cigars on a tray. Waddy walked up the rickety steps of the Airstream and Annalee showed him in. The front room held a serviceable miniature kitchen, a chair, a loveseat, and a small television set. In the center opposite the hall to the bedroom was a head the measured length of stool, sink, and a size-twelve shoe. To sit on the toilet one needed to move four pairs of skis—downhill, telemark, cross-country, and spring—for rocks, Annalee explained—out of the bathroom.

"No shower?"

"Outside. Solar. Attached to the trailer."

"How do you shower in winter?"

"Quickly."

Waddy hesitated. The prospect of chill didn't bother him nearly so much as the lack of modesty the arrangement suggested. He held his peace.

In the back room a double bed all but filled the space, leaving only a shin-tight margin around three sides. By a half-bed, he figured she'd meant a small space. His surprise showed.

"You get the side to the wall. I don't snore or toss. If you do, you'll have to leave."

"Sure," he mumbled, trying for casual. "That's only reasonable."

"One other thing," Annalee said. "No screwing around. Not with me, and if you get lucky, you'll have to go to her place."

Waddy became embarrassed anew.

"That's okay."

"Not that I have anything against sex, you understand. It's just ... I've sworn off."

Waddy nodded. He intended sympathy, not assent. Tacked to a corkboard were a dozen snapshots. Annalee and a second woman, mannish, awkward-looking behind a knobby nose. The two were hiking, kayaking, riding a chairlift. He started to ask, but Annalee plucked them down as he watched and gathered them together in a deck.

"That's ... ?"

"That *was*. That was Norma."

"Oh. She's ... ?"

"Gone. She's gone." Annalee's words ended in a soft, glottal gulp.

Waddy rubbed his hands together. He meant his gesture to say he approved. But he had a second reaction. That so pretty and kind a girl as this should be gay was disappointment enough, but gay and rejected ...

"Great," he said, looking about. There was nowhere new to look. "Just perfect. Okay if I try it for a month?"

Annalee studied him with maternal eyes. "Yeah, I think so. I think it's a good arrangement. I need the dough. And you ... " She shook her head. "Someone needs to look out for you, Brush. You're a furry little mouse who got off the train at Hawk Depot."

Waddy smiled. He liked the description.

Five

Justin Kaye was caught up in his own promote. Bars before the last dissonance of the afternoon concert, he rushed from the music tent, hopped in his custom Ford Explorer, and fired its 5.4-liter engine. (Custom in this case meant precisely its opposite: Justin's truck had no precedent. It was a rolling duck blind—full camouflage interior, walnut gun racks suspended from the roof, ammo drawers and two waterproof pads for dogs in the rear.) Justin gripped the goose call that knobbed his gear lever, reversed out of his parking spot, and sped toward town. He passed the other premature evacuators—Schöenberg. After all, who really cares about Schöenberg?—and headed for Pantagruel's.

Four-thirty, in time to catch Frankie. For Victor Grant, he needed the right table. Everyone there would know Grant, and everyone would have his own promote.

Justin's scheme was a natural. He smiled at his wit. A natural. It had fallen into his lap at a meeting of the board of the Friends of the Friendless Earth. He supported the Friends, supported conservation. Especially now that he had completed his fifteen-thousand-square-foot house on Red Mountain. Now that his underground storage tanks were topped off with propane, gasoline, and jet fuel, now that he had sufficient water rights for his closed-circuit trout-stream-*cum*-water-wheel. Conservation was the answer.

A thousand points of light, said George the First. There was an underappreciated president. With his eye for photo ops, the man should have been on Seventh Avenue. In the Bush One years, Justin had used a Barbara double to move size sixteens.

Justin supported FFE and FFE, Justin felt sure, would support his deal. FFE disdained plans that made money—Justin's plan made not a dime. It saved the land, created valuable duck habitat, and kept one of the valley's last pristine plots out of the hands of developers. It only did good. Almost.

Two hundred and thirty prime acres up Conundrum Creek were coming on the market. Zoned at full density, it would hold a few hundred units and would bring the price of an aircraft carrier. But no one could get that zoning anymore in Aspen. The gate had shut. To get any development, you needed a clever plan.

Justin had the plan. Sign a few of the town's richest fellows, those who liked to shoot, for a hunting club. He already had a name, the Isaak Walton Preserve, and a logo. Packaging maketh the man.

He had packaged this dinner. Victor Grant: Grant liked to hunt. He could buy into the Isaak Walton Preserve with the change between his sofa cushions. Grant was an odd bird—insisted he had a blind date, and Justin said of course, bring her along. A strange concept, the country's eleventh richest man needing a blind date.

"The table," he told Frankie. "Room to spread out the drawings. Hold the drinks until I've rolled them up."

Twelve investors, half a million each. Debt for the balance. One tax deduction for the interest and a second for the conservation easement. What's better than private shooting? Tax relief. Better than that? Publicity. Justin's staff did up a press release.

"Aspen Moguls Save Ranch." Always write your own headline.

> A team of Aspen investors, led by Justin Kaye and
> investment-banking giant Victor Grant, have joined
> together to save the Conundrum Ranch for posterity.
> Today Kaye announced plans for the Isaak Walton
> Preserve, an environmentally designed hunting club
> dedicated to saving a magnificent tract in the heart
> of national forest. In a display of unity, environmen-
> tal executives appeared at the first hearing to praise
> the project. The plan, with a single caretaker home-
> site as approved by Planning and Zoning, preserves
> the property and excludes future development.

Justin had talked with Planning and Zoning. One caretaker unit was okay with them. In fact that's what had given
him his idea for a private wrinkle. It was a way to cut the cake.
What good is being the birthday boy if you don't get the rose?
Tax benefits, leverage, good publicity, and daily bag limits.
And the little wrinkle. Justin shook Frankie's hand and went
home to change for dinner.

∿

"Indonesian Funds Suffer Drain."

Peyton Post glanced again at *The Wall Street Journal* and
repeated the headline to the mirror as he shaved. Indonesian
Funds Suffer Drain. He liked a headline for conversation. How
to turn it into a question? "Did you hear about the Indonesian
funds?" No. Open-ended. If the listener hadn't heard, he'd be
left with a lame follow-up: Oh, yes, they've suffered a drain.
"How are the Indonesian funds doing?" Too much of a setup.
"Do you think the problems in Indonesia will affect us?"
That's it. Anyone could answer that one.

Pleased, he finished shaving under his nose, washed away
the specks of lather, and inspected the result in a magnification

mirror. Rugged, tanned, clear-eyed. Some tiny lines around the lids and the corners of the mouth. Not unappealing. In the summer sun his hair grew lighter, and about this time of year a woman invariably said to him, "What I wouldn't give, Peyton, for your locks." Some of them went on to offer it anyway. It was nice to hear. Not that he would take them up on it. He was devoted to Chloe—she had taken over his life, his trusts, those squabbles with the bank officers over distributions. She out-skied him, abided his appetites, and never grew petulant about the investments that disappeared, the houses that didn't.

He combed back his hair and admired the way it lay in furrows. Establishing the part was a ritual—he inspected individual strands and decided to which side each belonged. Peyton recognized each one and knew its place. Where he shaved back his sideburns, the skin glowed a paler tone. A single day in the sun would even that out.

This was a glorious time of year. Absolute best. Maybe second to winter. In the winter you didn't need a headline, in winter one could always talk about the snow. Its depth, was it new or old, wet or dry? Crusty or corny or soupy or tracked? In the summer, mountains were a safe bet, walking up them or biking over them. Or the bikes themselves, their construction— aluminum, titanium, vanadium—their gearing, where one had been on them. And in the fall there were geese and ducks, various things to shoot. Spring was the awkward time, every-one still indoors. Spring was a conversational void.

Spring brought a second problem. The Posts were in an odd way homeless. It was too early for the house in Maine, and besides, the locals there talked only of unemployment. Too rainy for the Florida Keys, too crowded in Scottsdale, the Hamptons were empty. Forget New York. They were obsessed with current events. He was glad spring was ending and the season starting again.

Peyton filled a palm with bay rum and splashed it against

his cheeks. It was his father's choice of aftershave. If only Chloe were to grow keen on children, it could be his son's. Then he dried his hand, took a ballpoint pen, and jotted words on his palm. Indonesian Funds, he mouthed to the mirror, Suffer Drain.

~

Rod Hollister drove the rented car up the serpentine. He was sure he'd recognize the house. The real estate agent had asked to come with him, but he'd had a bellyful of her at the closing. He'd just spin up Red Mountain to see what $15.5 million looked like.

The same as the pictures. But empty. The sellers were in the middle of a nasty divorce; they'd removed every stick of furniture. The oversized rooms were empty. The few cartons his decorator had shipped, now stacked by the front door, made it emptier.

He walked around. Needs fixing up, but then, wow. Man's got to score in here. The sauna, the pool, the views, the projection room. He tore open the top carton and pulled out a box. It was from a New York jeweler. What the hell has the decorator been buying? He turned back the tissue paper. Crystal coasters. A set of twelve. Swedish. Hollister dropped the pale blue box back into the carton. Fifteen and a half mil. When he agreed to buy the house, it didn't seem like money. That was his take on a single platinum record, and he'd thought he could make them whenever he liked. Now he wasn't sure. Maybe she ought to buy coasters at Wal-Mart.

He opened the door and walked out on the deck that faced the ski hill. The rugged peaks showed the last of winter's snowpack. He tensed at the sensation of eyes on him. If the yellow dog hadn't lifted its head, he wouldn't have noticed it.

"Get out," he yelled. "Scram."

The dog lay in the sun at the corner of the cedar deck. At the sound of Hollister's voice his tail began slowly to thump the ground.

"I am not kidding," Hollister said, angry. He was afraid of dogs. "Fuck off."

This was a mix. Mostly lab, a long unkempt coat that was yellow with a brindle saddle. Barrel chested, wide forehead, lachrymose black eyes. The words were the first the beast had heard in a week. It rose and, ears tucked back to signal affection, walked slowly toward Hollister. He grabbed the collar and read the tag. He swore again. The address was his new one. "No way. You're not living here."

Hollister unbuckled the collar and removed it. The dog licked his hand. Hollister yelled a curse and jumped back. "Now beat it. They left you behind. You're not going to shit all over my fifteen and a half million bucks." The tail kept wagging.

Hollister went back to the door. The dog watched expectantly.

"Go ahead, beat it." Hollister held his arm back threateningly. The dog looked at him, wiggled its rear end in gratitude.

The first coaster hit the deck short and the dog reared at the shattering of glass. The second caught its flank. It yelped and scampered down the drive. "That's it," Hollister yelled after him, "keep going." The dog looked back at the voice expectantly, but when a third coaster whizzed by its head, it ran off.

❧

Etta Eubanks squeezed her plump rear into fresh jeans, slipped on the turquoise leather jacket with Choctaw beadwork, leaned on the bedpost to hoist herself into polished tan boots, and winked to her full-length reflection. "You kin brush the coat of a Poland white 'til it shines," she drawled country, "but she's still a sow." This dinner was on her. These characters seemed fond of that overpriced decorator place. She'd settle for a T-bone and a Bud any day, but Pantagruel's it would be. Just the four, Peyton and Chloe Post, Dooberry and she. Dooberry's restless wife was off buying a horse, and her own husband had gone in search of stone. Etta liked the symmetry of pairs. Pair 'em up and ship 'em out. Noah had the best job in the Bible.

Except of course for God.

Etta had news. After their first conversation, she went out on her own. That was her daddy's advice. "Honeybee, you can find out anything if'n you'll just hold on." Daddy brokered oil leases. He left her overrides on dust, ten dry wells, and some worthless acreage. A shrewd trader even at ten, Etta later parlayed them into the last major trap found in western Oklahoma.

She'd called two major airlines. The airlines were in trouble. Her calls were returned the same day. And both told her, you bet. They'd love to look at a system that identifies people so they could speed up security. They couldn't say what it would be worth to them, but the amount would reflect a portion of increased revenues. Which, they estimated, would be considerable.

Dooberry, that prissy peacock, is supposed to be the entrepreneur. You'd think he'd know to do this. If he spent more time at his work and less cooing over rich women, maybe he would. Still, she jotted down his number. The Posts would come too. First things first. She phoned Pantagruel and made Frankie promise her a special table.

❧

"All our tables," Frankie was saying to his staff, "are special." The briefing was conducted in the kitchen. Frankie described the day's du jour, a salmon for which Chef had made a *coulibiac*. "Tonight," he announced, pulling himself above his sixty-two inches and easing, as he did toward dusk every day, into a northern Italian accent, "tonight at second seating the great Milanese tenor. Seat him immediately. That means move out the first seating no later than nine fifteen. *Capisci?*"

Frankie saved his few Italian words for important guests and the occasional point of emphasis. The staff, it seemed from their nods, *capiscied*.

"In the first seating I draw attention to the following groupings." He read from a card. The chairman of the board of the country's second largest utility, a movie star with his sixteen-year-old lover, reservations in the boy's name. And four tables of tourists, Frankie's term for everyone unknown to him. At table six, by the men's room, would be Mr. Justin Kaye, the clothing manufacturer, and two guests, including *Forbes*-listed Victor Grant. At table seven, Etta Eubanks, who, he explained, was from Oklahoma.

~

Justin Kaye dressed from the JK Durango line—jeans and rattle-snake boots, a slate blue cashmere jacket, and a teal cowboy shirt. He loved the shirt's details: mother-of-pearl buttons, black piping on the seams, scalloped pocket flaps. A short, broad-bottomed woman was being seated at the adjoining table.

"Beautiful jacket," Justin said to her.

"Why thank you, kind sir," said Etta.

"Wouldn't that be a knockout with this shirt?" Justin parted the lapels of his jacket and stood up.

"It would be. I must look around for one of those."

"Look no further. I make them. I'll send you one with my compliments."

Etta smiled back. "How very kind. But my daddy taught me not to take candy from a stranger."

"Did he?" asked Justin, amused.

"Yes, sir. He said, 'Just take the stranger.'"

The appearance of Frankie, hovering like a rescue helicopter, ended Etta's fun. "A glass of white. But not that stuff you pawned off before. Tasted like mule piss. You got a drinkable Montrachet?"

"Of course, Miss Eubanks. But not by the glass."

"Well, Paul's balls, man, open up a bottle."

Justin wanted to stay in this conversation. But across the room came the disjointed figure of his guest.

Victor Grant's clothes set him apart. Even here, Grant wore a striped tie against a blue button-down shirt, khaki trousers, and a gray cardigan sweater. He had learned all he knew about dress during his years at MIT from an accommodating Wellesley sophomore. Once mastered, he never revisited a discipline. As it happened, his fashion complemented his character, it lent him a disheveled look, and his wardrobe—he owned ten gray cardigan sweaters, in weights for the seasons—graced him with the dazed and arrogant mien of an Ivy League professor.

Grant Opportunity Fund, the Street's leading leveraged-buyout performer, found companies with bankable assets, borrowed against the assets, and used the cash for their purchase. If the transaction didn't support the debt, Grant sold the assets and paid off the banks. Creditors won, so did investors. It is true that people who might otherwise have jobs were out on the street, but bankruptcy was a product of economic selection. The fit survive. On Victor Grant's desk high above Broad Street sat a brick of Steuben crystal presented by major investors on the occasion of his fortieth birthday. On it were etched the Fund's five-year return and the words, "If they don't ask, you can't turn them down."

Justin greeted him, Frankie pulled out his chair, lifted the swan napkin by its tail and snapped it open, matador-style. The promote was on.

❧

Etta's guests arrived in a chatty burble of bonhomie. Only Etta had attended the afternoon concert, but no one felt dissuaded from commenting on it. "We skipped it," said Peyton. "I can't keep up with modern music. Where is it all supposed to end?"

Frankie seated them promptly with an eye to the clock. A tall blonde moved toward them, then past. Her bustline ballooned like a spinnaker in twenty knots, urging its owner downwind. One of Grant's aides, one who understood that an MBA included the prospect of a little pandering, had met her on the Mall and invited her to dinner for his boss. The conversational buzz returned as she settled down behind Dooberry's table, at Victor Grant's, and propped the menu in front of her.

～

"Have you decided what you'd like, Mr. Hollister?"

The waiter recognized the singer even behind dark glasses. Rodney Hollister was not unhappy about it.

He *had* decided. He'd like the 38-C blonde who'd just blown by. His own date was asking questions about a sauce. He'd brought her back from Vegas thinking God knows what. What the hell was her name? It was a month—May? June? Undressed and splayed out before him she had all the appeal of a butterflied leg of lamb. And the sex—as if she were blocking a show. No, that blonde is what he wanted.

He snarled at the waiter, "It ain't on the menu" and walked to the men's room.

～

Victor Grant turned for a brief, chivalrous moment to Tiffany, the cause of Hollister's discontent. Tiffany had her own sale to make.

"It's a pleasure to join you, Victor. My life is usually taken up with other theater people. Very confining." It turned out she had briefly been a regular on daytime TV, where her character had survived two miscarriages, an annulment, Nembutal addiction, and poisoning from a tattoo needle. She was in Aspen, she told them, to network.

Justin unrolled an aerial view of the upper reaches of Conundrum Creek. The acreage was outlined in red. "We'll dig a couple of ponds to lure migrating duck. The fish are already there. 'Course you'd want to manage the stream. Holding pools, that kind of thing."

Grant listened. So did ears at the neighboring table. "Mergansers. Bag limit. Blinds. Twenty-gauge." Isolated words pulled Peyton Post from his own dinner talk.

Etta saw Peyton wandering and let him go. Chloe controlled the purse strings—Peyton could amuse himself.

As drinks arrived, Etta told her guests her news. This database idea could bring in money. She'd made a few calls. Dinners languished, despite the efforts of the busboy to see them eaten. Waddy—for indeed he had been assigned to the table—left Etta's chair to run for pasta spoons and glassware.

Tiffany noticed Waddy, lean, dark, insecure. Thought him handsome. That was one thing about Aspen, all the men were handsome. Tiffany Ashe: a Hollywood PR flack had truncated her name. The ancestral Latvian original, he told her, would not fit on a marquee. She didn't like her new name. It made her feel dirty and, well, burnt out.

৵

"Where will I find Ziploc bags?" Waddy looked up to find an unlikely busboy: a black man, quite bald, his dome mahogany in the kitchen's fluorescent light. What hair he had was silver and curled in dreadlocks that waved like a fringe of chenille. A zealot's beard, and a feral look in one eye as if it might be glass. Waddy showed the fellow the drawer behind the fryer.

The man took several Ziplocs. At the long table where the vegetables were prepared, he filled two with asparagus stumps and gathered discarded shells of endive.

"Good pickings," the man said cheerfully, examining a lemon stripped of its zest. The white smock he wore was freshly laundered.

"I suppose." Waddy pushed a dish trolley toward the washer.

~

Hollister felt better. A short line and a plan. If he got the blonde, he could ditch this woman. What was her name? April? No, later in the year. Someone tugged at his shirt.

"Rodney Hollister. I knew it." A middle-aged woman with a new face looked up adoringly. "Do you give autographs?"

"I don't give anything, lady. I get." He pulled free and returned to his table. When he sat down, his companion brushed her finger under her nose.

"What?" he asked irritably. He would move her to a different bedroom and in the morning, Charley would show her out. Charley was the perfect houseman. Vietnamese—no one understood what he said.

Again she ran a finger under her nose.

"What? Speak. You do speak, don't you?"

"Powder, Rod. You look like you been eating a sugar doughnut."

He wet his finger, dabbed at his lip, and licked off the tracings. "At these prices," he said, "I want it all."

~

"What we're missing," Etta said, "is uniqueness. Something only we have, that keeps subscribers with us." Chloe Post sat quietly, but her faint *Gioconda* grin gave her away. Etta called her on it.

"I've been considering fantasies," Chloe said. "They fit in patterns, but their details are individual."

The bread basket made the rounds. Dooberry, fascinated to watch his pigeons building their own coop, fumbled the basket. A pumpernickel bun rolled to the floor. Waddy was on it like a Cuban-league shortstop.

"So?" Etta goaded.

"So we get each subscriber to list his fantasy. His suppressed desire. We take it down, using his digital photos and his detail, and create a version of it. Interactive."

"Interactive meaning ... ?"

"Once he's downloaded it, he gets to land at Normandy, putt the putt, move her limbs about just the way he wants."

"I'm sorry," said Dooberry. "How does all this make money?" He was beginning to think the bus was leaving without him.

"It might be useful," Chloe whispered, "in purchase motivation."

"Give the lady a Kewpie doll," Etta said.

"What am I missing?" Dooberry asked no one. Peyton shrugged back cheerfully.

Chloe went on. "Motivation. If you know what someone wants, you can sell her most anything. If she yearns to be marooned in Tahiti with the *Tannhäuser* chorus, that's where the Lexus ad shows her."

"Bingo," said Etta. "We charge to make the movie for the customer, then we use it to sell the customer. We catalog his fantasies."

"Catalog fantasies?" repeated Dooberry. They nodded.

"Wow!" he said, louder than he'd intended. "Is that a money tree or what?"

The silver-haired busman emptied celery trays into a Ziploc.

"Where do the black olives go?" Waddy asked, meaning to be helpful. The man had left them in the trays.

"Damned if I know," the man answered. "I don't care for them myself."

It hit Waddy. "You're not a busboy."

"Never said I was," said the man, eyeing a stub-end of focaccia.

"What are you doing?"

"Foraging. The leavings of others."

"The white jacket?"

"When in Rome," the man answered with grace. "Gossage is the name." He put down his bag and stuck out a hand.

Waddy shook it. "Brush. Waddy Brush."

"Waddy."

"Wadsworth."

"After the poet?" Waddy nodded. "The Bard of Bowdoin. *Evangeline, Outre-Mer.*" His uvular *R* rolled easily. "My compliments to your mother."

"She favored poets."

"You must tell me more about her. Not now, though. I should be off." He collected the Ziplocs he'd stacked on the preparation table and let himself out the back door.

❧

Victor Grant finished with the business conversation. He'd do Justin's deal. The money was peanuts. His lawyers would check it over, do the club's papers. One of his young quants would vet the financials. If the numbers crunched, he told Justin, he was in. Then he turned to the lady.

"Sorry to bore you with all this," he said solicitously.

"Not at all. I think you learn something every day."

Grant smiled. "I'd like to think that's true."

"It is. What did you learn today, Victor?"

Grant thought a moment. Actually, he'd had a worthwhile early morning observation. "I learned that if you put it on the brush abeam rather than tip to tip, you save about sixty percent of your lifetime toothpaste expense."

She looked blank. Justin jumped into the pause.

"An actress," he said ingenuously. "What are you doing next?"

"I've been discussing a new production," she said eagerly, and touched her date's arm uxorially. "He's a film producer but he wants me to do a reading tomorrow."

"Really? What play?"

"*King Lear*," she enthused. "It's by Shakespeare."

At this instant Dooberry's "Wow" quieted the room, and the words *money tree* floated free. Victor Grant had skills beyond intelligence and courage that had contributed to his success. He read at high speed upside down, and he followed two conversations at the same time.

A money tree. Private venture funding for a computer deal. The plain-talking lady in turquoise wasn't doing the hustling. The pompous man with the affected accent was. The handsome fellow with the perfect tan Grant had seen before. Where? Easy enough to find out.

～

Wow, Dooberry thought to himself. Maybe it was a dumb idea. But good ideas and good money raisers do not often overlap. The Posts were nodding their amens.

" ... catalog your thoughts," Chloe said. "Or could you? Could you make one of those computer games out of it?"

The four of them eyed each other blankly.

"Sure you could," said a voice beyond the table. They looked around to find its source. There stood only the busboy.

"I beg your pardon." Dooberry believed the poor should refrain from discussing money.

"Sure you could," the busboy said. "That's what virtual reality is."

"What?" asked Etta. "What is it?"

"It's computer animation driven according to text. You put on a helmet and data gloves, you turn around and see a three-dimensional landscape. Three hundred and sixty degrees. Color, movement. You design a simulation around whatever's written."

"Individually?"

"I don't see why not," Waddy said. "Everything you're describing would fit a template. Sex, power, freedom, youth. You write four or five templates, do custom work for the individualized version. Maybe five percent more code. Same I/O devices."

"I/O devices?"

"Input output. Games use I/O devices that resemble the players' interface with the physical world."

"You mean to say, young man," Etta fixed on him, "that you could design software so that individual stories could be produced efficiently, as a computer game?"

"It would all depend on the programming," Waddy said, winging it. "But it could be done."

Etta wasn't able to get out her next question. The tenor had just arrived. Frankie needed table seven, but its diners were clogging the drain. Frankie applied the Roto-rooter. "A bill for Miz Eubanks," Frankie said, taking Waddy by the elbow. "We don't want to tie up her evening."

～

Helping Tiffany rise from her chair, a waiter slipped her a paper matchbook.

"Tell me," Grant said to Justin Kaye. "Computer games. Do you think they're a passing fad?"

Justin was conflicted. Money Grant invested in another deal was money he wouldn't see. "A past fad. Another way to sell unreality. I wouldn't put any money there. Not quite sound."

In Grant's experience, the best investment schemes were often not quite sound. Unhappily so were the worst. Still, he preferred the contrary to the accepted.

They moved across the room toward the door. Tiffany held her matchbook tight and scanned the room. Rodney Hollister removed his glasses and stared back.

She looked down. The matchbook had Hollister's picture on it. She opened it furtively.

Inside, seven digits. An Aspen phone number.

∾

Etta's group broke up. "I hope your wife gets her horse," she told Dooberry, who had completely forgotten Flavia. Peyton Post asked Frankie about the lanky fellow at the next table. He looked familiar, another sportsman. Perhaps Peyton would ask him about the duck club.

"Why Mr. Post, that's Victor Grant. Don't tell me you haven't heard of him."

"Should I have?"

"The Wall Street fellow? Last month's *Fortune*? 'When God Runs Short'?"

Peyton thanked him and shook his hand. Frankie's palms were moist from the busy night and their constant pressing of flesh. Peyton's grip had left his own hand with a blue inkblot, letters he could not make out, legible but backwards. Frankie went to the men's room and held his palm up to the mirror.

Squinted at the blue smudges and turned it this way and that, until he decrypted the message: Indonesian Funds Suffer Drain.

Six

Flavia Dooberry had indeed gone to see a man about a horse. Despite Dooberry's protests that they couldn't afford one, not until this latest scheme came in. "No harm in looking, dear," he allowed. "Go and enjoy yourself."

Flavia did both. She booked herself at a guest ranch toward the Flat Tops. The head wrangler could not have been easier. Who could blame him, thought Flavia charitably. Months on the ranch, the heat of horseflesh between your legs. "Y'all come back soon," he called after her.

Driving home she ached in the oddest places. A deliciously experimental partner. Like a gymkhana, she'd told him, without the ribbons.

She raced by the bus stop outside Basalt and hit the brakes. A pretty Hispanic girl watched her back up thirty yards. Was it the sight of someone familiar, or simply her good mood? She lowered the far window.

"Want a lift?"

"*Qué*?" asked the woman.

Flavia beamed, spoke Spanish. "Do you want a lift? I'm driving into Aspen."

~

"I don't like to be looked at that way."

"What way?" Waddy was embarrassed. He knew exactly what way.

"Like I am an order of crème brûlée with six spoons."

"Sorry," said Waddy. He averted his eyes. Annalee was wearing only underwear, and fetching underwear at that. Waddy's word carried sincerity and confusion in equal measure. Remember, he scolded his libido, she's picked another sex. Not the one we root for. Waddy fixed his stare on the poster of Satchmo. Of all the breaks, with only two to choose from.

"What are you going to do today?" Annalee asked. She slipped into jeans and a Jimmy Hendrix T-shirt.

"Nothing much. Day off. I thought maybe a jog up one of the mountain trails. How 'bout you?"

"It's the FFE garage sale. I thought I'd clear some room. Want to help?"

"Sure," Waddy said. He slid across the bed, still warm from Annalee's body.

"Would you mind?" he asked.

"Mind?"

"Turning the other way?"

Annalee left the tiny room with a smirk.

❧

Pantagruel closed every Monday. Frankie put the day to good use. He took inventory, planned and ordered for the coming week. The phone was under his hand, to call the greengrocer, when it chirped.

"*Buongiorno.*" Frankie liked to stay in character.

"Ah, Frankie. Glad I caught you. Victor Grant."

"Yes, Mr. Grant," Frankie looked in pride to the *Forbes* list, with its neat red check. "Your dinner okay last night? Everything okay?"

"Yes, yes. A question. Who was at that table next to us? The funny woman built like a fireplug and the scholarly chap. With a couple, a handsome couple?"

"Oh, you mean Miz Eubanks. Thassa' Etta Eubanks, the oil lady."

"And the couple? The tanned fellow. I know him."

"Oh, sure. Thassa Mr. Post." Frankie culled his accent from Chico Marx.

"Post?"

"The plumbing Posts. From the toilet?"

"Oh, yes. Of course. Peyton Post. He's in the book?"

"You bet, Mr. Grant. If not, you call me."

Frankie rang off. No explaining these people. They live in the same town but never introduce themselves. He was reaching to call the grocer when the phone went off a second time.

"Frankie?"

"Thassa me."

"Mortimer Dooberry here. Listen, I need a favor. The busboy we had last night. Do you happen to have a home number?"

Rusticana rummaged around in his files. Should he ask why? For a private party? To feed to Mrs. Dooberry? No matter. He gave the number.

"Do you happen to have a résumé there?"

"For the kid? A job application."

"What does it say about his education?"

"Computer sciences."

Eureka, thought Dooberry, in the tradition. "Thanks, Frankie. Great meal last night."

"Anytime, Dr. Dooberry. Always a pleasure to serve you. *Ciao.*"

∽

Flavia couldn't remember having so much fun. Carmen, it turned out, cleaned rooms at the Hotel Jerome. The stories she told, the stuff she'd found. The ropes and the paddles okay, but what, Flavia wondered, what do you do with a crescent wrench, a pneumatic tube, and a pound tub of chopped liver?

"Maybe," Flavia said, "we could meet again. Just talk, *chica a chica*, have some laughs."

"Any time," Carmen said.

~

Annalee wanted all Norma's stuff out. Near-new in-line skates, two kayaks (one high-performance and one for cruising), a Thule ski rack convertible for bicycles, a pair of telemark skis and two pairs of K-2 parabolics, a half-rigged Windsurfer, four pairs of Varnay sunglasses, an ice ax, a shoebox full of odd fishing pieces—lures, line, flies.

"You just going to give this away?" Waddy asked.

"FFE sells it. They keep half and give half to me. Anything you want?"

Waddy picked up a hockey gauntlet and set it back. The woman must have been the Jim Thorpe of her time. "Nah," he said. "Only ... "

"What?"

"This fishing stuff. I'd buy that."

"Take it."

They roped the kayaks to the top of Annalee's Jeep, stacked the VW high, and set out for town.

~

Flavia told Dooberry about the woman she'd given a lift, how they'd chatted away like magpies. "Maybe," Flavia said hopefully, "maybe we see her again."

"Dear, she's a chambermaid. What in the world would we have in common?"

"I s'pose. But, Doo. She's a scream. All we did was laugh."

"Dear," he said to her as she dried off from her shower. "I think we've happened on some good luck." He told her of the dinner.

"We have found ourselves some real pigeons." She wrapped a fluffy forest green towel around herself and tucked in the loose end at the chest.

"That's nice, Doo."

"These pigeons don't wait to be caught. They knock on the door."

"Yes, Doo." She was wrapping a second towel around her hair. Dooberry noticed with a tiny sigh the way her breasts rose against the terry cloth. He took the car keys from the table where she'd dropped them and headed for the airport.

~

Peyton Post's morning was nothing short of transcendent. It had begun it with a rum and tonic overlooking the prospect from his deck. Pyramid Peak, Castle Peak, and the Maroon Bells glinted across the way. To the east, in the lushness of summer, the ski trails were ribbons, green as U.S. currency. Not this new stuff of oversized etchings and electronic tapes but the good old greenbacks of an earlier time—a verdant path that flowed down to the town itself. He felt his tan deepen as the first of the rum—a brand he'd found in Martinique and now had flown in by the case—eased into his bloodstream.

Peyton was where he belonged. Look at the views. Not a flaw. His grandfather used to quote a poet: "'Say not the struggle naught availeth.'" Others might think he had an easy time of it, but Peyton's struggle had been his youth. Boarding school kids teased him. First year, they nicknamed him

Dummsy, from "dumb as a post," and it stuck throughout.

He'd left his tormentors behind; here he could walk the streets as Peyton. *Where I belong. Still, do Chloe and I know the right people?* His parents had spent great effort avoiding what they'd called "an element." Peyton was never quite sure what that element was. *Dooberry, for example, with his money-grab, money-grub schemes? Etta Eubanks with her dreadful clothes and headline art? Were they "the element"? Was Chloe? Was he?*

Peyton rose, walked to the glass trolley where the girl had set out a crystal bucket of ice and two freshly quartered limes, and poured a second drink. Admired its deep amber color. *When they crush the cane,* Peyton had been told at the distillery, *they leave the molasses. That's the difference.*

*Take this fellow Grant. Nothing nouveau about him. You can tell from the carelessness of his dress, the rumpled khakis and frayed collars. That's class. Grant is putting together a rod and gun club right here in Aspen, I overheard him at dinner, and I don't know anyone to put me up for it. We need to change our set.*

At which point, the phone rang. Victor Grant was on the other end. *Nothing short of transcendent.*

"As a matter of fact," Peyton examined his glass. Suspended in the dark rum the ice prisms resembled precious stones. "I *do* know who you are, Mr. Grant.

"All right, then. Victor.

"I agree we should have met before, Victor. You've been here a long time.

"Yes, us too. Yes, too bad the way it's changed, isn't it. I was just thinking that. A certain element, don't you think? Oh, not impertinent at all, Victor. No, we were talking and there's no secret to it. Yes, we are indeed thinking of putting a little money up. Dooberry. Dooberry. Good man. Cambridge. We're flattered you'd have an interest. No, no. I'm sure they wouldn't mind. Absolutely. Great. Will do. Right, right as rain. By all means, Victor.

"As a matter of fact, there *is* something. If I'm not mistaken, you're something of a duck man?"

～

The camo Explorer wound up the serpentine. On alternate switchbacks the June sun shone into Justin's eyes. He adjusted the gray polarized square on the windshield. He'd found it in an airplane catalog. Could it fit his ads? Accoutrements of the good life become the good life. That was, his ad manager had told him, synecdoche. The part symbolizes the whole. Synecdoche indeed.

He honked once, honked again. The horn made the sound of geese, a series of low *gronks*.

Peyton was taking his nap. Four midday rum and tonics have their price, and the first installment is several hours' unconsciousness. A Mexican woman appeared at the kitchen door and wiped her hands on her apron.

"Mr. Grant asked me to run this over. See that Mr. Post gets it, will you? He should have his lawyers look it over, and if there are any problems they can deal with my New York people. Can you remember that?"

"*Sì, señor.* New York people."

"Good," said Justin. "Good girl. I'll call."

The Walton Preserve was selling itself. This morning his new neighbor had come calling with a large Kentucky Fried Chicken box.

Hollister was in show biz. Was it rock or crossover? He and Rochelle were at breakfast. Was he bringing a neighborly box of thighs?

"Look, your land deal." How does word get around that fast?

"Yes?"

"I mean, these lots. They're a good deal?"

"Well, they're not lots. See it's a duck club and ... "

"Yeah, but if I need to get my money out there'll be buyers?"

"I'd certainly hope so. Of course ... "

"Great," Hollister looked to see whether there was anyone in the Kayes' spacious living room.

"Would you like to come in?"

"No, no. But here," Hollister handed him the chicken box. "Save me one. No paper, just save me a lot."

"You shoot?"

"No, man. Just want to park some cash. Nothing illegal. A divorce. You been divorced?"

"A few times."

"So you understand. No paper, if that's okay with you."

"You want me to save you a membership?"

"That's it." Hollister sniffed. "Save me a membership. That's not enough, you let me know." Hollister turned unsteadily and left.

Justin put the box down on the coffee table. He was particularly proud of the table, an old mining bellows that Rochelle had refinished. The box was sealed with packing tape, and Justin used a pocketknife to slit around the lid. Inside were thousand-dollar bills in packets of twenty, each packet looped with the paper label from a Vegas casino. Ten packets.

"Who was that?" Rochelle asked, spreading French blackberry preserve on her toast.

Justin reflected on the price of liquidity. "I think we just made a sale."

❧

Dooberry called from his cell phone. Once at the stoplight outside town and a second time in the airport lot. Astonishing, no answer. What will come of us if young people refuse to answer their phones? Civilization depends upon a shared responsibility. If everyone behaved that way, we'd have anarchy.

At the first call, Waddy and Annalee were at the booth of FFE, unloading a sailboard boom. A large military woman clocked in the gear. She wore a scout's outfit: khaki shorts, a Sam Browne belt, and a Smokey the Bear hat.

And a frown.

"A lot of clutter," she said. "The world doesn't need clutter." She picked up a shopping bag of Norma's clothes.

"Clean?"

"Just washed," Annalee answered.

Philida pulled out a football jersey. Washington Redskins. Her brow creased. "It's polyester," she said. "You know how much of our planet's hydrocarbon layer is converted into polyester each year?"

"Exactly," Annalee came to the rescue. "Exactly why we're getting rid of it."

The street bordering Paepcke Park was filled with booths. A woman with long black pigtails made pyramids from empty milk cartons, a rafting company offered to videotape your whitewater experience or, for an extra fee, film a double in your clothes. At the last booth young people in saffron robes were constructing a sand drawing on a table. Waddy and Annalee stopped to watch.

A beardless man approached them.

"A sacred medicine," he explained. "A Buddhist sand mandala to bless the community. We are Shartse monks, Tibetan. We travel the country to confer blessings and to remove obstacles to happiness and prosperity."

"Is that a good job?" Waddy asked. Annalee nudged him. "You're from Tibet?"

"The Shartse monks are from Tibet." Three of the brothers worked over the long table, carefully urging colored grains from funnels.

"And you?"

"I myself am from Winnetka. We also do readings, past, present, or future lives. You can find your next identity."

"Great," said Waddy. "I'm hoping for something useful. Maybe a salad bowl."

"Do me." Annalee offered her hand, palm up. "Present life." The young man took both hands in his, closed his eyes and concentrated.

"You send strong signals," he said. "You are close to meeting an important person."

"Important like on *Letterman* or important to me?"

"Important to you." He gave a winning smile. He had a shaved head and perfect orthodontured teeth.

"You're next," Annalee coaxed. Waddy held out his hands and the youth took them.

"Your life will soon take a sudden turn."

"Good or bad?"

"There is no good or bad. There is only the journey."

Waddy thanked him and turned to leave.

"Twenty dollars," he said happily.

"Hey!" Annalee's voice squeaked. "I didn't know there was a charge."

"There is no charge. That is a suggested donation."

She opened her wallet, gave him a ten. "Suggested discount."

"*Tashi delek*," he called after them.

◡

Dooberry made his third call. I need that busboy, keep the momentum going. He hung up angry and found a gas jockey at the executive hangar. The kid was willing.

"Afternoons, I've got the time. In the morning, when they're all fueling, I'm running scared. But now ... " He wheeled the tug at top speed. Dooberry clung to his seat.

"What kind of a jet are you interested in, Dr. Dooberry?"

"Just window-shopping."

The kid was a student of aircraft. "It all depends," he was saying, "on how hot you want to run. Most of these people, they don't worry about gas bills."

And a student of the owners. Dooberry made notes on who owned what. If their plane was here, they were here. He'd start tomorrow with Etta, she'd know every name. They stopped by a high-tailed craft with the portrait of a man on its nose.

"What is that?"

"It's a King Air," the kid told him. "Belongs to Rodney Hollister. The Vegas guy? Pilots it himself. Though he could fly without a plane."

Dooberry shook his head. All that money for indulgence and nothing for science.

"When you decide what you're going to buy, Dr. Dooberry, let us know. We keep 'em gleamin' and screamin'."

"Thanks," said Dooberry. He opened his billfold and took out twice what he'd planned on tipping. Propinquity to wealth had given him a buoyant feeling of security. "Thanks," he said again. "You'll be my man."

❧

Waddy declined Annalee's offer of a beer. He dropped her off and drove toward Conundrum Creek. Afternoon thunderheads were gathering at the high end of the valley, but they'd be another hour. That's all he needed. He turned the car off the main highway at a wooden sign and followed a creek toward the great massif of Pyramid Peak. Two miles up he crossed a slatted bridge past the No Trespassing signs. These houses were used a few weeks a year; there was no one around.

He parked in a glade of newly leafed aspen. At this altitude budding came late, and the leaves were silver green. He took the shoebox from his trunk and rigged a drop line. Mono on the spool, two quarter-ounce weights crimped a foot from the end, and a bait hook. No different from fishing for rock cod in Skakit Bay, just scale down and find the right bait. He took off his shoes and socks and waded into the stream. Flipped river rock and dug around in the tall sedge that bordered the stream. The water was so cold his ankles ached.

Atop a stone sat a black nymph the size of his thumb. It looked like something from a Japanese horror movie. He threaded the squirming hellgrammite on the hook and tossed the weights around his head, bolo-style. The bait plunked into a pool fifteen feet upstream.

A little fish smashed the hook before it could settle. A brook trout, no more than seven inches. Magical reds and yellows, a liquid look to its skin and a planetary stare to its eyes. They could come from Mars. He slipped it from the hook.

Some other world. He missed the computer game business. If he ever went back in, he'd use the wild way fish looked, the way they lived and moved, darting through three-dimensional corridors filled with undercuts, elodea floating like a Venuvian landscape. He cast again.

Just before Waddy had left Seattle, he made a call, punched in her extension. A metallic voice, "The person at this mailbox (pause, then her voice, equally cool), 'Lisa Laroux,' is no longer with the company. Please touch zero for an operator." She had moved on when he did, though she was doubtless in demand. Waddy cast again. In his mind's eye he saw her working in the next cubby—she used to hum while she programmed, old Beatles' tunes. He saw her lying in a king-sized bed, exhausted from their lovemaking. Chewbacca the Wookiee was bringing them a breakfast tray. "Rocky Raccoon," she sang, and he sang along with her, "came into the room ... " He cast again, the line splashed on the water, and the shadow of a ten-inch cloud fled upstream. Why hadn't he asked her out after that one night? He plugged his laptop into the phone jack and logged on. Maybe she had left him an e-mail. Nothing. Then he typed in her extension and—it was easy to hack—her password. The name of her cat. A crisp dialog box appeared on his screen:

> THIS SUBSCRIPTION DISCONTINUED. IF YOU WOULD LIKE TO RESUBSCRIBE, CLICK HERE.

A first fork of lightning, pink and jagged, split the sky and lit the dark water. Waddy wound the line back onto the spool, climbed to the bank, and headed for the car. The image of Lisa's nakedness stuck in his mind, with the dialog box fig-leafed over the pertinent areas. Funny how the mind works, he thought, as the starter cranked and fired.

Seven

Etta Eubanks disdained the spoils of wealth. Perhaps not the spoils—most of those she enjoyed—but what they did to people. People grew combative. Etta decided early in the money to eliminate combat before it got started. So she bought herself a Unimog.

Ever since that evening in the White House when she'd watched films of Humvees tracking across the Kuwaiti desert and the Unimog pulling them out of deep spots, she'd decided to have one. All four tons of it, sixteen feet of length and seven of width. On the vanilla-leather seat in the nine-foot-high cabin, she was riding the bridge of a great ship of fortune. And the gadgets: roller fairleads, a winch kit with the three-quarter-inch shackle and snatch block, six hundred thousand candlelight of high-intensity beams, a remote control to turn on the boosters and woofers from thirty feet. In for a penny, she figured, twice too much is just right, and she painted it pink.

The truck took up two parking spaces, so she took it to town only off-season or early in the day, before Aspen's streets filled up. Mortimer Dooberry's meeting was early in the day. Afoot were the joggers, bikers, practitioners of Shaolin. Women with athletic bras and softball-sized deltoids strode through the new sun, pumping chins for aspiration and hand weights for pectorals. Men in second and third bloom pedaled space-age bicycles up mountain slopes. It was the parade of Those Who Will Live Forever, timers to their pulse and calipers to their waist.

Etta roused Sherry from his bubbly doze and loaded him into the Unimog. The great pink truck picked its way through the healthy horde.

Dooberry had rented the ballroom of the Hotel Jerome. No breakfast—twenty-five people were expected and until he closed this sale he was on his own euphemistic nickel. Twenty-five, of whom last week's dinner guests, he hoped, were his base. Chloe and Peyton Post, Etta and her husband. The airport list produced several others, including, of all the luck, Victor Grant. If he could cage Victor Grant, the rest would be easy. In their East Side duplex or over their Lake Shore Drive dinner table, they'd get value enough. We've put a few chips on a software deal in Colorado. Victor Grant is in it. Do you know Victor?

Flavia and he ran through the slides before anyone showed up. Charts illustrated revenue sources (mass mailers, high-end merchandisers, banks, the subscribers themselves). Everything the company did, according to the slide show, generated dollars.

"Back one, Flavia."

He examined the budget. His fee was modest, the fat evenly distributed. Padding in every line, travel, entertainment, computer support, software design, interface access, wide-area networks, spread uniformly so it didn't bulge. The trick to these proposals was diversification. Dooberry figured his take on Wise Mother—for he had so named it—would easily see them through the year. He'd worry about next year after he paid for this one. Whose '47 Willys Jeep was pulling up by the Unimog? Dooberry recognized the rumpled, boyish driver in the gray cardigan from the cover of last month's *Fortune*.

❧

Washington was two hours ahead. Victor Grant, the boyish driver, had been up since five, applying the cornerstone of his investment philosophy. Not buy-low, sell-high—that was a mug's game with two flaws. One, it assumed you could predict the future. And two, risk couldn't be measured. Grant's cardinal rule on investments with unpredictable risk was to eliminate it. Sell high, *then* buy low. Get out before you get in.

He held his second conversation in as many days with the undersecretary. And the undersecretary had an answer for him.

"Absolutely, Victor. If it works, we'd be very interested. Let me get this right. It includes the individual's own suppressed desires?"

Grant confirmed. "As submitted by each subscriber."

"And why would he do it?"

"Because the venture converts it into a video."

"We'd be very interested."

Grant asked the ultimate question.

"No, I can't price it for you, but if it does what you say, then who else but us should own it? We're the logical buyer. If it comes to that, we'd want one hundred percent. Being who we are, we don't want partners."

Grant pressed.

"I can't give you a price, but on a per name basis we're thinking, ballpark ... " The sum the fellow mentioned made Grant smile. It was the precisely the ballpark in which Grant wanted to play.

~

Site plan rolled under his arm, Justin watched as the Ford pickup turned across the bridge and spewed dust on the gravel. He'd heard the old heap before he'd seen it, rattling as it left the asphalt of the Castle Creek road. You couldn't be sure Marco Campaneris would show. Eccentric and rich is one thing, hell, that was Aspen. But eccentric and poor was scary. It gave one a minatory air, a sense of nothing to lose. Marco was all he had. He needed to break ground by ski season. That way, he'd have Reliance. Once you build it, Justin knew, the courts won't make you take it down. Most Aspen townsfolk took their holiday during the fall. Attendance at the October P and Z meeting would be light. He'd get Reliance.

Hence Marco Campaneris. Construction in the valley was booming, and Marco was the only contractor available. Hardly a contractor. A crazy old coot with a truck and two blades for his John Deere. And the man's point of view—he hated developers.

The pickup clanged to a stop on the road below. Marco got out, put finger to one nostril, and cleared the other on the ground. Wiped his nose on his wrist, his wrist on his jeans, and walked uphill. Justin unrolled the site plan so that his own hands would stay occupied.

"Hey, Marco," he called cordially. "What's happening?"

꜒

To Victor Grant, 7 A.M. meant 7 A.M. He parked in the shade of a pink truck. A stray yellow dog, muddy and forsaken, peered hopefully from behind a car.

Dooberry, his staff had told him, was the weak link. The man had a track record of making money only for himself. A self-aggrandizing popinjay, not a manager. Still, everything else Grant learned was encouraging. Databases bloomed and faded in the nineties. Since then, threats to security had created new demands that so far no one had met.

On the software side, the staff felt less sure. Grant controlled one of the country's leading computer game companies; it would be easy for him to find good technical advice. But he would tread lightly. He would incubate the deal until the technical side proved up. Do the risky stuff with the other guy's money, step in if it worked. If it worked, he'd need one hundred percent. That suggested debt, not equity. Debt and foreclosure.

As he crossed the ballroom, he thought he heard a perfectly inflected Portuguese curse: *Puta que paril.* A beautiful black-haired woman was searching the Persian carpet on all fours.

"Can I help?" he asked the cantaloupe-sized buttocks below him.

"I drop a slide. My husban' kill me."

"We can't have that." Grant fell to his knees and covered the missing slide with his hand. "Murdering your spouse. Aspen courts would give him a month of hard labor, maybe two."

"Thass all?" asked Flavia. She turned to find him grinning. Grant's crouch afforded him an insight to more of Flavia's assets, for the top buttons of her cowboy shirt were undone. Grant looked away.

"What do you think? Is it worth it?"

"Same for me?" Flavia asked. "You think only two months for whacking The Doo?" Flavia had watched *The Sopranos* in two languages.

"The Doo. So you're Mrs. Dooberry?" He handed her the missing slide and they stood. People began filing in, and Grant heard his name whispered about.

"*Claro que sì.* And I know you." She looked at the celluloid in her hand. "You are a gentleman."

"Thank you."

Flavia crinkled her eyes. She didn't often encounter a blush.

"I must go," she whispered in a confidence that was equally unnecessary and intimate. "They're coming."

"Who?"

"The pigeons."

"I beg your pardon?"

"The pigeons. Thass what The Doo calls them."

"Does he?"

"*Exactamente*. He says these are good pigeons, open up their own coop."

Dooberry made his way over, balancing a prune Danish on top of a coffee mug.

"Victor Grant," he said triumphantly and extended his free hand. "Think of it."

"I do," Grant said, his eyes on Flavia. "Often."

"I'm delighted to meet you. I can't tell you how exciting it is that you're considering joining our little business. A man with your reputation. I'm Mortimer Dooberry."

Grant held his gaze and shook the offered hand. "Well," he said. "Coo."

❧

"What do you mean, homesites?"

Justin Kaye was surprised how aggressive the question sounded. Even hostile. He was standing on the crest of the ridge of the Isaak Walton Preserve, admiring his handiwork. God's too. A glacier had sculpted this moraine and on its retreat left mineralized earth. The topsoil supported trees and high mountain grasses. Blue spruce grew to timberline. Above that line, where the soil gave out, rose four thousand feet of schistose rock, the double-peaked massif that was the Maroon Bells. The Isaak Walton Preserve would be the most glorious land play in Aspen's history. And he would have a house in its midst.

As far as Justin was concerned, it was a job for hire. He didn't like the critical tone of the man's voice. He needed an earthmover, not a conscience.

"What do you mean, homesites?" Marco repeated.

"Homesite. Just one. Well, two. Here," Justin's finger went to the drawing. "P and Z will let you put in a caretaker's unit." He kept his voice steady.

"For a caretaker? That looks to be five thousand square feet."

"Six thousand two, actually." Marco had stumbled on Justin's little wrinkle.

"That's one fuckin' large caretaker."

"Well, the caretaker is actually over here, above the garage. We can get a single site plus caretaker, so I thought why not put in," he pointed to the plans and swallowed, "an owner's representative."

Marco's eyes narrowed.

"Sorry, Mr. Kaye. Get someone else." He began to walk down the hill to where the pickup was parked.

"Wait a minute. What do you mean?"

"Well, I ain't starting a dig that ain't going to happen. P and Z may be a bunch of pussies, but when this gets out, the town will go bullshit. And it should. Homesites mean a PUD, and P and Z won't approve. And even if they did, God knows P and Z has their price and you can afford it. I won't have no part it. I won't be fucking up this countryside. Not that I can save it, you understand, but you can fuck it up without me."

"You don't think they'll allow it?"

"No way. I'll sign on, and P and Z will change its mind, and I'll be left with no other work. Even if they don't, you'll get sued. This here site's surrounded by wilderness. Wilderness is as bad as Indians. The Sierra Club and the FFE will sue your ass, and I tell you somethin' else. I'll be with 'em. You want homesites, get somebody else."

Justin gazed out on the vast bowl, its U-shaped bottom riven by Conundrum Creek splashing ice clear. Maybe Marco was right: give up the wrinkle. The deal was tough enough without it. Dam up the stream, build a couple of holding ponds smack in the path of the flyway, a clubhouse. Permanent duck blinds down there, a shack for loading shells, storing gear. Some kennels to board dogs overnight.

But he had his heart set on a little cabin in the wilderness. Nothing extravagant, a moss rock fireplace and a cathedral ceiling facing those peaks.

There must be a way. Something Marco said had given him an idea.

"Tell you what, Marco. I get any opposition to a house, I back off. How's that?"

∼

"Yes, Mr. Grant?" Dooberry held the remote control, waiting for Flavia to dim the lights. He thumbed the button nervously and glanced at the numbers on the screen. He wished he hadn't been so greedy. He could do with half the travel. Less.

"You're going to need a site for your project, isn't that so?"

"Yes, that's true, Mr. Grant." How fast could he retreat? "Of course, property around here would be too expensive. So these projections use a lower rent. I'm trying to be conservative. I thought ... "

"Well, I tell you, Dr. Dooberry. I may want to be a part of this."

"You may?"

"Yes, I may. If I like what I see, I'll buy a unit. Tell you what—I'll do better. I'll lease your group the guesthouse on my property in Starwood. That way you, as team leader, can be nearby."

"You would?"

"I would. No need for cash, Mortimer, the money should go into science, and I don't need it. We'd accrue the debt, maybe it's convertible. Unless you're uncomfortable with that?"

Dooberry couldn't keep up. If Grant came in, everyone came in.

"That sounds very generous," he heard himself saying.

"You go ahead," Grant told him. "If I like what I see, do we have a deal?"

Everyone was watching. "Absolutely," Dooberry said, but more loudly. "A deal."

～

"Real beef stock," Sherry Topliff said a second time.

"That's the secret?"

"That's the secret."

"I don't know if we have any."

"You go ask the chef. Most chefs keep real beef stock. Then two ounces of vodka, fill a tall glass with half tomato juice and half real beef stock. Salt, pepper, a shot of Worcestershire. Tabasco. A Bloody Bull should make you cry."

"I'll ask," said the young man. He'd made Sherry's first drink using canned bouillon and the second with powder from a jar. Both had come back empty. Still, he was there to serve.

Sherry grinned at a dark-eyed woman. She smiled as she passed, kissed her fingers, and put their cool tips to his cheek. Who was that? he wondered. Didn't we have dinner together?

Flavia walked by him and out the ballroom. Her part in The Doo's presentation was over. She wandered into the hotel's lobby. Carved oak balustrades, heavy tapestries to cushion sound, sconces hand-fashioned to capture an era that never happened. Tourists were lolling about, their cameras at the ready. A rumor had gone through the streets that Madonna was around, and a couple from Indianapolis was quizzing the desk clerk.

"I don't know where you heard that, but we cannot give out ... "

"I heard it more than once," said the woman. She had yet to see a single celebrity, and this was their last day of a three-night package. Hollywood was better. In Hollywood you could buy a map and see their homes. On trash day, their garbage.

"That doesn't mean it's true," tried the clerk. The husband shot two pictures of Flavia. He knew she was somebody, from the push-up bra. They would study the prints back home.

"You seem to be a nice young man," the woman said to the clerk. "Just give me a hint." The nice young man shrugged, looked desperately for a guest to help. Behind him, white lettering on a felt board listed the events of the day. Dr. Dooberry had the ballroom at 7:00. Lions' weekly lunch at 12:30, all Lions welcome, and at 4:00 in the ballroom, the Aspen Institute. A lecture on Renaissance art, "The Madonnas of Florence." It was a natural mistake.

Flavia entered the elevator. Somewhere upstairs, Carmen was changing bed linen. The hotel had only three stories. It shouldn't be hard to find her.

~

The idea struck Justin as so innovative it might be divine. Others get revelations about original sin and the path out of the desert. Why not him? Why wouldn't God involve Himself in a little profit? People use Him for comparison: so-and-so has more money than God—you hear it all the time. Maybe He gets tired of losing ground, maybe He's picked me to help catch up. After all, one year W had called the JK Durango line heavenly.

Whatever the source, the idea was brilliant. Justin was standing on arguably the most glorious building site in all of Pitkin County. You wouldn't have to carve out much acreage, the crest of the ridge provided a natural footpad. Surrounded by fourteen-thousand-foot peaks, national forest on three sides, and rushing down its crease, Conundrum Creek, frosty as designer vodka. Marco was right. No chance in hell they'd allow a homesite. Not unless he could quiet the opposition. Not without a zig or a zag. Maybe both.

Justin lay the drawing on the ground and put a rock on each corner to prevent it from furling. Then he unfastened a brass shirt-flap button bearing the pressed shape of a bison and removed a mechanical pencil from his pocket.

∿

The lights came back on. So far, so good. But now ... Dooberry took a deep breath. "Any questions?"

Hands came down quickly when Victor Grant rose from his chair.

"I want everyone to know that my people have checked out Dr. Dooberry and they've checked out the science. Not that this proposal is without risk, but our assessment is that you've got an exciting venture here. I'm happy to say, Dr. Dooberry, you can count the Grant Opportunity Fund in." Victor Grant sat down. An audible rumble went through the crowd, the passing of reverential gas.

Dooberry understood the salient facts. Victor Grant was not merely buying into the offering. He was volunteering to house it on his own property. What endorsement could be greater?

"Well, Mr. Grant. I am swept away. To have someone of your reputation, your sophistication ... " In his excitement he let a page of notes fall to the floor. "I would say that the partnership accepts your offer with great pleasure."

"If it's all right with you, Dr. Dooberry, my lawyers will send you the papers," Grant said and retook his seat.

People turned to each other. The opportunity might be getting away. Checkbooks appeared from purses, pens from polo shirts. A slender white arm rose like a spring lily. It was attached to Chloe Post.

"Could I ask you to go back to the last slide? I had some questions about two or three of the line entries."

No one else was interested. People leaned over to congratulate

Victor Grant, introduce themselves, shake his hand. Peyton Post left the room. Dooberry pressed the Return button and the financial statements reappeared.

"Chloe, that's a great question. I'd be happy to take it up with you after the meeting."

❧

Peyton had followed the presentation early on, but when they got to numbers he left. *Numb* and *numbers*, they must have the same root. Besides, Chloe would decide. A condition of Peyton's coming into his money was the appointment of an individual co-trustee suitable to the bank. Chloe fit the bill. She had a Wharton degree, a good head, he was lucky to find her. Most of the women he'd known thought money was for spending. Chloe fiddled with it like Lincoln Logs. Called it capital. For that alone, the bank loved her.

In the hotel lobby he was immediately blinded by sharp flashes from three cell phone cameras. One of the shooters, a young girl, not, Peyton noted through the floating dot on his cornea, unattractive, asked for his autograph.

"I'm afraid you have me confused ... ," he started to say.

"Oh. I'm sorry. I thought you *were* somebody."

"Hey, listen," he said as she turned away. "You don't want to have a drink or anything?"

"Me? I'm fourteen."

He found the elevator and aimlessly punched the top floor. The questions would go on and on. The girl was right, too early for a drink. Maybe he'd take his mountain bike up toward Ashcroft this morning. Once you made the climb, coming down was a rush.

He got off on the top floor. All these closed doors—hotels made him horny. At the very end of the hall stood a service cart. It was bathed in light from an open door, its fluffy bath towels swelled in nappy amplitude. From within came the song of feminine laughter. Peyton approached.

Inside, a pretty woman in a maid's uniform sat on an unmade double bed. Across, lolling in a stuffed easy chair, a second woman, he'd seen her before. They were speaking Spanish. He took in the carnivorous look of her: the clingy pedal pushers in gold spandex, the deep vee of the cowboy shirt. "Hello," Peyton said. Where had he met her?

"Hello, Mr. Post," said Flavia. "Come on in. Unless you think you cannot manage two ladies at once?"

❧

"They tell me you can do anything, Christine."

"Anything."

"What I'm going to ask is a little, well, unorthodox."

"Try me."

"It's not illegal. I want you to know that. Only ... "

"Yes?"

"Private. More private."

"Sounds intriguing." That in a breathy voice.

"I'd really like it kept between us."

"JK, you're the master."

"I mean, I'd like you to keep this discreet."

"I know how to do it all, JK. I came up from the bottom."

Justin pictured his head of design. If only she were as attractive as her telephone voice. It changed registers, deepening like a shower as the water warms.

"There are two drawings. A site plan and an elevation plan. I want you to reproduce them, down to the architect's seal and everything. Just add a little square I've drawn in pencil."

"That's it?"

"That's it. And add some lettering to the square. To identify it." He spelled the three words out for her.

"That's it? Piece of cake."

"Great, Christine. I'll FedEx the originals to you today. Make sure the square is placed exactly where I have it."

"Done."

"One more thing. Make the lettering, how to say this? Old."

"Old."

"Antique-ey. It should look like it was done in the nine-teenth century."

"Got it. You want a counterfeit."

Justin hesitated. "That's what I want. Can you do it?"

"Soak it in tea, nuke it for ten minutes on low, it comes out ancient."

"Sounds good. You can do this?"

"Piece of cake. Who counterfeits the past better than us? And just those words? *Arapaho burial grounds*?"

"That's it."

"Done, JK. Piece of cake."

～

"*Es necessario*," Carmen was saying.

"You need," said Flavia.

"Muy apretado."

"To get it really tight."

"Like that?" Peyton asked.

"No, no. You show, Flavia."

Flavia came over to assist. Lifting, folding, tucking. She had wiry arms and her muscles showed under the skin. Not like Chloe. Chloe had no interest in fitness. Peyton watched the biceps move, firm as live animals.

"You got to get the tuck right," she said with a giggle.

Peyton let the corner of the mattress down. He giggled too. "Like that?"

"Ohh," said Carmen. "Like that." She took the last drag of the joint, stubbed it into the ashtray, waived her hand through the smoke.

"Now what?" Peyton asked.

"Now the top sheet. Same thing. Same folds."

Flavia threw the fresh sheet across the bed, and Peyton attacked his corner. Next, the down quilt. Carmen showed them how to hold it by its fringe and snap it out so the down distributed evenly. Peyton stripped the pillows and tossed them to Flavia for new cases. The faint mowed-grass scent of the linen took Peyton back to early summers on the Vineyard.

"What do you think," Peyton asked, "should we do another stick?" He dug a sterling Asprey cigarette case from his pocket. Flavia took it from him and read the inscription on the lid. "'To Phillip Post from his Board.' Who he?"

"That's my great-grandfather."

"'The king on his throne. August 1906.' He was a king?"

"He was an inventor. He was in toilets."

Carmen spoke in Spanish.

"What did she say?"

"She says good marijuana." Flavia used a long *A* and a guttural *J*. Māri-Whuana.

"The best," Peyton told her. "Kif, from Morocco."

"Kif," Flavia repeated.

"Does she want to do another?"

"No," Flavia translated. "This is a nonsmoking room."

Peyton put the case back in the rear pocket of his lemon yellow slacks and went back to work. "The old sheets," Peyton asked, stuffing them into the discarded pillowcases as he'd been taught. "Where do they go?"

❧

Mortimer Dooberry was jubilant. Seven sales and eight promises! He separated out the checks and slipped them into the inside pocket of his blazer.

"It could not have gone better," he said to his wife. She reappeared just at the right time, stood by the door with him as he said good-bye to his guests. "Could not have. How do you like what Victor Grant did for us? Isn't that fantastic?"

"Fantastic."

"And we're oversubscribed. We've raised it all plus some. What should we do? Turn someone away? Give everyone a little refund?"

"Give back?" Flavia asked. A last couple were just now gathering their papers and rising from their seats. "Give back? Doo, you outta you fucking mind?"

"Chloe and Peyton," Dooberry announced as the Posts approached. "How good of you to come. I hope you enjoyed the presentation."

"I did, Mortimer. I did." Chloe looked at her notes. "I want you to consider us in for one unit, if I can get the bank to go along. You must understand, we clear through New York."

"Oh, I understand. Of course."

"But I assure you, Peyton wants in. I'm leaving a signed subscription agreement with you. I'm calling this recreation, not investment. The money will be here by the end of week. Will that be timely?"

Dooberry nodded. "Timely, yes." This idea was dynamite.

"Very stimulating," Chloe said in her Public Radio voice.

Peyton came next, bussed Flavia's cheek and pumped Dooberry's hand. "Great meeting," he said vigorously, and meant it.

Eight

The scope through which Aspenites sight each other's social standing has two crosshairs. The first, as in any healthy American town, is wealth. Elsewhere, seven figures of invested capital ranks one as wealthy. Here it ranks one, in the easy condescension of the town, as mini-rich. Should the market turn, the mini-rich will need to find work. Aspen wealth requires a freestanding portfolio of at least eight figures; better nine.

The second measure is tenure. Last week's arrival finds himself explaining that he has recently returned, having first visited ages ago. That remark cues the comment that he remembers when Aspen was a better place, the days of Goethe not Givenchy. Grand to be rich, far better to be smug.

Marco Campaneris met the second measure. He got there first. How had he done that?

Marco's grandfather shot a man, or thought he had, and left his Basque village by way of Marseilles. When he landed in Boston, he went looking for familiar landscape. He herded sheep in the Bitterroots of Montana until the price of mutton fell. Then he went to work in the mines.

His son, Marco's father, inherited the pick and shovel. He dug silver in the loop by Creede and moly on John C. Frémont Pass. He was running a slurry in the Rock Springs coalfileds when he met his wife, whose dark skin and high cheeks reminded him of his Basque mother. In fact she was five-eighths Tesuque.

They raised three children. The oldest, a devout boozer, drove his truck off a bridge one night and drowned in the Ruby River, just when the water was clearing. Gasoline from the tank killed fish for miles downstream. The daughter married and, last Marco heard, was a glazier in Ventura, California, where she'd been told it never snowed.

Marco was born in Casper, Wyoming, with a short left leg. It was the night Gene Tunney whipped three men in the Casper auditorium, though not at once. At twelve, with a limp the only thing going for him, Marco quit school and took work no one else wanted. At twenty he wandered into the office of Summit Mining in Leadville, Colorado, and got a job underground. He learned to work an air drill, an overshot loader, and a slusher hoist. Until the accident, he made good money setting powder. But a blasting cap went off early and he lost three fingers and part of the meat of his left hand. Management offered him permanent disability, but he figured, hell, he'd rather work, so he went back under as a timberman. Those leathery souls plunge into a shaft soon as it's blown and shore it against slide. For the risk that the rock might run, they get an extra dollar an hour.

Marco spent twenty years pulling tin and tungsten out of the hills of central Colorado until the tin gave out and so did the price of steel and the company all but shut down. Marco could run most machines, and found a county job bulldozing snow off the Independence Pass road. When Lake County ran out of money, the folks on the west side agreed to pay him for both ends of the road. So it was that Marco bought from his old company a miner's shack high on the pass, no clear title, but back in the woods. In the next years the little town on the other side filled up. Folks were pulled in first by the setting, then by the powder snow, the Mahler, the conferences on world peace, the high-grade cocaine.

Marco cleared the road spring and fall—winter, the city fathers let it go. Summers he hunted and trapped and explored the mines. The hills are honeycomb around there, and they say if you're smart enough to read a compass and dumb enough to try, you can walk from Aspen all the way to Crested Butte and never see the sky. Marco saved up, bought himself a used Deere crawler-dozer, quit his county job, and became an earthmover.

He dug up the past. Whiskey bottles, lamp-oil cans, chain hooks, the occasional slurry bucket. He tossed whatever he found in the Summit Mines Quonset hut behind his cabin. Lots of bones, mostly cattle from the days when herds were driven up here for summer pasture, before parabolic skis and chanterelle mushrooms drove the economy.

Winters Marco signed on with the ski company, just to keep his hand in. He ran a snowcat to groom the trails, he made snow, and finally, because his stub fingers were vulnerable to frostbite, he ran a ski lift. That was a cushy job, inside a hut waiting for someone to fall off the chair.

This site that Mr. Kaye wanted him to dig would produce no treasures. Too far up the mountainside. Marco pretty much knew where the Utes and Arapaho had camped and where the squatters had settled. Conundrum Creek would yield nothing.

～

Waddy tossed socks and underwear into the tomato paste carton. He should be happy. This arrangement, particularly the sleeping part, was driving him up the wall. He was moving way uptown. Still ...

On the CD player, Satch and the Hot Five played "Belle Meade Blues," slow and pining. Annalee carried a box of his clothes out to the VW and came back for more.

"I'm going to miss you, Waddy. You're a dream roomie." She wore cut-off jeans, a T-shirt that said JK Durango.

"So the deal is salary plus room and board at Victor Grant's house?"

"Guesthouse, actually."

"A hell of a jump. From half a bed in a trailer to a Starwood house. Is this a great country or what?"

"Oh," Waddy sighed. "Oh, sure." He had found nothing about her that gave a clue, not the lingerie-model's body—or what Waddy took to be a lingerie-model's body, since he had never seen one, except of course in the lingerie ads, which he still read with care—not the fresh body or the slightly mismatched green eyes or the plain talk. If Waddy hadn't known, he'd never have guessed. Never. Every time he mentioned Norma, though, Annalee winced. She was still hurting.

"Anyway, this'll be good for both of us. I mean, you might want to, you know, have company over."

"Why, Henry Wadsworth Longfellow Brush. Are you worried about my sex life?"

"No, it's not that," Waddy lied. He studied the floor. Annalee was carrying a carton of his boxers. She leaned over and kissed him lightly on the cheek, filling his nostrils with the scent of a metallic spring. He realized it was fabric softener.

"So you're running this hush-hush deal?" She walked out and placed the box in the backseat of the car.

"No. They're going to hire a senior programmer. Mr. Grant has contacts in software design. And it's not so hush-hush." He followed with his CDs. "Maybe I should leave these. I don't have a player."

"Are you kidding? Victor Grant's house will have it all, a pneumatic corkscrew, electric fingers on the bed."

"It's not really hush-hush. They want to do computer videos from psychological profiles. The head programmer flies in tomorrow for the kick-off meeting."

"And the pay? Enough to take a woman to dinner?"

Waddy was packed. Except for the CD that was playing.

"I got a right to feel low down," sang Louis.

"Are you worried about *my* sex life?" He was standing by the door of the car. Boxes sat on the shotgun seat, in the back, tied to the top of the folded canvas.

"I'm not worried," she came close and took his hands. "My little chick may yet be a rooster." She kissed him a second time, this on the other cheek. Without the laundry, the only scent was the softer one of Annalee, her hair, her.

~

Hollister drove the starlet to the portico. She'd be his first piece in the Aspen house. Maybe he'd start a list, like a guest book.

She was impressed. God. She ought to be. Decorator had gone overboard, all this crap from Italy and God knows where. His eye roamed the living room, out toward the deck.

"Shit."

"What's the matter, Rod?"

"Nothing, baby. You get that sweet ass upstairs. There's a robe for you in the closet. Get into that. I'll be right up."

He went to the den. His idea, the gun rack. He'd bought the .22 in Vegas, he liked to plink at the crows.

He put three cartridges in the chamber and went out to the deck. That brindle dog was still there. It wagged its rear, stuck down its head, and made to approach.

"Scram! Goddamn it, scram." The dog looked up, confused. Its coat was caked with mud. "Scram!"

Hollister fired a round into the air. The dog started at the noise and turned to go. Then, perhaps from memory of a house where he'd been petted and fed, he turned a last time to look back. The second shot caught him in the left hind. He yelped and ran off, stumbling over the border of bark that had been laid to keep the flowerbeds free from weeds.

~

"Honest," Justin Kaye was explaining. "That parcel will not go into the duck club—the entire burial grounds goes to a foundation. No Arapaho ancestor will ever be disturbed. The Isaak Walton Preserve respects the sensibilities of our Native American ancestors."

The head of Planning and Zoning looked up from the plat on his desk. Was Mr. Kaye joking? Last year someone convinced him to allow an exemption to the thirty-thousand-square-foot limit on Starwood homes to put in employee housekeeping. The bastard had built two houses, ell to ell, and argued that his wife was the employee. The local newspaper had reamed him out.

Mr. Kaye stared back with palpable and practiced sincerity.

"And these structures?"

"Strictly one-story. No living quarters. Log cabins for the club, wood and shingle." He pulled eight-by-ten glossies out of his portfolio.

"The set designer for *Stagecoach* is long gone. The Fox people got us the next best thing. Man's a genius. Logs from authentic railroad cabins. Replicas of the original, when they brought in Chinese labor to cross the Divide? Dead on, except for the HVAC."

"Neat little setup. Memberships?"

"Limited to fifty members. We're already oversubscribed. We'd, uh, we'd be happy to make room for you if you like to shoot."

The man gave a short laugh. "Not on my salary, Mr. Kaye. Thanks for the offer."

"Well, you'll come up then. As my guest."

The man clucked in appreciation. Justin had covered his bases. An environmental impact study, sketches of the land plan, and elevations of the pond and creek.

"Your studies are impressive," he told Justin. "But you should know, this whole town will come down on you. These are hot potatoes, Mr. Kaye. A beautiful piece of wilderness, sacred Arapaho burial grounds."

"I checked at the library. There aren't any Arapaho left."

"No matter. You'll see so many Indians, you'll need John Wayne. And Friends of the Friendless Earth is headquartered here. They'll be on you like flies on shit."

"This is a sensible plan. They'll see."

Justin had resurrected the Norfolk jacket and two-toned shoes. Manhattan women who wanted the Rita Hayworth look had two choices: Justin's label or thrift shops. Real estate too. He had built a mini-mall around the church where John Quincy Adams had married Abigail Smith. He knew what he was doing.

෴

Tiffany knew what she was doing. She'd flubbed the reading. *King Lear* might be one thing—why the king of a country who had three daughters with clear complexions would rant around the countryside in a thunderstorm, she didn't understand—but when it came to fellatio, she knew her apples.

So it was frustrating to get no response. The more she tried, the further Hollister drifted. He didn't seem to have his heart in it.

"Shit!" he cried, confirming her suspicions. He climbed out of the bed and started rummaging through the bottles on his night table. She'd never met a man with as many vitamins. He unscrewed a top and poured something into his fist.

"How 'bout some music, sweetheart?"

"Sure, sure. Whatever you want." He mumbled the last sentence through pills. He pulled the open bottle of Stoly from the ice bucket on the night table and swigged.

Tiffany rose, put on the borrowed robe. Walked to the CD rack and read labels aloud. They were all Rod Hollister.

"You have lots of hits," she said cheeringly.

"Let me tell you. In this business, just when you're immortal, you wake up one morning dead."

Hollister's singing came into the room. The strings and eight-piece percussion couldn't disguise it. "Do do, you you, do do, you you ... "

Tiffany was no critic, but it didn't sound like immortality. It sounded like noise.

"Turn that shit off." He must have thought so too.

Tiffany hit the power button. Silence returned. She came up behind him and put a compassionate hand to his shoulder.

"Hush, sweetheart. Don't get angry. Come lie down and I'll rub your back."

∽

He announced himself at the guardhouse. It didn't mean a thing.

"Waddy Brush. I live in Mr. Grant's guesthouse. I'm going up for the meeting." The guard checked a clipboard, inspected the dent in the Bug's fender a second time, and lifted the barrier.

*Architectural Digest* had called the vast stone and wood construct that was Grant's Starwood home "a cosmic Tuscan graft onto the New World." Waddy's car chugged up the long drive. Workmen were replacing the original landscaping—the cypress, cistus, and oleander imported from Italy had succumbed to their first Rocky Mountain winter—with aspen and locust trees, their roots bagged in burlap.

At the top of the drive, Waddy came to the main house. It was more a village than a building, constructed of linked units. A chimney tower, stacked terraces, a stone-pillared porte cochere all gave the impression that a quaint town had been dropped, fully aged, onto this bench. Cedar eight-by-fours framed the marble facing. An effort had been made to nestle the structures into the hillside and reduce the silhouette, though it was hard to conceal twenty-six thousand square feet.

The guesthouse sat beyond the tennis court and out of the view line. It too was faced in marble. Under its shake roof were a full kitchen and three large bedrooms. The conversion of the living room to lab had begun: three PCs, connectors, and cables.

Waddy parked behind the main house amidst a Bentley, a Jag XK 150, and a fuchsia Unimog. He made his way around the gravel path to the front. The two barn-wood doors opened from behind.

He gave an order, mineral water, to a white-coated man. Straight chairs had been arranged in the two-story living room concentric to a conversation pit: a massive sofa covered in velvet paisleys, lounge chairs of beige leather, a zebrawood coffee table easily eight feet in length. The fireplace mantel was not a single shelf, but several brass ridges, each holding an array of votive candles. Waddy took a seat in the rear.

He recognized many of the guests. Mr. Grant for sure, Mortimer Dooberry, Etta Eubanks. Etta's husband had a glass of dark liquid in one hand and what looked to be a bar of soap in the other. Sherry returned Waddy's nod and wandered toward the doors. Also Mr. and Mrs. Post, two of the restaurant's regulars, and Mrs. Dooberry, who sat leafing through a magazine.

Double-story windows at the far end of the room displayed an alpine meadow and, beyond, the massive peaks of the Elk Range. Bright sun hit off their snows and reflected into the room. Victor Grant walked to the immense hearth, where unsplit logs lay stacked, turned to his guests, and cleared his throat.

"I'm happy to welcome you to the first, and for all practical purposes, the only necessary meeting of Wise Mother. Our head programmer is missing. The plane is running late, fog in

Seattle. Dr. Dooberry, you're the man of the hour. I'll get out of the way."

Dooberry was on his feet. "Thank you, Victor. Ladies and gentlemen. Here in this room are gathered the people who have made this experiment possible." His eye roamed the crowd and alit for a benign moment on each face.

"Our budget is in the bank. My task is to move this revolutionary idea as far as possible. I want to thank you all, but especially Mr. Grant for getting behind us, for the use of his house today and the guesthouse all summer.

"Also the people who will do the work. If the plane doesn't make it I'll ask Waddy Brush to say a few words."

The mention of Seattle had started Waddy daydreaming. Dooberry had a gift for tedium—was it the thump of his voice or the odor of pretension that clung to him like tear-sheet perfume? The sound of his own name brought Waddy back with a start. What had Dooberry said? I'd be called on? He sent his boss a look of panic.

Dooberry went on. "Most of you know each other. Back there, our programmer. Waddy?" Waddy rose a modest inch off the chair. Late morning clouds blocked the sun. The distant peaks turned gray, and the room darkened.

"I want you to hear as well from the software side of things," Dooberry went on. Waddy gulped. He was no public speaker and not much of a private one. "And the software side of things has just arrived. Again we're indebted to Victor Grant. Through a company he controls in Seattle, he has found us one of the leading designers of computer graphics. Just off the plane. I want to introduce you to ... "

Waddy saw the woman enter. Shocked, he inadvertently and silently lip-synched the words as Dooberry spoke them in the bogus cadence of a television announcer.

" ... Lisa Laroux."

~

Peyton slipped out unnoticed during the break. Why did Chloe care about investments? They simply made more money, and as he understood it, he already had a surplus. Still, everybody he knew had a surplus, and none of them shied away from more. The explanation might be in the shortage of dinner table topics. Peyton suspected he was on the verge of an insight about civilization, but, like the little silver ball from a key chain he had once dropped on his own lawn, it lay too deep in the cuttings for him to find it.

Rather than pursue these rogue thoughts, Peyton adopted the political attitudes that had come with his grandmother's crystal. He walked up the hill from the Grant houses. Could he smoke a jay here? The sun had come out again but the armada of clouds sailing up the valley signaled a June storm. It was a pretty sight. He reached for his cigarette case, prized it open, and sniffed the fragrant leaf inside.

"I'd be careful if I were you."

Sherry Topliff carried an empty glass and a bath-size bar of soap whose nub end had been shredded. "There's security all over the place. Most of them are busy scrubbing the rocks."

Peyton considered the advice. He tore open a rolled cigarette, dipped his finger in the flakes, and rubbed some on his gums. Offered the joint to his companion. Sherry wet his finger and stuck a pinch, snuff-style, under his lip.

"They wash the rocks?"

"They do after me." Sherry pointed down toward the west. On a massive granite outcrop he had chalked the face and shoulders of a bulbous woman. "I drew that earth goddess. On spec, see if Grant liked it. But security said Mr. Grant just had that boulder trucked in from Vermont by flatbed, they didn't want me chiseling away at it."

"Is that what you do? Goddesses?"

"Goddesses. Also gods, but breasts are the best part. I prefer goddesses."

"Me too," Peyton said thoughtfully. They turned back toward the house.

"What do you make of Dooberry?"

Peyton hadn't made anything of Dooberry. "I'm not quite sure. What about you?"

"Man smirks like a bedbug. Don't trust him. Still, Etta's going ahead. She can afford it."

Peyton considered this. He could afford it too, but the prospect made him uneasy. How does a bedbug smirk?

They walked the long way around, by the stone guesthouse. Two small boulders guarded its entrance. Sherry stopped, glanced around, and quickly sketched the face of a woman.

"What do you think, Post? We could call her *The Goddess of Money Is No Object*. Wouldn't a little deity improve things around here?"

Peyton didn't answer. A uniformed guard was hurrying down the path. The soles of his brogues slapped on the pea gravel. They went on.

෴

Not quite recovered, Waddy had missed Lisa's first words. She wore a white silk blouse, red sheath skirt, and black tights. The colors, the fit, whatever it was, perhaps the spike heels, made her look as if she'd been shanghaied from a singles' bar—the kind where the cheese cubes have turned dark at the corners. Why was he worrying about her?

"... and not much for speeches. We're designing this for the average Joe. No VR crap, no head-tracking device, no data gloves. The subscriber sends in computer images of the faces he wants, he gets back what looks like a high-grade home movie, with the fantasies he gives us.

"Any questions?"

Lisa pursed her lips. A perfect valentine.

"Miss Laroux. What do you see as the major risks in this project?"

She glanced over toward Dooberry. "I'm just software," she said. "I don't know anything about the validity of these sales projections." Dooberry squirmed in discomfort.

"The psychologists tell us people will reveal their fantasies to a faceless computer. It's why Freud sat out of his patient's sight.

"And the business people say that information gives a subliminal edge to folks who sell stuff. With it you can convince them of anything, a car or a candidate. If they're right, we have a business. If they're wrong, we have bupkus. I'm out a job and you're out your money."

Two questions later Dooberry regained center stage. Guests moved quietly toward the door. Waddy saw Lisa head toward the kitchen and caught up with her.

"Hi," he said.

"Hi."

"Waddy. Waddy Brush."

"Whatever," she said, opening one of the three refrigerators. "This organic?" Together they read the label of a bottle.

She twisted off the top and knocked back half of the guava juice in a long gulp. "We're going to be shacking up together."

"Excuse me?"

"We're down in the guesthouse. You're the other programmer, aren't you? Staying in the guesthouse?"

"Oh, yes. Yes, that's me."

"Well. I look forward to it, Brush. We'll be working together."

"Like old times."

"Old times?" She pointed a finger at him. "Rainwater?"

"Corridor F, Third Floor East."

She considered him a moment, slugged back the rest of the juice. "So ... "

"So," Waddy said hopefully.

"So we took a screwing together?"

He took a breath and replied. "Yes. In a manner of speaking."

❧

Grant's aide brought the Land Rover to the front of the house just as Etta drove by in her pink dreamer. She slid the far window down.

"Where you headed, Mr. Mogul?"

"To the airport. I need to be in New York."

"Hop in. I'll give you a ride."

Grant, conservative by nature, eyed the assemblage of metal that was the Unimog. In the high-country sun, it was the color of a strawberry frappe.

"Come on, hop in. You don't know what the world is like 'til you've seen it from up here."

He climbed the three chrome steps and turned to take a battered attaché box from the aide.

"That's it?" asked Etta. "No toothbrush and jammies?"

"No. I keep a pair of jammies in New York."

"I bet you do," she said as the machine rumbled down the gravel drive.

The Starwood road descended in acute turns, and Etta downshifted expertly for each. The truck held the grade with a satisfying whine of gears.

"Nice machine," Grant said. She was right. The world looked different. "Know anything about the engine?"

"A little. It's a Mercedes with overhead cam, six cylinders in line. Produces about 115 foot-pounds of torque." She smiled to see his lower lip go out.

"Five forward?"

"Six forward, two reverse. Fully synchroed, full-time rear-axle drive and shift on the fly front axle. You like machines."

Grant shrugged. "I'm trained as an engineer. The money stuff came later."

"Yeah," Etta said sympathetically. "It usually does. You get back from New York, come on over. You can take it for a spin. And I'll see what I can do to find you a nice woman."

"You do that too?"

"It's a hobby of mine. Rich man like you needs a woman. Not that silicone starlet I saw you with."

Grant's private life embarrassed him. He changed the subject. "What takes you to the airport?"

"Picking up a picture. Bought it yesterday." Grant leaned back so Etta could look to the right as she entered the highway.

"What did you buy?"

"Frenchie. Bonnard."

"Yesterday? Sotheby's?" Etta nodded. "*The Bather*," Grant said with a smile. "I bid against you."

"Victor Grant. You Yankee piece of shit. You cost me a million bucks." She gave a throaty laugh to show she'd bought at a good price anyway. Hit the *oogah* horn twice and passed a Wagoneer full of tourists. It was the transition she was looking for.

"I don't mind losing at auction. An auction's a game. But I'll tell you this: don't fuck with me on this Dooberry thing."

"Why, Miss Eubanks. What do you mean?"

"None of that bullshit. I see what you're doing. Do a favor, lend some money, get the secured position. My daddy used to pick up leases that way. Make the debt convertible, if it's hot you convert, if it's close you foreclose, if it fails you're out heat and light and soda pop. I'm on to you, Victor Grant, and I don't intend to be squeezed out."

"I wouldn't dare." Grant sounded sincere.

"Oh, I think you would. I think you'd dare most anything, 'cept maybe a new tie. I'm just saying, don't fuck with me." They made the turn into the airport. "You have that expression back East?" Etta asked.

"No. We're more genteel. We say pollinate."

"Fine. Then don't pollinate with me."

They smiled at each other. As they did a siren went off directly behind them.

"What on God's goddamn earth is that? I wasn't speeding, you'll be my witness."

Etta pulled over and took her registration from the map case. In the oblong rearview mirror she saw a woman in military blouse and khaki shorts coming at her. Her mouth was an em-dash between a jutting chin and aviator glasses.

"What's up, Officer Krupke?"

"Name's Post. And I'm an eco-cop. Friends of the Friendless Earth."

"Is that a cop?"

"It is around here, ma'am. The City of Aspen has empowered us to give summonses for crimes against the environment."

"Oh, goody. This man has a plane to catch."

"He'll wait," Grant volunteered. He had never seen anything like this woman, who now climbed up the three steps to look them in the eye. She studied Etta's registration and Oklahoma license.

"Got a local address?"

Etta gave her the number of her West End house.

"Know what this gets per mile?"

"Book says ten on the road, but it's closer to nine. Maybe six in town. Somethin' wrong?"

"We're running out of fossil fuels, ma'am. In case you hadn't heard. Not only that, but lugging two people around with three tons of steel ... "

"Four."

" ... four, is an undue use of the infrastructure. It takes highways and shoulders and bridges to support you, and all that burns up asphalt and more fuel."

"I know about fuel, lady. I figure, I find it, I can burn it."

"Well. I'm not going to cite you. There's no law. But I want you to think about your actions. This is the *Tyrannosaurus rex* of vehicles."

"That's why I have it, lady. It gobbles up everybody else."

"Just think about what happened to *Tyrannosaurus rex*." She put two fingers to the brim of her hat. Gave a quick cowboy nod to Grant and stepped down.

"Don't that beat all?" Etta asked, putting away her papers. When Grant didn't reply, she asked him again.

"Don't that beat all?"

"Yes," he replied. Absently but heartfelt. She dropped him at the FBO, where his GS-3 had already pulled up, its stairs lowered expectantly.

"Thanks for the ride, Etta." He got out and went through the gate.

Interesting, Etta thought. Must be the way the mind of a financial genius operates. He's off me and on to the next deal. His thoughts seemed a million miles away.

In fact they were less than a mile. They were with the woman in the military blouse and hat. Assured, powerful, decisive. All the traits he felt, in his secret moments, he lacked.

Nine

Pilgrims filled the road that followed Castle Creek. Like their brethren headed to Mecca and Compostela, the agonies of their faith showed on their faces. Walkers kept to the shoulders. Joggers, wide-mouthed as carp, ran by disdainfully. They were overtaken by in-line skaters, in turn eclipsed by bikers, uphill swaying from pedal to pedal, downhill squeezed into an *oeuf*. All joined in a single sneer as Waddy's Bug passed.

The pavement gave out at the Conundrum Creek turnoff. The pilgrims kept to the macadam, and Waddy had to himself the road less traveled. He passed a sprinkling of houses, none smaller than the average Purdue fraternity, and drove through the leafy green of August. Early storms had scoured the sky to a Wedgwood blue, and its glazed bowl fit amply over the glacier-carved landscape.

Waddy parked, was disappointed to find that he was not alone. There sat a pink *ur*-truck. From behind its gleaming sides a sorrowful mutt peered at him unsurely. Waddy called, but when he took a step, the dog turned and sorrowfully limped away.

Up the slope Waddy spotted the parker of the truck. A chunky man in his sixties stood over a rock outcropping and seemed to massage it. Waddy took out his drop line, stuck a few sinkers and an extra bait hook in his pocket, and walked up to investigate.

"Howdy," said the man, looking up.

"Howdy," Waddy answered. "Whatcha doin'?"

It was an understandable question. Sherry Topliff held half a shaggy bar of soap. Its tracings were left on the block of viara granite in front of him.

"What do you think?"

Waddy looked closely. The boulder was scored with three circles and a scrimshaw of cross-hatching and squiggles.

"I don't know," he ventured.

"Just some thoughts." Sherry's hand described a mound. "What I see for this hillside are women, scalp to navel, looking up at the sun. Earth mothers. Can you see them?"

Waddy wasn't sure where to look. As he wondered, there came a clatter of gear and spraying gravel. A dilapidated pickup braked into a yawing slip and popped to a halt. Its bowlegged driver was out the door before the rattle stopped. He covered the thirty-yard gap in seconds.

"Who the hell are you?" he asked and picked at the stubble on his chin.

Sherry spoke up. "My name's Topliff. I sculpt."

"You do, do you? And what the hell are you doing to that stone?"

Sherry started to explain his women. Marco Campaneris cut him off.

"What you're doing is trespassing, mister. You ain't got no right to be here, and you sure as hell ain't got no right to mess with that stone."

"Oh, I'm not messing with it. I'm just going to be removing some of it."

"Says who?"

"Says Mr. Kaye. He invited me to come up and take a look."

At the name, Marco's lids relaxed, then tightened again.

"He did, did he?"

"He said all this rock would go eventually. Magnificent stuff. Dates from the Devonian period, the age of the fishes. He said whatever I knocked off would save him the cost of blasting it out."

Marco bobbed in combat.

"So what's this?"

Sherry went back to the gathering of women. He pointed uphill, where his chalkings showed on other outcrop.

"Mr. Kaye suggests we do the sculpture in the ground and then decide whether any of it gets moved into the galleries. Or simply leave it in the ground, a motif for his development."

"Is that right?"

"That's right."

"Well, I tell you something. Mr. Kaye's got no development yet on this property. It ain't approved yet."

"So I understand."

"So if you understand, how's it you're up here drawing hooters on these rocks?"

"Merely ideas, my friend. All those markings will wash away in the first rain."

Marco was thwarted. "You got chisels and a air hammer in that there truck."

Sherry nodded.

"You fixin' to start chislin'?"

"I simply tote them around. I won't begin work until all the approvals are in."

Marco turned to Waddy. "And you?"

"Me? I just came to fish." Waddy held out the drop line as a shield.

"What do you know about fishing?"

"Nothing, I guess. I mean I used to do a lot of it in Washington."

"Washington?" Marco spat out the word.

"State of. Don't know much about it except I like it."

"Got a license?"

"No."

"Ever have one?"

"Nope. Never have."

At these words, the dark face inexplicably broke into a snaggled, conspiratorial smile. Something, it might have been years of knocking against crooked lips, had chipped his front teeth.

"Ever tickled for fish?"

"No," Waddy said, mystified.

"Wanna see how?"

~

"Go?" Tiffany asked when she finally figured out what it was the houseman was telling her. "Go where?"

"He no say, lady." Charley had a funny way of pronouncing *lady*. It came from the throat. "Jussay go."

Tiffany had come downstairs after a long night of flaccidity and rage. She thought her ouster unfair—she'd done everything she could think of. Her Adidas satchel lay packed by the door. Charley stood in a sleeveless undershirt, black trousers, black chauffeur's cap. He had stringy arms, and the oversized cap made him look like a prisoner.

"Is he here? Can I talk to him?"

"Mista Horrista go frying. Say, when he fry, you go."

Well, Tiffany thought. I've had worse Dear Johns. This business of screwing celebrities was no easy matter. "Did he leave me anything, a note?"

"No note. He go frying. Jussay, Challey, you take lady. I take."

Tiffany picked up the satchel. "That's all right, Charley. I've already been taken." She walked out into a glorious day.

~

By the time he reached the top of Independence Pass, Victor Grant was dripping with sweat. The climb had taken, he noted on his chronometer, three hours ten, not bad for an altitude gain of two thousand six hundred feet. A good seven minutes over his personal record, but not bad with no trainer to push him. He would get himself fine-tuned. The bike too. Maybe the Nishiki needed some oil. He'd have it taken into the shop.

He reached into a pannier and fetched a clean towel. In the pull-off at the summit, travelers were snapping the usual shots of each other against the tundra. West lay the Elk Range, east Twin Lakes, and the headwaters of the Arkansas. Must do this more often. He timed his heartbeat. On a pocket computer he entered the climb time and the rate of metabolism. Glanced at the day's appointments, looked at investment ideas. Text-messaged his AA, Isabelle—"Thinking abt impact of crude prices on consumption. Pls chart change in oil prices times percentage of GDP vs. same times share of disposable consumer income spent on energy. 30 years to present. Tomorrow's fine."—then pushed a button to retrieve his notes for the cruise down.

Here's the reason to make this bloody climb. There's nothing like the speed on descent to clear out the mind. He'd written an agenda of four items, in order of importance. Pacific Basin investments. Personnel: a fund manager out of control, performance excellent but personal life interfering. Third, this Wise Mother thing. How much money of his own to sink before pulling the plug. Finally, a private matter. He needed a woman in his life. "Expand," read his entry, "the pool."

Grant replaced towel and computer in the pannier, clipped his chin strap, and mounted the bike. By the first curve the speedometer needle was climbing through thirty. He leaned into the bank and focused his mind on the yen's decline. Sixty-one percent since its 1989 high. The U.S. Treasury was entering the market this week to prop it up. You bolster the yen, you increase Japanese purchasing power for our goods, but you make their exports more difficult to push. Result: eventual decline in the Nikkei Index, reverse in the balance of payments. Counterintuitive, he knew, but true. Landscape went flying by, he closed on a car with Iowa plates. Its wheels straddled the yellow line. To the right, the mountain dropped off into blue air. Grant braked gently fore and aft. The driver sensed Grant's cycle and reluctantly eased back into his lane.

Who benefits? Reverse in the balance of payments, stronger monetary unit, money going out of the country. Grant let up on the brakes and sped by. A separation of mind and body: body bent into the curves, finding the balance to keep the momentum at peak. Mind hit the obvious solution: an arbitrage. Short the yen, go long in Japanese bank stocks. They'll drop faster than the Nikkei, they'll become a bargain. All the while, their earnings will be up. He smiled into the next turn and the wind hit his teeth. It had the right elements. It defied logic, it limited risk, and it met his aesthetic of complexity and interest. Contrarian positions appealed to him, and he got bored easily.

Down he sped. Shifted gears as the landscape momentarily flattened out. What was next? The fund manager. For some reason he couldn't get into this zone on the climb. Too much work. That was why he put the tough problems first. There was less traffic at the top. Now to the fund manager.

By the time Grant passed Lost Man Creek, the man's job had been saved. Grant would send him to counseling. A good boss stays ahead of performance, not behind. Neglect now, suffer next quarter. What's next? He swerved to avoid a couple of kayakers unloading boats into his lane.

Wise Mother. Not a big dollar number. Easy solution. Dooberry signed the papers without thinking. Sink or swim. Until they run through their first tranche. That silly fellow is unlikely to come up with anything. If he does, I have part of it. If not, the lease gives me an inside position. If they go belly-up, they'll leave technology. If not, maybe a book deal. Either way, my money comes out first. Solution: stay ahead of the equity.

Grant was approaching the grottoes. Here, before it plunged down the valley into the canyons of the Colorado, the Roaring Fork, the fastest descending river on the continent, is hollowing caves and chutes in the sandstone. In the stretch of road by it, cars parked on the shoulder to unload fishermen and picnickers. Grant braked. Was there a correlation between the velocity of the bike and the velocity of thought? Maybe he should try skydiving. He considered stopping to enter both observations in his Blackberry. What was the last problem? It eluded him as he slowed for hairpin turns at the bottom of the pass, where tourist cars were likely to jam. You didn't want to come on them too fast, there was nowhere to steer the bike.

Oh, yes. A woman. How is it that the world's forty-seventh richest man—at least according to *Forbes* magazine, who had his numbers wrong, far too low, should he consider correcting them or was that just an exercise of ego?—how is it that the world's forty-seventh richest man can't get laid? It would be nice to find a woman. There again, his nature worked against him, his preference for the contrarian and his impatience. Still, human elements aside, this was like any problem. Gather the data, analyze the elements, match issues to ideas.

Traffic increased. He noticed his own rate of speed fall to fifteen. He had no ideas.

❧

Annalee knew him as one of Pantagruel's regulars. Frankie always told the staff, Be good to customers, be real good to real good ones. She saw no harm in what he asked. A table an hour before opening. "Tea for two," he said, smiling. "Like the song."

Annalee retrieved the tea service from the upper cupboard and arranged the tray herself. The walnut humidor with its rows of neat packets, sugar cubes in a porcelain bowl, lemon slices, and a pitcher of milk. By the time she had the tray set, Mr. Kaye's guest had arrived and was taking her seat.

Annalee could not have been more surprised. Mr. Kaye lived in a world of *Vogue* ads, the men freighted with rugged brows and shoebox jaws, the women leggy, flat-breasted, and hipless. What would Mr. Kaye have to say to this woman in khaki shorts and epaulette shirt? A Smokey the Bear hat that, as she removed it, revealed hair that sang the praises of laundry soap. Justin entered, pointed a pistol of forefinger and thumb at Annalee, and walked to his guest.

They selected their teas, black pekoe for him, chamomile for her. Annalee put a plate of little cakes on the white cloth and withdrew. A gross of scarlet napkins needed folding into swans for tonight's crowd.

Justin was at his best. He sparred and jabbed, he attacked Philida's cynicism with charm, sincerity, humor. None of it worked. Friends of the Friendless Earth was not about to commit itself to some plan so rich people could shoot duck in one of the last remaining wildernesses in the Elk Range.

"Why don't you just go downriver and shoot to your heart's delight? Or better still, why don't you just leave them alone? What have they ever done to you?"

Justin was frustrated. Also bloated. Four cups of tea, and the caffeine had begun to make him jumpy. He excused himself, used the men's, returned with a new dodge. Honesty. He would try honesty.

"Look, Philida, sweetheart. Let me square with you. Why do we have to shoot duck on private property? Why? 'Cause it's private. We're wealthy, and wealthy folk got their wealth for that reason. To shoot duck where no one else can, to ski the best powder, to eat the best cuts. To have a club that other people can't join. That's life. I didn't invent that, God did.

"Now, we have the land tied up. We can file a plat for twenty-three ticky-tack houses in the middle of this land, as it's zoned. Or we can file for the Isaak Walton Rod and Gun. If we subdivide, we'll all meet in court. I know that, you know that. But remember the Indian cemetery. If we win, there'll be volleyball on the sacred grounds.

"My plan saves all that. With Friends of the Friendless Earth behind us, no court suit, no volleyball. Those ancestors doze away like newborns on Nytol. Think about it."

Then, in case Philida hadn't understood, he pushed back and said it again. "Think about it. The world comes down to alternatives."

Seeing him move his chair, Annalee came to clear the torn packets. She leaned over the table. A site plan was spread out among the cups, secured by saltcellars and a cruet of balsamic vinegar.

"Oh, Mr. Kaye. Is that what you're planning up Conundrum Creek? Looks beautiful."

Philida snapped back. "You think so?"

"Sure," said Annalee. Real good customers—Mr. Kaye was one of the best. One fabled evening last season, Justin Kaye hosted simultaneous dinners, and, with facile table-hopping and a sunny disposition, not a guest had caught him out. And Justin Kaye was a good tipper.

"Sure, just look. Only one real building," she put her finger on the clubhouse, "and these cute little ones. What's this?"

"That's for the fish boy," Justin said. "We'll have someone on site to clean fish and pluck feathers."

"See that," Annalee said to Philida. "Jobs for the locals, minimum impact on the environment. And here?"

"That's the Arapahoe burial ground," Justin said and wagged a finger in the air. "No development allowed. Absolutely none, zilch, we're giving up a prime site. No infringement on sacred Indian territory."

"Out of sight," said Annalee. By Justin's plate she placed the bill, solemnly folded into a leather wallet embossed with the restaurant's name. Frankie was particularly proud of the wallets, the scarlet silk lining.

Justin watched Annalee walk away. Pretty little figure. Too bad I can't do something with her in print. The Dakota line. Too much ass, though, and the face a shade too Mediterranean.

"You should try," Justin turned his thoughts to Philida Post, "to take the locals' view. Too many of us blunder into this valley wanting to become residents but never taking the locals' view. That young woman, Philida. She sees the harmony of it all." He slipped cash into the wallet. They rose and moved toward the door.

"Thanks for the tea, Mr. Kaye."

"Justin. I hope you'll consider this."

"Oh, I will."

"Good."

"And after I've considered, if you turn a single spade of dirt, we'll sue."

He started to take Philida by the arm and thought better of it. He had a last card to play.

"I'm not sure whether you know this, but your brother will be a member of the Isaak Walton. Peyton. It wouldn't hurt to do something nice for your family."

"My brother? The clubman?" Her voice rose in a hook. "Listen, Mr. Kaye, our family was in toilets."

"Yes, I know."

"Well it's a family saying. Keep the water in the tank clean." Justin opened the door for her and she accepted his chivalry with reluctance. He followed close behind.

Annalee had fifteen minutes before the first seating. She bussed the dirty dishes and replaced the cloth. Under the wallet, she found two new one-hundred dollar bills, Ben Franklin looking for all the world like the kindly uncle she'd never had.

❧

The two followed Marco's example. Fifteen feet from the creek he hunched down and began to crawl. They watched his butt shifting from side to side. When it reached the bank, it stopped. Sherry and Waddy crawled to him.

"Now," he said in a forced whisper. "Upstream."

They crawled crabwise, Waddy first. They had gone ten feet that way when Marco touched his arm. He would fish here.

"Got to move upstream," he whispered. "Sound travels down."

He rolled the sleeves of his work shirt past the elbows. Slowly sunk his bare arms into the rushing water. Pursed his lips and studied the sky as he felt around. Pulled out and signaled for Waddy to move upriver five feet.

There he tried again. Hunkered his chest to the cutbank and lowered in his arms so he could reach back under. And, grimacing from the cold, slowly lifted out a fish. Startled to quiet. Its frantic eye searching the new air, it rested in speckled peace in Marco's hands. He rose to his knees and showed it to them.

"A brownie."

The fish was perhaps a foot in length. Its belly was shot with deep yellow, its sides dotted in phosphorescence. The two others watched it. Marco leaned back over the bank and gently let it go.

"You try."

Sherry went first. Held his hands under and moved them about. Nothing.

"You got to feel 'em. Then just tickle the belly as you hook 'em up."

He pulled his arms out and rubbed his hands together. Blew on them hard. When they opened, Waddy saw their thick palms and brown calluses. That man wouldn't feel a shark bite.

Waddy was next. When his hands went in he gasped at the icy water. Slowly he brought his hands under the bank and up, first directly in front of him, then a foot down. His hands touched the underside of the earth, root and cress, and his imagination made them squirm, but there was nothing there. He wiggled upstream and felt again. This time he sensed it. Faint, imperceptibly live. A length of something that rested on his rising palms for an instant and floated away. He had touched an angel. Marco recognized the look on his face.

"Had one?"

"I didn't hold him. Forgot to tickle."

"That's okay. You'll get the hang of it."

Marco's voice had returned to normal volume. When the fish moved off, it was gone, not coming back. Marco lay down again. "Anyone need supper?"

"Sure," said Waddy. Marco closed his eyes, felt about, and pulled out an eight-inch brookie. Dispensed it with a rock and handed over to Waddy.

"You'll want potatoes." Waddy thought when Marco said that and reached to his back pocket he might produce them. Instead, he took out a flat round box, twisted off its cap and offered snuff around. Waddy and Sherry declined with a shrug. Marco stuck a nip under his lip. Spat out the loose ends.

On the walk downhill, Marco picked up a calf's aitchbone.

"Now you two sons a bitches are still trespassing and I could run you in. But you want to come up here and tickle for trout or use that drop line, take what you can eat, why, you be my guest. Mr. Kaye won't complain. If'n I catch you using all that shit they sell in town, five-hundred-dollar fly rods and stomach pumps, I'll have the warden up here in minutes. Meantime, wash them tits off'n those rocks." He tossed the bone into the bed of the truck.

Sherry looked at him. "The rains will take care of it."

"You'll take care of it. I ain't comin' up here tomorrow to see naked ladies."

Sherry wasn't pleased. "I don't have any water."

"Tell you what. You take off that fancy cowgirl shirt and dip it in that creek. You'll find it has water, it ain't run out."

Sherry hesitated.

"Or I suppose you can try to fix the tires on that truck o' yours. Two flats and one spare."

"That truck doesn't have flat tires."

Marco looked at him evenly. "Not yet," he said, and again spat with the same sound, a soft *too* at the end of his tongue.

Waddy helped Sherry wash up. When the sculptor drove the cartoon truck down the hill, Waddy noticed the dog that had stayed in its space. Forlorn, the color of mud after days of rain. Sitting and watching.

"You want a ride?" The dog tensed to rise but didn't have the energy. "I'm going through town, I'll give you a ride." The dog rose, put weight on its hind leg, and yelped in pain.

Waddy filleted a slice off the fish Marco had given him and tossed it. The dog put its nose on it and snuffled it up without chewing.

"Hungry?" He sliced off a second piece. Then laid a trail of fish ending at the open door of his Bug. The dog went from slice to slice like a vacuum salesman. There was a ragged circle of blood on his left hind leg.

"You want to hop in, we'll have that looked at." Waddy tossed the carcass of the fish into the backseat. The dog followed, and Waddy closed the door.

Ten

The Grant guesthouse reprised the architecture of the main house, its grandeur subordinated in dimension. The living room was a miniature Romanesque vault. Lisa and Dooberry sat in the two oversized wing chairs, reading. Waddy was seated before one of the computer screens, in the tiresome job of programming the templates.

They had divided the labors. Dooberry was to arrange the ready-made part of the database. He simply found other bases to license so that, by overlay, or lifting the data to his, he accumulated buying habits, hobbies, addresses, and income brackets. His efforts would produce a massive amount of information, but nothing that wasn't available from a dozen other, recognized sources.

The competitive edge would come from the work Lisa and Waddy had undertaken. Lisa was reading—speed-reading, it turned out—psychology texts on suppressions and fantasies. She was to feed to Waddy the raw outlines of each, aligned in logical categories. Waddy would in turn design, first in text, then in computer language, ten or twenty substructure stories for each category, what they called their templates. The individual subscriber provided personal details that, when organized by template, were the heart of the Wise Mother database: the particular daydream the subscriber wanted to store in the privacy of his computer. Shared, of course, with Wise Mother.

Waddy picked up a text by Lisa's elbow and opened it at random. It listed over two thousand fantasies. He let his eyes rest and a sigh slip. He had underestimated the task. A further distraction was Lisa's rhythmic breathing, a breezy sound that brought to mind Japanese pen drawings, the erotic ones. His thoughts went to her apartment that night, her energies, the vindaloo. Was this job a stroke of great luck or his usual brand? She had moved into the room next to his, they were sharing two-percent milk, a pop-up toaster.

Lisa rose to stretch. Still he heard the provocative whistle of breath, only to realize it was Dooberry, who had dozed off.

Lisa began to structure some order out of the chaos. She divided the fantasies into working groups: simple, social, and exotic. One template would suffice for the simple phobias. Once identified, Waddy would add the graphics. He would simply plug in the object, be it a person (they started inexplicably with a current singer, whose lips made a perfect valentine), a place (Palau), or a thing (strawberry mousse) and produced visual examples. The social phobias and the exotica would similarly fit into brackets. Waddy began to see the task was achievable.

Using the universal computer code ASCII, he entered the first algorithms.

༄

"Etta is hosting a dinner for the investors." Chloe had her hand over the receiver. On the deck beyond, her husband reclined on the chaise longue, thumbing through the mail while the midday sun deepened his tan.

"Do you want to go?"

"I don't know," Peyton said laconically. "I need to visit Sinbad."

"Well we'll stop off before he closes and be at the restaurant for dinner."

Peyton didn't respond. Instead he reached over and took a draught from the Mount Gay sour he'd made. Had squeezed fresh lemons for it. He preferred to see Sinbad on his own.

"Peyton?"

"Yes? Fine. But I may drive down earlier. It's a sale. You have to be there first to get the good rugs."

Chloe returned to the phone. Etta's secretary was accustomed to waiting.

"We'd love to. Eight? At Pantagruel. Tell Etta we look forward to it."

Peyton came in carrying Sinband's postcard as if it were the winning lottery card.

"You should really stay out of the sun," she said.

"Yes, I suppose so. I think I'll drive in now. The best stuff goes early."

"Good idea," Chloe said supportively. "Get a short kilim runner if he has one." Peyton placed the mailer on the table, picked up his keys, and vacantly went through the causeway to the garage. Chloe looked down at the card. Another sale. Every fall she would clear out the house and ship rugs east for resale. The inevitable loss was well within her budget for Peyton's hobbies. But she wasn't profligate: kilims tended to be lighter, easier to ship.

Peyton flattened the rear seat of the SUV. The rug would fit in there. He wouldn't want to tie it to the top. Too chancy.

He headed down the mountain to Sinbad's Imports and Exports. Mostly, now that Peyton reflected on it, imports. To stay on the mailing list, one needed to respond. Miss two sales and you're off the list. Rule number two: pay the asking price. The rugs were mostly Moroccan, inferior quality. Not that Peyton cared much about rugs, though over the years he'd bought his share.

Sinbad was in front of his store, loading two Jerez weaves into a Bentley. A slight Asian man stood by impassively, in white shirt, black pants, black chauffeur's cap.

"Hey," Peyton said. "What's happening?"

Sinbad regarded him through half-closed black eyes.

"Mr. Post. I wondered whether you were still my customer."

"Sinbad. Don't joke. I'm a loyal follower. You my man."

Peyton intended his ghetto language to be fraternal. Sinbad shook the hand of Charley, Rod Hollister's houseboy. The Bentley drove off, and Peyton followed the man into his store.

"I appreciate your vote of commercial confidence." Sinbad spoke with precision.

"May I see the inventory?" The merchant did not move immediately.

"You are sure? I do not want you purchasing unnecessary merchandise, Mr. Post."

"Oh, no. I am sure."

"It's just that I haven't seen you all summer. I thought perhaps you have a surfeit, or you found another importer."

"No, no. You the main man. Believe me."

The storekeeper watched him squirm for a satisfying minute. "Just so," he said and turned. Peyton followed him into the back room.

In the musty space, colorful rectangles were spread out across the floor. Peyton quickly moved to pick one up.

"This one is nice."

"You have a good eye, Mr. Post. That is a prayer rug from the north. Near Khvoy. Very fine quality."

"Yes, I think I like this one."

"You would like a pad with it?"

"Oh, most definitely. I need a pad. In fact, I'd like two. Can I get two?"

"You don't wish to take more than your share, Mr. Post.

Pads are scarce. I have other customers."

"No, no. I don't want to take another's share. Only if you can let two go, Sinbad."

Again the proprietor made him wait for an answer.

"I think so. I think I can do this."

"I would be grateful."

"The pads, as you know, add to the cost. Two pads add twice."

"I understand."

Sinbad looked him in the eye. Mentioned a price. It was higher than Peyton expected.

"That is acceptable? If not, please, Mr. Post, just say so. I do not want you to feel obliged."

"Oh, no. Acceptable. Absolutely. It's cool. Copacetic."

"You wish to take this with you?"

"Yes, please."

"A fine prayer rug. A good specimen of the weaving from the south of the country."

"The south. Yes."

"Now you will wait outside and I will wrap this for you."

"Excellent," said Peyton. "Excellent."

In a very short time Sinbad came out. Peyton paid in cash. The rug had been rolled tightly and sealed with three rings of packing tape.

The tube fit neatly into the SUV. Peyton drove back, pleased with the way he had patched things up. This man was a treasure. Necessary to keep on his good side. Peyton drove slowly, savoring his cache. It was like that first drink of the day, right after it was placed in front of you. Frost just starting to run. The glass can't go anywhere, it's trapped. He had his packet, it wasn't going anywhere. He visualized inside the carpet, just as he could taste that first drink. He saw himself carrying it to the basement, cutting the tape circles. Inside he saw the two luscious packets. Paper toweling on the inside to keep the leaf moist, double plastic bags taped shut. Two fresh lids of the finest Moroccan kif. Peyton assumed it came in the same way—the Tangiers connection shipped and Sinbad distributed. Too bad, Peyton thought. Too bad he couldn't get Chloe to invest in *that* operation. That would be owning the candy store.

❧

"Most people won't put themselves through it."

Waddy gulped. "The pain?"

"The cost." He quoted a figure that was twice what Waddy expected.

"You can't save the leg, Doc?"

The vet shook his head. "Poor fella's been gimping along for at least two months. What the bullet didn't do he's done to himself. Brave pup." He scratched the dog at the base of the skull, and the dog closed his eyes in pleasure. "Most folks would put him down."

"Why?"

"For themselves. They don't like to see a cripple."

"He'll do okay on three legs?"

"He'll do fine. He's strong and healthy. But it's a lot of money for a pet." The men looked down into the dark and hopeful eyes. "They don't really have a use."

"Can I pay you half now and half over time?"

"Sure," the vet said. "That'll do. You'll need to fill out these papers so we can give him shots and a tag. He'll need a name."

Waddy studied the earnest face. "Brave and useless. I'll call him Hero."

❧

Annalee pulled the napkin by its swan tail and spread it on Waddy's lap. "You've come up in the world," she said and scratched the back of his neck playfully. "Back as a guest."

He nodded, his thoughts still on Hero and the operating table. Up in the world—you could say that of the sardine in the net. Dinner conversation bounced around him. When Chloe Post turned to talk the price of Louisiana sweet crude, he rose and sought out Annalee. She was at the greeter's lectern.

"The new job," she said. "Good?"

"So far."

"All you can ask. No reservations?"

"About what?"

Annalee pursed her lips. "I shouldn't have said. It's just ... "

"Just?"

"Making movies of people's fantasies. You don't suppose there's an evolutionary reason that our dreams are dreams? Fleeting?"

"I'd never thought of it."

"Or an aesthetic one?" She flipped through the night's reservations.

"You've lost me," Waddy answered.

"Maybe they ought to stay transient. Floating, where we can't get at them. Maybe if you put them in an album, we'll be something different."

"That's a romantic view," Waddy teased. He'd sought her out because of her nails on the nape of his neck. Now he was getting lectured.

"I suppose. Maybe it's like the guppies."

"What guppies?" Waddy had been programming so long, illogic confused him.

"You should be getting back," she said and went to greet an arriving four-top.

◞

Afterward, Etta invited her guests and the waitstaff to her place for dancing. The salmon-red house was packed, and she enlisted Waddy for errands. He stacked the CD player and carried three liter bottles of water as she went about filling humidifiers in every room.

"May I ask you a personal question?" he said.

"Of course."

"Why Evian?"

Etta looked puzzled. "Is there something better?" They continued on.

"Heat and humidity make an evening," Etta told him. "Summers at home, with the right wind, we get the smell of horseshit from the barn. I'm looking for Tulsa in late July," Etta said. They rolled the large Persian carpet and slid it to one wall.

Waddy searched for a face he knew. Against one wall, Lisa leaned somnolently while an earnest young man pumped her about the project. On a davenport, Peyton Post was assembling a joint on his knee. Across the room a tall blonde, radiating bustline and fresh looks, had cornered a man patched with a new hair weave. "Produces game shows," Etta explained. "TV."

Waddy helped Etta pour Champagne, sherbet, and Grand Marnier into a Cuisinart. Smoothies, she called them.

"It's exciting," Waddy overheard Tiffany say. "I think that show has a certain sexual tension." The producer nodded.

Now it was Dooberry who had Lisa in a corner. Waddy watched, distraught.

Etta came up behind him. "You need a woman, young man."

"I was thinking the same thing."

Etta poured herself another smoothie.

"Well, you're not going to find her sitting around with an old sow like me. The species must survive. Get out in the pit. Take a stand. That cutie? From the restaurant? She's here. She was giving you the old come-hither at dinner."

"Oh, no, Miz Eubanks. She's just a friend."

"You think so? Well, friends don't let friends sleep alone." She followed his sight line to Lisa. "That woman's not interested in you, son. Find one who is."

"I can't seem to do that."

"Nonsense. Stop being selfish. Heed the biological imperative, not some notion you got off John Denver records. We need a little life force humility. We're all drones in the hive"

"Drones are sterile."

"Don't pull science with me, young man. This is screwing we're discussing."

"I'm more of a self-determinist," Waddy said unsurely. "I think history is made by individuals."

"Nonsense. Need to get back in touch with our place in the evolutionary line. We're part of a mob, right along with fruit flies and spider monkeys. You think they fritter away their time, she loves me, she loves me not? They don't. They keep their eye on the evolutionary ball."

"That's a harsh view."

"Harsh? Hell, man. I'm talking about *Homo sapiens*. Competing for space on this planet. Who you rooting for, us or the cockroaches? Get in the game, son. You're one of our top draft choices."

❧

Annalee carried about her like a perfume a soft melancholy, borne of her intuition of intractable time. She was a peach on the limb, and she was ripening unplucked.

She looked out at the night and let go a sigh.

"What's the matter, little sugarbee?" asked Etta, who had come up behind her.

Caught with her blues showing, Annalee turned and moved the points of her mouth up.

"Oh, I don't know."

Etta leaned on the rail beside her. "I bet you do. I bet you're thinking, I have so much to give and no one to give it to."

Annalee looked down and let slip an embarrassed smile. "Something like that."

"Well I'll tell you something, sugarbee. You'll find someone to give it to. No doubt in my mind. And something else. They won't know what in God's gargled earth to do with it. The more you have, the more they splutter and stall."

Just then Sherry came up. "Etta, honey. You seen that young man pouring the smoothies?" Etta turned, grabbed him around the waist, and planted a loud kiss on his cheek.

"See that?" she asked Annalee. "See what I mean?"

~

Waddy made another pitcher and went about filling cups. He passed the dining room, where the staff had laid a considerable buffet. There feasting among the spiral-cut ham, the Stilton wheel, and the vegetable tray was his friend from the Pantagruel kitchen.

"Mr. Gossage?" Waddy tried.

"Ah, Brush. The mother inspired by poets."

Gossage wore freshly laundered jeans, a Levi's shirt, and bolo tie looped through a small turquoise slide.

"You're out of uniform."

"On the contrary, Henry Wadsworth Longfellow. We're all camouflaged."

"You look suitable."

The man bowed from the waist and his dreadlocks fell about his face. He pushed them back casually. "You know what Edison said about genius? One percent inspiration and the rest perspiration?"

"I've heard."

"Well, Brush. Survival is one percent perspiration and the rest haberdashery."

"Are you a guest?"

"I am indeed. Though not an invited one." Waddy's discomfort showed on his face.

"Don't worry," he said spiritedly. "It's merely an application of reciprocating surpluses."

"What are those?"

"Reciprocating surpluses, my dear Brush, are the basis of my Utopian model." He took a blossom of cauliflower, plunged it into a lightly curried dip, and popped it into his mouth.

"You see," he said when he had almost finished chewing, "the world is in imbalance. Floods in Bangladesh, droughts in Mongolia. Carbon dioxide over the Santa Monica Freeway and plants aching for photosynthesis in Manaus. There is no pollution, only supply wrongly placed. The trick is to balance shortage with excess."

"And you are helping with that?"

"I am indeed. The capitalist society, admirable as it is, continues to create excess without heeding the shortages. It is based on continued production, long after demand has disappeared. Tell me, Brush. Do you know how the Amazon jungle composts itself?"

"I don't think I do."

"The Amazon has no glaciation. There is no natural friction to break down the plant material. But as foliage dies, the ants take over. They munch the leaves into tiny bits. They chew up the jungle piece by piece. That is what we need."

"Ants?"

"We need an army of ants to consume the crumbs of our overindustrialized society."

"And that is you?"

"It is. I am an early enlistee in the army of the ants." A tray came between them, and Gossage helped himself to a bite-sized bun that held a slab of beef.

"You should have been a professor of economics."

"Oh, I was, my dear friend. I was."

Etta joined them, and Waddy, uncertain of his companion's status or sanity, introduced him simply as Mr. Gossage.

"I hope you don't mind, Mrs. Eubanks. I saw the party through the window and decided to pop in."

"*Mucho gusto.* We can use a few more straight males."

"How can you tell?"

"I witch 'em," she said. "With a forked stick. Like my daddy did gas traps."

Gossage was delighted. He took a handful of Chinese pea pods from a bowl and put them in the pocket of his jeans.

"You live nearby?" she asked.

"Across the street."

"Really? I thought I'd met all the neighbors."

"I'm what you'd call short-term," he said. Waddy at first thought Gossage had a glass eye, but on closer inspection one was merely off-color. Blue changeable to gray. The second, brown going to black, gleamed with excitement.

The CD player switched disks and an unmistakable horn slithered across the room. Satchmo's arpeggio introduced "Dippermouth Blues."

"Hey," said Waddy. "You like this music?"

Etta cracked a wobbly smile. "Louis? He's an old friend."

Waddy extended his arm and Etta took it. He led her about the floor, spinning in the two-step his mother had taught him, dips and twirls. Etta was as wide as she was tall and bore a remarkable resemblance to J. Edgar Hoover, but she could dance. The first number finished, and the Hot Five went into "Snake Rag." They danced that and "Terrible Blues." Finally, like two heavyweights in an August fifteen-rounder, they staggered onto the Victorian porch to cool off. Waddy held firm to the railing as the house pitched in what seemed freshening seas. Peyton Post came by and offered them a toke. Waddy obliged. The smoke burned his throat.

Etta shook Peyton off—"I've had enough fun"—and Peyton wandered on, trailing a thickly sweet smog. Etta resumed her coaxing.

"I want you to go in there and hit on one of those broads. You really stuck on that skinny one?"

"Oh, Miz Eubanks, I am. Her shoe size is seven narrow, she was born on St. Crispin's day, I've even downloaded pictures from her days at Harkness Hall School for Girls. Her yearbook photo and the championship field hockey team. She's a knockout in a plaid kilt."

"How do you come by all that?"

"Computers. We used to work together. I hacked her password. Read her e-mail. Solicitations from her college, the books she bought, department store accounts. I'm not kidding, every time she'd order lingerie, it drove me wild. Do you know what it's like to love a woman, a love that is entirely unrequited, yet know what color tricot she favors?"

"You're obsessing, son. Got to get over it. You're building yourself a masturbatory museum."

"Oh, how true, Miz Eubanks. A museum. A Louvre."

Etta tossed off the last of her smoothie and let out a ladysized burp. "Hells bells, son. Just move it over."

"Move what over?"

"All those cozy feelings. It's not the person that's important, it's the feeling. Just pack up the feeling and move it somewhere else. That cutie from the restaurant. I'm for *her*."

Waddy shook his head solemnly. The notion disturbed his semicircular canals. He steadied himself as the prow of the porch rose and plunged.

"Are you sure about that? I thought the object produces the interest, not the other way around. You really think love can be boxed and shipped?"

"Shee-it yes, son. Like a stereo. Easier, no wires. That feeling's in *you*, it don't matter who's on the other end of it. Think about it. If in the entire universe you had to find one woman and she had to find you, sex would happen about as often as comets colliding. Stop fretting so much. Take a load off. Go in there and nail one of those babes."

But when Waddy looked about, everyone had gone. The Posts, the crashers, Dooberry, Tiffany with a man she hoped was a television producer, the enchantress Laroux. Even the mendicant Gossage. He helped Etta clean up the glasses and replace the rugs. He took Sherry's ankles, Etta held the arms, and together they hoisted him onto a couch. Several smoothies to the good, Waddy drove home alone.

## Eleven

Storky, blinking, Waddy Brush descended from the stairhead bearing a bowl of Rice Krispies across which a spoon and a rolled paper napkin lay crossed. The excesses of the previous night jangled in his ears. Dressed in sky-blue cotton pajamas his mother had given him for Christmas, he peered uneasily into the new day.

For reasons he could not recall, when he came in from Etta's jamboree, he had decided to place the makings of his breakfast—milk, cereal, banana, appropriate flatware—on a tray and carry it upstairs. He fell quickly to sleep and awoke with the last of the Champagne bubbles popping behind his eyes. So he carried the fixings down, woozy but determined to set a place, brew a pot of coffee, and wait for his lost love and almost-roommate to appear from the other bedroom.

At the bottom of the stairs, he nosed what he thought was an aroma of decay. He started, confirmed in his guess when he saw the coffin-sized box. Someone had died. He peered uneasily at the markings: the carton carried the new servers. They were hooked together to form a single corpse-sized console. The fragrance was polyurethane.

He went to the kitchen and assembled coffee. Hero hobbled in and thrust his wet nose into Waddy's palm. The vet had cleaned him up, his coat was brushed to a shine, and he'd already started to fill out. Waddy walked him to the front door, and when Hero hesitated, gently pushed him out. On the welcome mat was that morning's *Aspen Leaf*. Waddy poured a cup and settled down to read.

The lead story was about his favorite fishing hole.

### Kaye Files for Club Approval

Fashion king Justin Kaye, who makes Aspen his second home, has filed with Planning and Zoning for approval of a private fishing club at the headwaters of Conundrum Creek. The application for the two-hundred-and-thirty-acre parcel comes up for first hearing in September. If approvals are secured, Kaye said, he intends to break ground as soon as the winter snows recede.

The parcel is located in one of the area's most scenic and culturally significant locations (see map). It is bordered on three sides by national forest, assuring privacy and views. Plat filings show the existence of an ancient Arapaho burial site on the property.

"We're going to ensure a minimum impact," Mr. Kaye said. "We're hoping everyone will get behind this responsible adaptation of the land."

The Isaak Walton Rod and Gun Preserve is expected to meet stiff opposition. Spokesperson Philida Post told this reporter that Friends of the Friendless Earth will oppose it at the hearings and is prepared to file suit.

In his youth Waddy developed the talent to create a kazoo from individuated Rice Krispies. Take a few from the top of the bowl, before milk made them soggy, and hold them loosely in your lips between the canines. Now he sat pondering the fate of his fishing grounds to a rollicking "Stars and Stripes Forever."

His attention to the march was so complete that the words startled him.

"You're cheerful, Bush. What is it, the Fourth of July?"

Lisa Laroux stood midway down the stairs. The black and silver football jersey she wore to just above her knees made her leggier than usual.

"The Oakland Raiders?" Waddy asked. He wanted to correct her, he thought it important, if they were to have a relationship, that she know his name, but first things first. The Raiders were enemies of his hometown Seattle.

"What?"

"The Raiders? You're a Raiders fan?"

She looked down and shrugged.

"Go team."

Lisa peered in an angry squint at the sunlight and proceeded to the kitchen. Waddy heard the refrigerator open and shut, pans banging, cupboard doors clattering. She reappeared, sipping at the lip of a mug.

"Listen, Bush. If we're going to get along, you need to know this. I can't stand perfection in a housemate. Coffee made, dishwasher dishes loaded in descending order. Me, I'm a slob."

Lisa pulled out a chair and sat cross-legged on it. Waddy looked at her.

"I mean," he managed, "do you root for them?"

"Who?"

He gave up. Just as he was about to offer her a section of the paper, the door of her room opened. He looked to Lisa in alarm—could it be an intruder? She went on sipping. Gray-flannelled trousers appeared on the stairs and hesitated. Waddy couldn't see their owner. The trousers paused and descended spryly. Atop them was a male torso, and atop that the sheepish face of Mortimer Dooberry.

"Well," he said and rubbed his hands together. "Well. Breakfast, eh?"

"Yes, sir," Waddy answered.

"What do you have there, Brush? Cereal?"

"Rice Krispies." Waddy pushed his bowl over a few inches, intending to demonstrate rather than offer. There were only a few grains left.

"I could go for a real meal. Bacon and eggs. Maybe I'll just drive into town."

Waddy didn't respond. Lisa took the sports section and turned to the results of the women's marathon.

"Lisa?" Dooberry's face glowed. For months his libido had been vacationing in a distant clime, and he'd assumed it had taken up permanent residence. Last night it had returned.

"Hmm?"

"How does that sound, a real breakfast?"

"No, thanks. I need to get to work."

"Work? Oh, yes," said Dooberry, embarrassed by the word. "Well then."

Waddy carried his bowl and mug to the kitchen. Hero waited patiently at the back door. Waddy went out barefoot. The dog looked up at him.

"That's it? Out the front and around to the back? So you lost a leg. Is that any reason to be a wuss?" Waddy read the dog's slow blink as an apology.

"Race you up the hill." Waddy took off. Hero walked unsteadily toward him. Waddy turned at the road and ran back down. Hero followed at a walk. Waddy rubbed him behind the ears.

"Not bad, but not a romp." After two more trips Hero was risking a trot.

Inside, Dooberry had gone. Lisa sat before two slices of wheat toast and was carefully blading organically grown raspberry preserves onto one.

"Look at this," she said to no one in particular. "Twenty-six miles over two mountain passes. This chick does it in under five hours. Forty-five hundred feet of elevation gain." Her mouth was filled with bread and jam but Waddy understood her clearly. "What a bitch."

~

He walked self-consciously through the main terminal. Usually, to avoid the public, Hollister reached his aircraft through the FBO, where private planes were serviced, but last night's pharmacology had left him dehydrated and he was desperate for a large water. Happily it was too early for a crowd. No one noticed him.

He got his bottle and turned to leave. A cheerful young man in a saffron robe blocked his way.

"We're trying to raise money ... "

"Beat it, asshole."

"We also do readings. Past, present, or future lives." The boy walked along with him as he went out to the tarmac.

"Like fortune-telling?"

"Sort of. We read your aura. No charge if we fail."

Hollister turned. "You're on."

"I'll need both your hands." Hollister obliged by putting the bottle down. He grasped the boy's extended fingers. The boy closed his eyes and stood silently for a full minute.

"You're giving off a strong sensation."

"Must have been the dope."

"Very strong. Very strong message."

"So what does it say?"

"You're going to hit a new peak."

"When?"

"Not too long. Maybe this winter."

"A new peak," Hollister repeated happily. Retrieved his water. It was a timely assurance—Hollister had been worried he was sliding from favor. He peeled a bill from a roll in his pocket.

"Hey, thanks." The money disappeared into the robe.

"No problem." Hollister broke the seal on the bottle and took a long and satisfying swig. A new peak.

~

The organizing committee for the annual Snow Ball held its first meeting in an anteroom of the Hotel Jerome. Mary Finch had agreed to chair the group out of frustration. The ball was an Aspen tradition, to end the winter social season. Lately it had run a loss, the organizers having overspent on what Mary considered frills. Her purpose was to get back to profitability. Never mind that the disease it benefited, while suitably unpleasant, had been surpassed by more fashionable ills.

The committee was thrilled. Mary and Gene Finch were old Aspen, rare sightings midst the bright plumage. They skied on old equipment, attended concerts for the music. The Finches kept happily to themselves, and the local society column referred to them, when it did so at all, as the Rosy Finches.

"I realize this may seem old-fashioned," Mary was saying, "but we should make money. That, after all, is the idea."

Rochelle Kaye was a supporter. "But, if you'll excuse me, Mary, I'd like to see a broader representation on our committee."

"Who do you have in mind?"

"Well, we need to attract all kinds. Aspen is becoming diverse. We need to get some diverse people in."

The idea was roundly praised, though no one took it seriously. The only black anyone could think of was a famous television newscaster, and he'd been asked to (and had declined) the board of everything from Rolfers for a Fur-Free Aspen to B'nai B'rith.

"Asian Americans," said one. "Victor Grant," said another. Mary wrote down Color and Money.

"Any other groups we should try to nab?" Mary asked.

"The Hollywood set," Rochelle volunteered. "The Glitzianas."

"Oh," said Tiffany. "I'd like that. Mix and do good at the same time."

"There's a significant Mexican population moving in," someone called.

"Trouble is," Mary said, "I don't know any of them. Do you?" The group looked around dolefully.

～

Flavia and Carmen found their pas de deux restful and satisfying. They enjoyed the time to themselves. Peyton was fun, but he hogged the mirrors. Besides, the women liked each other.

This meeting had been arranged after Carmen's hours. Flavia had brought her two valises of old clothes. She'd first packed them for Second Hand Rose, the used clothing store, but she preferred that they go to her beautiful friend.

Carmen was thrilled. The labels meant nothing to her, but she had a good eye and appreciated the excellent fabrics. "Maybe," Flavia confided to her, "that's why we're soul sisters. *Irmãs de coração.* I was *una mendiga,* a beggar, before I got into modeling. These are the last of what I walked off with. They look terrific on you."

And they did. On the first floor the women passed the assistant manager. He lowered his eyes in greeting.

Their path led them by the committee meeting room. Someone called out to Flavia.

It was the actress from Pantagruel's that first night. Flavia rummaged for her name, but remembered only that it was a famous New York retailer. For the life of her she couldn't get it. Not Ann Taylor, not Bendel, neither Hammacher nor Schlemmer.

It didn't matter. Tiffany introduced her around and Flavia

introduced her friend Doña Carmen Siquieros to women fully prepared to think the best of them.

Carmen made that easy. In her Ferragamo skirt, a mocha faux hide with an irregular and scalloped hem, and a Versace blouse of fuchsia silk, she clearly was someone to know. They sat and chatted. By the time they had downed two rounds, Chivas for Flavia and Kahlua and cream for Carmen, both had agreed to join the committee. Mary Finch drew a neat pencil line through one of her words.

~

"Just a minute, my other line's ringing." He hit the button on his cell. One of the world's leading designers of men's fashion, a name gracing the dearest of bespoke suits, waited patiently for his return. He punched back.

"Sorry, Lou. Listen, you tell Barney's they don't put your socks on the main floor they can put them where the sun don't shine. No ifs, ands, or buts." Maybe butts, Justin thought, but kept it to himself—puns don't travel well. Besides, Lou was in no mood. One of the six great designers, no one can touch him for that urbane Milanese look, but he can't handle a little spat. Designers should be kept on an island. "Third floor men's, that's a cemetery. You tell them first floor by the entrance and stick by it. Gotta run." Punched in line two.

"Philida. Sweetie. Sorry to keep you. You wouldn't believe the help grown men need. What's up?"

"Mr. Kaye, I simply want you to know that we're getting ready to oppose your application."

"I expected no less. I'm disappointed but not surprised."

"I wonder if you know that the plat on file doesn't show the burial grounds. The drawing you're using is really worse for your case."

"Well," and he smiled. "I believe in full disclosure."

They didn't call him the Clark Clifford of Seventh Avenue for nothing. He spread the elevations on his desk. The little cabins were coming in above estimates. They'd had to go to Wyoming to find the silvered planks that went so well with the forest green tile roof. If the buildings were up, he'd shoot his fall line there. Wonderful background. Deduct his dues.

"In the same spirit," Philida continued, "I should tell you that several Native American organizations are joining us. They have an interest in this too."

"Excellent. Every interested party ought to be represented."

"They won't simply be represented, Mr. Kaye. Their lawyer is the best in the country at this sort of thing."

"Philida, I'm delighted. I want a solution where everyone wins."

She didn't respond, and he waited briefly for her to say something. "Believe me," he added.

She gave out a skeptical "Hmm" and rang off.

Twelve

Waddy breezed through the base fantasies faster than he expected. He showed his work to Lisa. Just like the old days, watching the back of her head as she monitored the algorithms on the screen. He tried to visualize his infatuation leaving her shoulders, a cartoon angel floating free. Nothing happened.

Dooberry scolded them about exceeding estimates. The money he'd raised had to last through the spring—no results by then, he warned, they were all out of jobs.

Finished with her research, Lisa jumped into the programming with the enthusiasm of a Marine recruit. Up at five writing code, calisthenics at eight, a light breakfast, and back to work. She napped after lunch and followed that with an hour's tear on one of the road bikes Victor Grant had left for their amusement. Waddy watched her streak off from the Norman farmhouse that was the garage, her body bratwursted into spandex, her helmet bent over the handlebars in a pose of prayer. Exactly sixty minutes later she returned, read her vital signs from the LED strapped to her wrist, and announced her conclusions.

"Point three miles gain, a personal record." Or, "Just didn't have it today. Menses, I'd guess."

Waddy and Hero went out on their own. Hero's running lessons were beginning to show effects. He galumphed along beside Waddy on hikes up Conundrum Creek to fish and ahead of Waddy on lazy bike rides. Waddy told him of Etta's theory that Lisa was simply not the ideal romantic interest. Her single-mindedness, for one thing. "For a second," he told the bounding dog, "I find it difficult to overlook her inability to remember my name." Dooberry paid an occasional visit. He was, he explained, chasing money. More and more he affected the accent of an RAF officer in a war movie, the sound one might make trying to unstick a wad of peanut butter from one's palate. *Mnyaa.*

As a team, Waddy and Lisa worked well. They knew the shortcuts, they quickly filled the gaps. They dipped into the vast Web libraries of computer-generated 3-D images available to amateur and professional gamesman alike. Less Apollo, more Dionysus.

"Well," Dooberry told them. "It seems you chaps are hard at it. *Mnyaa.* I'll report in." Here he pointed to his temple as if he had imagined them, "to the potential investors. *Mnyaa.*"

∿

The strain in the telephone voice of his Aspen lawyer made Justin smile. The fellow is upset. He seems to think he's in a real life, there at the end of the yellow brick road. Let him come down here and wrestle the banks about the spring line.

"So they're turning on us. We don't need them. We'll win at the hearing. They're too late."

"Justin, believe me. The Friends of the Friendless Earth are never too late. They stopped Disney in the Sequoia forests, Del Webb in the Everglades. They have a following."

Justin took a handkerchief from the pocket of his silk tweed jacket and buffed finger marks from the glass desktop. Up Sixth Avenue, by the Time Warner building, an ambulance was trying to get through a blocked intersection. Beyond, the leaves of Central Park were readying their October turn. Poor sap. He's two thousand miles away from the action.

"So what's the worst they can do to me?"

"They've already started. They filed for an injunction. They say that either your old mining plat with the Arapaho burial grounds is accurate, in which case you can't disturb the sleeping ancestors, or it's inaccurate, in which case you can't disturb the environment."

Isn't that something? Every fall the trees turn the same color, and no one bitches. No columnist complains that it's last year's palette, that God has run dry and He should give way to the Italians.

"Listen. I don't know who came up with all these dead Indians. Maybe my plat is wrong. Am I to blame?" Of course, it'd be easier for God. No need to refinance inventory. And He could smite the Italian designers like He did the Canaanites.

"They think yes, Justin. They're hopping mad."

What about fall colors for spring? A paradigm shift. No, it's a dumb idea. Stick with what works. Still, the spring line needs a theme.

"What's next?"

"A hearing. Pitkin County District Court, full of tree huggers. And that's not the worst news."

"What is?"

"The Native American groups have entered an appearance and hired Silverheels Brumberger."

"Who?"

"Silverheels Brumberger? The most famous Indian lawyer in the country. The man who got the Tlingits three hundred million dollars for the Point Barrow pipeline and the Louisiana Cherokee royalties on every derrick in the Gulf of Mexico. Irving Brumberger? The old Indian fighter?"

"Silverheels his Indian name?"

"That's what *Time* called him. The Cherokee gave him a warbonnet and an unpronounceable name."

"They have Silverheels, we have you. We'll see them in court."

"Justin, you'll get murdered. A dozen rich guys from New York and Beverly Hills want to shoot duck, so they plan to dig up wilderness and trample dead Indians."

"One plat shows a cemetery, one shows none. Maybe there are no Indians."

"Not the point. Public opinion, Justin."

"So?"

"So we need to approach Brumberger. I should explore settlement."

Justin envisioned the Aspen lawyer, a callow lad, sitting underneath diplomas from some school where slalom is a major, his border collie waiting patiently for the conversation to end so he and his master can toss a Frisbee. That's not who should negotiate with Brumberger.

"This Brumberger, he's in the west?"

"No." The sound of papers shuffling. "New York City. Trump Tower. Do you know where that is?"

Justin spun his Bertoia chair and examined the building that housed his adversary.

"Yes, yes. Maybe I'll just walk over and see him."

"Well, Justin. I don't recommend that. Remember he's a highly sophisticated advocate. You should have a lawyer present."

Derricks in the Gulf of Mexico. Interesting.

"I'll take my chances." Man brings his family out on an old Chris-Craft launch to see his oil derrick. Three kids, a youngish father, Ben Affleck gone gray. Blazer with heraldry, brass buttons. Long white flannels, maybe a pencil stripe from the thirties. The mother? Fair, to show off strong floral prints, Blythe Danner as dame of the manor. Early in the morning, sun coming off the ocean. Lots of bright work on the boat. A couple of roughnecks stand on the derrick in my tees. Sleeves turned up, grimy, old money meets new.

They rang off.

"Christine," Justin rang his head of design. "See if we can find an antique motor launch. Lots of wood and chrome. And that model we used in Garmisch? The one that looks like Blythe Danner?"

❧

Victor Grant unloaded the Nishiki from the truck's rack. The cell was already Velcroed to the handlebars, his trainer had done that. He spoke "office" and got his administrative aide.

"Isabelle?"

"Yes, boss."

"You ready for me?"

"Ready."

"Go ahead and transmit."

The aide hit a button and the phone programmed the telephone numbers, in the order she suggested he make them. Grant checked the tire pressure. Just right. That Isabelle has a good future. She might think this is a waste of an MBA, but everything is in the details. Grant plugged in the earpiece from the phone and strapped on his helmet.

This was the time for eastern Long Island. No crowds, no invitations, just sea and sand. Dunmere Lane as it extended into Further Lane had new tar and only occasional traffic. Grant ran his thumbs around the hems of his biking shorts, swung onto the bike, and pushed off. He did a leg past the golf club, around Sagaponak Pond, the Dune Road cul-de-sac. He'd had his intern clock it, in a respectable fifteen minutes. A sprint to warm up. Now he punched the computer to a lower pace, steered himself onto the Montauk Highway where he could cruise, and hit the button for his first call.

"Grant here."

"Yes, Victor." The man had been standing by.

"I'm really interested in seeing our investment made liquid by the end of the year. I wonder what your plans are for getting us out."

"Well, Victor. The markets are off."

"Yes, I've heard."

"Sorry. I just mean it's not a good time for an IPO."

"I've heard that too. I try to keep up."

"We have an inquiry from one or two mezzanine funds, but the company needs the money. I was hoping you'd stay in."

"Which funds?" Grant asked.

The man gave the names grudgingly.

"We need liquidity. You can go ahead and try to sell them for yourself, in which case I'll block it and you'll starve. Or you can sell them our piece. Help us out. Then they'll be stockholders. You know what stockholders are? They're people in the stocks. Once they're in, you hit them up for more."

There was a moment's silence. Grant ticked up the rate five miles. If he fell below that pace the computer would beep. It didn't.

"Do you want out completely?" Grant heard retreat in the man's voice. "If you'd just stay in, say half, we could both be served."

"Completely."

"What's my choice?"

Grant ignored the question. "Tell the mezzes you're not looking for equity right now. The company's strong, you have me as a partner, an IPO's a year away. If they want in, they can call me. Tell them that at the right price, you think you could convince me to get out of the way."

"What price?"

"Leave that to me." He thought he heard the man say something in assent, but he couldn't be sure. He clicked off and hit the automatic call button. The undersecretary's name and number came up on the screen.

He was placed on hold. He relaxed. What the hell—his view was of breaking Atlantic surf, he could afford to be second banana.

When the undersecretary came on, Grant filled him in on Wise Mother.

"I'm expecting they'll have the usual financing bumps along the road. Those bumps are our decision points. If you want to buy in, we'll make mountains of those molehills."

"We want in. I have authority." He mentioned a price, a multiplier of each subscriber. That's how databases sold, as a function of names.

"I'll have my lawyers do up a contract," Grant said.

"How will you know about their bumps?"

"That's why I'm calling. Send me someone to keep an eye on them. You must have people trained to do that." Grant came to a part of the road that had been taken over by sand and sawgrass. He geared down and pedaled hard.

"I know just the fellow. How long will you need him?"

"Let's give them time. Say the first week in December? Let me guess. He's West Point."

"Corps to the core."

Grant ignored the remark. He didn't see the use of puns. "Name?"

"Don't know yet. He'll use an alias. We don't want him tied back here. But you won't have any trouble recognizing him."

"How's that?"

"He has benign symptoms of Waardenburg's Syndrome."

"I beg your pardon?"

"Waardenburg's Syndrome. Genetic, can result in deafness. Not in him, though. All he has is one white eyelash and a white forelock."

〰

It was the very last day of calendar summer. In the high Colorado Rockies, where interstitial seasons do not hold to script, fall had been in the air for weeks. On the valley floor the leaves of cottonwoods had turned to maize, and the deciduous groves on the hillsides were yielding gold by posture and altitude. The change came first to the north faces. Out on the Maroon Bells road, the sun shone low and bright through the translucent leaves and lit up the sides of the road. Waddy could have been driving through an MGM musical. Down by the lake, two lovers lay on a blanket, his head in her lap, she shielding his eyes as he read to her. Waddy watched them and felt a mild anguish—if only love would sink its gentle teeth into him.

He pulled in below the Walton Club site, laced on his sneakers, and set off to jog though the colors. They started down a game path that followed the stream, he keeping his eyes on the uneven ground. Hero regularly ran ahead and came back to urge him on. "Your lessons are over," Waddy told him. "And stop showing off. You're a leg up on me."

He almost ran over the man.

"Hey."

The kneeling fellow looked up—Waddy knew him: the man who tickled fish.

Marco held up his hand. Waddy peered over his shoulder. "Feeding."

Waddy searched the black water and saw nothing. Just as he was about to jog off, a submerged form broke the surface and disappeared.

"They feeding," Marco said again.

"Who is?"

"You see 'em? Two hens and a male."

Waddy peered harder. A shape black and liquid as the stream grew large, then small. He realized the trout had risen.

"They're feeding," Waddy said. "On what?"

Marco didn't answer. Continued to kneel, perfectly still. Then his arm went out, snared the air, and he opened his fist.

"Damselfly." There in his palm a speck of life unfolded its elliptical wings, fluttered, and flew off.

"Nice."

"Gimme a hand?"

"Sure." Waddy and Hero followed him up the hill. Waddy helped Marco load debris into the truck bed. A crushed five-gallon gas can, a bolt and nut rusted together, and, thick as a wrist, twelve feet of corroded cable. Last, a rusted iron and oak contraption, easily six feet long.

"What do you suppose it is?"

Marco wiped his nose on the sleeve of his work shirt.

"Pulley arm. For sluicing slag."

"Mining?"

"Sure."

"You find other mining stuff?"

"Yep. Piece of a bellows. Ore bucket down the stream."

"Valuable?"

Marco looked at him with surprise. "Not to me."

Together they hefted the arm into the truck bed. Marco drove man and dog to the Volkswagen.

"Lot of mines in these hills?"

"Enough."

"They ever strike it rich?"

"Here? Don't think so. Don't keep people from trying, though." The truck came to a ford in the stream and Marco got out to lock in the hubs. Motored across and up the other side.

"Want a hand at the dump?"

"Ain't goin' to the dump. Takin' it home."

"Home? What are you going to do with it?"

"Nothin'."

"Want a hand?"

Marco looked back through the window. "Sure."

Marco turned off the pass down an unmarked lane to his Quonset hut. Opened the padlocked door and pulled the chain on the bare light.

"Hey," said Waddy. Inside were row upon row of hand-hewn shelves, each tipped at a slight angle so one could view them from the single aisle down the middle. Arrowheads, hook-and-eye sets, geodes. Shovels and windlasses and bits of a derrick, a peg-tooth harrow, a hay rake, a lister, a swivel plow missing a handle, three meat grinders, and a fender from an Indian motorcycle. Hero found a stray bone on the floor and brought it to Waddy's feet.

"Hey," Waddy said again. "Look at this. You sell it?"

"It's just stuff."

"You collect it?"

"Yep."

"What for?"

Marco shrugged. Together they dragged the pulley arm to the back of the hut. They laid it lengthwise between Marco's dozer and a wooden spool that had carried electric wire.

"Thanks."

"No problem."

"That fellow was right." Marco scratched Hero under the chin.

"What fellow?"

"Fellow I met at the dump. Said if I'd help him move a box out to the airport, why, somebody's aunt would help me. Said we needed more aunts. 'Cept you're nobody's aunt. Maybe uncle."

Waddy smiled. "Ants. Black fellow, no hair on top?"

"Funny eye. That's him. He'd found this box, maybe six foot long. Wanted it moved to the airport. I hauled it for him."

Waddy studied him. "Say anything about reciprocating surpluses?"

"Can't be sure."

"What did he want the box for?"

"Can't be sure," Marco said. "Just said I'd be seeing aunts."

Waddy and Hero headed down the mountain to the Jerome. Weekly status meeting with Dooberry. The boss had given up visiting the guesthouse, was spending all his time looking for new investors. After Dooberry's single encounter with Lisa, she had dropped him. Waddy knew the feeling. In the parking lot, Mrs. Dooberry and one of the shareholders, Mr. Post, were leaving. Waddy honked and she waved.

Code was going in smoothly. Waddy had templates for six basic fantasies. At ten, they planned on a focus group, to test the concept. Would seeing yourself in the backfield of the Green Bay Packers encourage you to reveal all your other personal data? Would anyone bite?

He locked Hero in the car, its window rolled down so the dog could smell the world.

Dooberry sat at a corner table. In an English worsted suit, wide points on his shirt collar, a solid navy tie. Out of place as a panhandler, which of course he was.

Waddy gave him the numbers for the week. Each template could be individualized with about two hundred lines of ASCII. Estimated programmer time to bring a subscriber from template to product, less than an hour. They both ordered beer, Dooberry a Newcastle, warm.

"Well done, Brush. I'll relay this to our stockholders. Past and future. Must keep an eye to the future, you know." Dooberry took a sip and gave two fingers up, the Churchill victory sign. "Room temperature, don't you see. Brings out the flavor. *Mnyaa.*"

Dooberry jotted notes from Waddy's report on a pad he pulled from his inside pocket. "Perfect," he said. "We will capture that subscriber and his dreams for less than forty dollars. His data will turn at the rate of thirty-six times a year, at a buck and a half per. So, we'll have our money back in … ," and he squinted at the page.

" ... about nine months."

"About nine months. And we'll still own the data, go on selling it. That'll work."

Dooberry left and Waddy ordered a second. The summer crowds had gone, and the Jerome Bar was habitable again. Until happy hour, when the glib chirp of mating would drive Waddy, nursing a chronic melancholia, into the streets. Miz Eubanks was right. Lisa wasn't responding. He'd asked that very morning how she felt about the possible end of Wise Mother. She'd launched into a techno-philosophic answer, and he said, "No. I mean as a woman. How do you feel about it as a woman?"

"I don't think of myself as a woman," she said. "I think of myself as a man, except I'm smart and I menstruate."

He liked what he'd done. The templates met the need. To customize they would use a lot of freeware—canned backgrounds—and a little handwork. It wasn't the job that had him down, it was all this *life* around him. All this mitosis and meiosis, the to-ing and fro-ing. In his four Aspen months he had yet to meet an interesting woman. Except Annalee—she was terrific—but living with a beautiful woman you can't touch is torment. Like mermaids, he thought. Who thought that one up?

And as he sat contemplating myth and mermaid, the very source of his musings sat down in Dooberry's chair and touched a fingertip to the top of his hand.

"Hey! I was just thinking of you."

"And what were you thinking?" Annalee asked.

"I was thinking you were like the Sirens."

"I'm flattered."

Waddy hadn't the heart to correct her. "A beer?"

"Can't. On my way to work. I was passing by and saw you in the window, looking sad."

"Sad? No, not at all. I'm aces. The project is a great success. I'm enjoying it."

"I hear you're living with that woman Laroux."

"Yes. Lisa. I knew Lisa from Washington. State of."

Annalee frowned. "Overcast, I hear, State of."

"No need to be snide. And you? How are you?"

"Oh, I'm aces too."

"Yes? Oh, I'm glad. And have you found ... a friend?"

"You mean to replace you? No, you have proved irreplaceable."

"I have?"

"You have."

"You need to tell me," for her remark had stayed with him, "about the guppies."

Annalee pursed her lips and half-closed the larger of her cool green eyes in thought. "I don't want to discourage your career."

"My career will be discouraged when the salary runs out."

"Well," and Annalee balanced the cork coaster on its edge. "I'm all for mystery. It's the best thing we do. Memory, love, creation. I'm not a fan of messing around with them."

"And you think, by coding fantasies, we're messing around."

She made a quick sound with her tongue as if sucking a lozenge. "I do."

"And the guppies?"

"When I was maybe three, we had guppies. They have these little panels of color, when the sun hits, and my mother and us kids loved to watch those colors dart around. So my sister and I decided for Mother's Day we'd make her a bracelet of colors. Decoupage, you ever do decoupage?"

"Can't say as I have."

"We netted the guppies and left them to dry. When we came back that afternoon to do the bracelet ... "

"No colors."

Annalee smiled sadly. There was a sharp rap on the window by their table. Frankie Rusticana pointed urgently to his watch.

"Must go."

"Must?"

"Yes, yes. Tonight Pantagruel is proud to present Icelandic salmon *en croute*. I have the *en croute* yet to do."

"Well toodle-oo."

Annalee gave a damp sigh. "Toodle-oo." And off she went.

~

The very next day the arctic jet stream herniated across the Canadian border. From the south, moist air swept up the Sea of Cortez and spilled into the bowl west of the Continental Divide. The moisture crystallized into flakes, each conceived in its Maker's eye, a fastidiousness lost on those below. And these million inventions fell wetly, densely on the Grand Mesa, on the unpicked peaches in the orchards of Montrose, on the charging Yampa River flowing out of Oak Creek and west into the canyons of Utah, on the great peaks of Sneffles and Ouray and Taylor, and democratically—one of the few democratic events in the Roaring Fork Valley—on the rich and poor of Aspen.

Indeed most of the rich had long departed. Victor Grant had left after the music season. To celebrate Peyton's three-month stash and the double-digit returns Chloe achieved in a sideways market, the Posts had gone to sail the Aegean.

Etta spent the first day of autumn putting the Unimog on blocks. She did the dirty work: jacking up the ends alternately, sliding cinder blocks under the axles. She emptied the radiator, drained the crankcase into two gallon jugs, and unhitched the battery cables. Feeling the need for exercise, she rotated the tires. Sherry she shipped off to a Vermont seminar on the air hammer, and she herself headed to Tulsa carrying a stack of seismic data on a promising Jurassic trap in eastern Montana. Justin Kaye, considering the possibilities of taffeta for the spring line, concentrated on business and put off his rendezvous with Silverheels Brumberger.

And as the homeowners departed so did the barkers and buyers and hustlers and healers and stylists and drummers and dressers who served them. The woman who Rolfed for regularity and the man who chanted away arthritis went off together to Carmel, the peyote-cultivating yogi to Rancho Mirage, the pyramid-maker to Jupiter Island. The woman who counted the flecks in your iris to advise on wardrobe colors and life strategies opened up shop in the Keys. Having had a banner season, the canine therapist went to his home in La Jolla and took six months off.

The working class stayed on. Carmen Siquieros kept at making beds and cleaning toilets. Dooberry withdrew from the Wise Mother account a chunk small enough, he hoped, to go unnoticed and sent Flavia away to the equestrian center at San Miguel de Allende, where she could ride to her heart's content. Her appetites went with her. In the absence of their heated persistence, Dooberry could continue to believe it was her heart, rather than some other, but no less vital, organ, that was in need.

Dooberry himself stayed in town. Not that he had anything to do at the Grant guesthouse, but he was expected to make an appearance. Every time he sluffed off, the news of his inattention was reported to Mr. Grant by his staff. Annalee still greeted diners, though there were fewer of them. Bereft of celebrities and the *Forbes* fifty, Pantagruel closed weekdays until ski season.

Lisa extended her biking range to thirty-eight kilometers and sentenced her libido to hibernation. Waddy remained hard at work, spending long days in front of the computer screen. In the evening, while Lisa sped off to new personal records, Waddy began to help Marco sort through his summer's treasure trove. Marco Campaneris too went to winter ritual: when the snows flew, there was no earthmoving work. He signed on to run equipment for the ski company. He liked the night shift: no people, no boss, no hassle. But that job, like Aspen itself, would not begin until December. Until there was enough snow to ski on, Aspen closed down.

# II. The Winter

*The winter! The brightness that blinds you,*
*The white land locked tight as a drum,*
*The cold fear that follows and finds you,*
*The silence that bludgeons you dumb.*
*The snows that are older than history,*
*The woods where the weird shadows slant;*
*The stillness, the moonlight, the mystery,*
*I've bade 'em goodbye—but I can't.*

*—Robert Service, "The Spell of the Yukon"*

Thirteen

"Call me Irv."

A stunning size-four receptionist with mocha skin and an Afro left Justin at the door. Brumberger draped his arm around Justin's shoulder and pointed with a ringmaster's sweep to the view.

"Irv it is."

The offices overlooked the Deco splendor of Rockefeller Center and, in modest backdrop, riparian New Jersey. Below, early Christmas shoppers straywalked among the taxis and limos. On a clear day, Justin thought to say, you can see your clients' tepees. But didn't.

"This is very nice, Irv. Lovely taste." Justin took one of the crushed-leather club chairs Brumberger offered and his adversary took a second. "This is the way two men should talk," Brumberger assured him warmly.

"How's that?"

Brumberger flapped his hand. "At ease, face to face, reasoning together."

"Oh," Justin countered. "I thought you meant the Limoges and the zebrawood."

Brumberger nodded in appreciation.

"Don't knock it. If Geronimo'd had a better decorator, who knows? He might have had his own line of accessories instead of losing the West. But here I am telling *you*."

Justin Kaye bowed at the homage. He had selected a two-button that morning, midnight with a gray pencil stripe. One of sixty-four winter suits in his closets, all his design, this matched with an ecru shirt and solid aubergine tie. Not purple, a color he found excessive, but aubergine. The look was Averill Harriman—indeed he had used an Averill Harriman double in the *GQ* spread that September.

"Very nice indeed."

"I figure, Justin, treat yourself. If it only costs money, it's cheap. No reason to dress like a peasant just because you're from Pinsk."

Justin gave the slightest shiver. The words reflected his private canon. His fashion conglomerate—suitings, accessories, linens—rested on consumers' disposition to cling to a heritage they never had.

The meeting did not come at an easy time for Justin. The new line had been launched to dismal reviews. Justin had lost his gamble on peach as the color of the year—*Women's Wear Daily* called it a retro-stinker. Not a financial crisis quite yet.

Justin pointed to the wall. Facing him, identically framed pictures hung at eye level. Senators, movie stars, a vice president, tribal bigwigs, all embracing Silverheels Brumberger.

"I'll bet," he said, deciding the effect of his flattery would make up for its transparency, "I'll bet there's a story behind each of these."

"You'd win your bet. That is me with the Hopi, who were getting a screwing by Interior over a casino. That is me handing over a check to the Mohave for the rights to a marina by Lake Havasu. And there," twisting to see, "I'm being admitted as an honorary Cherokee." Justin rose to look closely.

"You know what it means to be admitted? They gave me my own name. In Cherokee."

"What is it?"

"Who can remember? It means, 'He who keeps every third row of corn.' You wear a warbonnet, sit on the floor, and smoke a pipe full of squirrel shit."

They laughed together. Justin understood this man. He was someone who could look charm in the eye and not be afraid. The receptionist returned, passed a plate of biscotti, and flashed Justin a glass-breaking smile. They all want into the business.

"So, Justin, tell me. What can I do for you? You didn't come here to suds me up."

"No. No, I didn't. We have a problem in Colorado, Irv."

"We do? Not me. How could I have a problem with you?"

"The Isaak Walton Rod and Gun Preserve."

"That? The sacred burial grounds? That's you?"

"I'm the developer. And that one house lot, that's for me. There's a lot of money at stake."

"Justin, don't bullshit a bullshitter. It doesn't work. This isn't about money."

"It's not? You have this on a contingency. What do you get if you win, a clavicle and a drumstick?"

"This is about principle." Brumberger shook a demonstrative finger in the air. "Your town is full of people who can afford principle. A principle of the Native Americans is threatened, and they're paying me to defend it."

"Poor babies."

"That's some town you have there. Nothing but millionaires."

Justin shook his head slowly. It was a common mistake.

"Millionaires leave Aspen in droves. They sell little businesses, come with fourteen, fifteen mil, and find they can't manage. They haven't done the math."

"What's the math?" Brumberger was interested.

"They need a place to live. Two million bucks buys a shanty. Someone who thinks he just got rich doesn't want to live in it. So he spends six or seven on a house and another mil fixing it up. Minimum. Average house price in town last year was six. Now he needs toys. What's the use of being there without toys? A couple SUVs, skis for powder, Nordic, hardpack. Another half mil goes to outfit him and the little lady. Instead of the wad he thought he'd have to invest, he's down to half. It scares him, so he puts what's left in munis. Now he's out of the market, he has nothing to tell his friends, and he's behind the averages. He can't live on it. His pool man costs five hundred a visit, and his gardener seven. He can't do it. If he'd stayed in Des Moines, he'd be rich. So after a year or two scraping by, ducking neighbors who hit him up for charities, a grand here, a grand there, a day's rafting with a credible *grand cru*, proceeds to MS, he packs up and heads home."

"Tough life. So who stays?"

"The ones with real money. Enough so life is perfect. No electric lines above ground, no cellulite, no excavated Indians."

Brumberger flicked at the lobe of his ear. "Let's get down to business," he said.

Justin was ready. "First things first. If I do a deal with you, I don't want those tree huggers to have a second bite. You have to control FFE."

"You want one spokesman for all the plaintiffs?"

"That's what I want, Irv."

"I can't promise ... "

"You can ask. Philida Post thinks you're the best. She told me."

"Justin, schmaltz gives me heartburn. I'll ask. Next?"

"You got the drawing?" Brumberger motioned him over to a library table by the south window. On it was spread a copy of Justin's revised plat.

"Here? Am I right? Here is where you want to build?" He had his finger in the square labeled Arapaho burial grounds.

"The issue is, what is there? That's where I want to build if there are no graves."

"But if there *are* graves, Justin. Be reasonable. You'll have your Jacuzzi smack on their *succah*. Be reasonable. That's our lawsuit."

This was going just the way Justin had planned it. He nodded and did a silent count so his eagerness wouldn't show.

"On the filed plat there's no cemetery, on this old plat there is. We don't need a lawsuit, we can do this ourselves. Tell you what, Irv. I'll do test holes. Not only here," Justin indicated the square. "As many as you like. If we find a dead Indian, we don't dig. We give them elbow room."

"Whose cost?"

"My cost. I pick up all costs. But if we don't find anything, you drop the lawsuit. Sound fair?"

"You'll need to be supervised. You can't go and disturb the sites without supervision. The shaman will need to be there in case you find his uncle."

"The shaman it is. He can stay in our guesthouse. Sauna, views of Snowmass."

Brumberger considered the offer. "Someone from the tribe will have to be there. Also the FFE. Miss Post."

"Anyone you like. Sound fair?"

Brumberger rolled up the plat and secured it with two rubber bands. "When will all this happen?"

"We can't dig 'til spring. There's two feet of snow up there now. You postpone the court hearing. As soon as the snow melts, I'll get my man up there, take a look. What do you think?"

"I'll have to speak to the tribal council."

In the reception room Justin returned the secretary's smile. She was a stunner. Too bad, not quite right. Something in the neck, too short. Otherwise he'd use her for the formal shoot. For formal they were showing crimsons, and a new sea emerald. That chocolate skin would show gorgeous off the shoulder.

∾

The pace of the season slowed in the cool air, and with it the progress of the Wise Mother database. Fantasies were turning out to be complicated. Lisa's studies showed they drew heavily on experience.

"It's basic Jung," she explained. "If a child's first viewing of his mother in a bath is associated with the mackerel they had at dinner, he may forever be eroticized by mackerel. But it's one of a kind. Fantasies are going to be tough to digitize."

Lisa told Waddy and Dooberry this at an early December meeting. The town was quiet and they were able to park on Main only yards from the Jerome Bar. While they waited, Lisa doodled algorithms in a notebook while Waddy thumbed through an L. L. Bean catalog. Dooberry arrived in a rush, smoothed out his cashmere blazer, and patted the small crest on its pocket.

They told him he simply would have to spend some money to get their problem solved. Lisa had already assessed where they might go for help. "There are major companies," she said, "doing software games. Including Grant's."

Dooberry reached into his jacket and tugged at his French cuffs. "Out of the question. They would take us over in a minute. Freeze us out."

"But," Lisa persevered, "we're at a dead end."

"That, as we say, is hard cheese. We're on a tight budget. Unless we have something to show, we're out of money by June."

"This June? You raised money for only nine months' work? This can't be done in nine months."

Dooberry folded his lower lip over his upper. He would not let this woman make him feel guilty over the considerable salary he had pocketed. This woman, who had told him when he called, the day he shipped Flavia to San Miguel, an innocent dinner invitation, Sorry, Mortimer. Once was lovely, but once was enough. I never repeat myself. The woman had no sentiment. And certainly no gratitude.

"I'll ask. But don't get your hopes up. Mr. Grant has said, No more dough, the Posts are on a sloop off Ephesus and won't be bothered. Without good news, I can't raise money."

Dooberry stood, left an inadequate ten-dollar bill for the tab, and walked out.

At the table behind them, his back to the threesome and his face in the prow of a *Wall Street Journal*, a man allowed himself a narrow smile. The man had dark hair with a distinguishing white forelock. Victor Grant had told him about the regular status meetings.

"Time to circulate my résumé," Lisa said, and sucked the last puddle of lemonade from below the ice cubes.

"Oh, I don't know." Waddy studied the catalog. A moss green anorak, marked down twenty percent. His mother said the solution to any problem was there all along, like the second sock in the drawer. Just look again.

"We need a device to translate words into pictures, right?"

"Right," said Lisa. Her eyes roamed the room.

"So maybe we do that. Maybe," he turned the catalog around so she could see the anorak, "maybe we just list all the words that a subscriber might use, include *mackerel*, and let the program pick from our catalog."

"All the words?"

"Sure. How many can there be?"

"Words? The *Oxford Unabridged* has about half a million. Your average desk dictionary under a hundred thousand."

"There," Waddy said comfortingly. "That's a start. And you wouldn't need all of them."

"No, you wouldn't. Shakespeare only used maybe twenty thousand."

"Exactly. You cull them, you pick out nouns. Let the rest go. A few adjectives to subclassify the nouns."

Lisa leaned forward. "So how does the brain access words from the computer?"

Waddy went back to the page of parkas. "Don't know. Yet."

Lisa nodded at him and narrowed her eyes. It was a menacing sight. "Bush," she began.

"Brush."

"Brush. You just may be about to earn your salary."

❧

He left the warm cab of the snowcat. On the short walk to the hut at the top of Lift 7, cold stung Marco's face. He squinted at the sparkling pinholes of starlight to bring them into focus. Fresh snow—they'll be out early to track it up. Only one sound, and that a cold one, the crunch of his Caribou boots. Inside the hut, he fired the propane heater and plugged in the hot plate. He would have coffee with his sweet roll.

He'd worked four hours packing trails. He liked the job—alone on the top of Ajax Mountain, the hum of the big diesel to keep him company. Below, the occasional glimmer of another Cat's headlight flashed among the white-caked spruces. Now inside, the heater blasting, he shed his quilted parka. Walked to the door, kicked his heel to the floor to jar loose packed snow, and unstrung his boots. The Caribous really worked—leather tops, rubber bases, lined with God knows what—but if you had to tramp around in subzero temperatures at ten thousand feet, they were made for tramping.

The bubble atop the tin percolator was showing earth-brown. Glad he'd brought it up. The kids working the day shift drank powdered coffees or that god-awful tea, but he liked a cup properly brewed. Kept fixings on hand, cleaned up after himself. On the day shift you got constant chatter. How's the snow? Another shitty day in paradise. Have a great day. Thin air must starve the brain.

Before this Marco had run the snow-making gun, a job that put him on the hill between midnight and six every day.

He liked the solitude, but the diesel compressor gave off an awful stink.

He balanced the sweet roll on the rim of the oversized white mug so the steam would warm it. He'd had it in his parka pocket since midnight, when he'd picked it up fresh at the bakery. A big disk with a glob of red jam in its center. Life can't get much better.

Marco flipped on the light. He preferred the dark; once you threw the switch, the outside magic disappeared. Never mind. It would reappear for him on his drive down. He still had to run the check on Lift 7. Now, stocking-footed and down to his wool pants and shirt, he opened the newspaper on the bare wooden table, spread a napkin beneath his mug and pastry, and pulled out the chair.

Justin Kaye and the Walton Club were back in the news. A settlement proposal had stayed the lawsuit. The story quoted his boss.

> "We'll not disturb a single bone of any Native American," Kaye assured interested parties. Philida Post, spokesperson for the Friends of the Friendless Earth, described herself as satisfied with this outcome. "We'd rather see this glorious meadow left intact. But Mr. Kaye's proposal is acceptable to us. A careful excavation of select sites will prove whether this area has any archaeologic significance."

They'd want him to work first thing in the spring, soon as the snow melts. 'Course, they don't know when the snow melts. They're not about to muck up that road during runoff, they'll leave that to me. I'll visit every so often, check snowpack, measure the ground frost. Late April, maybe May.

He folded the paper napkin carefully and put it into his pocket. Stuck the grounds in the garbage sack to pack down on the Cat, and washed up the percolator and mug in the sink. Good as new. Then he picked up the phone. The dispatcher, warm and cozy two thousand feet down the hill, answered.

"Campaneris. Top of 7. Eight inches new powder. Headed down."

Outside, the silent world had waited for him. The ski runs were cut to face north, so the snow stayed shaded. Even the December sun could take its toll. There it was, just cracking gray in the east. Feathery ribbons of cirrus, red and purple, mirrored its first light, still below the horizon. A shift in the thin air lifted snow pats from the needles of a nearby Engelmann spruce. They hit the ground with a pillowy plop, like the belch of a ghost. God, this is some country. Keep people off it and it's some country.

He ran the Cat down the edge of an intermediate run. Expert slopes you packed uphill. You didn't want the rear end of this thing beating you down the mountain. At the bottom, he stopped to cycle the lift once through.

By the housing, they'd built a cushy operator's cabin, floor raised off the ground to store the patrol's toboggans underneath. Marco walked to the motor house and noticed movement no more than a flutter, the snow resettling itself. He stuck a gloved hand into the parka's pocket, fetched a flashlight, and kneeled down to have a look.

A ptarmigan hen looked back at him. She had turned almost completely to winter dress, swan white, though on her back he could make out the remnants of the dappled brown she wore in summers. Off to the left, a rustle: there was her mate, sitting on a nest of pine needles and twine. Ptarmigan nest early, lay in spring. And this pair had chosen a corner not five feet from where thousands of skiers would board the lift.

He looked at his watch. There wasn't enough time to move the nest today. He'd have to do it after the lift closed, when the birds could follow and settle. But one day's crowds would drive these birds off. They'd hie out and miss a season. He went back to the snowcat and rummaged around for a Phillips screwdriver.

He started the lift. The noise shriveled his bladder. From within the housing came a screech like a rabbit caught by a coyote, then a series of clangings. In seconds a fuse tripped and the contraption shut down. The birds stayed put.

Marco looked about before picking up the phone. There, in a copse of naked aspen trees cordoned off from skiers, he would resettle the nest.

"Hey. Bottom of 7. We got trouble. Motor's out. Looks like one of the hinges on the box worked itself loose and fell into the gears. Flywheel's stripped. Must have been the vibrations."

Fourteen

A foul mood befell Etta. Back home they called it the Texas nicies. First Sherry had been expelled from the seminar in Rutland for taking his air hammer to the courthouse statue and undressing Justice to the waist. A few citizens petitioned to leave her uncovered—Rutland has a paucity of tourist attractions—but the movement failed. That prank cost Etta a five-hundred-dollar fine for drunk and disorderly and eleven thousand for remedial stonework.

The next day, the first of her Aspen Christmas stay, she discovered that the lift to her favorite ski runs had broken down. And to top it off, when she dropped by to see how her little scientific investment was doing, Mortimer Dooberry turned up his hands like a London butcher during the Blitz.

"It has risks, Etta. We'll keep at it, of course, but it's always been a long shot. Most new ventures are undercapitalized."

"Listen, Doo." The moniker had spread. Dooberry didn't like it, especially in light of his new inflection, which entitled him, he felt, to a greater dignity.

"Listen, Doo. You weren't talking long shot when you were depositing my check. Have you told Victor Grant that this project is foundering?"

"I left a message. Victor thought if we had good news along the way we might be able to raise more cash. Another tranche of capital. But we have nothing more than the outline of a computer game. Victor said he can't imagine sinking any more into it."

"Of course not. He wants progress."

"How much," Dooberry asked idly, "do you suppose is a tranche?"

"You'll be in that trench," Etta said sharply, "unless you get on the stick. I'm not prepared to call the hole dry until we're further down."

Dooberry removed a box of Players from the blazer's inside pocket. "Etta, I assure you, I'm exhausting my resources."

"You need help?"

Dooberry hesitated. Whatever he spent would come out of the stockpile he'd allocated at project's end for himself and Flavia. He took her hand in both of his.

"Etta, believe me. What needs to be done I can do."

"Just remember. Us investors are adverse to Grant. He's the creditor. Any news, good or bad, you tell me first." She called this out as she exited Dooberry's foyer to her truck. Parked amidst the fresh berms of snow, the pink Unimog looked for all the world like what an extraterrestrial might order for dessert.

❧

The first test. Waddy summoned the subscriber's screen and entered his personal data. For real. Social Security number, place of birth. Lisa had created an online extranet that accessed six databases rented for this purpose. In seconds the screen showed eleven pages on Henry Wadsworth Longfellow Brush of Skakit Point, Washington. They had his catalog purchases for four years (few), his complaint history (none), left thumbprint from Washington Motor Vehicle, his credit rating (excellent), newspaper articles on the Battling Crabs loss at State, an estimated earnings history (only percentage points off, and not promising), and a commendation from his landlord for a clean leasehold.

Waddy set to work answering the fantasy questionnaire. He classified his own from the primary level—Security, Serenity, Triumph/Domination, Humility/Subordination, Ecstasy, Mayhem—as Triumph. Subclass Athletic. At the image page, he transferred four digital shots of himself. Scanned and entered the basketball team picture from his high school yearbook. Adobe Photoshop and the Wise Mother software did the rest.

Waddy hit the Submit button, and suggested to Lisa that they take a break. But before they could leave their chairs, a tone signaled incoming e-mail.

They ran the attachment. Not bad. There was Waddy on the court with his team of a decade earlier. They randomly shot baskets. More scripting would be needed.

∿

Tiffany's car crept through the blustering day. Edgy clouds out of the north spit snow and, on the dirt road, dust devils lifted sand and grit and blew it against the windshield.

Just what Mother warned me about. He picks you up and dumps you out. Tiffany checked her calf-length boots. He'd made good on the wardrobe, a Chinese red Patagonia parka, the Bogner ski pants with the wet look. And the small Japanese four-wheeler. He'd told her to keep the car and drive herself back to Vegas.

But Vegas was where they'd told her to get her ass to Aspen. And place it into the hands of powerful people. She'd followed the advice to the letter, and what had it gotten her? A blind date with that Wall Street big shot who sent her home in a cab, a month of the cokehead singer, living from gallery opening to gallery opening on sparkling water and pâté while her savings disappeared. A stint as a *live-in*—Tiffany chose the word. A TV producer with two shows in the high Nielsens. First he was going to get her Chekov, then a sitcom, then board girl for a new quiz show. And instead what did she get? What started as a one-nighter became a week in Starwood, enduring the sexual gymnastics of a monkey on Viagra.

The fall season, he pleaded. It's bombing. I need to get back. It was a weak line—fall seasons always bomb. He can go screw himself, and she smiled at the thought. It was the only permutation he hadn't tried.

Plastic bags flapped on the barbed wire. With a theatrical flair, Tiffany had picked the county dump to think through her future. Maybe it was time to move. She inventoried her strengths. At thirty-three she was tending to overripe, the pores enlarging, the waist spreading. Possible roles were down to the abandoned wife or the scheming professional. But her eyes remained too wide apart and her face remained North Dakota Swede. Her CV opening credit was Miss Gouda Cheese, 1995. No, it was time to think about a new career.

She parked the car by an abandoned sleeper sofa and opened the glove compartment. Tubes of eyeliner, alpha hydroxyl, and Retin-A. She found the Helena Rubenstein gel and smeared her cheeks and forehead. Guard the asset, her agent had warned her. Bras for sleeping, sun cream in the sun, and this in the wind. Damaged goods don't sell.

Yet that's what she was. She looked about. Slabs of designer board fluttered in the wind, a leather hassock oozed its stuffing. She exited the car, treading to avoid any contact, and walked around a kayak with caved-in holes the size of dinner plates.

And realized she was being watched. A small, swarthy man on a pile of debris stood hefting a large metal sign. Beneath her gel mask, she blushed deeply. If she'd known anyone were here, she wouldn't have gotten out of the car looking like an extra from *Star Trek*.

"Howdy," he said.

"Howdy," she answered and smiled.

"Come junkin'?"

Tiffany thought a moment. "Yes. I guess that's what I'm doing."

"Not much here. Found myself a sign." He walked toward her. He had, she noted, the very limp Laughton had used in *Hunchback*. He held the sign up for her to read. Skiers Park Here.

"So I see. What will you do with it?"

The man weighed the question. Looked her over. From the quality of her outfit, she wasn't here to furnish an apartment. He'd developed of an eye for ski outfits: he saw thousands a day pass in line.

"Don't know."

"You could sell it."

"To who?"

"Decorators. In town. They buy anything."

"That so?"

"That's so."

"A sign?"

"Anything. If it says Aspen, or skiing, even better. Twice what it's worth. If it says bars or mining, three times." This pretty woman seemed to know what she was talking about.

"You have other stuff?" she asked.

He studied her again. Had she burned her face in an accident? "I got some shit. Want to see?"

~

Peyton was warmed by the sun toasting his body. Remarkable. The middle of December, yet here in the Ionian Sea the weather was ideal. Even the sounds he heard, the lapping of water against the hull, the shuffling of the crew on rubber-soled shoes as they straightened about, handsome little marine tasks, everything suggested relaxation and a good tan. The light was gentle, not so strong as the Rockies. By the time they returned to Aspen for Christmas skiing, he'd be roast-chicken brown.

The couple who had chartered the ketch, Pride's Crossing people, had motored into port to see the sights. Alexandria, they had told him, was historically important. To Peyton that meant crowded and smelly. He'd seen enough ruins to last him. Who cares about the past? He'd asked that question last night at dinner, squab with an excellent white Burgundy, and they'd jumped on him. Even Chloe. It was like criticizing God. "The past instructs us in who we are," someone lectured him. "It tells us what will happen."

Well, he hadn't said so, but he really didn't care to know more about either topic. As to who he was, he knew. And for the future, well, unless you were betting on horses, the hell with that. He liked the surprises of each day. There weren't enough of them. What possible benefit is there in knowing the future? Who cares?

A rhythmic beep answered one of his questions. Chloe. Chloe cares. He raised up and studied the way the lines of her legs converged to the trim rear end. She lay on her stomach, her cell plugged into a laptop, and punched expertly at the keypad.

"What's the news?" he asked diffidently.

"NASDAQ is down again. The Fed's move was twenty-five basis points short of expectations."

"And?"

"And the market anticipated a stronger statement. So the pros are selling. Not me," she said, mostly to herself. "They have nowhere to go. They'll be back."

Her thigh showed a white crescent where it met the bottom of her black one-piece bathing suit. The light was so clear, when he closed his eyes, he saw the crescent in negative.

"Chloe?" Her cell was beeping again. Or perhaps it was

the computer. She didn't answer.

"Chloe?"

"Yes?" He wanted her to turn and look at him, but she didn't.

"Let's go below. How 'bout a nap before lunch?"

This time she did scrunch around. He winked. He'd seen Redford do that to Debra Winger.

"Peyton. It's the middle of the day."

"So?"

"So the crew is about. Walking above our heads."

Peyton reconciled himself to a day of continence. Trouble was, with the cocktails and the wine and the ouzo, he never felt sexy at night. It was time to get back to Aspen. The snow would be flying, and with the snow came the party season. There was a party every night, if you wanted. Chloe would be delighted. This trip was an interruption in her schedule. She didn't care for the Pride's Crossing couple, and the time difference complicated trading. Perhaps he'd have a swim.

"Kris?"

"Yes, Mr. Post?"

"What's for lunch?"

"Eggs Florentine, Mr. Post. Spinach, ham, a béarnaise sauce."

Peyton rose. Better get some exercise. He removed his sunglasses and scuffs and stacked them on the deck chair. Walked to the bow. The water was a perfect turquoise; he could see the anchor chain tracing down to a mottled bottom. He looked back. Chloe was typing notes. Her small breasts were urging from the top of her suit.

"Kris," he called.

"Yes, Mr. Post?"

"I think I'll have a mimosa before lunch. Can you make a mimosa?"

"Yes, sir. Orange juice and Champagne?"

"Exactly," he said.

He turned and executed a perfect racing dive into the water.

～

Justin Kaye thought better than to honk. Not everyone liked the goose call of his SUV. If anyone lived the simple life, it was the Finches. He would knock gently on the door. Besides, he always enjoyed a peek in. These people were the genuine article, the folks on whom his entire sales philosophy had been modeled. They had that easy, aristocratic taste. They wore the clothes they'd always worn, used the blankets, suitings, and sheets they had always used. Precisely the look he was replicating. Except for the markup.

Gene Finch answered the door wearing a wine-colored chamois shirt. The rolled cuffs were lined. A shooting blouse. Gene Finch differed from Justin's clientele in that Gene Finch shot.

"Hi, Gene. My Rochelle here?"

"Meeting's still on. Drink?"

"Sure." Justin entered. Despite his immersion in design, Justin found the real thing a foreign land. It wasn't the trappings so much as the mores. Conversation, for example. The Finches talked only when they had something to say. It was an admirable trait in theory, though in a business driven by sales, it wouldn't work.

"Bourbon?"

"Scotch. If you have it." They were standing in the under-sized kitchen. It had been installed in the late forties, when the Finches' parents had found Aspen. The place looked like an old *Esquire* advertisement of the good life, one that would cost you three figures on eBay. Justin knew. He owned an entire set of *Esquire*s from 1940 to 1955, for ideas.

Finch took two bottles from a cabinet and poured a glass from each. Justin marveled at the insouciance. Booze in a kitchen cabinet, generic whiskey. If you're secure enough, you can save a fortune.

"Why are you smiling?" Gene asked.

"I was just thinking."

"What?"

"What a nice life we lead," Justin lied. In fact he was thinking about the estate tax. No need to eliminate it. You people spend so slow, the sun will go cold before you run out. Finch added ice, ran both glasses under the faucet, and added an inch of water. Justin followed him to a small room off the kitchen. In the living room a dozen women were seated around coffee cups, the Snow Ball committee in full bloom.

"Good of you to lend your wife to Mary."

"Listen. Good cause."

They lifted glasses at each other. Finch reached into a pine side table and found an opened bag of pretzel nuggets. Threw them on the table between them and gestured for Justin to dig in. The chairs were covered with Navajo blankets. The real McCoy. The table was a slab of glass mounted on a yellowing rack of antlers. God. How do they get away with it? Bolted to an ancient desk was a contraption he'd never seen. He asked.

"Shell loader."

"What for?"

"Pack your own shells. Big savings."

Finch got up, demonstrated. Loaded three shotgun shells and offered them to him.

"Hey, thanks." Finch was an investor in the Walton Club. Justin finished his drink and sucked on the rocks.

"Sounds like they're winding up. Mary appreciates the use of your wife."

"Rochelle's a smart lady," Justin said. "Took me three false starts to find her."

Finch looked confused.

"My fourth marriage. You?"

Finch laughed. "We're on our first."

"I've been through the Swedish beauty, the heiress from the convent, and the Jamaican model. They talk about the Jewish princess. Let me tell you, they're all princesses."

"That so?"

Justin wished he hadn't started. Mary Finch's wardrobe was mostly jeans and sweaters, and she'd probably seen a hair salon only through the window. "Princesses. All fairy tales and no pot roast. When I found Rochelle, I said, 'That's for me.' Stability, candles lit on Friday night. Know what I mean?"

"You bet," Gene said blankly.

"Stability. What's more important than values?"

"Nothing."

"Exactly. Nothing." They stared at each other. Thankfully, Justin heard the sound of rustling from the other room.

∾

"You a cop?" Hollister asked him. A scraggly beard, and shining through a border of long tresses, a dome whose ebony glaze seemed polished by the winter wind—the man looked more like a prophet. But Hollister's concerns were immanent, not theologic.

The man examined a vial and swabbed out crumbs of cocaine with his pinkie. "Good smack," he said.

"You're either a cop or a junkie, it don't matter to me, I'm calling my lawyer."

"Keep snorting this, your septum will dissolve like an Alka-Seltzer in water. Septum first, then the brain."

"You're no cop. So why are you going through my trash?" Hollister had had this before, garbage hounds. Usually groupies, looking to scrounge a piece of mail with his name or a shopping list. He didn't mind—it was a good way to meet chicks.

"Too bad no one's figured out a way to create a financial instrument backed by people," the black man said. He wore three or four sweaters against the cold, making his thin frame top heavy. "If there were, you'd be a natural short."

"Listen, what the fuck are you after?"

"Insulation. Your workmen threw it out." Hollister looked down. Beneath the man's foot were end cuts of the sheet insulation left over from the construction. Hollister was adding a pool cabana, after the design of the Parthenon.

"So?"

"So, I can use it. You have any objection?"

"You're insulating?"

"I am. My holiday digs."

"That won't cover much space."

"I don't need much."

He was adding the cabana because the last woman had proved hard to evict. He'd never again let them stay in the house. He'd stash them in the cabana. That way, he could screw when he wanted, park them out there, and Charley would evict them when he was out of town.

"Any objection?"

"No. No objection. Just keep off the personal stuff."

Gossage looped thumb and finger into an okay. Rolled the fiberglass and began down the hill. This would do fine for his holiday place. The man went back inside.

Holidays were the problem. The rest of the time his theory of reciprocating surpluses kept him warm. Gossage had his choice of homes. He looked for a good library, a conspicuous spare key, and a back door. These houses were occupied perhaps thirty days a year. Otherwise they stood unused, heated to keep the pipes from freezing, the only security a random check. Dozens of places fit his bill. Good reading was another matter. The average bookshelf held Robert Ludlum, *The One Minute*

*Manager*, and Tom Clancy. One simply had to persevere. In the house he'd just vacated, across from Etta's in the West End, he'd started *David Copperfield*. After the holidays, when the owners returned to St. Louis, he would move back. David had just headed to Dover to look for Aunt Betsey Trotwood.

When the owners had arrived, Gossage moved to Red Mountain, two doors down from Hollister. His new hosts favored experimental European fiction, not Gossage's favorite. It was an eclectic education. The hammering and sawing on the Hollister cabana had awakened him.

Gossage needed to find digs for the oncoming Christmas week, when every vacation house was in use. He packed a motion detector that lit a sixty-watt bulb. If a car came up the driveway or a door opened, he was out the back. But he was getting too old for midnight exits. He decided to yield to the supply curve. Never fight the curve. So he'd found a splendid carton at the dump, and with help moved it to Sardy Field. At the north end of the Aspen airport's single runway—arrivals were favored to the south and departures to the north—stood the HIRL device, high-intensity runway lights. Ten bright bulbs that remained lit twenty-four hours a day, more than enough heat for Gossage's new home. He'd fit the box snug against the bulbs, on the runway side so the view of approaching aircraft wasn't blocked.

A camouflage Explorer pulled around the curve. Gossage stuck out his thumb. It slowed and stopped. The woman in the shotgun seat rolled down her window.

"Where you headed?"

"To the airport."

"We're just going into town."

"Going to market?"

"Yes," she said. "Wine for the holidays."

"Better prices at the Airport Shopping Center."

The driver smiled. "I admire salesmanship," Justin called

across his wife. "Hop in. We'll take you there."

"Up for the holidays?" Gossage asked.

"Through the New Year. Then it's back to the grind."

"And that is?"

Justin smiled. He'd appeared in the fashion press and the business magazines so often he enjoyed not being recognized. "I'm in the clothing business."

"Ahh," Gossage sympathized. "*Shmata*. Tough margins."

"Not with the right goods," Justin said into a curve. "If you have the goods, they want it no matter what. That's something Adam Smith didn't reckon on."

"No, I suppose not. Adam Smith never anticipated the logo. But he anticipated a population of customers and a nation of shopkeepers."

"Is that such a bad thing?" Rochelle asked. "I mean, look at this town. Is this a bad thing?"

"Depends," Gossage said. "Some people think that we're screwing up the world."

"I don't think so," Rochelle said. "I think we're supposed to use it. John Locke said, 'Nature never makes excellent things for mean or no use.'"

"Well done, madam. That is one of my favorite quotes."

"My wife," Justin said apologetically, "she's a reader."

"You read John Locke?"

"I just read that this morning. I was hoping to put it to use."

"Bravo. Tell me," Gossage turned around to look out the back window at the imposing stack of brick and mortar that decorated Red Mountain like a Christmas tree. "Tell me, just which house is yours?"

❧

The truck rumbled down the road toward the turnoff. It was a private drive, not a county road, and Marco himself did the plowing. He cleared it only to the width of the truck and then shoveled a small mound across the entrance. No need to advertise he was there. On the turns Tiffany leaned inward, away from the window-high snowbanks.

"So," she asked, "you collect stuff?"

"Sometimes." The road juked around a patch of ponderosa and flattened out. A silver Volkswagen convertible was parked in the clearing.

"You have company."

Marco climbed out of the truck and walked to the hut. She followed. Below, she heard the trickle of a stream. The door closed behind with a clang.

Inside, three bare bulbs hanging from cords gave the only light. The hut seemed to gather the cold, and her breath showed as a balloon. When her eyes adjusted, she saw long rows of rough wooden shelving holding junk of every description. Old gasoline cans, perhaps two hundred bitters bottles, wood shards that had started to petrify, rusted metal signs advertising tobacco and Coca-Cola and headache cures. At the far end a young man in a heavy cable-knit sweater was intently brushing off rocks. She introduced herself.

"Something, huh?" Waddy asked. She agreed.

"See these bricks? They're a hundred years old. Fired down the road on the Frying Pan, when Aspen had a silver boom and needed buildings." Waddy walked her down the aisles and explained random items. What made geodes, why pyrite is called fool's gold, grades of quartz and tourmaline and basalt. Marco had disappeared.

Trays of bones. "We haven't figured out what are sheep and what cows and what us. He could sell the cattle skulls to that woman in Santa Fe who paints them."

Tiffany knew her name. "You're in the business with him?"

"There is no business. He just collects. And I'm kind of helping out. I like it."

He was a nice young man. Handsome and well mannered. Hadn't hit on her, even after she'd unzipped her parka. Then she realized she was still covered in gel.

"Here," Waddy was saying, "these are my favorites." A shelf held pancakes of gray rock stacked perhaps ten inches high. Waddy picked up one, dunked it in the water of a nearby coffee can, and showed it to her. Imprinted in the stone was a chambered oval, perhaps two inches long and horizontally striped. Under the bare lightbulb the wet outline shone like a gem.

"Fossil," said Waddy. "It's a trilobite, the great-granddaddy of the crab. It lived around here a long time ago."

"No."

"Yes."

"Where?"

"All this was under water. This old trilobite sat on the bottom of an ocean, just minding his business. Then the sediment buried him. Just bits and bits of sand raining down on him. The ocean dried out, the mountains thrust him up, and Marco found him."

"I never heard."

"Get Marco to tell you. It was several years ago."

The door opened and Marco entered. Tiffany looked over with growing warmth.

"Three hundred million years," he said.

"What'd I tell you? He knows. Invertebrate paleontology."

"Hey, kid," Marco said. "You want to use the outhouse, better take some paper."

Then, remembering his guest, "You too, lady."

## Fifteen

Victor Grant congratulated himself. It had turned out to be a truly providential decision. Often, he reflected as he strained, often we make decisions we consider trivial. They *are* trivial. And so we don't bother to revisit them. Neglect to assess, test, account for. On each verb he pulled at the oars. Assess (stroke), test (stroke), and account for (stroke). Fatal weakness. He could hear his professor. Insist on it (stroke). No matter (stroke) whether it's a business (stroke), a product (stroke), or a person (stroke). The image of the professor morphed into his father, a retired one-star general, who'd taught a variation of the theme: sloppy habits (stroke) don't fix themselves (stroke).

The trainer ticked up the rate to thirty-three per minute, and Grant responded with a burst. Across the tops of his Reeboks he saw a smile as his trainer acknowledged the effort. A providential decision. His assistant Isabelle had complained she'd never find the combination, a personal trainer with shorthand. It *was* unusual, Grant agreed, but supply follows demand. Dominic saw the ad, wanted the job. Found a course, brought himself up to office speed before he applied.

Grant was smiling at his own inventiveness. Synergistic multitasking. The cost of installing the gym was a trifle—one good idea would pay for it. *Mens sana* (stroke) *in corpore sano* (stroke). Dominic smiled back. He thinks (stroke) I'm returning his grin (stroke).

His heart rate showed in red on the screen before him. Real-time information: strokes per minute, time elapsed, time remaining, calories burned. Stroke rate crept up, leveled off. His breath was even. He inhaled on the return and spoke on the pull.

"Dominic, call Dooberry. Aspen. Cell memory. Lunch tomorrow. Same place. He makes reservations. Status report. Also he should. Bring. Names of the board. Something called FFE. Got it?"

"Got it."

"Next. My office. Isabelle. Washington. Testify. Technology. Committee. Talking points."

"Yes, Mr. Grant."

"Last, pilot. ETA."

"Save your breath, Mr. Grant. We're about to hit the sprints. Up to thirty-eight for three minutes, back to thirty-three, then forty before the cool-off. You game?"

Grant gave a quick nod.

"How you feelin'?" The fact was, he was a bit winded.

"Fine. Get it done."

Dominic left his client on the rowing machine and went forward to the cockpit. Grant continued to pull smoothly at the oars, thirty-six thousand feet in the air. He listened to the hum of the Rolls engines. What (stroke) is the relative output (stroke) of energy? Body (stroke) versus engine (stroke)? Comparative efficiency (stroke)? Heat loss (stroke)? Machines made pretty music (stroke). Maybe I'll sponsor a study (stroke). Not Mozart (stroke), turbines.

Dominic returned.

"The pilot says, 'Aspen at eighteen twenty-zee.' Mean anything to you, Mr. Grant?" Grant smiled. They call it universal time (stroke), but the universe doesn't use it. Beware technophiles (stroke) who forget the market (stroke). Grant felt in synch, triceps, oars, and quads all working together. He'd entered a zone. This was easy. On the LCD the number thirty-eight began to flash and a beeper sounded insistently. "Pick up the pace, Mr. Grant."

~

Waddy switched on the tape and his high school team appeared on the screen, inanimate.

"Let's add some details," he suggested.

"It's six thirty. I'm due in town for dinner."

"It won't take long."

Lisa headed up the stairs to her bedroom to change. She said something dismissive and closed the door.

Together they were wrestling with the translation of ten thousand nouns into pictures. They had a commercial program, meant to teach reading, that went the other way. If they could only reverse the translation, they would save a lot of time.

Waddy studied her notebook.

Lisa had a square and mannish script. She had printed her favorite quote from Thomas Hobbes. "We cannot think about things, only about the names of things."

He had no plans. He booted up the computer and mused over their inventory of programs. Minutes later Lisa emerged from her room, transformed: Stella McCartney snake black jeans, a metallic brocade belt of Chinese red, and a silver tube top that might have been peeled from a lunar module. Under the top there was no room for a garment, scarcely enough for skin. A translucent lip gloss that looked like spar varnish. Waddy squinted to assure himself that she had made up her eyes, not blackened them in a brawl.

She picked up his stare. "Impressed?"

Waddy was impressed. But not smitten—maybe he had graduated from his infatuation. Or maybe he'd just dropped out.

"Lisa," he said, "did you ever think you wanted to settle

down? Catch some soaps, cook French toast, make babies?"

She shot him a jagged look. "Bearing babies is the female equivalent of joining the Marines. I have nothing to prove. They don't give medals, and there's no enemy."

At the door she turned a last time. "Don't fuck with the programming unless I'm here," she said sternly. "If we short this out, there's no second chance."

"Maybe when you get home."

"Not tonight, sweetie." She affected a cowboy drawl. "Little Peggy Sue is a-goin' dancin' and a-partyin', she g'wan to find herself a bronco buster, and she don't intend to see this-a-here ranch 'til her plum's been tuckered out." She slipped into a forest-green ski parka. Outside it had begun to snow.

"Listen, Bush. Working here we've become friends, don't you think?"

"Yes."

"I can say this? Personal?" She toothed her lip.

"Yes," Waddy said expectantly.

"You might get out more." She went into the snow-spotted dark.

~

It was one week to Christmas. The birth of the prophet of the meek and powerless was nowhere celebrated with greater zest than Aspen. Jewelers placed their wares in glistening windows, each bracelet, each bijou freshly dipped in thiourea bath and lit by halogen bulb. Haberdashers set garlands and greens amidst their suede, crocodile, and snakeskin, their silks and pashminas. Family by family the absentee owners returned. Entire households disembarked from Gulfstream and Lear, in a protocol reminiscent of the Roman senate. First the freeholders themselves, followed by children, stepchildren, and household servants—those who watched their offspring watch television or taught them to ski or bench press or bike.

Down other gangways climbed advisors expert in municipal bonds, neuroses, and crows' feet, those who dressed, peeled, bleached, and manicured, highlighted and Botoxed. Following Victor Grant down the steps came a personal trainer, two new MBAs, a corporate lawyer, and a chap with a white forelock. The town was filling up.

Frankie was ecstatic. *The* slick monthly, the one that tracked Julia and both Toms and Bruce and Lindsay, had reviewed his restaurant. "Overpriced, oversauced, overfilled: an absolute must on your Aspen itinerary." Both seatings were full for the week. Every shop in town was doing box office. The photographers who shot you against an alpine backdrop had no openings. The dog therapist hired an aide. The Hatha yoga guru, who rubbed your spine with a ten-inch wooden wheel until you either saw Vishnu or claimed to, was booked solid.

At Sardy Field tower, the controller scanned the low-hanging sky and measured from end to runway end. The horizontal sight line, RVR it was called, was still legal, but at half a mile was at minimum. At the north end, he thought he saw a cardboard box jammed against the HIRL lights. Not a bad idea to check. The wind may have trapped it. No need to pursue it tonight. For although RVR was at minimum, the ceiling had fallen below. He recorded the standard message for the ATIS. "Sardy Field now closed. Instrument landings not authorized at this airport due to decreased visibility." He was eager to go home. It looked like they might get a pile of snow.

At the north end, Gossage was pleased with his innovation. He had fitted the far end of his emptied computer box into a Glad bag, the large garbage size, to keep out the moisture, and lined the inside with Hollister's insulation. The battery of lights gave off more than enough heat to keep him toasty. Until now, he had lacked a reading light. He unzipped the thermal sleeping bag—graded to minus thirty Fahrenheit—and with a single-edged razor blade he slit three sides to a square in the cardboard, making a flap behind his head. A warm ruby light flooded in, reflecting off the insulation. Toasty.

He lay for a moment admiring his handiwork and listening to the hush as high-country powder fell about him. Then he picked up the book and opened it. The title page was bathed in red glow and stamped in stencil that said "Property of the Aspen Public Library." Admirable, the library: a universally accepted model of the law of reciprocating surpluses.

He turned the page to Chapter One. "Emma Woodhouse, handsome, clever and rich, with a comfortable home and happy disposition, seemed to unite some of the best blessings of existence; and had lived nearly twenty-one years in the world with very little to distress or vex her."

∿

The man was self-conscious of the curl of white hair that fell over his forehead. "It's conspicuous," they had told him at Langley. "Disqualifies you for counterintelligence work. Of course, if you want to stay and ride a desk, we have to keep you."

He didn't want a desk, he wanted the field. This loan out to Mr. Grant may provide entrée to the private sector. West Point, army counterintelligence, then the Agency. Perhaps it was time to leave the government's payroll. Mr. Grant had constant need of an investigator. But he wasn't easy to please.

"Do they have the money to finish or not?"

"Inconclusive, Mr. Grant. The kids say they need more to do the fantasy port. Dooberry argues he can't get more unless the kids can figure out a way to demonstrate it. That's how it was left."

Grant squeezed his upper lip. It relaxed him.

"They need the fantasy thing. Without it they have half a balloon. Can you keep close?"

"They're cold."

Grant squinted to indicate he didn't understand.

"Cold. Unsuspecting. They leave the curtains open. So far, no one's noticed me." Grant nodded, closed his eyes. It was a specific gesture—it meant, the interview is over.

"Mr. Grant?"

His eyes opened in surprise. "Yes?"

"It might help if I knew what you wanted the outcome to be."

Grant considered. "I want them close but not there. When I step in, I want the technical work almost done, but not quite. If they succeed, they'll raise the money. I won't get a chance to get in."

The man nodded, fingered the black intaglio on his ring, closed his eyes.

"Got it."

～

Waddy worried about Lisa on the roads, drinking and driving. Of course, she probably wasn't on the roads, he realized, and worried anew.

Nouns were the key. The dictionary program did best on nouns. Concepts will have to be customized. He wished he'd paid more attention in the fifth grade when they were diagramming sentences.

He went to work on the reading program. Pulled up a drawing, typed in S-A-L-M-O-N. A buzz for failure. Typed in F-I-S-H, and that rang the bell. Now all he had to do was come up with an algorithm that permitted the specific to read as the general. Lisa said the fantasizer wouldn't care. She cited Jung. The fantasizer's thoughts were not on the mackerel but the mother.

The dictionary wasn't the answer. He needed to be able

to find related words, not the definition of words. The classification needed to be thematic, not alphabetical: he wanted to see all the kinds of fish so he could choose. He wrote down a sentence and went back to work.

Hours later, he'd gotten nowhere. Words needed to go both ways, specific to general and back, and they didn't want to. Finally, he sat back, exhausted, in the chair. In the confined air he had broken a sweat. His whistling sigh stirred Hero.

The dog opened one eye. "I would say, pal," Waddy told him, "that this is more difficult than I imagined. Then again, we didn't kill a single guppy."

Hero's tail gave three slow beats. "Let's you and I take a walk."

~

A trivial but satisfying application of his theory of reciprocating surpluses, Gossage's alarm was a Boeing 737 climbing out at twelve hundred feet per minute direct to Los Angeles. The roar thundered down from two stories above. Moments later he shook with the vortices of whirling air that were produced as the giant machine developed lift. The wake turbulence shuddered man and his meager belongings alike, as if a cosmic chef were dusting them *en papillote*.

Energy, Gossage mused as soon as his wits returned. Energy dissipating into the earth. Someone could use it. What about a turbine at the end of every busy runway to catch the wake of departing aircraft?

Gossage inched backwards out of his box. Naked and on all fours, he paused to slip his book into a Ziploc and search out his one change of clothes. The December sun that inched over Independence Pass lit his rump in umber.

He managed himself into long johns, two wool shirts, duck-blind socks. Laced up grommeted boots, snugged a black watch cap over his bald head, and trudged off to the fringes of the airport for his morning toilette.

As he stood wondering where the alkaline soil would best benefit from the nitrogen in his pee, he heard a metallic tapping. It came from the dump, in a far corner of the fenced grounds. Old tire husks, emptied oil quarts, car seat stuffing lay where the airport cleanup crew, admittedly ill-named, had discarded them. Just beyond was the border of the airport and a ridge that rose to a wall of obsidian.

Gossage walked to find the noise. A fellow wearing Buster Keaton goggles and a frown of concentration stood on a stepladder, thoughtfully chiseling away at the rock.

"Geologist?" Gossage asked by way of alerting the man to his presence.

The man sniffed back a runny nose and peered down.

"Sculptor."

"Mind if I watch?"

"Not at all."

Years hearing them in his classroom had taught Gossage to save dumb questions. He studied the rock but couldn't make it out. Finally he asked. "What is it to be?"

"Woman," the man answered. "Mostly I do women."

"That may explain why I didn't recognize it. Ancient memories." Gossage examined the wall. A white-on-black cartoon looked out mournfully, soap tracings of a face and upper torso. Conspicuously, he now realized, a woman. And massive in scale. The span between her eyes was, end to end, the length of a man.

"Do I see an expression of distaste?" Sherry Topliff asked.

"Not at all. On the contrary. I like it. Public art for an unsuspecting public."

"For a moment," Sherry took the goggles from his eyes, "I thought you might feel it overlarge. Vulgar."

"No, no. It can't be small. Largeness is needed here to

be noticed. And you remember what Oscar Wilde said about vulgarity."

"Actually I don't."

"'Vulgarity is the conduct of other people.'"

Gossage recalled his mission. He unzipped and relieved himself a respectful distance off. Grabbed a handful of snow to wash and took a toothbrush from his pocket.

Sherry had turned back to the rock and was chipping to define the top of the woman's head. Gossage watched him work.

"Obsidian is tricky," Sherry told him. "It's glass, it can split and run. Once you get the lines right and the fibers cut, here, in bas-relief ... " He let the sentence go.

"Do you have a name for it?"

Sherry looked at the drawing he had made on the rock. He studied the curves, as if written in them were the woman's words.

"I think I'll call it *The Goddess of the Conduct of Other People*."

"I like that. It appears she is to be nude."

"She is indeed. Nude and rude. Perhaps in ages ahead they'll come to worship here."

"They'll come and celebrate her feast day."

"Exactly." Sherry had gone back to chiseling. "In the ritual, her followers will buy offerings at the best stores, dress her, and make her beautiful."

Gossage smiled and looked into the soaped oval spaces that were to be her eyes.

"Are they going to object?"—meaning the airport and the neighbors. Sherry understood.

"Not if they don't see it. Once it's done, why I might polish it up. This rock looks mighty fine polished. And I'll clear out some of this hay. Give her a chance to breathe."

"Amaranth," said Gossage.

"What's that?" Sherry paused to look down.

"Amaranth. Not hay. Also known as pigweed. In the

spring, when it buds, you can eat the leaves. The Anasazi ground its seeds into flour. You can find it in health stores."

"Don't say."

"Do say."

"I thought it was just some weed."

"You ever stop to think about weeds?"

"No, can't say's I have."

"It's the name we give to something we don't want. Something that's welcome if it were only somewhere else."

"Never thought of that." Sherry came down from the ladder and stepped back to assess his work.

"Amaranth, you say."

"I do."

"Flour?"

"Flour."

"Well," he climbed back up, slid his goggles into place. "Well, maybe I won't cut it back. Maybe I'll leave it like it is."

Sherry resumed with the hammer and chisel. Over the noise of his taps came a ruckus perhaps fifty feet from where they stood, the clang of cans and bottles tossed about, the muttering of ardent curses. Sherry stopped and they both looked.

A young, familiar man parted the grasses and walked at them through the fresh snow.

"You assholes seen a Maxwell House can?"

"I beg your pardon," Sherry said from his perch.

"A Maxwell House can. My connection is supposed to be a Maxwell House can. Fifteen grand's worth of Colombian snow. Seen it?"

"Certainly have not."

The man studied Gossage.

"Do I know you?"

"Red Mountain," Gossage told him. "Insulation from your cabana."

"Oh, yeah. The coon garbage detective."

"Life takes odd turns." Gossage was looking at an empty Minute Maid carton that the man had carried in. Hollister dropped it at his feet.

"Listen, asshole," Hollister said and unzipped his teal parka. From the wide leather belt, rodeo king buckle, he withdrew a black pistol the size of a paperback book. Gossage had never seen one from that particular aspect. Peering into its small bore devoured everything behind it.

His fear was contagious. Sherry shrunk into the stepladder. Gossage saw Hollister's eyes flicker as a thought made tentative contact behind them.

"You a narc?"

"That's right." Sherry spoke from the second step. "He's a narc. He's Tom Grinch of Homeland Security."

Hollister was confused. He stuck the pistol back in his belt and retreated, facing them all the while. When he'd disappeared into the high grasses he shouted, "Better not be. Better not be, asshole." The man retreated angrily.

Sherry shrugged, fixed his goggles, and went back to chipping.

"Thanks," Gossage said. "That was quick thinking."

"No problem."

"It's Tom Ridge, isn't it?"

"Right" said Sherry. "I'm no good with names."

～

Mary and Gene Finch were first to the hut. The Corkscrew Lift serviced five double-diamond runs, the most difficult on the mountain, and it had been out of service for eight days. Engine repair, the problems of getting a new flywheel delivered and installed. For eight days powder had accumulated on these runs without a track. It was a morning the Finches lived for. The sky was the flawless blue of first hyacinths. Its color would wash out as the sun crossed the sky, losing its polarizing angle and melting the fragile crystals that sparkled on the surface. Last night alone ten inches had fallen in town, more up here. The couple waved to the operator, rode the chair up, and dashed to the bottom. Long ogee curves, effortless, the deep powder dissipating every bump, erasing the line between liquid and solid. To ski deep powder was to be a bird. Neither noise nor friction, only balance, lift, and cant.

By their third run others had arrived. No matter. They'd had the best of it. They kicked off their skis and sat on the hut's small porch.

"Marco."

"Mr. Finch. Hey, Mrs. Finch."

"Lift's been out?"

"So I heard."

"What happened?"

"Don't know. Monkey wrench."

"Those monkeys. Got to watch 'em." Gene Finch tried to meet his eye but failed.

"Mrs. Finch, you heard about Conundrum Creek?"

"What about it?"

"Fellow going to build a fishin', huntin' club. A house too."

"Yes, Marco. I did hear."

"What's FFE going to do?" Mary Finch was a trustee.

"Not much we can do, Marco. Fellow's got through P and Z."

"What about this Indian shit? That stop it?"

"Well, that's a long shot. But they've brought in a top lawyer. If there's anything to do, he'll do it."

"I dunno," said Marco. "Land never does well."

"What do you mean, Marco?"

"In court. Against people. Land just sits there, never seems to win."

"You said a mouthful, Marco." He wondered why city

folk always talked to him in slogans. Did they talk to each other that way too?

"Well. Anything I can do, let me know."

"Thank you, Marco. That's very kind." Mary Finch was touched by the thought, and immediately put it from her mind.

"One more run?" her husband asked her.

"One more. Then let's quit." They'd already had their perfect day.

~

Lisa Laroux knocked back a second bottle of protein-fortified grapefruit juice. A night of debauchery had left her dehydrated, sexually sated, and favoring a charley horse in her left gluteus medius. The pink juice reminded her of her excesses: cosmo-politans had been a mistake. Vodka, triple sec, and cranberry juice. They went down like a sports-ade.

No mistake with the ski instructor. A perfect specimen. Perhaps, she realized as she gingerly shifted her weight, she needed to pick partners a rung or two below perfect.

Over her first juice she discovered Waddy's work. He *had* run something on his own, damn him. The computer clock showed time. She couldn't retrieve it—he'd clearly not wanted it seen, but he'd noted something down. She would call him on it as soon as he got back. Dooberry had summoned her for lunch with the Grand High Purse, Grant himself, and she sent Waddy. She wasn't about to match wits with Victor Grant on three hours' intermittent sleep, a gimpy ass, and a hangover that could devour New Jersey.

~

Annalee seated the doctor, poured tap water, and offered Pellegrino.

"No, thanks. Just the still." Dooberry took the silk square from his jacket pocket, breathed on his glasses, and began to polish them. When, he wondered, did water become a scam? Restaurateurs are better at hustle than social scientists.

Frankie Rusticana touched his shoulder. "Will you start with our ostrich carpaccio?"

"I beg your pardon."

"Oh, Dr. Dooberry. Great to see you. How's your beautiful wife?"

"Fine, thanks."

"You expecting her?"

"I'm expecting Mr. Grant. I told the girl."

"Oh, *eccellente*." The pleasure of checking Grant off his list only days into the Christmas season gave a genuine cast to his smile. "You won't try the carpaccio?"

"I'll wait to order, Frankie." The trick with rich folks is to order down. Go cheap on the little things and they pay no attention to the big. Comfort Inns and burgers will get you an unallocated contingency fund.

Rusticana withdrew, sticking a mental Post-it in a dim corner of his brain. Dooberry was a possible. Just a possible. He hadn't flinched at the touch, as so many men did. Not that Frankie would press it. Not worth taking the chance to lose a customer. You only needed one lover, but you needed lots of customers.

Waddy found a choice spot half a block from the restaurant and gambled on an hour's worth of parking. He saw Victor Grant enter the front door ahead of him, watched Annalee steer him toward the back of the room.

Damn. If I'd been two minutes to either side, she'd be steering me. He leaned against the greeter's podium and decided to wait her out.

~

Silverheels Brumberger received with equanimity the news that his was a special table. He'd heard that line first at the Carnegie Deli forty years ago, when he was squeezed in between a three-hundred-pound man and the alto section of the First Methodist Church of LeMoille, Illinois. If your table was by Pantagruel's entrance in the summer season, you were conspicuous. In December, you were merely cold.

"I've never had ostrich carpaccio before."

"How is it?" Justin asked.

Brumberger grimaced. "Like Fleer's Double Bubble. With vinegar." He opened the menu and grimaced anew. "These prices, Justin. For these prices they should measure me for a suit."

Justin laughed. Nothing like hometown humor. "Order what you like. The lobster in sherry reduction is quite light. And delicious."

"You're not embarrassed, Justin? Wining and dining the opposition lawyer?"

"Irv. You think this is a schmeer?"

Brumberger rocked his hand in a Dutch roll.

"Irv, listen. If I could have bought you for the price of a penne pasta, I'd have done it long ago."

"This is more than a meal. A first-class ticket. Room and board."

Justin was unrepentant. "I thought it might help if you walk the property. See the plans, get the lay of the land. Why shouldn't you stay with us?"

"Your guesthouse is the size of the apartment building I was raised in on the Grand Concourse."

"It's adequate?"

"Adequate maybe for the New York Knickerbockers. And the meals ... " Here Brumberger spread out his hands to indicate the seven-grain roll on his service plate, the florette of wasabi butter, the remains of the appetizer.

"They're adequate?"

"Adequate."

"Complaints?"

"Well. Not a single starlet has asked me to dance. I haven't learned to ski ... "

"You want to ski, we'll ski."

"Are you nuts? And the land I'm supposed to walk is under three feet of snow."

Justin caught the eye of Victor Grant passing to a far table. They exchanged nods.

～

Grant nodded and, paces later, put the name to the face. Justin Kaye, the duck club. He'd bought in. Heard nothing since writing the check. Write a note to find out.

Joining had contradicted one of his cardinal investment rules: don't do the other guy's deal. If you want to hunt duck, buy your own place. Your own place, your own birds.

Grant hurried by. How do I get myself into these things? Here I am, about to eat too large a meal and listen to a dull man tell me about a deal I've already sold, all to find out the name of a woman.

But what a woman.

～

Brumberger was easy, thought Justin. Compared to the bankers, a cupcake. The bankers were clamoring. His women's spring line had gone down in a blaze of peach. And he had just seen the numbers from the men's line. Disaster. He was selling the casual look as the world went back to Bond Street. Wall Street law firms, investment banks, who would have believed it?

If he could only recut his inventory of blazers into three-piece cheviot. He hadn't seen the move coming. Forget that comfortable clothes made sense. When in history had common sense prevailed in the fashion world? Who would have believed it?

Certainly not the banks. For most of his career he'd been debt free. The very year he had a women's line that stuck on the shelves like contact paper, the year he had to borrow a little money—well, not a little—the world decided to redo its wardrobe. You can never tell.

❧

You can never tell. Waddy chewed on the thought along with a Cypriot olive. Annalee had seemed happy to see him, genuinely warm. Almost more than warm. Even though he'd never given in to those impulses to call.

And Grant didn't seem the least bit upset. You'd think he would object to his money going down the toilet. Waddy's progress report was that there was no progress. The early stuff was easy, the fantasies were proving insoluble. Too many.

Grant seemed bored. Only when Dooberry handed him a list of the trustees of the Friends of the Friendless Earth did he lean forward in his chair.

"Do we know any of these people?"

"Sure," said Dooberry.

Dooberry ran his finger down the list. "Chloe Post, her husband is an investor. Etta Eubanks you've met. My wife serves on a committee with Mary Finch."

Grant read over his hand.

"Do we need something from them?"

Grant ignored the question. "Know anything about their eco-cop program, who's in it?"

Dooberry shook his head.

"I do," Waddy offered. "One of them stopped me once for ... ," he flashed on his naked rear mooning out of the VW trunk, " ... for information. Tough customers."

Grant nodded thoughtfully. He folded the page and stuck it in the pocket of his cardigan. Then he left. When the considerable check arrived—Waddy'd eaten three courses, including a flourless chocolate cake topped with a white marzipan pagoda—Dooberry groaned.

"You didn't care for lunch?" Waddy asked.

~

Hollister completed his run-up, dialed in the ground frequency, and identified himself, "King Air One Romeo Hotel," to the controller. He shot his eyes to the vacant seat. This is the dull part. Waste of time.

"Advise when ready to copy."

"Ready to copy."

"King Air One Romeo Hotel depart runway three three. Lindz Three departure heading three four zero to eight thousand seven then left via heading two seven zero Gleno intersection at one six thousand then direct Las Vegas, as filed. Expect filed altitude ten minutes after departure."

Hollister read back the clearance. That was a standard departure, he didn't need it spelled out. The fellow was treating him like a moron.

"Have a good flight," the controller added.

Yeah, buddy. Right. You too, stuck in your windowless room and slug's job. He switched to tower frequency and was cleared for immediate takeoff.

Damn. Just when you want a minute's delay—here he rubbed his tongue along his upper lip and again eyed the blue coffee can on the seat next to him—you don't get it.

He aligned the aircraft so the runway centerline ran under his seat. Painted on the nose he could see the top lines of the G clef, the opening bars to his first Platinum, "Do Me, Roomie, Do Me." It was a customized job. On the far side of the nose, they'd reproduced his portrait from the album cover. Luminous paint—flying at night he could see its glow.

"One Romeo Hotel," the tower came on. "Cleared for takeoff." The bastards are trying to move me out. Fuck 'em. He popped the lid on the can and snared a pinch from the open baggie within.

"One Romeo Hotel rolling." With the heel of his hand he fire-walled the throttle. The turboprops built power. Airspeed passed rotation and in the thin air moved ten knots above before the craft lifted itself off. Hollister held the airplane in ground effect to gather velocity. The more level he held it, the greater speed he gathered and the steeper climb he could get. He wanted that rush of the high angle of attack. The aircraft cleared the bank of runway lights by ten feet, cars on the highway by twenty. He could see the drivers flinch and duck for cover.

Hollister adjusted the heading bug to 340 degrees, dialed in the steepest possible climb, and flicked on the autopilot. The plane rocketed up the Roaring Fork Valley amid freshly whitened peaks of fourteen thousand feet.

And a picture recurred to him, like the card the magician presents. As he'd left the runway, a man, standing by the end lights, bare to the waist and black as pitch, was scrubbing himself with snow. That bald SOB, the one who keeps turning up in my life. The fucker lives there! In the box!

"I'll nail him as soon as I get back," Hollister said aloud.

"One Romeo Hotel," the tower interrupted. "Heading two seven zero. Lindz Three departure."

What am I, a novice? This guy is on my ass. Hollister moved the bug, and the aircraft responded. Fuck 'em—he didn't need them. There wasn't a cloud in the sky.

He looked down at his fingers. With all the distractions, he'd forgotten the hit. He stuffed the powder in and sniffed hard.

Wow. Great. He'd wanted the rush to come as he peeled across the Maroon Bells, but the fuckers in the tower had distracted him. He made his last turn, identified the intersection, and turned to his final bearing to Vegas. He was through with them until he had to land.

Not bad. The speed, the angle, the way the blow makes your brain shrivel and stretch. The only thing missing was sex. That would be the trifecta. Speed, snow, and good head.

Still, not bad. When I get back, I'll nail that bastard. He flicked on a CD player. Through the Bose speakers came two chords he'd written himself. G seventh and C major. "Do me, roomie, do me."

~

Waddy knew something had happened when he walked in and found her smirking before the screen. Those rare times when Lisa was happy, her lips tightened to keep in the news.

"What's up?"

"Nothing much. How was lunch?"

"Great. I packed it in. You should have seen Dooberry's face when the bill came."

Lisa kept her attention on the screen, tightened her smirk so that the lips disappeared. It was behavior designed to get Daddy's attention, to prod the next question. Which it did.

"What's up?"

"Not much," she said and flicked a telltale tongue at the corner of her mouth. "Just ... " She turned the screen toward him and offered the keyboard.

"Type in a noun."

Waddy reached over, typed in W-O-M-A-N. Michelangelo's Eve appeared on the screen.

"Try another." C-A-K-E, he wrote. A birthday cake appeared.

"Again."

M-A-C-K-E-R-E-L. Lisa laughed. "Brush, you're a shill."

"Hey," said Waddy. "Of course that's really ... "

"I know, I know. Don't be so anal. A salmon will suffice. Double click on it."

He did, and a screen of fish subspecies appeared. "What ... ?" he started to ask.

"You did it. What you wrote. 'Not a dictionary, a thesaurus.' I just tapped into the Rainwater thesaurus. Available for $69.95."

Waddy found his mackerel.

"Now something else, something you'd fantasize about."

He could think only of Lisa in the tube top. He typed C-H-E-E-R-L-E-A-D-E-R.

She snorted. "Brush, I'm beginning to like you. You're kinkier than you appear." A pretty coed appeared, holding a megaphone over her head.

"I can't believe it."

"Now pick a part of her body," Lisa goaded.

Waddy's first thought was liver—he'd had an excellent vol-au-vent as an appetizer. But he entered L-I-P-S. They appeared.

"Now modify them. Big, crooked, wet, whatever you like."

"Heart-shaped," he wrote, and the lips complied. "Eureka."

"Not everything, but it's a start," Lisa said, and could not keep the smirk from spreading. Waddy wondered whether he should call Dooberry. Grant had explicitly asked to be informed of progress. Even before, he said, we had a chance to tell the stockholders.

No need. There was an investors' meeting coming up. They'd all learn at the same time.

Sixteen

No man is an island, entire of itself; every man is a piece of the continent, a part of the main. That is hardly news. Philosophers have long spoken of a metaphysical chain that connects humans each to each. Most folk, not given to conceit, consider the chain a figure of speech. Yet a link, the damaged link in an actual iron chain attached to a winch on a pier in Casablanca, set off events that soon reached into the Colorado high country.

A stray Moroccan nail flattened a tire. The wheel rim ran over a chain and cut halfway through a link. The link gave way, the chain snapped, and the wooden packing crate being hoisted by the chain fell to the pier and split apart. Rugs tumbled across the boards, unrolling like the tongues of frogs. They spilled their sacks of prime kif within inches of the toes of a member of the uniformed Casablanca *mekhezni*.

The policeman's job often required balancing the niceties of export regulations with the irresistible pull of demand, particularly since the pull paid so much better. But when contraband rolled to his mirror-polished shoes, in full view of departing tourists and arriving superiors, all were obliged to outrage. Shipper, expediter, and two growers in the mountains to the south were arrested and fined. The stern warnings kept them out of the market for a month.

The crackdown resulted in the loss of allotment to many

suppliers in the States. Down the line of distribution, customers suffered privation.

"What are you saying?" Peyton asked into the telephone.

"No rugs, Mr. Post. No rugs coming."

"I'll be right down."

Sinbad was trying to tell him something. Surely it could not be what he said, that the supply of Moroccan kif had vanished. Surely his words must be encrypted, surely they relate to price or procedures or amounts. After all, it was Christmas. Conversation took Peyton only so far, and the tonic that diluted his rum was beginning to make him gassy. How was he to get through without a little toke?

He drove down the mountain with brio and was at Sinbad's within minutes.

"I'm shut down, Post. S.O.L. Nothing I can do, supply has been cut off."

"Sinbad. I depend on you. What am I to do?"

"What are *you* to do? This is my living, man. You can buy on the street. Me? I'm out of inventory."

Peyton was untouched. One relies on one's providers. How do tradesmen get to be haberdasher to the Crown, except by dependability? He walked to his car disconsolate and peered into the shop windows. Kids would know. The pretty girl who seated people at Pantagruel stood by the glass door taking a reservation. Could she be trusted? Rumors of undercover narcotics agents were common in Aspen. Peyton thought through his Rolodex of acquaintances and failed to identify a single trustworthy person. Chloe couldn't help with this. This was a problem he'd have to solve.

He saw them cross, the fellow who had bussed tables and that angular, hard-faced woman, both involved with Dooberry's experiment. They're the right age. Perhaps they would have a connection. Get him through a month of skiing and back to the Hamptons in January. He knew a fellow in Sagaponack who could be relied on. Good chap. Lisa and Waddy ducked into the Jerome Bar before he could hail them.

~

"For God's sake," Lisa scolded, "keep your voice down."

But Dooberry could not contain himself. Just as it looked as though the project was out of money, these kids had come up with something. Whatever it was, and he wasn't at all sure, it would justify another slug of investment. He might squeeze out another year's salary. Flavia, back yesterday from equestrian school, wanted security. He'd pitch it to Grant: one year's budget. They couldn't begrudge him that.

Waddy recounted again what he'd experienced. Lisa described the images in the file. Dooberry was astonished at their progress. This was the dizziest scheme he'd encountered, albeit his own. He hadn't for a minute considered that it might work.

But Dooberry had never relied on science. His modest achievements had their roots in other disciplines. His formula for success neglected testable results. He believed that success depended on his being self-assured, dressing uncommonly well, and knowing a great many people by their given names.

"Shh," Lisa cautioned again, glancing about. By coincidence, she failed to look directly behind her, where sat a man with a white forelock. His chair backed on Lisa's, and even with his newspaper extended as the cone of his antenna, he had failed to pick up all of her words. Still, it was clear from Dooberry's reaction there had been progress. Dooberry was going to try to raise more money. Mr. Grant would want to know.

"Get on to the fantasies," Dooberry was saying. "The more lurid the better. This is sales, not science."

The man waited until they paid their bill and left. Mr. Grant wanted this project to have results, but not the appearance of results. If Wise Mother had any good news at all, the investors would ante up for another round and Mr. Grant would go penniless. In a limited use of the word.

I'll never criticize you, Mr. Grant had told him on meeting, for an excess of initiative. It was time to surface. To surface and infiltrate. How, he thought as he left the Jerome Bar, how and where? Sitting across the street, in front of the Explore Bookstore, where Aspenites gathered for coffee and crab Armagnac, sat a pink four-ton clue to his questions.

❧

Marco did not intend to piss away his day. He told her as much but, in that girlish voice she must have learned in beauty-contest land, she insisted and teased and put his coat about him and dragged him. Here he was in his truck heading into town, the day before Christmas, to shop.

He didn't give a fart in the wind about town or about whatever it is they sold in there, but Tiffany seemed excited, and he was getting used to having her around. He parked his pickup, ignored the meter—damned if he was going to pay to park on streets that belonged to the citizens—and followed her into Second Hand Rose. They sold anything at Second Hand Rose, dresses and whirligigs and God knows what else.

"What are we supposed to look at?"

"There." She pointed. On the counter by the register sat a small cheese box that he'd found at the dump, a foot square. In it were three railroad spikes that had come from his collection, dressed with red velvet ribbon.

"You done up those nails with bows? That's what you brought me in to see?"

"No, you stubborn mule. What I want you to see is what's *not* there. I brought in a *dozen* spikes, all with bows for the Christmas season. And ten of those insulation globes you had lying about."

"Meaning?"

"Meaning they've sold ten globes and nine spikes. At forty bucks per."

Money made Marco suspicious. Put in the mix that it turned ordinary folks to fools, no matter whether they had it or spent it or wanted it.

"You shittin' me?"

"Marco, what did I tell you? People buy that stuff."

Marco snorted, pulled a handkerchief from his back pocket, and blew his nose. "Forty bucks per?"

"And half of that is yours."

"Who gets the other half?"

"The store, silly. If you had a store, you'd keep it all."

Marco considered this. If I had a store, I'd be like every other poor bastard. Tied up indoors, see the light of day when you leave off work, when there *is* no light of day. Poor buggers. Imagine Adam saying, "Well, it's a mighty sweet Eden you got there, Lord, and I'm eager to take a look, but instead I'm going to open a little shop. Sell apples and keep the profits."

Still, three hundred and eighty dollars, you got to take notice.

Rose, the store's owner, was in the back room, arguing in loud and broken Spanish. Tiffany went to find her and returned holding a check made out to Marco Campaneris. He stuffed it in the pocket of his flannel shirt.

"You always thinking, ain't you?"

Tiffany looked at her feet. It was a novel compliment.

"Do you mind if I ask you a few questions?" A black man spoke to them from a rattan chair by the front window. His voice was friendly and polite. Where had Tiffany met him?

"Excuse me?"

"I'm interested in who buys and sells here," he said. The top of his head shone, a phrenological billiard ball. The span of baldness stopped at a fringe of ropey gray locks. Where had she met him? He wasn't the kind of person you'd forget. He sat with his legs crossed yoga-style. A large, imposing looking book rested on his lap, his fingers holding a place. Of course! The dump.

"Do you mind if I ask you a few questions?"

～

Waddy reached the bottom of the hill and fell back into the snow. His thighs ached from the long telemark turns. Fresh snow, two feet of it. A skier's dream. Hero thought his master was playing, licked the sweat from his face.

"Get off." The dog raced ahead to find what the forest held, bounding in powder to his withers. Waddy lay looking at the sky. He mind was stuck on the problem of Annalee. Was he making too much of it? For weeks he slept on the bed's edge so there'd be no accidental elbow or heel. Now he could think only of the recent contact, her nails on his neck, her fingertips alighting on the back of his hand. What could it mean?

She could of course be a toucher—the way some people are bores and some spitters—without intending anything. But what if she was signaling him?

Bi, that's it. Maybe she's bi. Waddy thought of himself, accurately, as broad-minded and, inaccurately, as a man of the world. In his delusion he was not unlike the happy diners at Pompeii, or for that matter the rest of us, who go blithely on, unaware of the mountain of seething evidence that swells until, like magma, it overruns beliefs dearly held. What's wrong with being bi? Nothing.

Though on reflection he wasn't sure what it meant. Do you switch off, as you might between sneakers and boots, depending on the weather and the activity? Do you outgrow it, like a childhood reaction to chocolate? He had friends who changed their magazine subscriptions regularly, didn't get locked in. He wasn't one to judge.

Rose had her hands full. Two customers wanted to rent dresses. They needed them only for the Snow Ball, and they could afford only one night's use. She wasn't in the rental business, Rose told them, but they wouldn't accept it. As they came out from the back, Rose was explaining it again, in measured tones.

"Look," said the curious man in the rattan chair. Rose had watched him for most of the day as he alternately read and wrote notes to himself. She would have chased him out long ago, but he was so distinctive. Dressed equivocally—bums in this town looked like ski bums—in sheepskin vest and hiking boots, he brought a hipness to the store window. Besides, better to seem busy.

"Look, let's work this out. This is an interesting application of my theory. They need dresses, you have dresses."

"What the hell is this, *Let's Make a Deal*?" Rose didn't con easily.

"Am I right?"

"What theory?"

"I'll get to that. Am I right?"

"I have dresses."

"So what we have is not an issue of economics, but of semantics. They buy the dresses, use them for a night, and resell them to you."

"I've told them. I'm not in the rental business."

Gossage thought a minute. "What is your business?"

"I sell shit. Anything I can."

"Dresses?"

"Exactly."

"So you occasionally buy dresses?"

"Yeah, but ... " Rose had left in Flatbush neither her skepticism nor her inflection.

"Now what if they bought the dresses? So far, so good?"

"Yeah?"

"Would you buy these dresses from me if I owned them?"

"I s'pose."

"So. Let's say you write me a contract to buy these very dresses at a price you pick, assuming they are delivered on a certain date."

"If I sell these dresses to them, you got no dresses."

"Ah. True. I will lend them the money to buy the dresses, a loan they repay in kind by delivery."

The woman wrinkled her nose. "A loan? What's your collateral?"

Gossage gave his most inside smile.

"The contract you wrote for me. What do you say, do we have a deal?"

Rose studied Flavia and Carmen. "Yeah. I s'pose."

~

Matt Hempel had been a cop less than a year. He was only twenty-three, and this, his first job out of Montana State, with a degree in criminal justice, was a dream. Aspen, Colorado. Beautiful women, blue skies, Champagne powder. Best of all, undercover work—no uniforms or haircuts, he just had to look like himself. On the downside, he had over an hour's commute each way, to a trailer wedged between trailers. But he didn't need a view there—he had one at work.

The dealers in town made him within days of his arrival. The city published its budget monthly in the *Aspen Leaf*. They simply came to the open council meeting and inquired. Matt wouldn't be surprised if they had reviewed his résumé. But so far, he was no threat. So far, the only arrests he'd managed were kids he'd met in the bars, kids looking for a few sticks to smoke on the slopes.

Dust busts: simple, quick, economic. Matt took them

down, their parents hired the town's drug lawyer, who copped a lesser charge, fines were paid. Average elapsed time, three months, no county cost for jail or prosecution. The sectors of commerce that radiated from this appetite—buying, selling, arresting, arraigning, bailing, defending, bargaining, and sentencing—continued to thrive. It was the model of a vertically integrated industry.

Job security too. It was a dream.

Matt used method acting for his cover. He snowboarded through the days, frequented the clubs at night, hooked up with his share of women. Be natural, the chief told him, so he lay himself on the tracks and waited for the inevitable solicitation to run over him. His one concession to the job, his cell, had sounded only once until now. This fall *Air Force One* had landed at Sardy Field. The president drove to Starwood for an elegant fund-raising lunch, catered by Pantagruel, oddly fresh turbot. On the return trip the motorcade ran into down-valley traffic. Hempel had been summoned to help.

So now, as he lounged on the deck of Little Nell in the company of two Bryn Mawr seniors, the cell's ring startled him. So did the orders, dispatching him to the riot at Second Hand Rose.

By the time he arrived, the ruckus had been resolved. The two women who had drawn the crowds were gone. The sight of them in bra and panties, unnotable throughout summer on any beach, had in the winter snows gathered a cheering crowd. Rose was promising the uniformed officer to make her customers use the dressing rooms. There were, of course, no dressing rooms.

Single-minded, Peyton Post overlooked Matt Hempel's officialdom, focused instead on the snowboard, the baggy woolen trousers, the long locks. Only the malicious would suggest that Peyton had ever judged a book other than by its cover.

"What's happening?" Peyton asked, arriving late.

"No big deal," Matt said. "Two foxes in their underwear."

His thoughts returned to the dormitories of Bryn Mawr. "You'd think nobody had ever seen a naked woman."

"Right," said Peyton. He walked beside Matt.

"Goin' boardin'?" Peyton prided himself on speaking a universal tongue for any caste, simply by eliding his G's.

"Beautiful day for it," Matt answered, on low alert.

"Sure is. I was thinkin'. I might light up and take a few runs myself."

Whoa. Is this guy for real? He looks like a local, he must know who I am. So he's putting me on. Matt restrained his enthusiasm and reviewed in his mind the law of entrapment.

"Sounds good."

"Don't know where I can get some stuff, do you?"

This guy could be my father. Would my father buy shit on the street? God, he's smarter than that.

"What did you have in mind?"

"Just a couple of jays. More, if you've got it."

Matt couldn't resist. "You're not a narc, are you?"

Peyton looked offended. "Do I look like a narc?"

Too good to be true. I should give him a stupidity dispensation. "I can do that," Matt said, "here." He stepped into the alley behind Pantagruel and fished two loose joints from his pocket. He'd been planning to smoke them on the first run down after lunch.

"Ten bucks."

Peyton removed a fold of bills held by a gold paper clip and paid the man.

"Hey, it's nice to make your acquaintance. My name's Peyton."

"Hi, Peyton. I'm Matt."

"Maybe we can do some regular business." It was exactly one month since the chain snapped on the Casablanca pier. Hempel took the ten spot from him, found his wallet, and deposited it. Then he turned the wallet and flashed his photo ID.

"I don't think so, Peyton. It might disrupt my career path. You're under arrest."

## Seventeen

News gets around, though several blocks behind gossip. By the day before Christmas, every investor had heard something. A dozen different stories in all. Dooberry's group is transforming fantasies into movies. They ran into a brick wall. They cut you a DVD, you can show it on your screen at home. They read your dreams; don't volunteer, and if you do, don't bring your wife.

The invitation for the investors' meeting at the Grant guesthouse was SRO. Better SRO, thought Dooberry, than SOL. A great audience, what in hell will I show them?

❧

One hundred and twenty-six million dollars is a lot of chopped liver. Justin searched his balance sheet a sixth time. Selling the Aspen house, the New York co-op, and the cottage in the Hamptons wouldn't be enough. Even selling JK Designs wouldn't do. How much would the banks take not to pull the plug? They wouldn't say. They weren't talking rollover, and they weren't talking work out, and they weren't talking compromise. All they'd say was, pay up.

The pressure came at the worst possible time. The preserve was going well—local and national press. Somewhere, Justin thought, somewhere on this eight-page balance sheet an asset is hiding. Something I've undervalued or overlooked. Underexploited. Under, over, and under. It sounds like the footpaths at the Walton Preserve.

What am I missing? In Justin's business, if you had one winner in the pack you canceled all other bets and put your wad on the favorite. My spring line is down the toilet. My houses are overleveraged. The only thing I've done right in the past year ...

Of course! The Walton Preserve!

❧

If she entered the When Did You Arrive? tournament, the editor of the *Aspen Leaf* would be a top seed. She had lunched with the Paepckes, had learned to ski with Freidl. But of course, she wasn't a player, just as she didn't waste time decrying Aspen's lost soul or the depth of its veneer. When a chance came to put a small nick in the parquet, that was different. That she did with delight.

So she put the story of Matt Hempel's latest bust on the front page. The offense was trivial, but the offender was copy. She rummaged through the photo morgue and found a picture of Chloe and Peyton dancing at last year's Snow Ball: she in spaghetti-strap black, he a dashing figure in jeans and white cretonne tie. How does he manage that tan year-round?

Readers would remark over their morning granola that poor Peyton couldn't spot a narc at a policeman's ball. They would laugh a comradely, benign laugh. And no one would be hurt.

Everyone in Aspen read the *Leaf*. The assistant manager of the Hotel Jerome read it. And when he read this story, he realized that Peyton was an Aspen resident. Not a hotel guest. So how is it I regularly see him coming out of an upstairs room with that Dooberry woman? And, as often, the maid. The short, attractive one. What's her name?

He began to pull personnel folders. His security chief had insisted on photo IDs. Here she was. He studied the snapshot and read the down-valley address. Easier to wait until she's on shift.

~

Dooberry put on an expression of affability with his cologne, an English lime. This morning, as he answered the bell, that expression brightened naturally. Etta was early for the investors' meeting. Behind her, a man whose name he didn't register. Who introduced himself as Victor Grant's man.

Etta made herself a tall bourbon and water and sat down in front of the large television screen. Grant's fellow didn't drink. He stood toward the rear, twirling a white forelock.

"Understand," Dooberry cautioned when the guests had settled, "understand Waddy here is our Alan Shepard. No full orbit yet, just a safe but historic first flight." Dooberry felt that the language of NASA added a certain gravitas to the venture. "Please keep your expectations in check. We have no way of knowing whether we have a moon landing or, as we say, simply hard cheese."

~

"I shouldn't take these, Justin. I shouldn't take gifts from the other side."

"What other side?" Justin asked dismissively and threw an arm around his pal. "We don't have two sides. You represent Native Americans with a devotion to the land. I head a team that respects that devotion. Wants to preserve the land for the very activities of their ancestors, hunting and fishing."

Irv Brumberger would not be persuaded. "I mean, staying at your house, that's one thing. But if I start wearing these shirts with the Justin Kaye logo ... "

"Don't be silly. Everyone wears my shirts. You'll look like the kids in *Vanity Fair*."

Brumberger unzipped his carryall and, with a bashful grin, packed all three shirts, each with the distinctive bucking bronco on the breast pocket.

"No one can criticize. We have a deal, we're partners. You don't schmeer your partner."

"No, I guess you don't."

Brumberger handed his bag to the airline agent and stepped up to the counter.

Justin was running the numbers in his head. Twenty lots, seven million a lot. Seven minimum, maybe more. "Soon as the snow clears, Irv, I'll let you know. You'll come out for the digging?"

"With my clients. They'll want to be there. If something shows up, they'll say *bruchas*."

"Now, I want you to approve who does the digging. Impartial and all that. My contractor is Marco Campaneris. He's reliable, ask around. Or we can use anyone you want." Justin neglected to mention that every other bulldozer in the county was booked.

"No, no. He'll be fine. He's impartial?"

"Impartial? He's on your side. Hates developers."

"We'll accept him. I'll wait for your call."

"And you'll stay with us again? Rochelle would be insulted."

"I don't think so. Just for appearances sake. Though I'll miss the meals." Brumberger patted his flexing belly. "Great breakfast." Rochelle had had the bialys flown in from Zabar's, the smoked sable from East Houston Street. Justin put an expression on his face—masculine, fraternal, genuine. The one he'd directed for a hundred shoots. You're manly, he would tell the model. But you're not afraid of strong emotion. He took

Silverheels's hand in both of his. They were standing on the shoveled walk outside the airline terminal. Brumberger liked to be early.

"You're sure you won't stay for the afternoon concert?" Justin asked ingenuously. He was fond of this man.

Brumberger gave him a wise smile. It acknowledged that Justin was a master of many worlds, and that he, Brumberger, had no such complex and alien ambitions.

"Justin, let me ask you something. Have you started to sell lots?"

Justin shrugged. "Irv. I can't sell lots until I know whether we have dead Indians. We have dead Indians, I have nothing to sell."

They shied back as a young man came between them wielding a pair of skis. "So. Whose money do you use 'til then?"

"Whose money?"

"Don't tell me it's yours. I'd guess you're preselling. Not that it matters. But I guess you're doing some preselling?"

"Let's just say, Irv, I may have some friends who want reservations. I do favors for friends."

Brumberger shook his hand. They understood each other. "Godspeed, Irv."

❧

The investors left the meeting satisfied. They liked the software that translated psyche into pixels. Not perfect, but a hell of a start.

More than satisfied. Pleased. If Wise Mother needed a second round of financing, they told each other, why not? It had a shot. Look at the progress they've made.

The man with the white forelock trailed behind as they left. To overhear their enthusiasm—just what Mr. Grant feared. And to study the guesthouse, particularly a casement window that reflected the high and white-glazed peaks.

"That," Dooberry offered, following the man's sight line, "that is the master bath. Even in the guesthouse you can sit in the tub and watch the sun set over the Rockies. Nice living."

"Nice," the man agreed. He was unconcerned with the view. He simply wanted to assure that the window he'd left ajar—first-floor bathroom—couldn't be spotted. He kept his thoughts out of his expression, he had trained to do that. But it gave him pleasure that his work was undetectable.

～

News gets around. That afternoon the audience settled into Harris Hall for a chamber concert. Everyone in Aspen had been exposed to Justin's deal—three articles in the *Leaf* and one in the real estate section of the Sunday *Times*.

How could he not attend? How could he not give friends the opportunity? Brumberger assumed he was collecting down payments. Why not?

Harris Concert Hall neighbors on the great tent of the Aspen Music Festival. Most of the hall had been set below grade, both to minimize its impact on the hallowed site and to enforce its audience's sense of security. We are safe amid the *Lieder* of Schubert and the quartets of Beethoven. We are in, the world is out. With its fan-design seating and low ceiling, the hall stands as both an acoustically superior space and a credible bomb shelter. If the world ends between movements, we'll be here long after you philistines have perished.

Justin knew exactly how to play it. Always dress for the occasion—make sure you're noticed. His lemon yellow Peruvian sweater tagged him as one of a kind.

A smattering of students gathered in collegial knots, clutching scores to their chests and waiting for the music. A few serious concertgoers spoke softly to each other or studied the program notes. The happenstancers—they had tickets, they had no alternative party, they might find one here—counted movements. There were people in cashmere socks and people in lined alligator loafers without socks. There were people who spent lives in drab apartments except for this week each year, when like a rare desert succulent, they bloomed in the Aspen air. There was a man whose fortune derived from deodorant and who annually gave a sizable sum on the condition that the festival annually play the 1812 Overture. There were rich and poor people, wise and foolish people, there were people whose lone issue with eternity was how their assets would remain intact for its duration.

And in their midst, standing while lights blinked to urge the crowd to be seated, the cruisers, those great frigates of personality who sailed about under full canvas, on display, smiling and signaling, announcing their presence. Their broad faces semaphored genuine pleasure in being present, in being so enabled, so perspicacious to attend this performance of a Brahms trio where their grandeur eclipsed all others, Brahms included.

No one could cruise like Justin. More than once he urged Rochelle to stand, to return the wave of a friend. In a plum spun-silk JK Durango classic, she drew viewers like a distress flare. Minutes before the baton fell, Justin had drawn four interested buyers.

"When will the money be due?"

"The tribes hired Irving Brumberger. Do you know him?"

"Will you appeal if you lose?"

Justin handled them individually.

"I won't take money until the risk is out. These are my shooting pals, not my customers." ... "If they find dead Indians, we give up, I swallow the loss. No Indians, they give up. No appeals. The preserve is for hunters, not lawyers." ... "Irv? He was at the house last week. We go way back."

The lights dimmed. A woman in the row behind waggled a score and shushed at him.

"Let's take our seats," Justin said happily. "Time to be quiet for Mozart."

"Brahms," whispered the woman with the music.

"Yes, yes. Brahms."

∽

Lisa didn't kid herself. It was pagan. Worse than pagan. Sentimental, jejune, old-fashioned. Traits that in others made her flinch. Superstition was the enemy of logic, science either worked or it didn't, and she was a scientist. Give me Euclid over hope, Newton over love. Still ...

She slipped on a lilac peignoir to cover both the Joe Cocker T-shirt, which read Let's Do It in the Road, and her ambivalence. The house was dark. She tied a quick bow and checked to make sure Waddy was asleep in the room next door. With the coast clear, she crept to the stairwell and went down.

The night was starless. Often winter nights in the high country were lit to the glow of a false day, as starlight pooled on the snow, but tonight a low cloud hung over the valley, adding to the faintly sinister mood. She moved to the kitchen. In the light of the refrigerator's low-watt bulb, she prepared the offering of the faithful. The very same ingredients for two decades.

That done, she retreated up the stairs, set the travel alarm for 3:30 A.M., and nestled hopefully into her bed.

Across the meadow, from a perch even higher than the estate of Victor Grant, a solitary watcher noticed the brief and low light. His first thought was a bathroom, but he considered the floor plan and deduced the kitchen. Someone up for a snack, possibly a timer light? He reminded himself, Don't panic, follow the plan.

The plan was to move at three o'clock. Both residents of the guesthouse would be in deep sleep. The watcher pulled the arctic sleeping bag up to his neck. From his car, parked in the drive of a neighboring and vacant estate, he could see the north- and west-facing sides of the Grant guesthouse. He would wait.

Time moved slowly. The elevation gave him the advantage of watching not only his target but the long road up from the Starwood gate, so that he could spot any roaming guard long before he'd be seen. He would simply let out the brake, put the car in neutral, and roll backward, behind the garages. But he did not need to fear. On Christmas Eve, even the partygoers had gotten themselves home by midnight. The roads were empty.

It would have been easy to ask Mr. Grant for permission to station his surveillance at the main house. But he understood Mr. Grant would not want to know anything about this project. He had been trained for just such action, he had a steady pulse, his body pumped surplus adrenaline. Engaged, on alert, cool. Ridiculous that a white forelock kept a pro like him out of his country's service.

At long last, the car's clock read 2:50. Close enough. Without starting the engine, he released the emergency brake and began the slow, noiseless descent toward the Grant houses. He parked pointing downhill so he could escape without cranking the ignition. Then he got out and quietly closed the door.

Now the tricky part. He had checked the guesthouse for contact alarms and motion sensors. Were Waddy and Lisa light sleepers? Did the guards of the main house keep a night surveillance? No covert operation was without risk. He was counting on a bit of luck.

And he got some: no one had found his casement. He forced it against the crank, squeezed his hand through, grasped the brass handle, and wound the window open as far as it would go. Then he boosted himself up and in. He came down in the oversized marble tub. Peered over its edge and felt an unworldly wetness on his face—the shock of a warm flush. Hero's tongue welcomed him. He dried his cheek and managed a soothing word through clenched teeth.

Slowly he made his way to the living room, to the project computer. From inside his parka he took the cloth that he'd brought especially for this purpose and draped it over the screen. Then, like a turn-of-the-century photographer exposing gelatin plates, he stuck his head under and switched on the power.

His Quantico training included basic computer programming and cryptology. In no time he cracked their software and grasped its architecture. Fairly simple stuff, question and response, preassigned with merge code.

A crunching sound brought him out from the cloth. The dog was eating from a plate. Damn him.

The program language was ASCII, the American Standard Code for Information Interchange. In ASCII, each letter of the alphabet is represented by a seven-digit binary number: 1100001 stands for lowercase *a*. To find what instructions sent what signals would take hours. His bladder was pressing up against his ribs and his heart thunked like a thrown rod. Best simply to sabotage the code. He looked down to his hands—the stone of his West Point ring glowered black in the night. That gave him the idea. A few random alterations ought to do it. He inserted the six letters, then checked to make sure it stuck. It hadn't. He needed to do something more. There, in the menu, was the key: Make Changes. He opened that window, repeated his dirty deed, and saved it to disk. It stuck. He reopened the program and repeated the alteration.

He quickly searched for all earlier revisions, the backup, and found them secured in the Q drive. Muttering an old college chant, he made the same fixes.

And heard, where before his pulse was the loudest sound in the snow-dampered night, a tiny electronic beep. Twice. Breathing deeply to control pulse, he pulled the cloth from his head to make sure. It was an alarm. He checked his own watch. Three-thirty. The noise was coming from upstairs. Hastily he exited the program, shut down the computer, stuffed the cloth in his pocket. Then he retraced his steps, Hero wagging behind him. At the bathroom he was sure he heard a footfall on the stairs. He dove through the window and landed headfirst in the snow.

～

Why she awoke exactly at three she couldn't say.

There were two possibilities. She and Sherry slept with windows full open, under a down comforter. It was a toasty arrangement, but only for those it covered. Etta was shaped like a milk carton and didn't turn freely. Sherry had almost the same dimensions, but he more resembled a top. On nights that he was particularly restless or insecure, he wound the comforter about him as he tossed. Tonight she looked over at him, asleep in his feather cocoon, and the bready warmth in her heart overcame the chill in the night air.

It wasn't temperature that awakened her but conscience. She could hear her daddy's voice. Honeybee, your wells are pumping, still, look at you. All you and that husband of yours do is overfeed yourselves. You're becoming one of them folks we used to laugh at. Do something, honeybee, do something useful. Tomorrow, she could hear him, tomorrow is the birthday of our Lord. Haven't we had His guidance to find all those producing traps? Do something for your fellow man in His name.

She *would* do something. She would put on a huge dinner and invite the poor. Of course, there were no poor in Aspen. By the time she could have them imported, Christmas would be over. If you can't have the poor, who's second best? The meek. After all, they're going to inherit a share of the earth, so it might be nice to know a few. For one thing, included in that share might be drilling rights.

To Etta the meek were synonymous with the single: no one with enough gumption to find a partner chose to sleep alone. It was a gift of God's gregarious earth that everybody, male and female, gay and straight, Jew, Christian, Hindu, Zoroastrian, or Parsee, had a cosmic imperative to hook up. She didn't much care whether it was for a night or a lifetime. Solitude was depressing and, until Judgment Day, which promised to be crowded and a bad time to meet new people, easy to fix.

Well, that's what I'll do. I'll give a damned Christmas dinner and invite every sad sack I can find.

She swung her legs out of bed. Sherry, bless him, snored through his sleep. His breath carried the faintly citrus smell of the evening's old-fashioneds. She flicked on the light and began to make a list.

༅

This time the premonition was undeniable. Premonitions made no sense, they weren't testable or replicable and she didn't believe in them, but one night a year she gave herself over to magic, and this night the feeling bowled her over. She shut off the alarm on its second ring.

She shivered in the chill and tightened the peignoir around herself. There is someone in the house. The excitement widened her eyes and quickened her pulse. There *is* someone here, it's he, I know it, and I don't know what I'll say. She crept to the top of the stairs and paused. A draft rose up the well, and on it the sound of feet on snow. She froze. That's not imagining, that's real. She waited. Next, she heard a heavier sound, a crumbling of packed powder. It could be two iron runners bearing weight as they began to move. She bounded down and looked out. Nothing. There was no moon or stars to reveal a silhouette. But she had heard it.

Excited, she went to inspect the offerings. They were on the living room table, among the code books and computer logs. Two of the cookies were gone! She took the plate and glass to the kitchen, sat at the table. Outside, flakes floated down like the innards of a snow globe. Absently, she screwed off the top of an Oreo and ate the frosting. She dunked the cookie expertly, so it absorbed the maximum liquid without disintegrating, and popped it into her mouth. Then unscrewed the last cookie, ate the filling, and drank off the milk.

He *had* visited. Just as her father had promised. Could it mean that her Christmas wish would be granted? No one, no one but she, could know her Christmas wish.

Eighteen

Etta was on the phone at seven. The assistant manager apologized: the butcher didn't arrive until nine. He took her order.

"I don't know how many. I'd say at least four. Four hams, spiral-cut, and carve four smoked turkeys. Good-sized and sliced thin. Better yet, why don't you set aside six of each. What we don't eat we'll take to the homeless shelter.

"No shelter? Well, we'll freeze 'em. You can't have too much food." She would pick it up.

She had promised the staff the day off, and they would have it. She'd get some volunteers to help, that was more in the spirit of things. The first people she tried were the Finches.

"Oh, that's great, Mary. Let's say two o'clock.

"No, I don't know how many, I'm just about to go start a-hollerin' invites. And you all invite anyone you see. 'Specially people who are alone. Say, I didn't wake you or anything? Really? To church? What church do you go to? Oh, certainly I know it. I thought it was a gallery."

Too early to call the Posts, so she went to work on guests. The police chief was glad to pass the word, and so was the woman who ran the AA meetings. At eight she roused Sherry and got him dressed. Together they gulped breakfast and rolled out the truck. They invited the staff at Carl's Drug and the two gas stations. She hit a gusher when she picked up groceries.

All the checkers and stockers were on short shift, and the two o'clock time suited them perfectly.

Sherry had a friend who filled the bill. Odd fellow who seemed to move around a bit. Etta parked by the north end of the airport, on the shoulder, and followed Sherry to the hole in the fence. Gossage was cozily tucked into his box, thirty pages from the end of *Northanger Abbey*.

"Y'all'll come, won't you?" she asked, her drawl deepening with her sincerity. "This is just ah-deal for the down-and-out. Y'all may not be down, but you are assuredly out."

Gossage accepted. Indeed, agreed to return with them and make stuffing. They drove off. As they neared the highway, Etta turned an acute angle up the hill.

"I have two stops, side by side."

"Was Starwood mentioned in the Sermon on the Mount?" Gossage asked.

"Etta doesn't think money has anything to do with loneliness," Sherry said. "She's out to cure people's pain."

"I see myself," she explained to Gossage as she double-clutched into the first serpentine, "as a blend of Billy Graham and Heidi Fleiss."

Waddy was still in pajamas, watching "A Charlie Brown Christmas." He couldn't speak for Lisa, uncharacteristically still abed, but he'd be there for sure.

"Ask that strange fellow with the bulldozer. And anyone else you can think of."

The second stop was next door. They waited in a sitting room while Victor Grant finished a telephone call to a florist.

Grant was pleased to see Etta.

"Etta, that's the nicest thing I can imagine," he told her. "But no, I'm afraid I have work to do."

He insisted they stay for an eggnog. Made, he reassured them, with Egg Beaters.

"Now, Victor, I assume you know the good news about what

they're doing next door. They've had some tentative results."

"I've heard something along those lines," Grant said cautiously.

"Well, it's exciting. They'll need more capital, but we knew that, didn't we?"

He smiled, a kindly, avuncular smile. "We did."

"And I assume if this news is real progress, all of the investors will pony up. Isn't that what you say in the venture capital world: 'Pony up'?"

"We do, Etta."

"And don't you think everyone will?"

"If they have real progress?"

"If they have real progress."

"Well, if they have real progress, I'll certainly take a look. Their debt is mounting, you know."

"What debt?"

"To me. All the value we've put in. The services, the office space, the work our lawyers did for them. All that gets expressed as debt."

"It does?"

"It does. At appraised prices. Etta, surely you read the documents."

"Well, I'm not sure."

"The debt is at appraised prices. An office in Starwood is expensive."

"Are you saying, now that you know there's progress, you're going to try to foreclose? I warned you about that, Victor. We won't stand back and let you take this deal away."

"I won't take it away, Etta. I don't need to foreclose. All I need to do is convert."

"Convert what?"

"Convert the debt. If there's progress and my people think it's a worthwhile venture, we'll convert our debt. You'll still be in. You'll just be diluted."

"This debt is convertible?"

"Etta, I'm surprised at you. You should always read the documents."

"Victor Grant, on Christmas morning, too. You are a prick of misery."

Grant gave the smallest of grimaces. He rose from the sofa and placed his glass on the table.

Etta stood as well and led the two men she'd brought toward the front door. "If you can't make our party, you send over that nice man who came to the meeting. The one with the funny hair?" Grant said he would pass the invitation on.

"Have you ever thought," Gossage offered, "how much space and energy you have here? Look at it. This house must be twelve thousand square feet."

"Sixteen."

"Sixteen. Have you ever considered whether assets you have that lie fallow might benefit others without your even noticing?"

"No," Grant said.

"Victor, can I make a suggestion?" Sherry asked.

"Of course."

"A little sour mash would perk up that eggnog."

Etta was at the door. An athletic man in a collared T-shirt beat her to it and stood ready with his hand on the knob. "Victor, I'm going back to read those papers. If they're not what you say, or if there's wiggle wide as a flea's ass, why I'll bankroll it and we'll sue."

"I think that's wise, Etta. Do look at the papers. And listen. Thank you for driving up here and for the invitation. That's just about the nicest thing anyone has done for me in, I don't know how long."

"Right," said Etta. The door opened and she and her men departed.

Grant called after her, "And Merry Christmas."

For others in the valley, Christmas morning was not a-jingle with quite the cheer and activity. Frankie Rusticana awoke alone and melancholy. He had closed Pantagruel for the day, and now he wondered why. What was he to do with himself? He stared across the faux zebra comforter. Holiday bouquets from his suppliers surrounded the dressing table. The fish man had sent asters and gardenias, the greengrocer azaleas and baby's breath, the laundry a Dean & DeLuca crate the size of a tenor, packed with French chutneys and terrines, all cushioned in festively green excelsior. Frankie sighed and pulled the covers over his head.

Matt Hempel also had the day off. He poured himself a bowl of Grape-Nuts, ate them dry, standing in front of the small television set in his trailer. The pope was speaking from a window in the Vatican. When the pope finished, Matt put on his coat to take a walk. He was only steps into the gentle snow when he heard from the neighboring trailer a small, furry sobbing, constant and durable. Matt had gone into law enforcement because he believed there *were* maidens in distress. Maidens and others. He knocked softly.

"*Quién está?*"

"Hi. My name's Matt. Are you okay?"

Carmen cracked the front door—it had no window—and peered out. Who was this man? Hadn't one of her neighbors pointed him out as an Aspen cop?

"What you want?" she asked through the slit. Matt could see only her front two teeth and an alluring gap between them.

"I just wondered, are you all right?"

"Yeah. Okay."

"I just wondered."

"You a cop?"

"Actually," Matt didn't quite know how to handle the

question. He wasn't on the job, so technically he wasn't under-cover. There was something compelling about the gap in those teeth, the way the tongue darted behind it.

"Actually, I am. But I'm not here on business. I live next door." He pointed to his rental trailer to prove what he said.

"So?"

"So I just wondered. Listen, I didn't mean to disturb you." He turned to go on his walk. "*Feliz Navidad.*"

"Hey," said the mouth at the door. "*Habla español?*"

"No. I got that from the 7-Eleven. They had a sign up."

The door opened a palm's width and revealed the pretti-est face Matt had ever seen, the blackest eyes from which ran parallel and wet lines down to a perfect chin.

"A sign?"

"In tinsel." The tip of the tongue moved up to the gap to cover it self-consciously. But the door opened wider.

༄

The Aspen Town Council had declared FFE a quasi-municipal agency. So the FFE eco-cops were allowed to buy into employee housing, particularly the long gray-blue buildings behind the art museum. No one asked Philida Post to provide her finan-cial statement, and no one thought to connect her name to the toilets in all sixty-three units.

Philida too had the day off. But she answered the door in uniform. She preferred it to civilian dress.

"Yes?"

"Philida Post?" asked the FedEx man.

"Yes?" Philida pulled herself up to military height. She resented these companies. They burned fuel to bring pack-ages from all over the country to one city, then burned more fuel dispersing them. A package from New York to Bronxville might travel two thousand miles. She thought to mention it, then decided that this fellow most likely was not responsible.

"Delivery. Refrigerated."

He went to the truck. Returned with a four-foot-high polystyrene box and opened it. Inside, wrapped in a plastic sleeve, were a dozen calla lilies.

"My God," she said. "Are you sure?"

The boy showed her the address. "Wait," he said. "I have three more."

"Lilies?"

"Dozen."

He went to fetch them. She found the small envelope and opened it. Inside, on the white card, had been printed in ink, "A Secret Admirer of You and Your Work."

"Who sent these?" she asked.

"Sorry, Miz Post. I just do what they tell me."

"How do I find out?"

"Sorry." He handed her a clipboard and she signed. "I just drive the truck."

"Where do they get calla lilies this time of year?"

"Costa Rica, I believe. Gotta run. Truck's full."

"Costa Rica?" Cutting down rain forests to keep me in flowers? She turned a raptor's eye on the driver. "Are these natural or hothouse?"

The driver looked at her, mystified.

"Are there import restrictions? How do we know the grower is licensed?"

He kept retreating. "Gotta run. Merry Christmas."

ॐ

Rod Hollister struggled to free his arm. The blonde lying on it never stirred. He swung his legs over the bed and levered himself up. Across the foot of the bed lay a second woman, also nude, but brunette. Shit. Where the hell was he?

He went to the window and searched for the cord. Shit, he thought again, and this time said the word. More high tech. These blinds had no fucking cord. He seemed to remember they worked on a switch. He grabbed a center slat with two hands and snapped it.

Outside, neon lights flashed even though the sun was high. Vegas. Of course. Vegas. I've got a six o'clock lounge show and then the dinner show at nine. The brunette looked up and grinned.

Double shit. I need some sleep.

He called the front desk.

"Listen. This is Hollister. There are two women in my room. I want you to send up the bouncer and get them the fuck out of here."

"Mr. Hollister? In the Bob Hope Suite?"

"Yeah, I guess."

"Sorry, Mr. Hollister. We don't have a bouncer."

"Fuck you don't. I don't know what you call him, but I use him in the show. The thug who tosses people out. It's in my fucking contract."

"Yes, sir, in the show. But we don't have a bouncer on duty at the moment. He'll be here for the show."

"Well, why don't you have one at the moment?"

"We gave him the day off, sir. It's Christmas."

"It is?"

"Yes, sir."

The brunette rose and covered herself with his tux pants. The suspenders hung to her thighs. She went over to the little jewel box on the dresser and opened it. It was empty. "Bullshit," she said at him, and he knew there was going to be trouble. Sitting on the table in the living room was a brick of shed-cured Molokai pot his dealer had given him as a gift. An entire brick. He'd better stash it before she got into it.

"Tell you what," he said to the kid at the desk. "You get

me another room. Send a bellman up with a key."

The brunette said "Bullshit" again and held the empty box up for him to see.

"Well, I don't know, Mr. Hollister."

"You got any more of this blow?" the brunette asked sulkily and wiped her nose with a dangling trouser leg.

"Listen, asshole. Put it on my bill. I'll pay for it."

Now the woman turned and, for the first time, saw the blonde, face to the pillows, sleeping cozily across the width of the bed.

"Who the hell is that?"

"We don't have another suite available, Mr. Hollister. Only rooms."

"You heard me! Who the hell is that?"

"Rooms would be fine."

"And no kings. Only two queens."

"Two queens it is."

"Who the hell are you talking to? Are you bringing more women up here?"

The jewel box came flying across the room. It wasn't much of a throw, and his duck was superfluous.

"Perfect," Hollister answered. "Just make sure they're empty. And hurry."

❧

Of the invitations Etta extended, none was more welcomed than the last.

"But there won't be anyone for me, Miss Eubanks. Holidays are so lonely for people like us."

"You never know, son, 'til you show up. I got a mess o' folks coming. Some of them must like boys. The odds are with you."

"But that's just it, Miss Eubanks. I'm *not* a boy. I'm well past the best-used-by date."

"Now Frankie, stop feeling sorry for yourself. You get dressed and haul your abused ass over here. We'll be gathering about two. And call any of your waiters and waitresses, 'specially that cute girl who seats people."

"What can I bring? I have oodles of chutney."

"That's the spirit. You can bring nothing but your old hide."

"No, I insist. It's Christmas. I'm going to make you a special dessert."

"Fine. You bring some cookies or something."

Frankie hit upon the idea as he hung up. His pastry chef was a Bellini with meringue.

~

Peyton wanted Chloe to concentrate on the issue, but she was distracted. The Finches, he explained, were to serve the food, and he and Chloe were to handle the bar. Peyton owned a red vest that he loved to wear for Christmas parties, didn't she think it was just the thing?

"I need to make this one call."

"Aren't the markets closed today?"

"They are," and she dialed the lawyer's number.

Peyton laid out the vest on his bed. Would a white shirt and bolo be better than a denim shirt? He put both of those out as well. But he couldn't catch Chloe's eye.

"I don't care what the fine is," she said into the phone, "and I don't care what the offense is. Plead it fast, so long as there's no jail."

The lawyer assured her he'd have a deal by Twelfth Night. Chloe took a sharpened number three pencil and drew a neat line through the lawyer's name.

Peyton was in the three-headed shower, happily shaving and lustrating himself. Chloe's conversation, even the half he heard, made him cozy. Like when his mother telephoned to have him excused from school. It was pleasant to be watched over. Outside, a Yule snow fell, adding to his buoyant nostalgia. He squeezed a washcloth over the shaving mirror to wash off the fog. When he stretched his eyes, the crow's-feet disappeared. They were, he had been told, easily erased. He thought not. A few lines matured him. No, he wouldn't have them done. Besides, he didn't like what the surgery had achieved for his friends. It made them appear not so much youthful as astonished.

Hmm. Serving punch he would likely avoid conversations. Still, one ought to be prepared. Yesterday's *Journal* lay on the bed where his wife had finished with it. He glanced over its front page, took a ballpoint pen from the telephone table, and wrote on his palm.

"Senate Passes Diluted Tax Bill"

෴

He took a club soda from Chloe Post. Perhaps it was his Academy training, but he believed two o'clock meant two o'clock.

"I'm sorry Mr. Grant couldn't make it," Chloe said.

The man apologized for his boss. Too much work to do.

Etta thought he was excusing himself. "None of that," she interrupted. "No business allowed. The day is set aside to love one's fellow man. Or fellow woman, dealer's choice."

"You're going to have some single women here?" Chloe asked her as the handsome young fellow waited to move off. "To match these hunks?" The man eyed the ground and his hand involuntarily touched his hair.

"Am I ever. Some of the best fillies in the stable. I missed out on that Lisa gal, you need to meet her, son. But she's working too. Can you imagine?"

The house filled quickly. Hungry, delighted to be sprung from the solitude of the holiday, they came to celebrate. They stamped their feet on the wide Victorian porch, knocking snow off mukluks and boots, off Caribou and Timberlands. Inside they were greeted by a twenty-five-foot Douglas fir that the florist had garlanded in white lights no larger than a cuticle and bows of cream satin. They shed their parkas and anoraks and Norwegian sweaters, received a glass of punch, and were left to warm themselves with Barbados rum and the news from Nazareth.

Kidney-shaped slices flew off the ham, florettes of cauliflower and broccoli were drowned in the curry dip, wheels of baked brie disappeared. The mix of shop clerks, waiters, gas jockeys, and town singles had an incendiary chemistry. Like the punch—Gene Finch and Peyton worked constantly to replenish the three bowls, and Peyton never got to utter his observation of the Senate action—the recipe of personalities was refreshing and volatile.

The Finches enjoyed themselves. This was their kind of holiday. They believed in block parties, AA-rated bonds, and good will toward men. Mary assembled a group around the piano to sing carols.

With everyone replenished, Chloe left her duties. She tracked down the one person she thought interesting: a black man dressed in turtleneck and jeans. He was talking with, of all people, her sister-in-law. Chloe had sensed that he was a sympathetic soul, and she was confirmed when the conversation turned to economics.

"You're saying we have enough in the world? That surpluses would balance the shortages if we could simply redirect them?"

"I'm saying that the competitive markets don't deal with them. If the world economies cooperated just a bit, they'd find a different configuration. And I'm saying the only way to gain that adjustment is for the consumer to make it."

"Sounds like socialism," Chloe stuck in.

"No matter if it does. It's not socialism. I'm not changing who owns the assets. Just where they are."

"I like it," Philida told them warmly.

"Philida," Chloe chided. "You like anything that makes you poorer. You should get over your embarrassment at being wealthy."

"Oh, I don't know," Gossage offered. "Embarrassment is a good emotion for the rich. Keeps them humble." The words brought smiles from both women. Gossage went on. "You see how nature, in this case human nature, counterpoises excess. What you call embarrassment. Others might see it as a sense of duty, or of charity. Whatever name you use, it moves those who can do something about social excess to action."

"It keeps the system in motion," Chloe said.

"Exactly. Any organism, whether it's societal or biologic, needs to moderate its behavior. When an organism injures itself, it needs to recover. When it overeats, it needs to digest and disgorge."

"So we need to be protected," Philida offered, "from our appetites."

"We need to understand our appetites, so they don't lead us to destruction."

"Like the dinosaurs," said Philida. "Devouring all the leaves on the trees."

Someone passed a tray of Swedish meatballs and both women, newly ascetic, declined. Gossage took two and placed them in a plastic bag in his pocket.

Philida put them her problem. "I've been considering excess in a different context. You tell me whether this is anti-social. A man wishes to impress a woman. He orders four dozen calla lilies. They are rare even in summer. In winter they need to be flown great distances by jet. Isn't that an excess that needs to be stopped?"

"And," Gossage asked, "you feel he's showing off?"

"No. He does it all anonymously."

"Oh," said Chloe, her hand to her breast. "That's not

antisocial. That's romance."

"Romance perhaps. But wasteful. Don't you think?" Philida asked unsurely.

"Philida," Chloe put her fingers to the woman's forearm. "Romance *is* wasteful. Lighten up."

"But killing forty-eight flowers, blooms in the prime of their productive capacity ... "

"Philida, these are hothouse flowers. They're grown to be cut."

Gossage smiled. He had overheard Grant's half of the telephone conversation that morning. There could not be a second suitor in Aspen ordering four dozen calla lilies.

"I agree. Look at all the good he does with his purchase. Paying a grower, a cutter, an exporter, all doubtlessly living in some impoverished country. Love is good business. And think of this poor man's imbalances. Here's someone too shy to send flowers in his own name. He fights off the urge to do nothing, he comes forward and proclaims his heart. It's a market correction against celibacy and for propagation. Dante has Beatrice say, 'Love moved me, so I speak.' He says, 'Love moved me, so I FedEx.'"

Philida sipped at her unpasteurized apple juice. Perhaps Gossage was right. The words were so gentle, so assuring. Philida was in fact bursting with pleasure, for being courted was a new experience. She had done her share of great gestures, but the object was always an endangered crustacean or an unloved cactus, never herself. If this man's emotions were genuine, and they appeared to be, and did no harm to the environment, well ...

～

Lisa was glad to have the house to herself. Glad, and not so. She built a fire, made herself a cranberry juice and protein powder shake, and settled in to read. The top book on the pile was psychobabble about living your daydreams. The second, understanding the psychology of romantic love. She went through both in half an hour.

The next book was, the flap said, simply an extension of Jung's work on dreams. The center section grouped fantasies into twelve categories. From it, Lisa realized, one could form a matrix of possible fantasies. Exactly what she needed. She finished the book in a single seating. It was midafternoon, and the winter sun began its roll across the silvered horizon. She rose, threw two logs on the fire, and fetched pad and pencil. The book laid out the logical relationship between fantasies and dreams and why these twelve categories served both. She flipped to the index, intending to chart the categories, and found something equally interesting: the author had done her work.

There in an appendix was the Universal Dream Key. Fantasies were divided into separate scripts, and each one of those subdivided for particular applications. It was ready-made.

She wanted to celebrate. Perhaps that party was still going on.

❧

On the far side of the house, his plate of turkey and potato salad set before him like a spinnaker, Waddy Brush sailed through the crowd in quest. He'd looked in vain and was about to give up when he noticed a small room off the pantry. Its walls were lacquered in forest green, and in it, where the color set off her fair complexion to advantage, was the object of his search.

"I thought you might be here."

Annalee didn't glance up at his words. She was examining a foot-square picture on the wall. A nude woman prepared to enter the bath she had just drawn.

"Look at this," she whispered.

Waddy squinted. A plaque had been attached to the frame with brass screws.

"Bonnard. Is he famous?"

"I think he is." Under the oil sat a carved credenza. The room's only other furniture were two club chairs, placed around a terrazzo table whose top was a chessboard.

"Do you like it?" Waddy had never looked much at pictures.

"Yes," she said simply.

"Why?"

Annalee looked quickly at him. He wondered if she didn't resemble the woman in the painting. You couldn't tell, because you couldn't see her face.

"Look at her." Annalee spoke as if the merit was evident.

The intimacy of the scene made Waddy shiver. They were peering at a beautiful woman. Perhaps not Annalee's equal, but lovely. She in turn was unaware of them. They were, he secretly thrilled at the word, voyeurs.

"She better get in the tub or she'll catch cold."

"Look," her voice was husky. "The porcelain of the tub, its whiteness. How cool it is. Its curves. The water inside. Look at her."

"She's on tiptoes."

"Yes. The tile floor is cold. She's absorbed. That's what makes it so ... "

"So?"

"Erotic."

"Erotic? How?" He knew, but he wanted her to say.

"It's so private. Private is erotic. And here he's painted it. For everyone to see. But still, it's private, between him and her."

"You think he knows her?"

Annalee lowered her eyes.

"I think he loves her."

Waddy stood there. The potato salad sat densely on the plate.

He didn't know what to say, and finally chose the wrong thing.

"You really miss Norma?"

She gave him a long glance. "On days like this, holidays, especially."

He went back to the painting. "When do you know you like a picture?"

"When I want to be in it."

Waddy looked about. There was one other frame in the room, a modern collage with the headline of a French newspaper.

"How about that?"

"No," she said with a smile. "I don't want to be in that."

"Me either. I go bonkers when someone messes up my paper before I've read it." That brought a laugh.

"Abstract art is supposed to spur your imagination."

"My imagination," Waddy repeated.

"Why do you say it like that?"

Waddy began talking. He told her about the Wise Mother project, the threshold of using other people's fantasies.

"No second thoughts?" Annalee asked. "No sense you're endangering those guppies?"

They found themselves sitting on the arms of the two chairs. On his lap Waddy balanced the plate of uneaten food.

"Lots of second thoughts. We're extracting fantasies. They go in the mix with people's hobbies, their credit cards. Just another statistic. Soon they're being used to sell a Lexus SUV. The more the database succeeds, the more data it adds. It takes on a life of its own. Begins to propagate itself."

"I prefer the old-fashioned way."

"You think we're messing with Mother Nature?"

"I think, once you get started, you forget about the real thing. Like playing tennis with a ball machine. I know folks who've given up normal sex for masturbation."

"It's the oddest feeling," he told her. "Digitizing your suppressed desires."

"Could I do it?"

"Anyone can do it. It doesn't take any skill."

"No, I mean, would you let me? Record my fantasy?"

Waddy started. He'd love to. "I don't know," he said nervously, and cut an overlarge bite of turkey.

He wasn't sure he knew her well enough for this conversation. "You have to let someone watch your intimacy," he said at last as he stared at the picture.

"Well," and she watched him chew. "It would be like being your model." Annalee flashed a mischievous eye at her friend in the picture, then added a remark Waddy contemplated for several nights, trying to decide whether it was said ingenuously or with regret. Either reading was possible from her tone.

"Without, of course, the skinny dipping."

They were interrupted. Waddy would have paid a month's wages not to be. Someone insisted they join the announcement in the living room.

"Everyone gather round," called Etta. "No speeches. But before we serve dessert, I want you all to see this piece of art created by our own Frankie Rusticana."

The Finches carried in an immense tray. On it, constructed on a field of the tiramisu for which Pantagruel was justly famous, Frankie and his chef had fashioned a crèche. The tableau was passed around, and the crowd ogled it. The donkeys and cows were caramel fondant and Cockaigne, snow of divinity surrounded the manger, and the logs of the humble inn were a combination of meringue and fruit paste. The holy family itself, marzipan of seven colors, hid inexplicably behind a barricade of profiteroles, and there in a crib of spun sugar and gingerbread lay a toffee baby Jesus. This was the most eloquent touch, for the delicacy, there known as *rahat loukoum*, was a favorite on the streets of Bethlehem.

Frankie received a hip-hip-hooray and responded with a brief and misty-eyed speech of thanks. When he was through, the crowd placed Frankie and Etta in the center of a circle. Their hands locked in each other's and raised over their heads like boxers after a championship fight, they were serenaded as Jolly Good Fellows.

~

Lisa Laroux was the last to arrive. There was ample food: turkey and rolls, coleslaw and potato puffs, still three kinds of cranberry sauce, even a final spoonful of the manger. But not what she'd come for.

She had walked in the snow for an hour this afternoon, considering her earlier visitation. If it were a sign, even a sign of her imagination, it still signified. That's what virtual reality taught: the imagination is real. And there was physical evidence. The missing Oreos, the sounds, the open window. She'd even found tracks in the new snow, one set coming to the house and a second going away. No, it was a sign, she was sure of it.

And that certitude pushed her to the party. Reason had to give way when the evidence was overwhelming. That was only, well, reasonable.

But if today she were to get her wish and the man of her dreams *had* been at the party, he was gone by the time she'd arrived.

~

Waddy walked in Lisa's steps and Hero in his. From the guesthouse through the wide meadow out back, up the road past the oversized homes. Twice a security car slowed to flash its spot on the two—walkers in Starwood were a suspicious sight. Not joggers or skiers or Rollerbladers, but a pedestrian suggested—what? Theft? Revolution? The guards recognized the three-legged dog and allowed them to go their way.

The interruptions barely disturbed Waddy's thoughts. It had been a wonderful day. His talk with Annalee had awakened in him a reservoir that held more than memories. Somehow he had tapped into a stream of powerful feelings. Their force was revealed only now, in the tranquility of recollection. He could explain it no better to himself.

The only comparable experience he could think of was his first pair of skis. A year's wages, from his mother's catering business, a year squeezing pâté onto crackers. The skis cut turns without effort, they tracked the snow and seemed to glide not on the surface, but above it. His feeling was like having those new skis, the world zipping by and him snaking through it with grace, and all the world changed.

As he walked, flakes the size of quarters floated out of the blackness and brushed his face. The temperature was well below freezing. He came to a single street lamp marking a neighbor's long drive and stood under it watching flakes dapple the beam of light. The snow seemed to take forever to fall; it must be coming from heaven itself. For reasons he could not say, the air put him in mind of the day he'd graduated from Skakit Point High. His mother had addressed him, as she did on birthdays and holidays. Putting her hand up to his shoulder, looking him dead in the eye, and squeezing the trapezius until he squirmed.

"It's a big world out there, Wadsworth. You have trouble keeping track of things. Your watch, your gloves. That's fine, but don't let go of who you are. If you put that down, sometimes it's hard to find again."

The strains were connected. He knew it. The illimitability of the snow, his mother's words, the high school diploma in its azure simulated-buckram binding. Should he be messing about with people's private thoughts so that someone could sell them a car? He *hadn't* lost track of who he was, and when he thought on his mother's advice, he felt unshakably secure.

## Nineteen

Blank. Waddy dutifully typed out his fantasy to fit the new format Lisa had programmed. Clicked the Submit button. No response. He went back and opened their first file—Waddy's basketball team. Blank. He sat puzzling in front of a screen on which fell a perpetual mint-green snow.

What was he overlooking? The day before Christmas the state finals worked. Three days later, nothing. Perhaps a wire worked loose in the power toggle, perhaps an investor kicked out a plug. This was major glitch—nothing was responding.

Lisa and he went to work. They listed every component and every switch, and tested them all. The failures could not have come at a worse time. January's payroll was in the bank, but that was all. On February first, the well went dry. Christmas Day, Etta and Grant had squabbled over control. If either knew that the early results might be the only results, they would be fighting just as vigorously to be first out.

Etta hired a lawyer she'd met during the holidays, a fellow named Brumberger, to send Victor Grant an intimidating letter. Dooberry's copy arrived by FedEx, the day after Christmas. "Irreparable harm ... unwarranted intimidation ... breach of significant fiduciary duties ... steps that may surprise you." There would be a response, Dooberry knew. Grant had an accordion file of lawyers equally articulate, equally anal. Maybe,

Dooberry thought, they could cadge another six months' funding by keeping the news of the breakdown to themselves.

Wouldn't work, Dooberry realized. Those two Eagle Scouts, Laroux and Brush, kept journals. He hated problems like this, where the only option was to find the solution.

"Okay, team," Dooberry said. Lisa and Waddy sat across the conference table in the guesthouse. Etta, naked and tabled at her twice-weekly Lomi Lomi massage, was on the speaker phone.

"Can you hear us?"

"I can," Etta answered.

"What do you suggest?"

"Well, let's brainstorm. Mortimer, you act as secretary and take down every idea. Everyone with me?"

Three yeses. "Lisa, honey, you start."

"Electrical connections. Check every one."

"You've done that," Dooberry said.

"This isn't a debate. Write it down. Other ideas?"

"Cosmic irregularities. Sunspots," said Waddy.

"That's ridiculous," answered Dooberry.

"Mortimer, please. Just write."

"Program," suggested Waddy. "Maybe this new format doesn't fit with the existing programming."

The programming was Lisa's handiwork. She took offense. "Can't be it. Same platform. Maybe someone opened up the computer at the demonstration and screwed with the code."

"Write them down, Mortimer," Etta grunted from the masseuse's exertion.

By the end of the session, they had listed possibilities from a power failure to a spell of astrological malevolence—Lisa's spectral vision on Christmas Eve had nudged her toward the transcendental. They would test each one.

Dooberry handed out the jobs. "How do we check the programming?"

Lisa spoke. "We print out the source code and compare

it to the master. We can't do it electronically. It's a long, dirty job. Manual."

"Manual means?"

"Brush and me. We are the *man* in *manual*."

"Fine," said Dooberry in a manly voice. "Get to it. If we can't show results fast, you're both out of a job." As, he thought as a gurgle of self-pity rose in his throat, am I.

～

Gossage was late getting started. The sun had disappeared and the clouds up the valley showed an ominous pewter underbelly as they drifted in low for carpet bombing. He'd arisen with the arrival of the seven-fifteen from Denver, a United 737 that shook his box as it thundered down to Runway 33, twenty feet overhead, full flaps, speed brakes deployed.

No, his alarm was not to blame, his own fascination was. He'd gone out and watched Sherry chip away at *The Goddess of the Conduct of Other People* as she began to emerge from the stone. Working as the mood struck him, he had finished the outline of her head and the left ear.

"You can't imagine," Sherry let his goggles fall to his chest, "how sensuous it is to spend an entire morning on an eighteen-inch nostril." He stood looking at the expanse of gleaming stone with an expression at once lubricious and proud.

As Sherry tapped and dusted, Gossage lay on a piece of cardboard and watched. Every so often, the sculptor took a break. They would open the thermos, sip coffee fortified with Jameson's, and nibble on the biscotti and fruit that Etta's staff had packed in a wicker basket. Red-checkered napkins, the everyday Spode.

"Listen, I must get to town," Gossage said when the coffee was gone. "It's a long walk, and today is moving day."

"Where are you going?"

"I'll let you know once I'm settled. Several possibilities, all good locations. I'm leaning toward a West End Victorian with the complete works of Trollope."

"We'd be neighbors."

"Exactly."

"You're welcome to stay at our place. We have lots of room. Besides, in a week we head back to Tulsa until the Snow Ball."

"You mean as your guest? Thank you, but that would be cheating."

Sherry gathered up his tools. "I see your point. But I'll miss our morning chats."

"Me too."

"Let me give you a ride into town."

Gossage examined the lowering sky and considered. He had to transport a single change of clothes and the six major novels of Jane Austen.

"No, I'll hoof it."

"Due date?" Sherry indicated his books.

"Due date. I'm off. May I mention something? It's a bit sensitive."

"Please."

"It looks like she's stuffed up." He pointed.

"Oh, yes. There's a fissure in the stone. I need a small-gauge chisel before I blow her nose for her."

"You might reconsider. Perhaps *The Goddess of the Conduct of Other People* should have a permanent sniffle. There are some who see a tear in the eye of *La Gioconda*."

Sherry turned to mull this about, and Gossage, with a glance toward an increasingly minatory sky, set out for Aspen, an hour's walk up the road.

◞

He could attempt it on the takeoff. He had brought the blonde with him for this very reason—she was the less belligerent of the two, and God knows she'd try anything. But the departure in Las Vegas was on the flats. No mountain, no real danger. It just wouldn't be the same. No, it was Aspen or nothing. That was the trifecta: drugs, sex, and a blind mountain landing.

He copied his instrument clearance from the controller: cleared from McCarran International direct to the Blue Mesa VOR as filed, then direct to Aspen. Flight level two three zero. Clear sailing most of the way. A stationary system sat along a line that ran from north of Ogden to Farmington, and the clouds were thickening. He'd been told to expect instrument conditions and low ceilings on arrival. Even better. Flying down through the soup, a nose full of dust, and a trusty blonde attached at the groin.

"You got the plan?" he asked her.

"I got it. How 'bout a line now?"

"Not now. We'll party at the initial approach fix. A fix at the fix."

She glanced over her shoulder. The brick of pot sat on the row of seats behind them, still in its Christmas wrapping. Reindeer and sleds. Like a kid with a toy, he knew what was in there but couldn't help peeking. Hollister had torn through just enough of the top fold to inspect its contents. It was quality shit. Even unlit, the aroma was unmistakable. Whoever gave it to him, and he swallowed the saliva that gathered in his mouth, he owed a favor back. Trouble was, he couldn't remember.

"Maybe just a joint." She licked her lips.

"Not 'til we're cleared for the approach. Timing is everything."

"Let me ask you something."

"Shoot." He taxied out to the active runway.

"Timing. How do you intend," she motioned with her hands, " ... at the right time?"

"Listen," Hollister became impatient. "You do your part. I'll worry about that."

The voice of the tower interrupted. "King Air One Romeo Hotel. Cleared for takeoff. Fly runway heading, I'll call your turn."

"One Romeo Hotel," Hollister replied. He switched on the CD player and considered the format. He set up "Do Me, Roomie" on the changer, ready for the big moment. All he had to do was press a button.

~

All I should have to do, thought Waddy, is press a button. There must be a digital way to examine two hundred pages of code.

The integers for each character had to be compared with the sourcebook. Sometimes he could simply scan and transliterate; he knew ASCII, he could recognize the characters. But he didn't want to go through this process twice. He moved slowly.

Why did I get stuck with this duty? Didn't Dooberry say it was Lisa and me? How is it she's doing the tasks that require a phone call and a night of sidecars, and I get the midnight oil and bleary eyesight? It's a class struggle. The ruling class against the remedial class.

He didn't expect to find anything. The possibility was illogical. If the algorithms worked three times, and they had, if they got results on the flat run, and they had, the sudden failure could not be the fault of the program. Unless, of course, someone had altered code. And they hadn't. After all, who would do that, and how? So his was not only the most tedious task, it was the least likely.

Fresh powder. I could be out telemarking the pasture, or up Conundrum Creek, as the snow begins to fall. Up on Justin's property, the elk coming down to forage, stripping the low bark from the aspen, no one around but me. I could call Annalee, she breaks after lunch, we'd ski to the high ridge to watch the storm come over Castle Peak, then glide down to where the road starts. We'd be exhausted, I'd suggest here for a tea, we'd come in and I'd build a fire. We'd be soaked through. We'd strip off our parkas and the wicking long johns, I'd suggest she shower first. She'd say, Waddy, you're a conservationist, aren't you? I'd say, Yes, I am. Well, we should conserve water, share a shower. Yes, that would be good for the entire earth, people showering together. Waddy, she'd say, and she'd look up at me, the fire would be crackling, and I'd get out Lisa's robe to put her in after we showered, Waddy do you suppose sexual preference is like voter registration, I mean, you're not committed, you can change right up until election day, isn't that right ... ?

Waddy looked at the printout. It read

1001000 1001001 1001101 1000111 1010100

With both hands he slapped at his cheeks to waken himself. Where did I leave off?

↷

The man walking toward him brightened up, intending to catch his eye. Gossage obliged with a smile.

"Hi."

"Hello," Gossage said warmly.

"I met you at Etta's. Etta Eubanks?"

"Of course," Gossage said, though he had no recollection. The man looked familiar, like so many middle-aged men about here. A winter tan, the peculiarly local combination of enduring fitness and enduring indolence.

"I'm Peyton Post. You talked to my wife."

"Ah, yes. Philida?"

"No, that's my sister. You talked to her too. My wife is Chloe."

"Of course. Short, pretty, pixie cut."

"Yes." Peyton was pleased. He thought her pretty too.

A bike path ran parallel to the road from downriver. Gossage had picked it up at the airport and encountered Peyton at the golf course. He carried six books under one arm and over his other shoulder a stick from which dangled a bundle of clothes. Peyton had seen the device only in the Sunday comics.

"Are you moving or going to return books?"

"Both, actually. You're very observant."

Peyton was pleased a third time. The compliment, the remark about his wife, and here he was talking to a black man. That was unusual, made him feel modern, and got his mind off the misfortune in Morocco.

"You're the fellow who doesn't believe in free markets."

Gossage chuckled. He had a low baritone, and when he laughed those who heard him laughed too.

"No, no. That's not quite it. I don't believe *only* in free markets."

"You have something else in mind? God perhaps?"

"Actually, that's quite witty. Some mathematicians think randomness *is* God. Or at the very least, His footprint. You see, I believe in forcing randomness on contracting markets. To prevent them from stagnating."

Peyton pursed his lips. "Look. If you don't mind, I'll turn about here and walk back to town with you. But I'm afraid we'll have to change the conversation. I can tell this will be something I won't get."

"Don't sell yourself short. It's easy to understand."

The black man moved the stick to the other shoulder and they started off, stride by stride. Peyton listened. He had a party this evening and if he could grasp a single sentence of what the man was saying, he wouldn't need a headline.

"Let's think of the market system as if it were a natural law. Supply and demand, the survival of the strongest. Just like gravity. Always at work."

"In a way it is natural law," Peyton offered.

"Exactly. Now let's look at devices that rely on natural law. The laws of physics. A centrifuge, say. It uses density and Newton's laws of motion. We measure the force by multiplying mass times the square of the velocity, divided by the radius. You remember high school physics?"

"It was an elective," Peyton said apologetically. They quieted while a large airliner came across the road and landed.

"No matter. What happens to material in a centrifuge?"

"It sorts itself out."

"It sorts itself out. Exactly. And then?"

"Then?" Peyton considered that it might be a trick question. Like school. But this fellow seemed too kind. "Then nothing."

"Precisely." Gossage flashed a white-iron smile. "Nothing. Stasis. Natural law has worked itself through. We could find other examples, the death of stars or the expanding universe. It's called entropy. Basic quantum mechanics."

"Entropy." Peyton wished he had a pen.

"Now," Gossage made to shift his books and Peyton, his hands free, took a load from him. "Now let's apply this to the markets. What happens when the strong compete with the weak?"

"They win?"

"They do indeed. And on the second day?"

"They win again."

"And again and again. The more they win, the stronger they get. The stronger they get, the more they win. Eventually, monopoly. Markets sort themselves out, to stasis. Oh, there are forces that upset the stasis, invention for one, and obsolescence. But not many. My theory uses randomness as an upset force. To keep vitality. I want *people* to step in, give the market something it hasn't predicted. Human nature helps the system."

"I'll say." Peyton thought of his beautiful wife, whom he loved and desired, and who spent her every thought parlaying an excess into a still larger fortune. "Human nature," and Peyton spoke with a wistfulness born of experience, "is pretty random."

"Not really. Not in scientific terms, compared, say, with the pattern neutrons make as radioactive material decays. Or atmospheric noise, or the lava lamp. Those give you mathematical randomness. But human behavior adds an unknown to the equation. Think of the universe as tension between order and chaos. Physics gives us order, random behavior gives us chaos. You don't want either to get the upper hand."

Peyton preferred his science usable, like the fellow on PBS who showed kids how to make invisible ink.

"Random behavior," he said.

"That's it. In mathematics those episodes are known as normal deviates."

"Normal deviates," Peyton repeated. "Good name for a book."

"I agree. *Normal Deviates: My Life in Aspen*." Gossage again flashed his molten white smile. They walked on silently, past the Nordic center and the Prince of Peace Chapel. On their left was the municipal golf course.

"Still with me?"

"I think so. Order and chaos. You take someone who follows the stock market and wants to be one step ahead. He goes on the basis that the market is reacting to known forces. If he can just figure them out ... "

"That's a force of order."

"And someone else who wants to hang out and enjoy people, smoke a little dope if it's available, and ski." Here he looked to the sky. "At least on sunny days ... "

"That's chaos. You want to keep both around. Those two are well matched."

"You think so?" Peyton was encouraged.

"Oh, I do." Gossage pointed to the steady line of trucks on the highway.

"Look at them."

"The traffic? How does it figure in?"

"There is nothing the supply chain can't deliver so long as the demand is funded."

Peyton melted. His new friend had hit upon the very engine of his melancholy. He let out a sigh. "I wish that was true."

Gossage glanced sideways at his companion. "You have something in mind?"

Peyton could not bear it. His privation was too painful. He unloaded the story, how Sinbad had lost his supplier, how every customer had scrambled about, down valley as far as Salt Lake to the west and Denver to the east, how there wasn't enough pot in town to scrape together a butt.

Gossage listened intently. He was particularly interested in agricultural economies. Here was a living example of a crisis that the free market was ignoring.

"How will it all work out?" Gossage asked sympathetically.

"I can't imagine," said Peyton. And he was right—he could not. But then, neither could anyone else.

~

Salt Lake Center handed him off to Denver over Glen Canyon, and Denver started him down.

"One Romeo Hotel, descend to flight level two one zero."

It's about time. Typical underpaid, underbrained government slugs. They recognize my call sign. (He couldn't resist using his initials for his tail number. One Romeo Hotel translated to Rodney Hollister in the number one position, this week and next. A new peak.) They're making a buck fifty a week, it drives 'em crazy someone like me has money. Hollister could take or leave the adulation, but he loved the envy.

They got the grades in school. Now they're on the ground and I'm up here with a sex toy, two million bucks of power, and a cube of Mary Jane.

He peered through the windscreen. Starting at the San Juans and reaching north as far as he could see nestled a low-lying cloud mass. The color of a dirty nickel, it lay over southwest Colorado like mushroom soup spilled from the can.

He checked the GPS. Eighty miles from Blue Mesa, another sixty miles to the Red Table VOR, which was the initial fix. He'd nailed this approach dozens of times, many of them sober. What the hell was her name? They could get started early.

"Okay, sweetheart," he said and undid his four-point seat belt so he could reach into the pocket behind her seat. "Let's do a quick line to warm up."

～

If you let your eyes unfocus, the zeros and ones made an irregular picket fence. Waddy got up and stuck a CD into the player. Louis's horn led with an arpeggio, then the band and a husky-voiced Thelma Middleton.

"Gimme a pigfoot," Waddy sang along. "And a bottle of beer." That won't work. I need to say these numbers out loud or I'll lose my place again.

"Oh one one oh oh one oh. Oh oh one oh one oh oh. One one oh oh oh one oh." He looked down. By his right index finger, just as he had said his last "oh," stood a one. He looked again. Could it be?

This exercise was futile. He wouldn't find anything, he was sure of it.

He checked the sourcebook against the printout. Could it be? It was. The sourcebook must be wrong. He stuck a Post-it in the margin, then went into the hard drive to read the code off the screen.

By Blue Mesa she wanted a second line. She got out her compact mirror and he poured from the leather pouch. He checked the autopilot and again released his safety harness, this time to unbuckle his belt and slip his jeans and underwear down to the hips.

"King Air One Romeo Hotel, cleared to one four thousand for the approach. Switch to Aspen tower, one one eight dot eight five."

Hollister struggled back to hit the mike button and said, "One Romeo Hotel to one four," dialed the new frequency, and finished disrobing. This ought to work out just right. With no more Center to talk to, he flipped on the autopilot to hold the vector into Sardy Field. All he had to worry about now was altitude. He was entering a corridor of mountains. He would simply step down the plane while she did her work, sniff a last few grains, and enjoy the ride. Make sure he could see the runway when he broke out of the clouds. With a little luck and good timing, he'd be zipping up on the taxiway.

He removed the armrests between them.

"You're on, sweetheart."

She leaned over and began her ministrations. This blonde knew what she was doing. The enthusiasm of youth and a little flip at the top of the stroke that was downright inventive. He reached across the undulating head and hit Play on the CD.

*Do me, Roomie.*

"Oh, Rod." She looked up. "I *love* that song."

"Thanks."

"We can make it *our* song."

"Back to work," he said with some urgency. Timing was everything.

"Aspen Tower. King Air One Romeo Hotel on final for three three."

"One Romeo Hotel cleared to land. Caution, ceilings may be below minimums. Welcome home, Mr. Hollister."

Minimums hadn't stopped him before. He had good reflexes, he could take this puppy down to the ground. The law on this approach required the pilot to decide at ten thousand two hundred feet whether to land. Without an uninterrupted view of the runway at that altitude, he must execute a missed approach. But the runway was still two thousand feet below that. These wusses gave you more than enough clearance. That's for old fuckers in nonperforming aircraft. More than once he'd sunk to tower height to get his uninterrupted view. He could do it again.

She worked away. Right on schedule. He stepped down to twelve seven and again to twelve two, cued by the mileage. *Do me, do me again.* If that jerk off in the tower could only see me. What's he get paid? Less in a month than I clear for a lounge show. He reached back into the open brick, took a pinch of leaf, and licked it from his thumb. And I haven't done lounges in years. Where do you suppose she got that twist?

Now would be the perfect time to break out. Nothing ahead. He checked his altimeter. Nine thousand six, sinking at five hundred feet a minute, a little dicey. He was below minimum decision height, everything else was on schedule. God, she is good. Give me breakout now, just a few hundred feet and I'm there.

"There!" he yelled.

"One Romeo Hotel?" asked the tower. In his urgency Hollister had squeezed the yoke and depressed the mike button. His enthusiasm was broadcast on the tower frequency. He ignored the controller and let the button go.

"There. There," he said again. Still no runway.

The airplane was at eight thousand seven when the controller heard a spent voice.

"On the missed. Going around. One Romeo Hotel."

The Aspen missed approach is intricate. After a climbing right turn to fourteen thousand feet, on a heading of three hundred degrees, the pilot must identify two navigational aids and find the intersection of their beams. For a solo instrument pilot, the workload is significant. For one who is stoned and getting expert head, it is excessive. Hollister began his climbing right turn, a maneuver airmen call a chandelle, but he had started low to the valley floor. He also had allowed his airspeed to creep up. His turn swept a wide curve. The King Air entered a standard bank and cleared the first ridge to the south of the airstrip.

Behind rose a second ridge, which it cleared, and a third, which it cleared. And a fourth.

On the fourth, an unnamed saddle that stood ninety-one hundred feet, the lowered starboard wing caught the top of a piñon pine. The impact jarred the wing down into a boulder and snapped the spars where they joined the fuselage. The crippled aircraft cartwheeled twice in the air and once on the ground. Jet fuel sprayed everywhere. The explosion knocked out windows from Starwood to Basalt.

~

"I can't imagine," said Peyton. As they looked at each other, trying to imagine, an apocalyptic boom shuddered the air. Their gazes caught in mutual terror. Before they could speak, a hot wind broke over them, as if a coal train was passing inches from their skin.

"What ... ?" said Gossage, and Peyton said something similar. The gust was followed by the patter of debris. Pieces of material began to fall on the highway, charred and smoking flakes dropped on the whitened golf course by their path. The sounds against the snowpack were soft, not metallic, like a rain of large drops.

In the terror of the explosion, all their senses went to work. Even smell. Peyton recognized the aroma and smiled.

Perhaps twenty feet behind where they stood, on the golf course side of the split-rail fence, on the edge of the eleventh fairway where the tall grasses force you to hit up not out, lay a smoldering cube. From it drifted an ancient scent, an aroma of memory, spices, and Lethean dreams. Peyton passed his athletic body through the logs. He walked toward the package and stepped gingerly on the smoking fringe that had been its wrapper. Christmas paper. It was hard to tell from what was left, but it looked to have been reindeer. And sleds.

❧

Sherry's hearing was diminished from a life of chiseling and jackhammering. Still, the explosion made him flinch. He was working at the time on the widow's peak of *The Goddess of the Conduct of Other People*, and he stayed on the ladder. The ladder jumped ten inches.

"What the hell was that?" he said, holding on to his perch, and then he ducked. Debris rained about him: bits of cloth, a shard of wing, two ovals of chrome that were cowling off the engine mount. Sherry climbed down and walked to where the chrome lay on the snow. It had a satisfying found-art look.

Later, the National Transportation Safety Board reconstructed the crash. Inspectors combed the surroundings and labeled and identified every piece of the aircraft and its occupants. They rented a hangar in Grand Junction and on long tables set out the parts of the King Air. The morticians set out the parts of the pilot and passenger. Both were scrupulous. The only items missing were Hollister's left leg from the top of the fibula down and the two chrome rims from an engine's trailing edge.

Waddy looked a last time at the numbers on the screen. Then he inserted the prized DVD, the one that contained the entire program, and searched as a final check.

"Bingo!" he shouted.

"Boom!" shouted the world.

The house, faced with Carrara marble from a quarry outside Pietrasanta, shook. The double-paned windows, marketed as environmentally sound for their insulation rating summer and winter, bulged but did not break. Waddy saw the computer blink, power itself again, and go into a lengthy reboot.

Despite the distraction, which might have been the end of the civilization, Waddy had it. The glitch. Someone had corrupted the trunk program by inserting, several times and apparently at random, two words. They used the same letters as a block—G-O A-R-M-Y. The spacing made the contaminant easy to find. Waddy saw neither motive nor malice in his discovery, but then he saw neither motive nor malice anywhere. He found all the intrusions and quickly corrected them.

Lisa and The Doo would be pleased. In his enthusiasm, Waddy forgot the explosion. Whether it was earthquake or bomb, there was nothing he could do about it.

*Twenty*

"Twenty-six homesites?" the head of P and Z was incredulous. "I thought you wanted a duck club?"

"We do, we do," Justin said. "But twenty-six homesites will hardly be noticed. It's not as if anyone drives by. It's a cul-de-sac."

"What happened to Isaak Walton?"

"He's still here." Justin pulled out a four-color rendering of the entrance gate. "On the sign."

"I don't know, Mr. Kaye. I'm not sure this doesn't need another notification procedure. Don't you think people will complain?"

"Not at all. Not at all. That's the beauty of it. Mr. Brumberger's suit names all interested parties, and here," Justin reached into the mock Pony Express pannier he used as a briefcase, "here is his stipulation. This is not some bum who sleeps under a bridge. This is Irving Silverheels Brumberger, attorney of record for all objectors. So you don't need a notice. Everyone's represented by competent counsel. Fifty-third and Fifth."

He showed the man the negotiated settlement. "It's quite simple. Dead Indians, we quit. No dead Indians, we proceed. Read it."

The man felt frazzled. He couldn't think fast enough to figure why Justin wasn't right. Why won't these developers stand still? They were like reef fish, nibbling at what you gave them, moving around, attacking from behind. Although, by anyone's definition, from one homesite to twenty-six wasn't a nibble. It was a major banquet.

~

"*Mi hermana cara*, I insist." Still, Carmen had reservations. She'd always paid her own way. Her looks gave her daily opportunities to travel free, "travel on your back" was the Spanish idiom, but she had always earned her passage. Now, fired from the hotel, with no savings and no job, she considered the hand Flavia held out. Why not? Flavia was her dear friend, her only friend north of the border until Matt. And she could work off room and board.

In the days since her arrival at the Dooberrys, she cleaned the house top to bottom. She did all the grocery shopping and prepared every dinner. Dr. Dooberry was so cute, he devoured so much of her posole that he had to sneak off to Clark's Drug for Mylanta. He couldn't be nicer. Solicitous of her every wish, sometimes coming to her room first thing to see if there was anything she needed on rising.

~

Waddy verified each switch twice and checked it on the list Lisa had printed out. Lisa liked lists. What had he ever seen in her? By comparison, Annalee was so soft, so—there was no better word—feminine.

Lisa and Dooberry were out for the day chasing money, leaving him behind to make sure there were no other snags. He pressed his fingers to the bridge of his nose. Proofing pages of ASCII could drive a monk to unnatural acts. His thoughts returned to Annalee. He'd better get some fresh air. The snow had crusted from thaw and refreezing—cross-country skis would be difficult. It was too cold to fish. Hero had cabin fever too, they needed to get out. He didn't finish his sentence, "Let's go see Marco," before the dog's tail was batting at the door.

If Waddy had hoped to escape from problems of commerce, he was disappointed. At the Quonset hut, Marco and Tiffany sat hunched like chess players over a yellow pad on which Gossage scribbled.

"I think it could work," the former professor was telling them. "In a new venture sales are always the problem, but your numbers are credible. Remember, you'll need twenty-five thousand for tenant improvements."

"Ain't gonna get that selling trinkets," Marco said flatly.

They looked up to acknowledge Waddy and Hero.

"I've been offered skin movies," Tiffany said. Marco grumbled his disapproval.

"This is no time for false modesty," she answered. "What are our options?"

Marco was silent. She went on. "I have three thousand in the bank, and you have that project for Mr. Kaye. Can you get an advance?"

"Don't know."

"We can ask."

"He's called," Marco told them. "Wants to see me."

"We'll ask," Tiffany said.

"Can't do that. We shook on it."

"Marco. He placed the call."

Gossage jumped in. "She's right, Marco. If he wants to see you, it means *he* needs to change the deal. You listen to her."

"It's blood money," Marco said and wiped his sleeve across his nose. "That property shouldn't be dug up by nobody. He's fixing to put a subdivision up there. Fucker ought to be arrested."

"Houses," said Waddy. "It's a shame."

Everyone agreed mournfully.

"It'll go eventually," Tiffany consoled them. "The market gets what it wants."

"Funny you should say that." Gossage spoke as if to himself. "Somewhere in a Santa Fe pawnshop is a medal with my name on it, from a European monarch. I got it for saying just the opposite. It comes with a red sash."

"How does all this affect the Walton Preserve?" Tiffany asked. "I don't understand."

"You will," Gossage assured her and gestured for Waddy to pull up a chair.

~

The memorial service for Rodney Hollister was packed. Like many entertainers, he had lived his life on the road. Those few in town who knew him uniformly disliked him. But fans came from around the globe to pay last respects to the man who had penned *The Fool in School*, *Gang Bangin' for Profit*, and the evergreen *Do Me, Roomie*. The service was held, so went the day's gag, at the Chapel Formerly Known as the Prince of Peace. It exceeded nondenominational—it was nonspecific. In the absence of anything good to say about him, the local youth choir did a medley of his tunes, their two repeating chords well within their capacity. The agent with whom Hollister had most recently settled a lawsuit delivered a eulogy that highlighted his innate good nature and eleven platinum CDs. Omitted was any mention of the trashed Carreras, the deflowered high schoolers, and a septum reconstructed as often as Hadrian's Wall. Outside the chapel, fans built altars to him. They carved soffits in the snowbanks, now yellowing from passing dogs, to display dried flowers, CD jewel boxes, underwear, and photos of the surly troubadour himself, his mouth often obscured by a blot of lipstick.

Hollister left no will and no survivors. Within a day of the accident, his stepmother arrived from Marfa, Texas, and with startling dispatch took charge of the estate. She sold the remaining aircraft, a Bonanza, for quick cash. She needed liquidity for the suite at the Jerome and her fleet of Dallas lawyers.

Real estate agents knew the house on Red Mountain, and she wasted no time acting on their recommendations. The day of the funeral she pumped out both underground storage tanks so that as soon as she could find a bulldozer, she could have them removed. Speed, she'd been advised, was her ally. Tanks tended to upset the local environmental nuts: if she waited, they would make her pull permits.

After the service, she and Charley, the houseboy, boarded a stretch limo to return to the Hollister house. It was a tactical error. Hollister's fans had come from distances, and all they'd had so far was a bland church hour, an off-key medley, and the Lord's Prayer, straight. Not a *People* mag celebrity, not even veggies and dip.

Filing out of the church they recognized Rod's houseboy and followed the limo like gulls behind a garbage scow. Security didn't help: they turned on their headlights and in a cortege of curiosity sailed past the gate. Soon the Hollister grounds bulged with adolescents ordering take-out and pizzas by the dozen, scavenging the drawers, and liberating Rod's collection of silk scarves and sex aids.

The only onsite authority was Philida Post. She had heard rumors of a peremptory strike on the tanks. In the uniform of the Friends of the Friendless Earth, she'd arrived to serve a court order that allowed FFE to inspect.

Not that she didn't have other distractions in her life. To her dismay and secret joy, the flowers had continued to arrive, exotic and excessive. Her conscience wrestled with the predicament. Why work for a better world when you privately encourage profligacy in others? It was a conflict, and as she watched the first tanker suck out 94 octane, she promised herself to resolve it.

Inside the house, Hollister's stepmother ranted at the intruders. The incidentals scavenged by these hooligans could have some value. She tackled one bestudded youth as he was making for the door carrying a blow-up doll that, other than the exaggerated orifices, resembled Paulette Goddard. When she got to her feet she recognized two of Rod's spangled shirts walking arm in arm down the hill.

It was too much. She reared back and shouted at the top of her lungs, "Everybody out!"

She had a piercing scream. There followed two beats of silence.

"Hey," came the answer. "Rock and roll."

She lurched out the back door and across the south deck. Three youths were standing at the rail, peeing for distance. Beyond the cabana, by the garage, the second of the two tank trucks was finishing extracting jet fuel. A mannish woman in a Sam Browne belt stood by.

"You. You an officer of the law?"

"Not exactly," said Philida.

"Well do something useful and call one. These mother-fuckers are stealing me blind."

Philida Post believed in law and order. She flipped on her two-way radio and reached Aspen P.D. Within minutes, four Saab sedans were rushing all eight on-duty officers up Red Mountain to quell the disturbance.

～

"So what is it you're doing?" Annalee had come to pick him up for a backcountry ski. She made him explain the Wise Mother project and listened thoughtfully.

"So the computer takes what you've given it and rewrites a happy ending. In this case a win for the team."

He nodded. "That's what's supposed to happen. So far all

we have is the game, without the ending. It's a beta test."

"What's a beta test?"

"I'm not sure. It's something financiers say."

"Sounds pretty mild." Annalee took her place before the screen. "Can I watch?"

"Gee, I don't know. Fantasies are kinda personal."

"That's why I want to watch. Who wants what's impersonal?"

Waddy hesitated. "We're not supposed to show. Lisa and Dr. Dooberry have done theirs. The software is still under construction."

"You show me yours, I'll show you mine," she said, and licked her lips.

Waddy thought for a minute. He went to the kitchen, came back with a large bag of Fritos and a DVD. Opened the one and stuck in the other. When he leaned across her to use the DVD player, he inhaled her scent—fresh, outdoorsy. Annalee wore no perfume. It was laundry day and she smelled of fabric softener. Also, as she hit the chips, a hint of corn. He hit a few keys, typed in a password.

Two seconds of blank screen. And then, clear as if it came from the mother cable, a basketball game.

The unsteady sound of an amateur band came through the speakers. Two snares, a trumpet, three saxophones. A trombone played in quarter tones. The instruments achieved a *dimuendo* one by one, like paratroopers out of a plane, and were joined by adolescent voices, fervent and reedy:

> Battling Crabs eternal,
> Pincers held on high,
> Hearts fixed on the goal and
> Eyes fixed to the sky.
> Battling Crabs eternal,
> Battling Crabs supreme,

We're fighting the fight and
We're dreaming the dream.

"It's the state finals," Waddy explained. The bag of Fritos was between them, its mouth gaping like a carp. He reached into the bag for a nervous munch.

The camera flashes on the scoreboard. Skakit Point High is seven down with fourteen minutes to go. The face of the coach fills the screen and looks out accusingly at Waddy and Annalee, who sit, chips in hand.

"Brush," he says, and his eyes widen. He might be exhorting an assassin. "Brush, you're hot. Keep gunning."

A towel is thrown over the screen and Waddy realizes he's wiping the sweat from his face. He can hear his heart beating. Is that in the program? A brunette with a pageboy approaches. She wears a white sweater on which a felt megaphone and the initials *BC* are sewn. The letters flex alluringly across her ample bosom. The present Waddy gulps for air like a beached shad. She closes her eyes, purses her lips into a perfect heart, and whispers to the camera, "Do it, Waddy. Do it for me."

The game has resumed and the ball whirls about. Waddy sits on the couch. Sweat appears on couch Waddy exactly as it does on screen Waddy. The gap in score narrows, disappears, reappears after a one-and-one: the Battling Crabs are a single point down.

The last time-out. The captain of the cheerleaders returns, squeezes his arm. "Please, Waddy, please," she whispers as if they were alone in a parked car. She turns to her mates and leads them in a Motown shuffle.

Waddy, Waddy, he's our man.
If he can't do it, no one can.

There's a break in the action. Waddy leans forward on the couch, sucks air at the bottom of his Slurpee, the sound of a dead engine.

"Okay," the coach says to a bunch of bowed heads. "I want you to get it to Brush. He's on fire. Waddy, you get free any way you can. One shot is all we need. It's all come down to this, men."

Waddy hits Mute. He asks Annalee whether she's seen enough.

"Are you kidding? Get back the sound."

On the court Waddy takes his position to the far left, sees the other guard walk casually to the keyhole to set up his pick. The ball is inbounded to his right, a second pass to the corner. He makes his break. As he rounds the pick, the ball is coming at him, hands high. Perfect. He doesn't hesitate. He is in the air, he launches.

Click. The screen goes blank.

"Is that it?"

"No," Waddy answered.

"What happens?"

"He misses."

"He misses? That was you, wasn't it?"

"Yes."

"And you missed the shot? You were open ... "

"I know."

"Perfect setup on the high post."

Great. Just what I need. Beautiful, gay, and a basketball expert.

"I missed it."

"You sure?" Annalee asked. "That shot looked good to me. Soft, good angle ... "

"It rolled in and out. Believe me."

They both sat back and breathed deeply. Waddy was drenched.

~

Justin stuck a cold Moosehead into Marco's fist. "What I'd like you to do is get this digging underway as soon as you can."

Marco tugged at the beer. Tiffany had sparkling water in a glass. They sat in the Kayes' living room, on belting leather sofas that faced each other. Antique Crownpoint rugs hung over the furniture. Though Marco didn't know it, the look was Arts and Crafts, the very look that had anchored Justin's home furnishings campaign that fall. Indeed the cost of the rugs had already been deducted from federal income tax as an ordinary and necessary business expense.

"Snow up there, Mr. Kaye. Couple of feet." Marco pointed out the window at the couloirs of white that striped Ajax Mountain, in case Mr. Kaye hadn't made the connection.

"Construction goes on in the snow. Right here in town, people are building."

"They're out of the ground," Marco countered. "Can't start until the ground thaws."

"Marco. What if cost wasn't a concern? Is there some equipment you could get to break through the frost?"

"Cost ain't a concern? But it is."

Justin eyed him cautiously. Is he playing me?

"What if? Is there something you could get to break through?"

"Well, I suppose you could. You could wait 'til the frost was down to eight or ten inches and then bring a 320 BL up there. A 320 BL could break through."

"Exactly. A 320 BL."

"But it would run you a pretty dollar."

"Like what?"

"Well, it would run double what I quoted you."

"Triple," said Tiffany.

"What?"

"Triple. There's site reclamation. Whenever you use a 320 BL there's site reclamation."

"Young lady," Justin turned a pale look on her. "Would you like another Perrier?"

"I'm fine, Mr. Kaye."

"Well, triple," Justin said. This job was peanuts compared to what he could raise selling homesites. Three times as many peanuts, so what? Justin's bankers had raised the stakes. "Let's say triple. When could you do it?"

"Still have to wait for the weather to warm up. But maybe third week of March?"

Third week of March. Justin closed his eyes. Third week of March. Rochelle had that dance, the Snow Ball. He'd have to be in Aspen anyway. His note came due the twenty-first, but if he could show contracts with names like Victor Grant on the bottom, he could get a rollover. Especially if he started early, showed the banks a plan. Banks liked plans more than payment. He had names from the concert, he'd get letters of intent. He could collect ten in a single evening working the tables at Pantagruel's. Give the bank a reason to meet. That's how you hustle a bank. Give them something for committee. The committee meets midmonth, considers a request for a rollover, sees the letters of intent. An out—they agree, let's give him a way to pay us off. Do they sue? No, they work with me. They cry about how tough an asset this is, how the feds are making them classify it. But they work with me.

Once the test holes are done, I'm in the clear. I don't care if Brumberger makes me plough the whole hillside. Once I pass the test, I'm in the clear.

"Find a 320 BL, Marco. Let's plan to dig as soon as we can."

The curves on the Red Mountain road switchback on themselves one hundred and eighty degrees. Coming up, both tank trucks negotiated the turns in first gear. But on the way down, the drivers were tired. The man hauling gasoline had boogied for an hour. The other had downed a few beers, the first keg having arrived shortly after the moo shu pork. He forgot he was fronting thirty-two hundred gallons of jet fuel, a shifting load over nine tons. He braked for the last hairpin, but not enough. The truck carried into the snow-covered shoulder and its wheels sunk to their hubs. The trailer jackknifed at the hitch and came to rest across both lanes of traffic. The road was blocked.

A crowd gathered. Rodney Hollister's fans, who had worked through their grief in time to pilfer his house of every condom and bar of soap they could find, now ambled down the hill to see what the trouble was. Four of the policemen left Hollister's, abandoned a pepperoni and endive pizza half-eaten, and were soon on site. They sent out a call for a wrecker, but there was none strong enough in Aspen to lift the load. An hour passed, a second. The lines of traffic lengthened. People were trapped.

Uphill of the roadblock, the Chinese delivery van began selling off its cargo. Tiny white boxes appeared up and down the line. Kung pao shrimp, lemongrass chicken, assorted dim sum. It looked as if he'd recover his costs after all. At the head of the queue, cozy in the cab of their pickup, sat Tiffany and Marco.

"What site reclamation?"

"I don't know. I thought he was desperate." Tiffany hoped Marco wouldn't focus on her expertise in dealing with desperate men.

Marco reflected on the negotiation. Justin had agreed so quickly. "Marco. We're trying to bank some money. You need to consider our future."

"Well ... ," and he swallowed his thoughts. He'd never considered before.

An untidy young man walked by carrying a snowboard.

"Hey, Marco."

"Hey, Matt."

"How you doin'?"

"Good. You?"

"Good."

"Marco, don't you have a Cat up the pass?"

"Sure do."

"That Cat be able to pull this truck out of the ditch?"

"Sure would."

Marco walked behind Matt, around the splayed tanker. The fire chief picked up Marco on the other side and, sirens blazing, took him back through town.

～

Philida eased her red Lambretta scooter between the semi's wheel and the mountainside. It was a short drive into town to the FFE headquarters, where she alerted Legal to the possibility of an illegal UST removal tomorrow on Red Mountain. Filled out an affidavit they'd need for the temporary restraining order. Wrote a note to herself to check whether a man named Marco Campaneris had the permits to operate a diesel engine within city limits. Checked her diary for tasks tomorrow. Only one entry:

"Call V. Grant."

Why wait? Pushpinned to the paneling of her workstation among the posters "Earth: One Spaceship" and "Let's Arm the Deer" was a bumper sticker that read "Do the Tough Jobs First."

Victor Grant took the call.

"Mr. Grant?" She identified herself.

"Philida. How good to hear from you."

"Mr. Grant, I want you to stop sending the flowers. They're

rare and expensive." Yesterday he had birds of paradise delivered, the day before cattleya orchids. "I know they're expensive. The earth can hardly afford your looting simply to impress me."

"I send them in the best spirit."

"That may be, but motives are irrelevant when the environment is plundered."

Victor Grant was candid in both business and the little social intercourse he allowed himself. He was simply too busy to be otherwise, and he had found that, in both endeavors, candor was so rare as to be the best guile.

"I want us to be friends," he said. "It seems I've done the opposite."

"If you want us to be friends, do something I admire. Do something to help the community around you."

"What do you have in mind?" Grant took a mechanical pencil from his desktop and with the fingers of the same hand rotated its point.

"Mr. Grant ... "

"Victor. Please call me Victor."

"Victor. You're a man of the world. I shouldn't have to tell you what needs doing. Get involved, leave your mark on your community. We're all living on the same spaceship. Don't foul it, beautify it."

"Yes. Yes, I'll do that."

"And promise. No more flowers."

"No more flowers."

❧

Even with a police escort, it took Marco an hour to maneuver his bulldozer from the Quonset hut through town and up the mountain. During the wait, the stepmother reclaimed the sex doll, a sports jacket, and a painting, oil on black velvet, of Rod Hollister standing in front of an approving Jesus.

Once Marco arrived he hooked up in no time. The truck came popping out like a cork. Tiffany wrote up a bill from stock she found in the glove compartment of the pickup and presented it to the city's undercover policeman.

"That's a little pricey, isn't it?" Matt asked her.

"We need the money," Tiffany replied.

Traffic was restored. The stepmother was relieved. All the debris that had backed up at her house could now be flushed down valley. She approached the gnarled man in the seat of the bulldozer.

"Say, this your business?"

"One of 'em," said Marco.

"You busy tomorrow? Can you come back up this hill and dig out a couple empty storage tanks?"

"Where?"

"Just up the road. The Hollister place."

"Sure," said Marco.

"Rush job," said Tiffany from the open window of the truck as she reached for the billing stock. "Cost you extra."

~

They drove the Castle Creek Road to its end and skied past where the road ended. He broke trail, but she followed close behind and he felt she was eager for him to move along. At the top, looking down on the ghost town of Ashcroft, they emptied what she'd brought in her pack onto a tarp. Sausage, cheese, fresh water. When they stepped out of their skis their legs disappeared into the snow, and they sat where they were.

The meal was perfect. Hot potato soup from a thermos. She broke the heel off the baguette and offered him the loaf. He threw crumbs under the branches of a large Douglas fir, and soon they had accumulated a crowd of feasting sparrows.

"Funny to think of that as a town."

There were several cabins, what the sign said was a saloon, a mercantile, a schoolhouse. Hand-hewn logs. Mostly it was old boards lying about at random.

"Let's get one of those houses," Annalee said. "We can fix it up. We'll have three ghost children and send them to the ghost school. You can be the ghost blacksmith."

"We wouldn't have any friends," Waddy said.

"We'd have spirit friends. The neighbors. We'd have them over for dinner and bridge."

"How much can spirit friends eat?"

"Exactly. And after they left, we'd wonder why we ever invited them. We'd promise each other that we needn't do that again and hurry into bed."

Waddy leaned back and looked overhead. Horsetail clouds swirled about the sky. He was perfectly happy and perfectly sad. God, thought Waddy. She's wonderful. She has so much to give.

They smiled at each other, put what was left of the fixings back into the rucksack. The smile didn't last long—Annalee looked away and put her goggles back on. Waddy didn't see the tear that was forming in her eye. God, she thought. I have so much to give.

## Twenty-One

Justin pursed his lips in a delicious and rare glimpse of self-recognition. There weren't too many people he would drive out here to fetch. The airport was busy with arrivals. He left his car at the curb and walked into the terminal. He would treat Brumberger right. Curb service.

A handsome young man in a saffron robe approached him as he entered the sliding doors.

"Can you help our monastery in Gaden?" He held out a can.

"You have a monastery in Gaden?"

"My order does. We're the Shartse monks."

"That's funny, you don't look black." The boy gave him an empty look.

"Never mind. It was a joke. Where the hell is Gaden?"

"Tibet."

"Listen, to me charity begins at home. Why don't the Shartse monks help with my monastery in Aspen?"

"Would you like a reading? The future? A next life? Twenty dollars."

Justin took out his wallet. The banks won't miss twenty bucks. The lad took the bill, closed his eyes, and took Justin by the hands. "No next life," Justin instructed. "The way I'm going, I'll have to mortgage it. Just the immediate future."

The boy concentrated.

"Thine enemies will leave you."

"That's it? Mine enemies will leave me? What will they leave me with?"

"That's the future I see."

"You see mine enemies?"

"I do."

"Tell you what. Next time, get the twenty off them." Justin turned on his heel and retreated to the car. The hell with Brumberger. Let him find me.

❧

From her perch, Etta surveyed the entire airport, threshold to threshold. The Unimog was a miniature control tower. She looked over the hurricane fence and beyond the line of aircraft parked on the apron. She could see down to iron pickets that were the high-intensity runway lights where Gossage had built his Christmas home and across to the irregular black scar on the hillside left by Hollister's exploding jet. There ought to be a panorama highlighting points of interest for the tourists. Maybe I'll donate one, with a telescope platform. People could view Sherry's sculpture.

Across from where she sat, the Goddess was emerging from the black glassine rock. The work filled her with pride. She watched passengers disembark the United Express from Denver and recognized Irv Brumberger, rumpled and squinting in the late winter sun. He was her lawyer in the dispute with Victor Grant, but she knew he was here on a different mission: Monday was the viewing of the Indian burial grounds up Conundrum Creek.

Why then was he carrying a suit bag? Etta lifted her Leica glasses and focused. Through the bag's plastic window she made out black satin. Of course, the Snow Ball. Silverheels

Brumberger came toting a tux.

The tuxedo changed hands. Etta watched Justin Kaye take the bag, give Brumberger an awkward embrace, and stow the luggage in the mobile duck blind that passed for Justin's SUV.

Her subject would come out of the northeast. She had found their flight plan. Any minute. She let her thoughts meander to Sherry's idea. He had saved the chrome rings from the Hollister crash and wanted to incorporate them into the sculpture. Hammer them flat and install them as the eyes of the Goddess, or—better, Sherry thought—her nipples. Etta hoped he wouldn't. Sure, it would be a public relations coup— Hollister fans still came on pilgrimage, many took home a charred clump of buffalo grass from the fated hillside—but as Leo the MGM lion said, *ars gratia artis*. Art over commerce. Chrome aureoles were a bit of flash.

Finally, the flight she was waiting for. She'd equipped the Unimog with a midrange receiver so she could monitor cops, fires, and the tower frequency. Victor Grant's pilot announced himself: Gulfstream Two Three Delta glinted silver in the western sky. It cleared Red Table Mountain, lined itself up on final, and eased down to the runway.

The airplane taxied to the FBO and let down its stairs. First down was Grant, in all-occasion cardigan and khakis. Next came that nice young man with the distinctive hair. Grant employed him for God knows what. And a third man, medium-gray suit with a chalk stripe, wing tips, lavender Thomas Pink tie. "Odds on," Etta said, "he's the man Grant found to buy this deal."

"Can't say for sure," she said out loud. "Daddy, I can hear your voice. If a man's wearing cowboy boots that have never seen cow shit, honeybee, be careful. He's most likely Wall Street."

◡

"You'll come as our guest, Irv." Rochelle Kaye could not bring herself to adopt the nickname that the media so loved. "We'll find a table with some eligible women."

"Is that wise?" Brumberger asked. "After all, I'm here on the Walton matter. Justin and I are adversaries. 'A man should be upright,'" he quoted Marcus Aurelius, "'not be kept upright.'"

"Not to worry," Justin called from the next room. "By the end of the evening, no one will be upright." Justin's mood was high. He'd found solid interest in the lots, real buyers. Tonight he'd find more. One had provided him with the perfect sales pitch.

"You're screwing up the prettiest valley left, Justin. If I ever want to enjoy it again, the only good views will be from inside those houses." As soon as the inspection was over, Justin would cash that man's check with the others. The timing was near perfect.

Rochelle showed Brumberger to his room. He removed the tuxedo from its bag, hung it on the closet door, and took a travel whisk to its lint.

"Is that what you're wearing?"

"The invitation said black tie."

"*Mountain* black tie."

"Which means?"

"Almost black tie. You need a spoiler. You can wear the jacket with jeans, or the tux with a cowboy shirt."

Brumberger frowned. A New Yorker's singular fear is to appear a rube, and he faced the dilemma that the night's custom called for him to appear as one.

"I don't own a cowboy shirt."

"We'll think of something. Do you have any trinkets from your Indian clients?"

"They've given me a warbonnet of feathers and muskrat teeth. A kachina doll that I suspect is me. In blue serge."

"Any of that," Rochelle said enthusiastically.

"They're on a wall in midtown Manhattan."

"We'll think of something."

～

Ned Quinlan's glacier glasses cut the glare off the crust. By midmorning, the snow began to melt and water drained through the cover with a low crackle. He located the USGS brass plate on the corner of the quarter section from the paint mark on the road. From it, he established a monument pin. He set his transit over the pin, its legs sinking inches into the snow, pushed the glasses to his forehead, and squinted through.

The first job was to center the levels. Then he'd shoot a north-south line. The job would have gone faster with a helper—you can shoot a line in seconds if you have someone to plant a stake—but this was a simple plane survey. He would save a few bucks, do it alone. Besides, he liked the solitude.

Corn snow, the skiers called it. Spring conditions, crystals that had melted and refrozen so that each granule was a rounded, tiny pellet. Looked like snow from a machine.

He took pains to follow Mr. Kaye's instructions. Don't trample the field. It needed to be fresh. Just stake its borders. We don't want be accused of tampering, Mr. Kaye told him sternly.

He lined off the remaining boundaries with an invar tape. Steel tape would vary from contraction, depending on whether it was touching the snow or suspended in the air. Then he set a blaze orange stake every ten feet. The field was fresh as a hospital sheet. The top layer of corn snow glistened in the sunshine.

～

"Just checking on you," Annalee said when he answered the door. "I haven't seen you since we made our plans to populate the ghost town."

With ghost sex, Waddy thought to say, but instead asked her in. It was Hero who showed how they felt, standing on his single hind leg to lick at her face.

"I thought you ought to know. That fellow who works for Grant came around. Knows we're pals. Asked whether you were making progress."

Waddy was discouraged. So far the programming didn't complete the fantasy part.

"Lisa and I have been tinkering with the software ever since the glitch. We haven't had a chance to test it."

"So, Alexander Graham Bell, will you be first? Will you make the famous, 'What hath God wrought?'"

"'Watson come here.'"

"Whatever ... "

Waddy smiled and agreed. "Whatever ... "

That shy concession spurred Annalee to action. She stood on tiptoes to kiss him. Waddy saw her eyes close, and, not completely without experience, he took her gently by the arms and lowered his face to hers. Annalee was short and he tall, and he had calculated the relative altitudes correctly. Her kiss surprised him, landing intentionally, he realized by the bemused expression she wore, now that he opened his eyes, on the tip of his nose. Twinkling at her own mischief, she scratched Hero's ears, patted master and hound on the flank, and rushed off to work. Pantagruel's catered the Snow Ball. Annalee had a long night ahead.

The kiss left him muddled. Maybe he should try to get her to enter her fantasy. That would give him a clue. Without it, he was, well, clueless.

∿

The three men, from three different tribes, had Pantagruel to themselves. Most of the staff were home, dressing for the long night. Emmanuel ordered for the table.

"So," asked Robert. "What is the purpose of the meeting?"

"The purpose of the meeting," said Morgan, the oldest of the three, "is the same as the lawsuit. To clear as much as we possibly can, net of expenses." Two of the men represented tribal councils with an economic interest at stake. Robert, the third, came from the Northern Cheyenne, Plains Indians from the Dakota Territory, renowned for their warrior traits and forensic skills. Irv Brumberger rarely tried a case without finding a reason to call Robert Yellowknife as an expert witness.

"But this fellow Kaye. He wants to see us before they do the digging. What's our strategy?" Robert had the beginnings of an ulcer and was nursing a Pellegrino Lime.

"The same. Lay it on him. Let him know we deal in the base currency."

"PFG?" asked Emmanuel.

"PFG," Robert confirmed.

"Another thing," Emmanuel leaned forward as if he had a hot tip. "If you see him smile, look out. They always smile when they're about to nail you."

"The wolf smiles. Have you ever noticed? Dogs, wolves, and the white man: they're the only animals that smile." Robert gave them a confident look.

The waiter brought the caviar torte, with which Emmanuel had ordered a white Bordeaux. For the lamb he had picked a Chambertin that he knew to be ready for drinking.

The waiter went through the uncorking and tasting rituals, and Emmanuel, used to the elaborate conventions of the ruling class, obliged. Odd people, these Anglos. For wines, they have ceremony. For birth and death, they go to hospitals.

"Groundhogs," said Morgan.

"What?"

"Groundhogs. Sometimes you see a groundhog smile."

They waited until the waiter had backed off.

"That's another thing," Emmanuel said to Robert. "You get a chance, bring up wolves. Shit, man. Do that and Kaye will have stories for his grandchildren. They love to hear us talking wolves, raven spirits. Drives them bullshit."

～

The Snow Ball signaled the end of the season, and those who had stuck out the long, dark winter, plebeian and plutocrat alike, congratulated themselves. The event also intended to generate monies for an arcane disease, although since its founding— every year the event growing more lavish—the costs eclipsed that amount. One wanted the best, even if charity was paying.

This year they were spending a bundle on entrances. The ball was held at the midway lodge on Ajax Mountain, a fourteen-minute ride up the Silver Queen gondola. Style must attend the way in. Guests found increasingly elaborate ways: snowmobile, heated snowcat, a Clydesdale-led surrey, a team of Iditarod huskies.

Although an Aspen ordinance banned the wearing of fur, the ski hill was outside the town's borders. This night men and women alike shed shoulder-to-snow mink at the door. Underneath, originals from Balenciaga, Calvin, and Dior. In keeping with an antic elegance, some women designed their own dresses. One starlet stole most of the press coverage by appearing in silk and Saran Wrap.

In the midst of the kitchen, Annalee stood in white blouse and black skirt, swirling raspberry sauce onto plates of roast pork loin, arranging slabs of ahi in nests of garlic mashed potatoes, and overseeing the monumental task of placing a hot meal in front of four hundred people, each of whom expected to be served first. Three bands played—two spelled each other in the main hall; the third, on the downhill deck, quit early when the alto player froze to his reed. The staff passed hors d'oeuvres in Trimalchian quantities, and at eleven the guests sat down for a six-course meal.

"You need some help?" Carmen asked Annalee from her chair.

"Oh, no thanks. Guests are supposed to enjoy themselves."

Silverheels Brumberger, seated next to this pretty Spanish lady, was impressed with Carmen's selfless gesture toward the caterer's assistant.

"That was a lovely thing to do." Brumberger sent his jury-sincere smile. Alone and uncomfortable in a borrowed bolo tie, he at last had found his opening. Rochelle had put him with the Dooberry party.

"Oh," Carmen said. "*No es nada.*" It was nothing.

"To be sympathetic to her distress amidst all of this excess, it was lovely." Brumberger exercised the range of his voice. Flavia began to translate for her, but thought better of it. After all, attraction had nothing to do with comprehension. Carmen's beauty would respond for her. This *loco* project of The Doo's was running short, Flavia knew the signs: squabbling, the thickening of her husband's English accent, a budget ticking down. If Carmen got lucky, with effective foundation garments and the right seating chart, she would never have to see a trailer park again. Maybe, Flavia thought, maybe I ought to be in the market myself.

"Have you ever wondered," Brumberger was speaking to Carmen, "what gluttony says about us?"

"Yes?" Carmen answered. It was one of the three answers Flavia had given her.

"Don't you think it says there is something eating at us?"

"Oh," Carmen said. "I do." All three answers were positive.

Flavia watched approvingly across her husband's plate. She wasn't sure who this man was, but from her years on the runway, she knew good tailoring.

Dooberry was oblivious to the mating buzz around him. He

loved sitting between these two remarkable women. Flavia was striking in emerald green, if a bit on the muscular side. Carmen, on the other hand, looked caramel-soft, her skin set off by the rose-cream gown. Like the maja in the Goya painting. Alluring, available. How much can a man be expected to take?

Or was it El Greco?

Close the gap, he reminded himself, between the realized and the idealized. That mote of wisdom will convert the troubled man to the actualized man.

Oh, God help me, he thought as he cut into a mushroom torte. That's not wisdom. Those are lines from my book.

~

Justin stood outside on a small deck behind the lodge. He'd picked the spot not for its view of the tin-snipped moon that now dangled behind the peaks, but for the prevailing breeze. The southerly wind would waft the smoke from his Monte-cristo No. 3 into the main room. Within minutes he had drawn a crowd of cigar fanciers.

"Yes," he said to no one in particular, "it left me speech-less." Justin was continuing a story he'd never begun. His audience, each offered a Cuban in the crisp air, was content to pay the price.

"No sooner had P and Z approved the plat than I had fifteen friends asking me to set aside a homesite for them. Victor Grant, Peyton Post. Men used to the best."

"What did you do?" someone asked. Give that man, Justin held back from saying, a cigar.

"Well, fortunately I have a few sites left. Not many. I want to get this lawsuit out of the way. That happens Monday—if they find bones, I'll eat this stogie. Once we have our list—it has to be the right people—I'll get the paperwork done. We'll be out of the ground by the end of summer, the blinds will be ready for goose season."

Only a few sites left? Used to the best? The right people? Irresistible. In the night air the mossy scent of tobacco stayed fresh. Justin converted six Montecristos into five business cards, home numbers on the back.

Two more smoke breaks, Justin checked his pockets for cigars, and I'll have the bank loan covered.

～

Etta wore a gown of carnelian satin with a contrasting cowgirl scarf. She had taken time to make up her face and eyes and had achieved the bright mien of an Easter egg. Now, seated at a patron's table with a view of the room, she enjoyed the sensation. Queenly. She looked about and cataloged her guests' blessings. Sherry will finish the Goddess before they return to Tulsa. Peyton seems to have survived a difficult Christmas, mellowing suddenly, almost as if an inner peace fell out of the sky. Chloe's decision to move to bullion, guessing at a market fall, is looking prescient. The Finches, well they're simply the Finches. Holding hands, rising from the table to dance the slow tunes.

Even the mussed Brumberger seemed to be making progress. Etta watched the next table, and as the space between him and his dinner partner narrowed, she let out a sigh. This must be how Noah felt after everyone bunked down for the night.

If only she could solve this dispute with Victor Grant. Dooberry was playing it close to the vest: no news about the problem that had had them broken down since Christmas. And he wasn't saying whether anyone was ready to pony up for the next round. Either the damn thing worked or it didn't. Why fight Victor Grant for the right to put more money down a rat hole? Let him have it. Maybe, and she watched the lawyer cant off his chair toward the Latin beauty, maybe I'll lasso that Brumberger fellow and talk a little strategy.

But Brumberger was lost in Carmen's cool and limpid eyes. Best leave it. The love bug had clearly bitten Silverheels Brumberger in a sensitive spot, and calamine lotion was not going to relieve the itch.

"It is a curious thing," Brumberger was saying softly, wondering all the while how he could turn the conversation from ideas to the warmth in his heart, and having no idea what his words meant, "it is a curious thing about the food chain. It cycles, but it only goes one way. A frog will eat a fly, but not vice versa. A snake will eat a frog, a pig will eat a snake, a man will eat a pig, and worms will eat a man. If the worm gets flattened on a highway, a fly will eat the worm. But not vice versa."

"Oh, yes," said Carmen, down to her last gambit. "I agree."

⌁

A sorrowful Wadsworth Brush strapped on a pair of touring skis and glided onto the paths that ran east from Starwood. Hero kept to his side. A moon followed them, halved as if it had been handled too often, and it set the landscape in a blue light. Against a sky scrubbed clean of clouds, stars stuck out as random dots. Across the valley, Waddy heard the final notes from the ball. At his distance, some ten miles, the volume was properly adjusted.

What is the value of this device, the brain? Writing fantasies that we suppress—what for? It doesn't do any good to illustrate them, even colorized. They reinforce our inadequacies. The whole project is screwed. I don't much care whether it succeeds or fails. There's no point in any of this except how it makes you feel, and I feel lousy. Oh, to be a Dooberry. Someone who doesn't anguish between success and failure, so long as his bills get paid. A wife to love him and a roof over his head, what difference to him what happens with this?

Waddy watched a swarm of lights slide down Ajax

Mountain. Last June he'd been fishing with Marco and they'd seen what he thought were fireflies. Marco had caught one to show him: a pink glowworm, Marco said. They glimmer three or four nights a year, only when they're mating. What if we shone phosphorescent in the night when we were mating, Waddy wondered. The lights on the mountainside jigged and slid about into two lines.

Maybe we do.

It was the grand recessional. As the party ended, guests piled into sleighs and were escorted between the glowworms. Which in fact were skiers, each carrying a butane torch. Snow-cats towed the sleighs down the hill.

Electric bulbs shone through the lodge windows and lit up the surrounding snow. It would be a late night for Annalee. He thought of her and his heart lightened. Of her on tiptoes, his eyes shut tight, how the heat of her shoulders seeped through the thin white blouse. The memory of this very woman had dipped him into the muck of wishing himself Dooberry, anyone, and now this second visit cheered him out of it.

❧

The guests held themselves tight under furs and blankets in the sleighs. In the last seat of one, Carmen and Flavia whispered in Spanish.

"So what did he have to say?"

"A great deal."

"Tell me, what?"

"He talked without stopping. I understood nothing. Except *gusanos*."

"*Gusanos*. Worms? Are you sure?"

"I am sure."

"Strange."

"Strange, yes."

"He's a rich lawyer, Carmen. And he's sweet on you."

"Phooo, my sister. I don't want him sweet on me, or sour on me, or on me any other way. He's old and ugly."

"Carmen, choose wisely. We have a lot invested in this night, and I tell you, you have made a conquest."

"I do not care. In a marriage there must be love."

"I agree, sister. But not necessarily with one's husband."

Dooberry leaned back to ask whether they needed more blankets.

"You see? Husbands keep you warm in other ways." Carmen laughed, but she wasn't hearing of it. She sang a little song to the stars. On her far side, certain that he felt the pulse of her body through two Pendleton blankets and a black bear rug, Brumberger listened. These were the sweetest notes he had ever heard. The sleigh made the last turns down Ruthie's Run and deposited them at the base of Ajax Mountain. It had been a beautiful night.

He was still listening to the soft voice when Dooberry interrupted.

"Why," he asked, "why are the police here?"

~

Waddy and Hero made their way back toward the house. They crossed an open field dotted with the tracks of squirrel and snowshoe rabbit. Cold night to be out. Hero stopped short and mewled. Waddy scanned the blue-black spaces between the far trees. Twice-reflected light colored the landscape in strangeness.

He was ready to move on, but Hero stood in a frightened point. Waddy traced his line of sight and only saw the coyote when it moved. At Hero's second whimper it lifted its head and stared, then returned to nosing the snow.

Waddy looked over in a fraternal bond. The three of us are in tough straits. Slim pickings for carrion, garbage doesn't stay garbage long. It goes through the disposal or onto the compost pile. Or into cans specially made to keep it from hobos like us.

"If I were you," at the sound of Waddy's voice the coyote stiffened and the points of its ears stood erect, "I'd find a nice lady coyote, move down valley, and build myself a den. Easy street. Real garbage there, and the rabbits aren't registered with the homeowners' association."

The coyote sniffed at the air, turned, and walked without a sound into the blackness at the base of the pines. Hero's hackles didn't settle until they were home.

～

The red-and-yellow strobe of the flasher atop the Saab patrol car gave off a harsh and alien light, but enough for him to recognize her.

"I came for Carmen."

"What's wrong?" Flavia stepped in front of her friend to shield her from this unlikely looking policeman.

"Nothing. I just came to offer Carmen a ride home."

Dooberry spoke up. "In a police car? Is she in some sort of trouble?"

"Let me handle this," said Brumberger, pleased to be able to show off. "Carmen, dear, I should advise you that you're not required to say anything."

"Is she in trouble?" Dooberry asked again. "She told us she had papers."

"Be quiet, Doo," Flavia instructed.

"No, no trouble," Matt Hempel said. "Just a ride."

"Well she's living with us. She doesn't need a ride."

"I didn't mean to your home." Carmen had no difficulty understanding Matt's English. She looped her arm through his.

"Oh, the gown," she said in Spanish. "It's supposed to go back tomorrow." She reached around to grasp the zipper.

"Not here, sister." Flavia restrained her. "I'll pick it up at Matt's tomorrow."

Justin and Rochelle Kaye caught up with Brumberger just as the police car drove off. He seemed dazed.

"What was that, Justin?"

"I think that was her white knight."

"Goodness. Wouldn't you think a white knight would get himself a shave and a haircut?"

"Apparently they don't wear them these days."

"And me?" He turned to Rochelle. "A nice Jewish boy from the Bronx? If she's the damsel, who am I? Do I look like a dragon?"

He didn't. In Justin's bolo tie and Stetson a size too large, both of which Rochelle had insisted he wear, he looked silly, but not draconian. She and Justin each took an arm.

"Never mind, Irv," Rochelle comforted. "Come. We'll take you home. I'll make us some tea."

*Twenty-Two*

It was the Sunday morning after the ball, and the streets of Aspen might have been a Universal International sci-fi set. The spaceship has landed, aliens have eaten every person in the village and washed them down with Liquid Plumbr, the benighted army has yet to arrive.

A hardy few tourists huddled in the boutiques. Skiers breakfasted and waited for the sun to warm the icy slopes. The high-speed lifts operated smoothly, their cables clanging around the giant base wheel to tug their quad chairs, empty, up the mountain. Doughnut makers spat out doughnuts in seven styles. The Sunday *New York Times* sat in waist-high stacks at Clark's Drug, awaiting the town's wake up.

A lonely convoy of vehicles rendezvoused by the ranger station and wound up the road toward Conundrum Creek. There was no one out to see Marco's John Deere crawler dozer, its scoop held high, its owner sitting in the boxy cab wrapped in scarves and a Navy peacoat. Beside Marco's seat, in the space between the gearshifts and the far window, a tarpaulin covered a large, irregular mound.

There was no one to see Marco's truck, following closely, driven by a handsome black man, merriment showing in each of his unmatched eyes. Nor, behind the truck, did anyone see the ancient silver Volkswagen convertible, the young man behind its wheel driving with determination. Had someone been afoot, he would surely have noticed the attractive woman beside the driver, blowing on her hands with excitement. Movie quality you'd say, or beauty contest at the least.

The bed of the pickup was loaded to its gunnels with equipment: a snow-making machine with the stenciled logo of the Aspen Ski Corporation, metal rakes, shovels, and a long coil of four-inch-diameter fire hose. The dozer's grading blade was propped against the truck's gate. Finally, an air compressor and a one-cycle gasoline engine. It might be cargo that the Ski Corporation was moving from shed to shed. The season for snowmaking had long past. You made snow at the beginning of winter, not at its end.

The day was perfect. The blue porcelain bowl that rests inverted on the back of the Giant Tortoise had not a blemish. The long couloirs of the Elk Range were warming in the sun on this, the day of the equinox, and the earth made a lit-kindling sound as new melt filtered its way through the snow. Black-headed juncos, winter's bird, had departed, and the first towhees had taken their place. Towhees didn't carry the harbinger press tag like the robin, for they were shy and hard to spot, but they were indeed the first sign of spring. In the backcountry, away from the roads and houses, bull elk were moving their cows from spare grazing to the higher slopes, where the thaw daily revealed new aspen trunks. The fragile trees were still a month from bud, and their tender, spongy bark was now at its sweetest.

Waddy had fixed a picnic lunch. Three thermoses of hot coffee; a gallon of lemonade; prosciutto, yellow and red peppers, and Bel Paese cheese, all to be spread on club rolls and slathered with olive oil. It was a festive event, so he baked two tins of his mother's special raspberry-lemon bars, cut one up for his compatriots and left the other with a note for Lisa. From the snore in her bedroom, he figured she had a soft-palated guest.

The bulldozer set a slow pace. Finally, the line of vehicles arrived at the site of what was to be the Isaak Walton Preserve. A local construction yard had delivered the 320 BL on rental. A massive affair, it was known in the trade as an excavator. Marco would use it to break the hoarfrost in case the bulldozer couldn't get through. As it turned out, the dozer proved sufficient, but the excavator had helped to triple the price.

There was a lot to do before the sun set. Tomorrow was the test, everyone was in town and Mr. Kaye had called three times to remind Marco. Yes, he thought they would be able to break ground. No, he didn't mind that Mr. Brumberger had invited representatives of the tribal councils. Yes, he could move topsoil on the whole tract if they wanted him. And no, he didn't mind the press, just so long as he could finish in time to watch his television shows.

The bulldozer pulled off the road and clanked to a stop. The truck and car parked behind. Marco's three friends came up to his cab—he hadn't let them see under the tarp—and began to coax and cajole him.

Hell, he supposed it was all right, now that they were on site.

He and Gossage unfastened the rope, loosened the canvas throw at its grommets, and pulled it back. They all grinned broadly.

❧

Rochelle set out brunch fixings on the breakfast bar. She had planned to serve only sausage and eggs, in the chafing dish with the fictive coat of arms that came from Justin's line of home accessories. Where had she heard that certain tribes kept kosher? Had she read it in a checkout line? Better be safe. She'd called, and Zabar's agreed to airlift whitefish and bagels.

Her husband was busy with their guests. Justin spread documents on the Queen Anne dining room table. Anasazi mugs, also from the line, weighted the corners and kept the survey from springing back into a roll.

"The cross-hatching signifies the alleged burial grounds. We've had the surveyor shoot the site, and he'll stake the lines for tomorrow's test." He handed a certificate to Brumberger, who read it carefully and nodded.

"All according to the stipulation between Mr. Brumberger and me." Justin spoke slowly and too loud. He had retail outlets in Saudi Arabia and Kuwait; he'd personally sold to Congolese royalty and Chinese commissars. Loud and slow. Here were the three emissaries of Brumberger's tribes. Morgan Atencio, of the Southern Utes, wore jeans and a flannel shirt. His sterling belt buckle, the size of a rearview mirror, was studded with turquoise and cat's-eyes. Justin never let the stomach on which it sat out of his sight. Whenever Morgan approached the black walnut table, Justin stepped in like a boxing ref. Robert Yellowknife was financial officer of the Northern Cheyenne. He wore a gray lambs' wool suit with a blue pencil stripe, an ecru shirt of pima cotton, initials embroidered on the sleeve, and a solid maroon tie. Only the third, Emmanuel Johnstone, wore trappings of office: a deerskin jacket sewn with seven rows of beads, one for each clan of the Shoshone Nation.

"Now, we are prepared to test"—Justin had been cautioned not to use the word *bulldoze*; while these remains were hypothetical, they were nonetheless revered—"to test any or all of this site, as you wish. We'll go as deep as you like, although the anthropologists have told us that three feet should be sufficient. So long as the work is concluded by 6 P.M."

Johnstone's stomach growled. Last night's Burgundy hadn't agreed with him. Emmanuel Johnstone lived in Grand Junction, where he was a successful stockbroker. Red wine always made him dyspeptic and bearish. His major customers were the other two tribes, whose casino profits were surprisingly constant. All his accounts had done well in large cap value stocks—perhaps he ought to take some profits.

He wondered where the profit was in this day's adventure. You never knew where things would lead. PFG—pale face guilt—was a growth business. You never knew. If this developer turned up a few remains—How many bones did it take to make ground sacred? There was no commentary on the subject, no authority—their tribes stood to make a few bucks. The theory was trespass, Silverheels had told them, or the Reliquaries Act, or defacing a cemetery. We'll worry about a theory when we get some facts. And Silverheels knew whereof he spoke. This was the man who had parlayed a pelvis and an ulna on a New Mexico mesa into mid–seven figures.

"Now or later," Justin continued. "You can pick your boundaries now, or you can wait until tomorrow. We want you to feel totally at ease."

"You sound sure we won't find anything," Brumberger said.

"Not at all, not at all. No one knows. That's why we're conducting this fire drill."

Brumberger turned to address his clients.

"I'd suggest we wait 'til we get there. You may have a feeling for the place, and this way you can pick and choose."

All three agreed. Johnstone passed on the conclusion. He was not only a registered securities representative, he was also the tribal shaman. His followers thought it a great combination for picking stocks.

"That's just fine," said Justin. The commercial loan officer at Morgan Chase had copies of every letter of intent. His committee hadn't yet given the green light, but they would recognize the signatures. That loan was as good as rolled over.

Justin smiled expansively. "This way, you can wait until the spirits move you." He felt the slightest chill in the air as he smiled. While the faces remained impassive, he was sure he sensed long muscles tensing. He wanted them to know he meant the remark as a good-natured quip, so he repeated it.

"This way, you can wait until the spirits move you."

Brumberger shuffled in undisguised discomfort. Johnstone's stomach growled a second time.

"You mind if I use a land line?" Johnstone asked. "I should check my e-mail."

~

Victor Grant thought it the oddest coincidence. That was the third child he had seen, this a boy, leading a black pig on a leash. Maybe it was a saint's day. Or a Walk the Pig contest.

"*Buenos días,*" he said as his bike rolled close. His words broke the stare and brought an instant smile. The stare was understandable—Grant knew he was a sight. Lycra jersey of silver and green, black spandex racing shorts, a Plantronics headset and microphone that sat atop his European-style racing cap. It wasn't everyday dress for northern Ecuador.

He sped south down the *Avenida de los Volcanos*. His trainer was having trouble in the thin atmosphere, and Grant had opened a three- or four-mile lead on the man. The new vanadium bike saved six pounds, and all those mornings climbing Independence Pass were paying off. This was a ride in the park.

They'd started in Otavalo, planning three days on the road. The first night they spent outside Quito, the second was to be in Latacunga, then bike to the airstrip in Riobamba. An extended weekend—he needed some time off, had several deals hanging, and he always did his best thinking by himself. This spectacular road flies down a cordon of volcanoes that grow from a valley floor amidst plantations of agave and eucalyptus and rise to the clouds. It was the ideal spot for a retreat—no one knew him, he knew no one, he'd be able to concentrate.

Oddly, the children distracted him. He found himself thinking conventional thoughts. A family had always seemed like the most precarious of ventures—never mind that he made his living in high-risk enterprise. In telemetry or software, you could isolate the variables, quantify the risk. Competition, innovation, asset coverage, management, control. The process was rational and the objective—return on investment—was simple. Opinions on how to achieve it differed, but the objective stood uncompounded, fixed on the horizon while the winds blew you and the markets about.

Simple, especially by comparison. What exactly was the objective in raising a family?

Isabelle had programmed his cell by remote, and he had hooked the receiver to the handlebars. There were two calls left, the first on a peripherals deal that needed more money. The second to his New York lawyer on that Aspen thing. After those he'd take a break, let the trainer catch up. His pack carried a small loaf of *masapan*, a chewy local bread, and a bottle of spring water.

He hit Send. Waiting for the connection, he snuck a look at the speedometer. Don't let it fall below thirty. His AA picked up.

"How's the weather?"

"Fantastic, Isabelle. Fields greener than you can imagine. The peaks are over twenty thousand feet high, and the air is so full of moisture there's a perpetual cloud cover. And the children. The most beautiful children on earth. It's like driving through someone else's dream."

Isabelle's window at 44 Wall overlooked the Brooklyn Bridge entrance to FDR Drive. Traffic was moving swiftly.

"Isabelle?"

She watched a taxi hit the ramp too fast, jam on the brakes, and rear-end a black Lincoln limo. She winced.

"Yes, boss. I'm here. I was just wondering." Not about the rear-ender. That happened once a day. She was wondering whether Grant had come down with some tropical disease. His usual response to the weather question was, What's on the list?

"I read their proposal on the plane," Grant said. "I think we say no."

"No? They seem ready to break out. With this latest tranche for marketing, they should be profitable. Ahead of projections."

"I understand."

"We've never had one come in ahead of projections. Not since I've been here."

"I know. But let's not make it easy for them. Nothing worthwhile comes easy."

"Is that in the Talmud?"

"I don't like the pricing."

Now her boss was back to normal. "You want to squeeze?" The turbaned driver of the limo pushed the cabbie in the chest. Traffic backed up to Centre Street.

"I want them to feel the pinch. Their cash flows—have you seen them?"

"Sure." Isabelle had finished second in her class at Kellogg. Of course she had seen them.

"They're out of money end of next month. They don't have time to find a new investor. We're the only game in town."

"So we should squeeze?"

Grant slowed up. The road ahead was blocked by milling pedestrians. He was approaching a street market. People clustered about tables. Farmers sat on blankets on the grassy shoulders, showing their crop, some sat on the asphalt itself. There weren't any cars. He got off and walked his bike. There were squash the size of footballs, gourds that shone yellow and red, flowers he'd never seen before. There were baskets full of radishes and corn and pink cabbage, and a long stringy root that inside—a woman broke one in half so he could see— was royal purple. He walked through, talking on his headset. People made a path. In close quarters, he lifted his bike, a

Morati custom-made to his dimensions, to his shoulder.

"Let's propose a new class of convertible. Half the price of the last round, and warrants."

"For what piece?"

A black-eyed girl came up to him with a carton. *"Mira, señor. Te gustan?"* Inside were six ducklings.

"Piece?"

"Yes. Warrants for what piece of the company?"

"Isabelle?"

"Yes?"

"Forget it. Let's take what they've offered."

"You sure, boss? Take what they offered? Us? They'll have a coronary, we'll need a whole new management team."

*"Quieras comprar, señor?"* A man joined in the negotiation. Was he a shill or just an interested bystander? He wore a white hemp hat and smoked a black cigar. Grant looked around. Every man wore a white hemp hat and smoked the same cigar.

*"Gracias, no."*

*"Estes patitos son muy salubres. Por veinte miserables sucres usted puede comprar todos los patitos."*

*"Digame, amigo,"* he said. *"Vivo en un ciudad grande. Nueva York."* Grant's Spanish had been exhausted. "Here I am half a world away on a bicycle. *Una bicicleta.* What am I going to do with six healthy ducks?"

The man broke into a beaming grin. He laughed. He repeated Grant's words in Spanish for the onlookers. They laughed too, and patted him on the back as if he'd won a Tony. They parted to make an aisle for him. The girl with the ducklings looked up shyly as he said good-bye.

"Boss, what was that about ducks? Are we still connected?"

"Yes, Isabelle. And I'm sure."

He sped off. Do something for your community, she had said. Trouble is, these people don't need me. Besides, if I do something here, I'll never get credit. He was ten miles down the road, passing the shore of an enamel blue lake, when he remembered he had a last call to make.

"Your Mr. Brumberger is serious, Victor."

Grant heard the disdain in the voice of his counsel. Avoid lawyers who believe where they took their degree makes a difference. Grant thought to make a note of his observation but had no pad or pencil. "He's not my Mr. Brumberger."

"That may be. Nonetheless, he feels he has a right to stop you converting the debt and taking over the project."

"And?"

"Victor. This firm drafted the documents. They're rock solid. I stand behind them. I don't think there's a court in the nation that will turn its back on the words of a contract between sophisticated parties properly represented. And it says you can convert."

"But?"

"No but. I just want you to know there's the possibility of a fight. And where there's a fight, there's always a possibility we can lose."

"What's at stake? Does this contraption work?"

"Well, that's exactly the right question." The lawyer sounded pleased with himself. "I've proposed to Mr. Brumberger that we find an answer. A summit meeting. For Monday. Show and tell. Gather the forces together, find out from this charlatan Dooberry what he has for results. Then we assess whether there's anything worth fighting over."

"Sounds like a good idea."

"You should be there."

"Aspen? Monday?" Grant looked sadly at the mountains around him. Clouds were separating and Cayambe, the highest volcano in the line, was beginning to reveal its snow-covered peak.

"You should be there. I don't know anyone else prepared

to make a judgment on what they find."

Grant caught a glimpse of the cup of the crater through the parting clouds.

"I suppose I can." It would mean getting up early, having the aircraft meet him in Latacunga. Clear customs, maybe McAllen, Texas. Then direct to Aspen.

"Okay. Listen, call my office, relay my plans, will you? And tell them to let the Aspen house know. We'll give them an ETA from the air."

He gave the man one last task. A number to call and a man to bring up to speed.

"That's Washington," said the lawyer, puzzled.

"Exactly." At these rates, Victor suppressed his urge toward sarcasm.

The lawyer hung up and shook his head in amusement. Not many clients were rich enough to have their errands run at his hourly rate. Still, he liked to think his firm offered every service. They did the client's bidding. He'd bill the time.

～

The sausage gave Justin heartburn. The meeting with the Native Americans wasn't going well. The more he smiled, the faster they backed away. He introduced Rochelle and smiled. He showed them the view from the sun deck of the otherwise Tudor house and smiled.

As they gazed upon the mansion ghetto of Red Mountain, it occurred to Justin that perhaps they were contemplating how the white man had improved the landscape so far.

Brumberger tried to assure him. "We have a deal. My guys will stick by the stipulation."

What are you telling me? Justin thought. That they're not Indian givers? A beneficent fairy kept the words in his mouth.

They left. Justin was fetching an antacid tablet when the

phone rang. His office never called on a Sunday. But his VP of distribution had big news. Big and ugly.

He crunched a second mint and washed it down with a pink digestive. Then he took a drive, pulling in by Woody Creek Canyon. A groomed path fringed the river. Maybe a walk would settle his stomach. The Roaring Fork River was undammed. From its origins high atop Independence Pass to its confluence with the Colorado, it fell faster than any other river on the continent. Its power, constant and measureless, tended to round off granite and polish the chips of red sandstone into almost recognizable shapes. At spots the path came within feet of the bank, and the air was cool and misty. An early runoff had begun, and the water, usually clear as vodka, now ran the color of weak tea. In another two weeks it would be mocha.

The roar still sang in his ears as he came out from the canyon, and he didn't notice the man sitting at the weathered picnic table.

"Hi."

"I know you," Justin told him. "We gave you a ride once. Don't you live on Red Mountain?"

"I used to."

"By the Hollister house?"

"There too. I recognized the duck blind." Gossage indicated Justin's SUV.

"Conspicuous, huh?"

"Let's say distinctive."

Well, Justin thought, it's owned by the company. JK Durango. In a month, with everything else, the bank will own it. What will Morgan Chase keep in the shell drawers?

"You look like you've had a tough day," Gossage told him.

"A bitch. You?"

"Couldn't have been better. Ever drive a Caterpillar tractor?"

"No."

"Neither had I. Ought to try it. You feel like God."

"I'll keep it in mind when I send out my résumé."

"Business troubles?"

"You don't want to hear."

Gossage indicated a space on the bench beside him. Justin sat. They leaned back against the tabletop and watched the waters course through basal rock.

Justin found himself talking about the vice president's phone call. Bloomingdale's had gotten wind of the company's troubles. If the bank called the loan, inventory would be frozen in the warehouses. There would be no manufacturing and no deliveries until they could sort things out. Bloomie's didn't want to be stuck with goods on the floor that were distress at every other retailer. Sales, markdowns. That wasn't the Bloomie image. Starting next week, they were cutting his New York floor space by half.

"It's a house of cards," Justin ended. "Trouble with banks gives you trouble with stores gives you trouble with banks."

"Sounds as if you've had experience."

Justin absently raised the book the man had been reading. "I've been on the verge of bankruptcy half a dozen times," he said. "Once we'd even drafted the papers and cut a check for the filing fee. No cash, no credit."

"What happened?"

"We met with the lawyers. It was either file for protection or file for a public offering. We gambled. It worked."

"What am I missing?"

"That was a different market. You can't do that today."

Gossage stretched. He rubbed at his palms where he had blisters from working the Cat's levers. Justin replaced the book on the bench.

"Have you ever thought of the advantage books have over life?" Gossage asked.

"No." Justin looked up, amused.

"Well, all stories, whether they're in a book or you're living them, have endings. In a novel, you know when you're getting close. You can feel the weight, there aren't many pages left on the thumb side. You know it's about to get wrapped up. Even with all these loose ends. In life, not so."

"You're trying to tell me something."

"Take the long view. The story will get resolved. It's the lack of resolution you find troubling. But that will end."

"I don't like novels," Justin said. "They're not real."

Gossage laughed. "I'll bet you don't like still lifes either. You can't eat the fruit."

Justin considered this. Nothing better than a good insult. Despite his gloom, he broke into a smile. Gossage giggled with him. Once Justin started laughing, it flowed, deep and long.

Twenty-Three

Victor Grant asked to postpone the summit meeting. He had arrived at dawn, overnight from Quito, and wanted to shower and change.

"I'll agree to the delay," Silverheels Brumberger told the Grant lawyers, "so long as I can be on my way by noon." He was in town at the behest of a second client, the Southwest tribes, and they expected him at the Conundrum Creek site promptly at one.

The investors in Wise Mother gathered in groups. Chloe used the time to quiz Etta Eubanks about predicted shortages in domestic crude. Long in oil and short in defense, Chloe's portfolio was exposed to the threat of peace.

Peyton invited Sherry Topliff to go for a stroll. He shared the story of the cube that had dropped from the sky like manna in the book of Exodus.

"I'm telling you, Sherry. The similarities were awesome. I was undergoing my own exile in the desert. If a Higher Power had thrown in cigarette papers, I'd be a believer today." He also shared the last of the cube. Its depletion did not alarm Peyton; with the April sun the Posts intended to leave for the Hamptons.

Brumberger called the investors to order and explained what was at stake. Victor Grant was threatening to convert the debt he held into equity, at a highly advantageous ratio. The conversion would give him control of the project and would dilute all their interests. Etta had instructed Brumberger to block the conversion. If he succeeded, Grant would likely call the debt. Then investors would have to step up with more money or let Grant foreclose. Before they spent considerable sums to fight with each other, Grant had suggested this meeting.

Brumberger turned the program over to Mortimer Dooberry.

Dooberry stood up front, where he had rigged a large portable screen so the computer documents could be seen by all. He was dressed as a land commodore: white ducks, blue blazer with emblem, small-patterned tie. He thanked his wife for her sacrifices and managed to find some reason to acknowledge everyone else in the room. Sherry Topliff and Peyton Post walked in during his talk. Sherry turned to his pal.

"Have I been away? Has he won an award?"

Dooberry returned to the computer terminal and manipulated a Lotus Notes program. Figures floated onto the screen. The audience nodded politely.

Not Flavia Dooberry. Lacking a university education she had not learned how to appear absorbed while letting her mind roam. As her husband took a flash-pointer to the screen, she went to the back, where the laptop sat.

Flavia knew generally how a computer worked, but it didn't occur to her that this machine, listing names she knew—one her husband's—had any connection with what was being shown on the screen. Dooberry was drawing parallels between their challenges and those of *Apollo 13*. A man with a white forelock raised his hand and asked if there were anything wrong.

"No, not at all. Why do you ask?"

"Well, we're here to see if your technology works. And you seem to be stalling."

Dooberry smoothed the front of his shirt. "I was simply

waiting for Mr. Grant," who with another had slipped in during Dooberry's talk, "out of common decency."

It was on the word *decency* that Flavia, idly circling the cursor, clicked on the icon marked Dooberry. The screen sprouted a dot of light that blossomed into a screen of snow. Two flashes of horizontal white, then a scene.

In which nothing was ambiguous. Perhaps the room: it could have been anywhere, a cheap motel, a transient hotel. What was distinct was the woman in view. She was absolutely lovely, and the expression with which she regarded the camera would have been familiar to any reader of those men's magazines that dwell on superficial beauty. The gaze blended lubricity and the devotion of a Rhenish Madonna. The black crepe de chine of her dress emphasized her dark eyes. The audience responded with a gasp. The sound came as a single voice, masking the emotion of any individual gasper. Warm guesses would include envy, desire, shock, and a readiness to participate.

Flavia was the first of several to recognize Carmen Siquieros. She had given the very dress to Carmen after two wearings, since it showed so much better on her friend. The woman reached down to its hem and raised it slowly to her waist, and then, in one lovely and breath-suspending moment, over her head. She stood before the gathered investors and advisors in a moss green chemise. The camera (all the fantasies were rendered in first person) looked down. White deck shoes were removed. A flannel blazer with a crest was pulled from the arms of the wearer, then tossed, sleeves wrong side out, onto the bed. Flannel ducks were unbuckled and pushed rudely to the floor.

"Enough," screamed Dooberry, whose clothes gave him away. "*Bastante*," screamed Flavia, though several present thought they heard a close homophone.

Lisa was sitting next to the terminal and leaned over to close the file. Flavia marched to the front of the room.

"Flavia, my dearest. Please believe me. That never happened.

Not that I didn't think of it. But it never happened." Dooberry held his hands clenched by his chin like an outclassed Golden Glover. He appealed to the guests. "It never happened. That's pure fantasy. That scene ... "

His defense was cut short when Flavia let go with a splendid right hook. Sherry Topliff later observed that the punch had been telegraphed. Sherry knew his fisticuffs, but most looked upon his criticism as a quibble.

Dooberry went down as if dropped from a gallows. The scene was chaos. Why, some wondered, were we being shown these blue movies? Why, others wondered, had they been turned off? What did all this mean for the investment?

The issue soon became clear. Was it science or nonsense? Was this Dooberry's memory or was it something else again, an oddity but a useless by-product of the quest?

"Waddy." Victor Grant found him in the kitchen, unscrewing the lid of a jar of papaya juice. "Is there any way to test Dooberry?"

Waddy hadn't focused on the issue. "You mean like a lie detector? We'll have to revive him first"

"No, no." This from Brumberger, who had followed Grant in. "Is it real or is it fantasy?"

The living-room clamor bounced into the kitchen. It echoed off the mock clerestory windows, off the oak beams and faux Tuscan vaults. Grant stood close to hear.

"We wrote software to turn a fantasy into a narrative. To make what you imagine come out looking like a film."

"But how do we know," shouted the man who had entered with Grant, a man no one recognized, since undersecretaries of cabinet offices rarely make the news, "how do we know it's a real fantasy?"

"Fantasies aren't real," Waddy said, perplexed.

"I mean fantasy produced by your program, not porn he made with a video camera."

Waddy considered a moment and walked back to the laptop. They followed. He brought up the file index, right-clicked on a document to find the exact spot he and Annalee had shut it down. Nodded to Etta, who gave her rush-hour taxi whistle.

The noise subsided for a second test.

Though a test of what, they didn't understand.

On the screen floats a basketball at the apogee of an arc. An unseen crowd sighs. The ball, its trajectory slowed so we see the backspin imparted to soften its impact, lands upon the back of the rim and bounces gently. "Ahh," the crowd says and "ahh" the crowd repeats as the ball bounces a second time, this off the front rim.

The ball mounts the rim with gyroscopic balance. Rolls about the inside of the hoop, pebbled orange rubber on orange metal. Gains speed around the curve like a carnival ride. Then, as Waddy, the undersecretary, Victor Grant, the investors, and a staggered Dooberry rubbing his chin watch in the present and a gymnasium of fans watch in the past, the ball falls through the depending net. Two points.

Waddy closed his eyes and clenched his fists. When he opened them, the eyes of the room hung on him.

"Fantasy," he said without a beat. "Fantasy. It never happened."

Chaos shattered the hush. The crowd acted as the analog fans might have, had the Battling Crabs won the game—cries of joy, cheers for Waddy, rampant confusion.

Chloe Post wanted to know about a patent application. Wasn't there a commercial use for this? Victor Grant was waving his lawyers into a huddle. The undersecretary was calling the department solicitor.

Waddy snuck out the front door and walked to his car. It was grand to see that ball fall. No matter that it changed nothing. The day was cloudless, full of clarity and promise.

The Rocky Mountains. Brumberger and his clients emerged from the SUV and met them face to imposing rock face. Conundrum Creek trickled down, bubbling into Castle Creek, then through the Roaring Fork Valley to join the mighty Colorado. Newness and freedom and farness—the gifts of the West. People seek possibilities here, and if some are disillusioned, if some don't find their dreams, it is in part because here they dream grandly. That is the West of our history and our myth.

"Goodness," Silverheels said to his clients as he gazed on the craggy peaks. "No wonder prices west of them are slightly higher."

Cars lined the road to the site. This was a major local event. "Spading for Spirits" read the headline in the morning's *Leaf*:

> Town mucky-mucks will assemble at Conundrum Creek at 1 P.M. today to see whether twenty-eight lucky billionaires get homesites in this verdant pasture. Rags king Justin Kaye has proposed a development on what some say are sacred Indian lands. If the spirits have moved on to the Happy Hunting Grounds and taken their bones with them, the deal is on. If instead the remains of Native Americans turn up in the shovel, the deal will be nixed, and Kaye will find himself up Conundrum Creek without a paddle.

It was the end of March. Those who'd come for the skiing had gone. Mud spots blotted through the snowy trails like psoriasis. Not much doing in town, so many locals came to see the show. Those who'd signed a letter of intent came too. If the deal was a go, it was a slam dunk, double your money in a year. People sat on tailgates and bumpers. The catered set placed camp chairs by the road and picnicked on sliced meats, imported cheeses, baguettes, all washed down with a chilled white. Gossage, Waddy, and Tiffany blended in. Across the untrod diagonal waited a bright yellow bulldozer, its scoop held high as a tomahawk.

Brumburger's group was last to arrive. Emmanuel and Justin walked the perimeter to inspect the surveyor's flags. They traced each leg of the staked rectangle, Johnstone's head nodding in contemplation. Was he, the bystanders wondered, hearing voices? Did the spirits speak to him? He was known as a good picker of equities—was the netherworld in the market and, if so, was it in large caps? After the dig, he would be asked by several onlookers for a business card.

Emmanuel returned to the bench that had been set up for him and his companions. "The Indians' dugout," the reporter called it in her story, but the rewrite man struck it. A few words passed among them in Paiute, their common language, and Johnstone translated for Brumberger.

"We have a first site," Brumberger announced. He took a red pencil and, on a copy of the filed plat, described a swath from midway down the westerly border, south and east.

"Wait a minute," said Justin. "That's not the site I showed you yesterday."

"We changed our minds," Brumberger said. "You staked out one spot, we want another. Not that we expect any hanky-panky."

Justin studied the markings and nodded. It didn't matter—one was like another. He had to remind himself that the whole concept of Indian burial grounds had been created in the art department of JK Durango.

Justin and Brumberger tramped up the hill to find Marco, saturnine and impassive. They explained the change. To their consternation, it upset Marco. He insisted on huddling with his friends, the black man, the blowsy actress, the young man who used to wait on tables downtown.

"But you agreed," Waddy protested.

"Ahh," Brumberger countered. "The stipulation says it has to be in writing."

"Besides," added Justin, "what possible difference? Why do you care?"

"Well," Waddy said, scrambling. "This is the sight we thought you'd dig."

"So?"

"So we've all settled in. We have our seats." He pointed to the folding chairs and portable picnic tables. By them Philida Post was setting up portable seats for her friends from the tribal councils.

"My friend Silverheels has his rights. I wouldn't worry about it." Justin was careful not to show confidence. There's no profit in gloating.

Marco looked to Waddy, who shrugged. There was nothing to be done, their work had gone for naught. He turned to Justin Kaye.

"Now?" he asked.

"Please. Now."

Marco took the survey on which Brumberger had drawn and fired up the tractor. It clanged around the northerly edge and down the far border. Marco positioned the machine downhill on a forty-five-degree angle and looked to his boss. Justin checked with Brumberger, then nodded okay.

Marco's first pass removed the snow cover. Adept as a surgeon, he stripped a swath perhaps six feet long and the width of the scoop—it measured precisely one hundred and twenty-four inches—so that underneath, the fragile mountain tundra peeked through. He deposited his load of snow in a neat pile behind the staked line, as if he might want to use it later. Then he lined the tractor on the same path, lowered the scoop, and moved forward in earnest.

The ground gave easily. In one short stroke, perhaps a

third of the way down the path, the shovel's maw had scooped two cubic yards. Marco turned the tractor around and gingerly deposited the load of earth in a mound by the first pile.

Even bystanders across the tract could see the results. Sticking out of the conical pile of soil like needles, atop it and falling off at the sides, were bones. Long bones, flat bones, short knobby bones. A gasp passed through the crowd. Either unhearing because of the diesel's roar or, as likely, uncaring, Marco realigned his tractor and made another pass.

This time you could see bones in the scoop itself. The crowd murmured in a churchly whisper and looked at each other uneasily. The three tribal representatives broke into a chant.

> Hyu hi hi hi
> Hyu hi hi hi
> Hyu hi hi hi
> Hyu hi hi hi.

Robert Yellowknife rose from the bench and began stamping the ground in rhythm. Marco repositioned the tractor and was about to gouge out another stripe.

"Stop!" someone yelled. "Enough!"

The chant went on. Sympathizers joined in, and the effect was a crescendo in surround sound. The entire office staff of the Friends of the Friendless Earth chanted in earnest. Two of them began their own shuffle dance. A cloud—Where had it come from? The sky had been flawless—a cloud passed in front of the sun.

"Enough," said Justin.

"Enough," ordered Brumberger. Marco reached down and turned off the machine.

It took almost an hour for the last of the cars and trucks to negotiate the narrow turn. The throng that stood about in wonder blocked the shoulders of the road. Justin Kaye was among the first to get out. Viewers inched back to make way for his camouflaged SUV, the way funeral hangers-on stand aside for the mourners. Alone and shaken he drove down the hill. What would he say to the bankers? The letters of intent were worthless, he would have to return the deposits. His note was due in two days. He was lost.

All the way down and for days later, in his inner ear he would hear, like the fragment of a song on the dentist's Muzak, the rhythmic *Hyu hi hi hi*. Justin was decisive. When he lost, he lost. No sentimentality. He didn't stay to see the traffic unsnarl or to supervise the reburial of the bones. He quickly agreed to Brumberger's suggestion that Marco put the place back in order—perhaps that would stop the insistent chant—but he didn't need to supervise.

Those present buzzed about it for days. The environmentalists were gratified—the old plat had saved the land. And you had to admire Justin Kaye for doing the right thing, folding his cards. Gossage bought pizzas and beer and treated the bulldozer team to a dinner at the Quonset hut. Over longneck beers they laughed: Who had worried that the oversized scapulae and the femurs the size of baseball bats wouldn't pass? And who would have believed that most of Marco's cattle bones would be buried in protected earth?

It was a miracle, a secret miracle. Only Justin Kaye understood how extraordinary. How many times, he wondered, does that happen? Probably more than we realize. The three Indians didn't seem surprised. After all, the old chart showed the site. They didn't know Justin had created it; besides, they chanted for miracles. So, he realized, do we. Blessed are you, Sovereign of the Universe, who brings forth the fruit of the vine. Not that He makes wine from water, but that He makes it from grapes. That's miraculous enough. Justin thought of the sudden run on cretonne that had saved his bacon in '92, and a warm flush came over him. Well, he smiled sadly, one for and one against. In the miracle department, I'm even-steven.

## Twenty-Four

On that afternoon, when the fate of the planet took one of its few turns for moles and voles and jays and against the dominant species, Waddy was among the last down the hill. He stayed and puzzled with his friends over the events. As he came to the highway that would take him back to Starwood, a young man in hiking shorts and rag socks stood with his thumb out.

"Don't I know you?" Waddy asked after the stranger had thrown his kit into the backseat and slammed the door. The man had a delicate face and long eyelashes. A delicate but abidingly familiar face.

"I used to live here," he said. "Down valley. Two years ago."

They talked Aspen talk on the way, the crowds, the antics, the usual stuff. It wasn't until Waddy had let the man out, reluctantly, for they got along well; stopped by the side of the road where he had to turn up the road to Grant's guesthouse. It came to him.

"Didn't you used to be a girl?"

⌁

Waddy returned, flushed with what he had learned, to find the guesthouse emptied of bedlam. When he had made his way to the door and driven off to Conundrum Creek, the arguments were at full tilt. Dooberry was tearing about to locate his wife, to explain that she had seen the prelude to an imagined adultery, not a flesh-and-blood one. Since Flavia had disappeared with the car, Peyton and Chloe gave the frantic man a ride back to his house. Chloe tried to settle him by musing on the questions his dilemma posed: Does history trump desire? Can we be faulted for our dreams? Neither man was interested.

Waddy opened the door to silence. Before the computer, Lisa sat quietly, running programs.

She looked at him blankly. "We've been shut down."

"How's that?"

"The lawyers got themselves a temporary restraining order shutting us down. A judge will sort it out. We get one month's severance, and we're on the street."

"Whatcha doing?"

"I'm not doing," she said wearily. "You'll do the doing. Me, I'm having dinner in town with that guy who works for Grant."

"Forelock man?" She nodded. "What's to do?"

"Court says we're to dump everything on the hard drive to DVDs. I've already filled one with source code. You put all the algorithms onto a second. Then the lab notes, anything else you can think of, on a third. Once the DVDs are done, they will be the only copy. It's all spelled out in the order. Erase everything else. Check to make sure it's gone. Nothing in memory."

"Why?"

"It's the lawyers' idea. They want one version, no copies. When the judge decides who owns what, they don't want any piracy. There'll be an affidavit for us to sign."

"That's it?"

Lisa stood up and stretched. She looked at her watch.

"That's it. I'll be late. Look, it's been a good run."

Yes, he thought. I suppose it has. "Where are you for dinner if I need you?"

"Don't know. I invited him, so I'm looking for cheap." She slipped on a suede jacket, checked her lipstick in the hall mirror.

"Try the Wooly Gulch."

"Perfect. I'm unemployed—got to save my pennies. Besides, I'm tired of all this arugula and reduction shit."

She was out the door and out of his life.

Do the nasty stuff first, his mother had taught him. Waddy shelved what he'd learned from the hitchhiker and studied the screen. He was in for a long evening. Files to copy, check, translate. He went into the kitchen and retrieved the wok from the top cupboard. Poured in a button of olive oil and swirled it about. He'd make himself a stir-fry, open a beer, and settle in. It had been a hectic few days.

He was sitting before the computer, Hero on his feet, when it hit him. Tapping chopsticks on his kneecap to the rhythm of *Gut Bucket Blues*, finishing his meal. What he was doing and what he'd learned from the hitchhiker fit together with the logic of a computer program. All it lacked was him.

Hero beat him to the car and leaped into the backseat. Nothing they both enjoyed more than a race. They flew down Highway 82 to the trailer court on twenty-two-inch wheels of love. If only she would be home.

"Hearts fixed on the goal," he sang in full voice, "and eyes fixed to the sky."

At several bends in the road, tires squealed, shrieking their fear of the steep banks of the Roaring Fork. Hero was never content in the car until it hit fifty, and now at each squeal he yelped contentedly. But Waddy had a steady hand. Ardor and a refreshed will to stay alive countered the physics of centrifugal force. If only she would be home.

Battling Crabs eternal,
Shellfish supreme,
We're fighting the fight and
We're dreaming the dream.

The Bug careened into the trailer court. Followed the tongue-in-groove painted fence, fishtailed through the muddy lanes among the double-wides, and juddered to a stop in a spray of dirt and pea gravel at Annalee's Airstream. "She better be home," he warned Hero.

Hero said nothing. "She better be home," he said again.

She was.

❧

She wasn't at the house, so Dooberry searched in town. Her favorite discos weren't yet open. Would Flavia have driven down valley to Carmen and Matt's place? He'd stop once more at home and call from there.

He could not have been more miserable. His equation of despair had not yet computed the fact that the project was over. They had been hopelessly broke before—that didn't bother him. To Dooberry, the next deal always lay becalmed, just around the promontory, awaiting a fair wind. No, the cause of his misery was the distress of his beloved, whom he cherished, and the guilt that his fantasies adhered to lower standards of fidelity than did he.

He walked through the portal of his house. There sat his Brazilian beauty, examining a Tom Collins and munching on its orange slice. The court fight over Wise Mother, the anger of the investors, the plague of lawyers, all dropped away at the sight of the woman whom he had always loved, though lately not in the carnal fashion.

"Dearest."

"'Allo, Doo."

"Dearest, that ... that thing with Carmen. It never happened."
He held out his hands as if he might be offering a watermelon.

"I know."

"Only in my imagination. It happened only in my imagination, and I'm sorry for that."

"I know, Doo. Carmen told me too. Is okay."

"Is okay?"

"Is okay." He walked to her and she rose to meet his reaching arms. Planted on her a distinctively carnal kiss.

"Better than okay. Is giving you back your *caralho*." She used the street word.

"Absolutely," Dooberry blurted and confirmed his passion with a second kiss. They moved hand in hand to the staircase. On the banister, retrieved from the body where they had looked so good that they got themselves a role in Dooberry's fantasy, were the crepe de chine dress and the moss green chemise.

~

"What inspired this rush of passion?" Annalee asked. They lay in the trailer's bed, no longer roommates.

"Actually, it was Hero." He would tell her of the young man with the eyelashes later.

"Hero?" asked Annalee and screamed. At his name, the dog had climbed from the floor and stuck his cold nose between her lower two ribs.

Waddy scolded him off. "When I first got him, he'd bark and cry in his dreams. He still does it occasionally. I asked the vet. Seems humans do it too, when they lose a leg. They still have pain in the ghost leg. For the rest of their lives."

"So?"

"So I didn't want to wake up the rest of my life with you as my ghost leg."

Robert Yellowknife too had had his fill of reductions. For the celebratory dinner, he booked the Wooly Gulch Tavern, a locals' hangout beyond town and across the tracks. The tavern was one dank expanse. Close by the booths sat two pool tables, and experienced diners stayed alert to sharp elbows, shoes lifted in buttress, and the pumping butts of cue sticks. There were no visible windows at the Wooly Gulch. Only the June monsoons freshened the air, and in that single month the breezes supplied the room with its oxygen to last the year.

Robert wanted a dinner to remember. Though his specialty was a chili that numbed microbes of the gastrointestinal tract, the chef was persuaded to import Apalachicola oysters and a case of a good Taittinger. In the tradition of his tribe, Robert invited everyone who had contributed to the success of the day. His two *dineh* brethren and Brumberger, of course, but also the surveyor Ned Quinlan, the ploughman Marco Campaneris, and, since they looked upon them as talismanic, Tiffany and Gossage. He included the couple who owned his motel and two Anglos who ran a tchotchke shop in Basalt—milled kachinas, Taiwanese concha belts. Of course the broad-shouldered woman, the eco-cop who had maintained order at the site. Finally, Justin and Rochelle Kaye. They were friends of Silverheels Brumberger. Once your opponent is vanquished, Robert explained to Brumberger, you must restore his dignity. Otherwise, you beget a new generation of enemies.

During cocktails, Gossage and Johnstone lost money to Quinlan at eight ball. Quinlan, after all, made his living measuring angles. The main course was steak fried in onions and butter. In the midst of dinner, Robert Yellowknife quieted the conversation. He wanted everyone to know everyone else in the room, and the Northern Cheyenne way to bring that about was for everyone to perform. Tell a story or sing a song.

Silverheels began with the tale of the eminent domain suit he'd won on behalf of the Hopi. Tiffany did a surprisingly convincing Blanche from *Streetcar*. The Champagne disappeared. Gossage spoke for three minutes on Kondratyev's Long Wave Theory, lucidly, although only Emmanuel Johnstone paid attention. During Gossage's talk, Robert Yellowknife rose silently and began to shuffle about the room. When the time came for his contribution, he began to chant, a song not unlike that for the revealed bones.

> Hyu hi hi hi—
> Hyu hi hi hi.

"Are you praying for ancestors?" Philida asked him as he two-stepped by.

"No, miss."

"Good weather?"

"No, miss."

"What, then?"

"More wine."

Someone recognized Lisa dining at a small table with the Grant detective, and they were brought into the party. Philida sat in deep conversation with Silverheels Brumberger—she was captivated with his observations about the food chain.

Which Brumberger interrupted only to order the next bottles. In a sweet soprano, Rochelle Kaye sang a tune from *The King and I*. Justin sat morose and quiet. In the vintage movies that he loved, disappointed heroes turned to drink. He was not usually a drinker, but the fate of the Isaak Walton Preserve, buried as it had been in Marco's first scoop, had pushed him to an extra glass.

Everyone had to perform, Robert Yellowknife announced, and even in his gloom, Justin was not let off. He erased pool scores from the blackboard and chalked in the balance sheet of JK Durango. He listed cash uses and sources. He explained leverage, inventory financing. He got a standing ovation.

∽

"And so," the man said and frowned with resolve, "I believe the Lord created one man for every woman."

Lisa listened in equal tedium and dismay. Part of her feared that this man with a white blaze of hair might be right. "Tell me," she asked. "Did you happen to be at a Christmas party last December in the West End?"

"At Miss Eubanks's house," the man said excitedly. She considered his words. It was certainly possible that what she believed had been a transcendental moment of insight on Christmas Eve had in fact been a slight temperature.

The moment was interrupted by a handsome, dark-skinned man who pulled up a bentwood chair, turned its back to the table, and straddled it to sit down.

"You need another drink," he said. It sounded more like an observation than an offer. Lisa's date must have thought so too, for he rose gallantly to fetch her a Chablis. Once they were alone, the newcomer said little. She asked and he answered as if waiting for the real test to arise. He was in investments, he said. He lived in Belle Fourche, South Dakota. He handled moneys for the Northern Cheyenne, his tribe, an amount, between casino profits and awards for reclaimed lands, that was considerable. He also testified on economic issues as an expert.

"Did you study investing at the Indian college?"

"I went to no college," he said darkly. "After high school I was trained by my people."

"Your people trained you in what?"

"In the rites of manhood."

Lisa took a moment to regain her balance. "Making a fire, stargazing, scarring your arm with a knife, that sort of thing?"

"No, our rites involve a study of human behavior. I concentrated on sex."

"Sex," Lisa repeated the inflexion. Inadvertently her head tipped like a sparrow's. For the first time, she focused on the cobalt eyes deep in their sockets. They were not easy to read in the smoky air.

"Sex," Robert Yellowknife repeated and paused. "We believe that to become a man, a youth must learn the ways of pleasing the female. This is what the animal world teaches us."

"It does?"

"Among other lessons. How does a bull elk command a herd of ten cows? Because he has learned, best of all the bull elk, how to please. It is a great obligation. He will get to sire the next generation. But he must use all his ingenuity, everything nature has given him."

"How much ingenuity can an elk have?"

"The scent of an male elk travels for miles. In the spring of the year, his antlers are covered in velvet. The elk knows forty-seven ways of pleasing his cow."

"Forty-seven?" Lisa asked and tried to sip from the emptied glass.

"And in my apprenticeship I had to perfect them all. But then, the raven knows sixty-two, entirely different, and the otter seventy. I learned them as well. There is no unhappiness in the otter world among the females."

"That's ... ," Lisa stumbled.

"One hundred and seventy-nine. But only a few of the species."

"How many animals did you study?"

"I studied them all. The woman I find will never have to make love twice the same way. I also studied the birds, the butterflies, the salmon in the stream. We can learn a great deal from the salmon in the stream."

"Can we?" asked Lisa, and for the first time noticed how

deep and smooth the lines were that ran from his wide nostrils to the corners of his mouth.

The man who worked for Victor Grant struggled back carrying a bowl of taco chips in one hand, a fresh light beer and her Chablis in the other.

"Bar's a zoo," he said, tugged at his forelock, and looked about for his chair. Someone had taken it for another table. "There are all these," and here he lowered his voice, "people here."

Lisa had forgotten his name.

❧

One waiter distributed bowls of apple brown Betty and a second served grappa from a Safeway shopping cart. It was Marco's turn.

He tried to rise to his feet and failed. That brought great applause. He insisted that standing was his talent, though not a constant one. Emmanuel and Johnstone propped him up.

He described the process of making artificial snow. In the middle of his speech, Victor Grant made an appearance. Brumberger asked that a chair be brought—he was, Brumberger explained, an adversary in a different fight, but an adversary nonetheless. Grant begged off. He simply wanted to speak with Mr. Kaye.

Rochelle took a firm grip of her husband's steel gray hair and pulled his head from the table.

Justin opened his eyes. "Hello."

"You own that tract?"

"I sure do."

"I want to buy it," Grant said.

"Sorry. Not for sale. Can't be developed."

"I don't want to develop it. I want to buy it."

"Not for sale." Justin returned his head to the wooden table.

Rochelle Kaye, allergic to alcohol, was fortunately church

sober. "What do you want it for?" she asked.

"I just want it."

"It's Indian holy land. You can't do anything with it."

"Oh yes, I can."

"What?"

"I can give it away. To the Friends of the Friendless Earth."

"You want to buy the preserve, it'll cost you," Rochelle said. She was looking at the amount of the bank note, accrued interest to date, chalked on the blackboard. Justin was in no shape, but she could calculate what it would take to save JK Durango.

"I'm prepared to pay."

"Why?"

"I want to do something for my community." Rochelle gave him her best subway squint. She'd been around, no one could sell her a skybox at Ebbets.

Grant hesitated. It was a corny line, but he had resolved to say it. When he'd tried it on his assistant, Isabelle had said she better bring her résumé current.

"We all live on the same spaceship." To his right, Justin Kaye gave out a brief, musical snore.

"Call us," Rochelle said. "Call us tomorrow."

Grant left. Those awake realized that Marco was still on his feet, waiting patiently, his head rolling in a circle the circumference of a dinner plate.

"Go on," said Robert Yellowknife. "So, you have the hose in a source, like a stream or a pond, then what?"

Marco took them through it. How you throttled the nozzle for the right mix of air and water, how you kept it open in freezing weather and pointed the spray downwind.

"And when you're done," asked Gossage, who could not remember an evening when he had learned so much, "do you have snow? Or is it some phonus balonus stuff?"

"Oh, no," Marco was insistent. "It's snow all right. Little

pellets, not flakes, but you can ski on it, it looks just like the real thing. Fool most anyone."

# III. The Spring

*There's a land where the mountains are nameless,*
*And the rivers all run God knows where;*
*There are lives that are erring and aimless,*
*And deaths that just hang by a hair;*
*There are hardships that nobody reckons;*
*There are valleys unpeopled and still;*
*There's a land—oh, it beckons and beckons,*
*And I want to go back—and I will.*

*—Robert Service, "The Spell of the Yukon"*

## Twenty-Five

The cell phone gave a soft, glottal click. Almost human, Grant thought, and satisfying. He enjoyed this conversation, ending as it had ended with an insight. And exactly the kind of insight he favored. Precise, discrete, ironic. It lacked only a quantifiable return on investment.

The insight was this: Philida would think that his donation of the Walton Preserve was an act of sacrifice. The conversation he just concluded, before his breakfast date with Philida, confirmed the sale of his entire holdings of Rainwater securities, off the tape and at a significant profit. The charitable donation of the Walton Preserve would help to shelter the tax on that profit. Do good and do well.

He glanced at his Seiko as the digits flashed 8:00 and looked up to see Philida approaching. Right on the dot. Punctual and uniformed, what a knockout.

Philida was on guard. She expected Grant to serve his own purposes as well as hers. Not forgotten was the barrage of calla lilies, green gardenias, amber tulips that had flooded her small apartment. Given his professed interest in acquiring the Walton Preserve for the Friends of the Friendless Earth, she expected to endure some gentlemanly flirtation. Besides, Victor Grant was not unattractive.

On guard and well prepared. Philida briskly outlined how

to complete a gift, guidelines for maintenance, the environmental safeguards the FFE would require. She handed him a budget. "An endowment will be needed to fund it," she warned. "I thought you'd like some projections."

"The budget is reasonable," Grant said without hesitation. "What's next?"

"Next is for you to decide whether you want to do this. It is not an inconsiderable sum."

"I've decided. I do."

"The land or the endowment?"

"Both."

"Then next is for you to negotiate with the owners. To see if you can buy the property."

"I've done that. They've given me a price. It's acceptable."

She had not taken him to be reckless. "Victor. This is a lot of money. Perhaps you should make sure you're not overpaying."

"Philida, dear. Thank you for looking out for me. I just cleared a transaction that will net me three times the price of that piece of land. I want to do more."

Philida was moved by his decisiveness. The smile she offered was cousin to a puppy's rolling on its back in surrender.

Grant's shyness had, until now, deflected his passion away from romance and toward business. But in either endeavor, he knew how to sell a deal.

"I want to do more with you, too, Philida. I've stopped the flowers, but I want to find another way to show you my honorable interest."

The waitress came over. "Anything wrong with that?" she said. Philida looked down. She hadn't touched her yogurt.

"No."

"You want I should take it?"

"Sure." Then to Grant, "What do you have in mind?"

"You're fond of the outdoors, I know. And the mountains."

"Yes, I am."

"Let's take a bicycle ride."

"I don't own a bicycle."

"We'll find one for you. What do you say?"

"When?"

"Tomorrow, if you can pack. Italy is lovely in the spring. The hills of Umbria. Separate rooms, of course."

"Italy? I don't know what to say."

Grant reached across and took her fingers in his. "Will you think about it?"

Now it was her turn to be shy. She had never been to Umbria, it sounded ideal. She retrieved her hands and put them to fidgeting with her Sam Browne belt.

"I'll think about it. I must be getting to work."

"Busy day?"

"Nothing special. I'm in the field today. I enjoy that."

Grant gathered up the forms she had brought, FFE's statement of purpose, a pamphlet explaining charitable trusts and how best to designate FFE as beneficiary.

"And you?"

"I? Oh, the usual. I need to close the sale of a software company and decide whether to sue on some local investment."

"Wise Mother?"

He looked up, surprised. She seemed so unworldly.

"Yes, Wise Mother. Do you know of it?"

"My idiot brother is an investor. It sounded zany, a complete zero. But maybe not?"

"Maybe not. Maybe something can be salvaged. I have the preferred position."

"What does that mean?"

"I can foreclose and sell the assets. Two, I can sue the promoter." He glanced at the bill and multiplied the sixteen dollars and fifty-five cents by point one five. Rounded down.

"You ought to let it go, Victor. You don't need another battle on your hands."

"Another battle?"

"A lawsuit."

"You're against war?"

"I'm against unnecessary war. Do you disagree?"

It was too early in their courtship to offend her over a point of principle.

"I'm not sure. Usually the people against war are those who will lose."

"That doesn't invalidate their position."

"No, I suppose not. But it makes them unpersuasive. Does it help the lamb to argue for vegetarianism when he's dining with the wolf?"

"I'm not concerned that the wolves will get you." The waitress brought back his credit card and he signed the slip with a straight line.

"You'll think about Italy?"

"You'll think about letting the suit go?"

"And we'll compare notes this evening?"

"This evening, then."

Philida squared her Smokey the Bear hat and pulled her kneesocks taut. They walked out together.

❧

Mortimer Dooberry had studied statistics, though not successfully. He was particularly fond of the idiosyncrasy that no matter how many times one flipped a penny, the odds of heads on the next flip remained fifty-fifty. It seemed to him a hint of good will in the universe. It suggested that every day, regardless of how lousy the past one, you awoke to the chance that the coin would come up heads. The same possibility, as he understood it, applied to tails.

As a result of this weltanschauung, Dooberry was not surprised when the breaks began to fall his way. His marriage digested the incident of the rogue file, and to his delight, the experience became an aphrodisiac. Flavia was inspired to find that her husband had some libido. She did not begrudge his imagination—instead, she dipped into her repertoire to re-create the passion of their early years together. Since Carmen had moved to Matt's place, her own house was private again. The Doo, out of a job, had no other calling for the mornings but to lie abed. He did just that, and enjoyed being under her considerable powers. She cancelled her summer plans for an equestrian seminar.

Her decision to stay home also helped the budget. With Project Wise Mother ending, they would need to conserve cash until something came along. And, true to Dooberry's peculiar even-odds determinism, the U.S. mail brought that something.

A man wrote from northern California to hire Dooberry as director of inner thought at the Shasta Center for Spiritual Unity. The SCSU, its color catalog explained, was a destination complex. The faculty was trained in acupuncture, transcendental transmogrification, a diet of the less aggressive vegetables, and foot massage. The campus included classrooms, a sweat lodge, two regulation bowling alleys, and a clinic for substance abuse.

They immediately flew out to see the founder. He had known of Dr. Dooberry long before the latest debacle. He wanted to affiliate with someone like him, someone with a broad background, academic credentials, and three *Oprah* appearances.

The atmosphere was tailored for Dooberry: mystery and asceticism, with a pinch of science. Hoping to find a post where longevity stood independent of skill, Dooberry inquired about security. The SCSU agreed to deposit two years' salary in an account against Dooberry's term of appointment. It looked as if the Dooberrys' ship of fortune, at least for two years of dry dock, was out of the shoals.

∿

Waddy returned to his empty house, dizzy from passion. On the desk, the source code printout sat where he'd left it, the DVDs stacked on top. Waddy was drifting on the high-octane fumes of discovered love, so when the doorbell sounded, he didn't immediately recognize it. The delivery woman smiled at his disarray, shirttail flapping, hair sticking out in the random angles of a desert landscape.

"Sign here," she said, handing him a carton, and though she tried, she could not catch his eye.

Or any other part, for that matter. Her Lear had touched down lightly and resumed flight. Waddy was dreaming on his great good fortune: Where will he and his beloved float on this flood tide that was his heart's outpouring? And where will they pull themselves ashore?

The carton contained the first printing of the brochure. Dooberry had spent a good deal of money on a marketing firm, they in turn had spent a good deal of money on a plan, and the agency that would implement the plan had spent a good deal of money on layouts, space purchases in the trade magazines, and this, the first Wise Mother Database mailing piece.

Waddy lifted one from the box and held it by its corner. Slick. Bullet points, demographics, statistics. The Wise Mother aggregated six major indexes, to give the purchaser of information every possible way of cross-checking not merely interest groups, but specific individuals. It would make a hell of a tool, Waddy realized, if a malign government wanted to know about its friends and enemies.

And the lead page made him shiver.

> Welcome to the Wise Mother Database. All the Wise Mother needs to know about her own child—and everyone else's.
>
> You'll get verified ID. You'll get age, sex, vocation, income (down to $5,000 brackets), catalog and

online buying patterns, credit card membership and buying histories, Social Security info, home ownership ID, zip codes tied to median income.

And MORE! Two categories never before thought possible: dreams and fantasies!

What could be more powerful selling tools? Is your business burglar alarms, locks, garage doors, window screens? Are you a developer planning the next gated community? Would you like to know qualified buyers with a deviantly high fear of breaking and entering? No matter if you're baker or banker, tinker or tailor, here's data your business can use!

And FANTASIES! The world's most powerful persuaders, from Genghis Khan to Stalin, have understood that reality is ugly and unpleasant, that an appeal to truth produces anger and disenchantment. Not sales. Those who manufacture romance and spin fantasies control the general public, whether it's the voting public or the buying public.

There exists no more powerful information. We don't know your business—you do. But we know what you can do with these tools in your hands: Anything!

Hero dozed in the corner. Waddy replaced the brochure glumly and put the carton with Dooberry's stack of mail. The night had been unrestful, and he felt unfocused. He turned his diverted mind to downloading the remaining programs.

Waddy finished by half past two that afternoon. The entire project reposed on three freshly burned DVDs. As instructed by the court's order, he labeled and signed each disk and placed it in its own jewel case. Then he dialed Annalee.

"No, dearest. I cannot go for a run. I'm due at the restaurant at four."

"Why are you working there?" He asked himself the question as he asked her.

"Only for the money."

"Why is it that you and I, who know so much about restaurants, don't have our own restaurant?" The idea came to him fully formed, with all the graphics. Shrink-wrapped.

"Waddy. Do you know the cost of opening a restaurant in Aspen?"

"Who said anything about Aspen? We'll find a place where chanterelle sauce is unknown. How hard can that be?"

"Go for your jog. It will cool you down."

Waddy threw his running gear into the trunk of the Bug. What had the computer business done for him? At Rainwater, he had helped make others wealthy. At Wise Mother, he had written brilliant formulas in record time and produced a federal court case and a sales pamphlet that demonstrated just how invidious his efforts could be.

He went back into the house, removed the three cased DVDs from the desk drawer, and put them beside him in the right front seat.

Hero and he drove down the valley to the interstate, turned east, and parked in the lot by the Shoshone Power Station. The path that followed the Colorado River was his favorite. An hour up the canyon, an hour down. The sun would soon fall over the canyon's walls.

He returned to the car sweating and loose, and toweled off. He would not again make the mistake of changing in a parking lot, no matter how isolated it seemed. The river burbled past. Why *didn't* they find their own place? He turned the key to engage the battery, put a favorite disk in the CD slot, pushed the Play button. Then, with the door open to listen, he leaned against the rear fender and stretched.

Hero woofed happily when he heard the intro. He was especially keen on Bessie Smith.

"Nobody loves you," sang Bessie, "when you're down and out."

Waddy took the three jewel boxes from the seat and walked to the railing. Hero followed. The river ran fast in this channel, the bottom of Glenwood Canyon. From here it meandered through the dry West. Supplied by the Green and the Yampa it cut through Utah, slicing sandstone of the great canyons. Finally, what water was left after evaporating in reservoirs behind great dams and being sprinkled over the lawns of Los Angeles dumped into the Sea of Cortez.

The water below churned red from neighboring clays. It was a river that could bury a civilization. He removed the first DVD from its case and, with an easy Frisbee motion, sent it sailing into the water. Hero gave a little yap to protest a game he couldn't play. The disk slipped away, silvery side up, like a feeding trout. So did the next two.

Man and dog turned and walked toward the parked car. A woman in khaki shorts and shirt, Sam Browne belt, stood with one booted foot on the VW's front bumper.

"What do you think you're doing?"

"I beg your pardon?"

"What do you think you're doing, throwing litter into the river?"

He had no answer. "It's a beautiful day, officer."

His vision couldn't penetrate her wraparound shades—she might be a bat, sensing direction from sound.

"You look familiar, mister. Do we know each other?"

He read the name from the brass plate on her asexual chest.

"No, Officer Post."

"Still. You look familiar. Littering is a misdemeanor in this state, punishable by five days' imprisonment, a fine of $500, or both. Do you have any idea why?"

"Why what?"

"Why it's against the law."

"I certainly do."

"You do?"

"I do. It's an execrable act. It shows disregard for oneself and one's fellow"—here he stumbled—"fellow persons. We all live on the same spaceship."

"That's right."

"I have no excuse. What's my penalty?"

"No excuse?"

"None. I was overcome. You see, I've just fallen in love."

Waddy couldn't say for sure, but he thought behind the lenses the invisible eyes widened. The music stopped, Hero nuzzled her hand, and the three of them listened to the gap between songs. Then from the open door came a clarinet riff and the first bars of "Heebie Jeebies."

The cop gave the slightest sniffle. "I tell you what. I'm going to let you go. This time."

"Thank you, officer."

"I'm off to Umbria tomorrow. I don't have time to write you up. But I don't want to see you again."

"Vice," Waddy said, although it seemed a bit flip, "versa."

She turned to go.

"Why Umbria?" he asked.

"A bicycle trip."

"Listen. Have a good time."

"I will."

"Be sure to try the osso buco. Umbria is famous for Caciotta cheese, the Cannara onion, and osso buco."

Philida gave him a thoughtful look. She was unaccustomed to solicitude.

"Thanks for the tip."

## Twenty-Six

As the boy walked the length of the bar toward him, Frankie picked off clues: black curly hair, light eyes, powerful shoulders. He wasn't a boy, really, he was a young man, perhaps twenty-five, but his amble and his clothes made him seem callow and easy. He wore mountaineering boots and gray rag socks, hiking shorts—it was early April, for God's sake, and here he was in shorts—and a tan cable-stitch sweater. Frankie appraised him as carefully as a casaba in the crate, wishing only that he could squeeze for ripeness. The way his broad neck came out of that sweater ...

"Hi," the young man said affably and walked within range.

"*Buongiorno.*"

"I'm looking for Annalee."

"You just missed her. She's quit."

"Where'd she go? Is she home?"

"Her boyfriend came to pick her up. They're moving down valley."

Disappointment turned the corners of the boy's mouth and dimmed the light in those lovely eyes. They were, Frankie could see at this distance, pale as Orvieto.

"She's a friend?"

The lad nodded and let slip a sigh. It wasn't lost on Frankie.

"My only friend in Aspen. I was hoping I could put up with her for a few days."

"Try to call." Frankie lifted the receiver from the hostess stand and proffered it.

"No. If she's moving, she's moving."

"You're new to town?"

"Not really. Returning. I used to live with Annalee." He offered his hand. Frankie could not help but notice how it protruded from the cuff of the sweater, the strong wrist, the long, slender thumb.

"My name is Norman."

❧

It was the perfect space. Second Hand Rose was packing up and going home to Scarsdale. There simply wasn't enough business in Aspen year-round, and the bear market had halved her alimony. Tiffany and Marco were her best suppliers. That's why she called them first.

"It's the perfect space. You do it over any way you like, do it so it's you."

And Tiffany did. The store reopened a month later as The Miner and the Maiden. It's still there. Tiffany has a natural ability for pricing, and she brings flair to converting trash into architectural specialties. What used to be in the Quonset hut is now cunningly displayed at retail, in pickle barrels and raffia baskets and ore carts. The Miner and the Maiden does not, however, carry bones.

Rose had been pinched by a high cost of goods against occasional revenues. Tiffany and Marco have no cost. Working the crawler dozer summer and fall, Marco brings everything he unearths to his wife. She prices it, adds a hand-lettered tag in cursive (description and date—*Late 19th C.* is her go-to), and puts it on the floor.

They do well. Marco could give up his winter job, but he likes being up on the hill. He declines the snow-making detail, he prefers to be home at night, and sticks to operating the lifts. Even that has turned out to be a source of supply. He saves whatever he finds under the chairs. There's nothing to be done with the candy wrappers, trail maps, roaches, and Chap Sticks, but the solo mittens gave Tiffany an idea. She's designed a lanyard that attaches a skier's glove to his parka, not unlike the yarn our mothers used to get us through grammar school winters. The patent application, the label reveals in small and hopeful print, is pending.

～

"I can't believe I'm doing this!" The top of the Bug was down, and in order to be heard against the wind she had to shout.

"Why not?"

"Waddy!" She said the word as if his name explained everything. "Waddy, we've spent one night together!"

"Nonsense. We've spent two months together. Remember me? I lived in your bed."

"That's not what I mean. We've spent one night together as ... "

"Yes?"

"Man and woman!" Annalee held a potted aspidistra on her lap. When she shouted, its leaves trembled.

"And?"

"Well, just that!"

"It wasn't so hot?"

"No! It was wonderful. But here we are, giving up everything on the basis of one night?"

"And two months. Don't forget those two months." Waddy took her hand and kissed it. Hero leaned forward from the backseat and lapped her ear.

"I can't. I wouldn't." Annalee hesitated, then decided to make a shouted confession. "I thought you were gay."

"What? I can't believe this."

The Bug sped down Highway 82 carrying everything they wanted. The rest, well, as Waddy said, it was just stuff. Wherever they went there would always be stuff.

"Well, I don't know. I thought you were gay. I mean, you never made a move, and I don't think I'm bad looking ... "

"You told me, No fooling around. So I didn't fool around."

Annalee saw him as if through a lens smeared with Vaseline. It wasn't merely the perception-jarring effect of true love. They had driven off before she had time to put in her contacts. Waddy plucked her from the restaurant, she said her goodbyes in minutes, they stopped at the trailer to pick up a sack of belongings, and they were off, coins scattered on the street.

"Yes," she said, admiring the very restraint that had, only last autumn, driven her mad.

"Look," Waddy pointed as the car approached the turnoff to the Wooly Gulch Tavern. "Isn't that Mr. Gossage?"

The question was rhetorical. No one within fifty miles resembled him. Over his shoulder he carried a stick from which swung a bindle. The other hand hung casually in the air, its thumb pointed downhill toward tomorrow.

They stopped the Volkswagen.

"Can we give you a ride, Mr. Gossage?"

"Oh, just Gossage will do," he said as he squeezed into the backseat. Hero panted at him happily. They moved a cardboard box that held Annalee's thermal underwear, some Teagarden CDs, and a bakery sack of fresh croissants that Frankie had insisted they take with them for the road. Once Gossage settled in, they replaced the box on his lap. "Where are you headed?"

Gossage twisted around. Something in his pocket was jabbing his ribs. He took out a dilapidated paperback and set it on the back ledge. "I don't know. I thought I might head south to the Four Corners. Visit one of those tribal fellows who came for the big dig. What about yourselves?"

Waddy mentioned a town west and north of Glenwood Springs. It happened to be the very place a helpful waitress had recommended to him as he wandered through Utah, though he didn't make the connection. A cowboy town, its motor vehicle records show the title of not a single Bentley, a place where dope is a name kids call each other and silicone is used in print shops.

"Why there?"

"We're not sure," Annalee replied, smiling. "We think we'll open a restaurant."

There was no traffic. Behind they heard the building sound of a large engine, and Waddy glanced in the mirror, trying to find its source.

"Excellent. I'll come to dine. What kind of food?"

"Nothing to remember. Chili burgers, chicken-fried steaks. Breakfast with home fries and refills on the coffee."

"Sounds perfect," Gossage said. It wasn't a car they had heard. It was a low-flying jet. It buzzed them, wagged its wings, and began to climb. Hero yapped it away.

"I've been thinking," said Waddy.

"Yes?"

"Well, I know some good recipes. I was thinking maybe we have one dish a night that's special. I was thinking, maybe we open with osso buco."

Annalee turned to the rear seat to relay the news. "One special a night. Open with osso buco."

"Sounds ideal." The road plunged down through red clay cliffs. "Tell me. I've been wondering."

"Yes?"

"I've noticed that hitchhikers are most likely to get rides from people with the least space in their cars. What do you make of the correlation?"

～

When *The Goddess of the Conduct of Other People* rose in full glory from behind its field of dry amaranth, not a single voice sounded in protest. This in a town where battles over zoning issues—the shade of teal on a sign, the length of shake shingle—are waged with a Saracen zeal. Sherry's thirty-foot sculpture was the cat that shows up on the back porch and stays—everyone assumed the Goddess had been invited.

You can see her today. Passengers on the port side of departing aircraft are often startled to encounter her open face at liftoff. Everyone finds something personal in the Goddess's expression. Her large, lugubrious eyes seem to follow you like a full moon through a forest of trees. Perhaps it's the absence of pupils. From her ears dangle hoops of chrome. Some say they came off the airplane that belonged to Jim Morrison, some say Buddy Holly. The force of lift from aircraft of sufficient weight causes them to vibrate on their stone posts, and for a moment the meadow fills with a tiny tintinnabulation.

The Eubanks' Citation is not quite heavy enough to set them off. When it rose to end Etta and Sherry's season, en route to Tulsa, Etta was sitting by a portside window. She studied the Goddess vis-à-vis.

"It's wonderful," she said and reached across to squeeze Sherry's hand. "The scale is just right. And the look, well, it's perfect."

"What kind of look, would you say?"

"Well, she's obviously a woman who gets things done. And her expression says, Today I've done fine but there's more tomorrow." The airplane began an easterly turn.

"Am I right?"

"You're absolutely right," Sherry said and squeezed back.

"Oh, look." Etta peered down valley. "There's that cute silver car of Waddy Brush. He called last night to thank me.

He's whisking away that lovely girl from the restaurant. Sherry, tell the pilot to fly over them and waggle the wings good-bye."

Sherry picked up the intercom phone and relayed the instructions. The airplane banked left.

Etta pulled a large leather purse to her lap and opened it up for the day's work. She had a development deal to read— in-fill drilling in the Denver-Julesburg Basin. But first the mail: a wheel of Caciotta cheese, a wedding invite from the Latin gal who'd worked for the Dooberrys and that nice policeman who'd arrested Peyton, a note from Flavia and Dooberry asking how she was and whether she'd consider an investment in an anxiety-reducing kiva. Last a note from Rochelle Kaye. They had refinanced JK Durango—it would live to see another season. Justin was thinking spring colors for the fall line.

The Caciotta was from Philida, who somehow had gotten Irv Brumberger to take her biking in Italy. God, thought Etta. I'm glad she didn't go off with that prick Grant. Maybe, if he keeps behaving himself, I'll find him someone next season. She looked at the photo, Philida and Brumberger in knee-length shorts on a bridge in Perugia, and stuck the snapshot back in the cheese wrapper.

A good morning's mail. Perhaps she'd start a scrapbook.

～

Frankie insisted Norman stay for lunch. It was the restaurant's last day until it reopened in June for the design conference. Only three tables. The Finches always celebrated their anniversary on the last day of Frankie's season. A mother and daughter on vacation. And a couple who looked familiar, the man telling an angular woman about life in Belle Fourche, South Dakota.

The chef served whatever he had. Frankie called it a smorgasbord, and put a bottle of Meursault on each table. What the hell, he could do with a celebration. It had been a long season. Successful and lonely. He gave himself April and May abroad, he could write it off. Two months in a foreign country alone—the specter depressed him.

The Meursault disappeared. This large man who was Annalee's missing friend seemed to have neither palate nor gullet. Wine went in like gas from a nozzle.

Not without effect. The wine made him loquacious, and he poured out the story of his unhappy life. Norman had wandered from male modeling to movie extra to Aspen river guide. That itself was not so extraordinary a voyage as one might think. But once here, ensconced with Annalee as his girlfriend, he found himself in a morass over his own identity.

"I simply hadn't figured out," he confessed as a second bottle was uncorked, "my own sexuality."

"Really," asked Frankie, trying his best to sound ingenuous.

"Somehow I feel I can tell you these things."

The man had wild, luxuriant eyelashes. "Oh, you can. You can."

"I began cross-dressing. Changed my name to Norma. Began to investigate the idea of a sex change. You know they're done right in this state."

"I do. But I certainly hope ... "

"No, no. I never went through with it. Annalee was a great help. She got me to a shrink, I figured out I wasn't weird. I was simply gay."

"Bravo," Frankie called out, rolling his *R*. "An important discovery."

"So I came back to thank Annalee and tell her. But here I am, with no money and no prospects."

"Oh," said Frankie. He leaned forward and caught the swag of skin at his throat. Then he signaled a waiter to bring the dessert list. There must be something in the refrigerator. "Oh, I wouldn't be so sure about prospects. Tell me, is your passport current?"

~

Waddy braked the car to a stop. They had come to the point where the roads divided.

Gossage unfolded himself from the rear and placed the carton he'd been holding back on the seat. He retrieved his stick and bindle and the battered paperback book.

"What are you reading?" Annalee asked.

"I'm finally finishing *David Copperfield*. I relate to him." He stuffed his book into the pocket of his tweed jacket. "We must each of us turn out to be the hero of our own lives." The dog heard his name and wagged merrily. "Do you think it possible that Copperfield was a black man? Dickens was playing to the white market and glossed over it?"

"That copy is falling apart."

"It's a bon voyage present. It was discovered under a ski lift. Soon as I find the right home, I'll go back to hardcover."

He shook hands with both of them. He had to reach through the aspidistra to get Waddy's.

"There's no need to wish you luck," Gossage said with a warmth that was assuring.

"No," Annalee said, "but we'll take it."

"I have a feeling," Waddy offered, "our paths will cross again."

At the suggestion, Gossage beamed.

"You mean there's to be a sequel?"

"Exactly."

Gossage assembled his pack and stick, hoisted the device to his shoulder. He was only steps down the new road when a Jeep approached. It had a torn canvas top, mostly opened to the elements, and it was painted, roll bars and all, a mustard yellow. It stopped and the front seat pulled forward to allow him to squeeze into the rear. So it was that Gossage disappeared around the bend to the left. Waddy sighed at the variety of human conduct. It pleased him. He steered the Volkswagen right at the fork.

He and Annalee were sucking on the same lozenge of thought. She spoke first.

"A sequel," she said. "Just imagine."

They both tried, but for all their optimism and youth they could not come up with a trace of what the future might hold. The warming failure hit them at the same time, and they turned to each other, as long as the road allowed Waddy safely to disregard it, to exchange a smile.

Ahead, the sky was bright. Quick brushstrokes had daubed traces of cirrus cloud across it, and the wisps of vapor divided the sky like mortar into parallel bricks of floating blue. Add Rothko's signature, and the picture would have been worth a fortune.

"You're sure this is the way?" Annalee asked. In her years in Aspen she had never ventured this far. The landscape was horizontal and serene and seemed to have space for every dream. "You're sure it's the right road?"

Of all the questions she might have asked, this one was the easiest. "It is," he assured her with a broad smile. "It is the right road."

# Acknowledgements

For their help in reading this book in an unedited, unintelligible form, my thanks to Alix Beeney, Sosua, Dominican Republic; Stephanie Garman, Los Angeles; and my wife, Jaren.

## About the Author

© Jackie Daly Studio

The poems and short stories of Bruce Ducker appear in the nation's leading literary journals, including *Poetry* and the *Yale*, *Hudson*, *Sewanee*, and *Southern* reviews. *Dizzying Heights* is his eighth novel; *Home Pool*, a book of his stories, will be published in the fall of 2008. He lives in Colorado.